Praise for Ra

'Modern issues, relatable characters, wit, intelligence and so much warmth—an absolutely unputdownable story.' —*Better Reading* on *The Work Wives*

'Looks at the power of female friendships, family ties, the search for love and the recovery process after significant trauma. A wise, discerning and entertaining tale, *The Work Wives* is a great addition to the Rachael Johns collection.' —*Mrs B's Book Reviews*

'Johns is one of Australia's most popular authors, and for good reason—she tells great stories. She always takes complex themes and then delivers them in a page-turning combination of heart, wit and wisdom ... *How to Mend a Broken Heart* is yet another cracking read from Rachael Johns ... in fact, it's her best yet.' —*Better Reading*

'Imbued with an adventurous spirit, and ultimately hope, this book transports you mentally to a vibrant and unique city a world away ... I highly recommend this book. I finished it feeling warm and cosy, if I'd just shared a wonderful adventure with two good friends.' —*She Society* on *How to Mend a Broken Heart*

'Rachael has delivered another realistic and relatable tale with everything from spooky old mansions with ghosts, to cultural culinary delights, to life lessons and the opportunities to start anew all in the iconic New Orleans.' —*Great Reads and Tea Leaves* on *How to Mend a Broken Heart*

'A brilliant read from one of Australia's most popular authors, this will have you hooked from the very beginning.' —*Who* on *Flying the Nest*

'With her typical humour, empathy and wisdom, Rachael Johns has once again created characters you can't help but fall in love with and wish the best for. *Flying the Nest* might just be her best novel yet!' —Tess Woods, author of *Love at First Flight*

'Writing with warmth and insight, Rachael Johns is brilliant at capturing the joy and sadness in all of our lives. I hope she has many more tales to tell!' —Anthea Hodgson, author of *The Drifter*, on *Flying the Nest*

'A really good book makes you feel like you've found a new friend—one that resonates with you, and one who you can learn from. That's exactly how I felt in Rachael Johns's new novel, *Flying the Nest* ... This is a book that women will want to bond over, share laughs and tears over—a must read for every woman who has had their life take an unexpected turn.' —*Mamamia*

'Rachael Johns really gets women and is able to express the multilayered internal conflicts that so many of us experience, lay it all out on the page, and still make it deeply personal ... She's masterful at telling the stories of everyday heartbreaks ... *Flying the Nest* is wonderful—Rachael Johns never disappoints.' —*Better Reading*

'If you like your chick-lit with a dash of intelligent social commentary, *Just One Wish* is the perfect summer read. Rachael

Johns's latest novel is sparklingly funny, quirky and totally of this moment.' —*Herald Sun*

'Johns knows how to weave the experiences of different generations of women together, with nuance and sensitivity, understanding how competing contexts shape women's choices ... Exploring themes like motherhood, the roles of women, and lost love, *Just One Wish* will make you look at the women in your own life and wonder what stories they haven't told.' —*Mamamia*

'Johns draws readers in with her richly complex characters.' —*The Daily Telegraph* on *Just One Wish*

'Rachael Johns writes with warmth and heart, her easy, fluent style revealing an emotional intelligence and firm embrace of the things in life that matter, like female friendship.' —*The Age* on *Lost Without You*

'Heart-warming and compassionate ... Any book lover interested in life's emotional complexities and in the events that define and alter us, will be engrossed.' —*Better Reading* on *Lost Without You*

'Full of heartache and joy with a twist that keeps the pages turning ... *The Greatest Gift* will appeal to fans of Jojo Moyes and Monica McInerney.' —*Australian Books + Publishing*

'Rachael Johns has done it again, writing a book that you want to devour in one sitting, and then turn back to the first page to savour it all over again. I loved the characters of Harper and Jasper; their stories made me laugh and cry, and ache and cheer and ultimately reflect on all the many facets of that extraordinary journey called motherhood.' —Natasha Lester, author of *The Paris Secret*, on *The Greatest Gift*

'The bond between Flick, Neve, and Emma blossomed as their sons grew up, but even best friends keep secrets from one another … Fans of emotional, issue driven women's fiction will welcome Johns' US women's fiction debut.' —*Booklist* on *The Art of Keeping Secrets*

'… a compelling and poignant story of dark secrets and turbulent relationships … I fell completely in love with the well-drawn characters of Flick, Emma and Neve. They were funny and flawed and filled with the kind of raw vulnerability that makes your heart ache for them.' —Nicola Moriarty, bestselling author of *The Fifth Letter*, on *The Art of Keeping Secrets*

'Written with compassion and real insight, *The Art of Keeping Secrets* peeks inside the lives of three ordinary women and the surprising secrets they live with. Utterly absorbing and wonderfully written, Johns explores what secrets can do to a relationship, and pulls apart the notion that some secrets are best kept. It is that gripping novel that, once started, will not allow you to do anything else until the final secret has been revealed.' —Sally Hepworth, bestselling author of *The Secrets of Midwives*, on *The Art of Keeping Secrets*

'A fascinating and deeply moving tale of friendship, family and of course—secrets. These characters will latch onto your heart and refuse to let it go.' —*USA Today* bestselling author Kelly Rimmer on *The Art of Keeping Secrets*

Once upon a time (briefly) Rachael Johns was an English teacher, then her dreams of becoming a novelist came true. Now she spends her days writing romance and women's fiction in the Swan Valley, Western Australia. She is the bestselling, ABIA-winning author of *The Patterson Girls* and a number of other romance and women's fiction books including *The Art of Keeping Secrets*, *The Greatest Gift*, *Lost Without You*, *Just One Wish*, *Something to Talk About*, *Flying the Nest*, *How to Mend a Broken Heart*, *The Work Wives* and *The Other Bridget*. *Outback Reunion* is the sixth in her series of rural romances set in Bunyip Bay. When she's not writing, you'll find Rachael reading, hanging with her adorable sheepadoodle, listening to audiobooks while cleaning up after her three teenage boys, or running the Rachael Johns' Online Book Club on Facebook. Rachael loves to hear from readers and can be contacted via her website rachaeljohns.com

Also by Rachael Johns:

TALK
TO THE
Heart

RACHAEL
JOHNS

TALK TO THE HEART
© 2023 by Rachael Johns
ISBN 9781038923547

First published on Gadigal Country in Australia in 2023
by HQ Fiction
an imprint of HQBooks (ABN 47 001 180 918), a subsidiary of HarperCollins
Publishers Australia Pty Limited (ABN 36 009 913 517).
This edition published 2024.

HarperCollins acknowledges the Traditional Custodians of the lands upon
which we live and work, and pays respect to Elders past and present.

A catalogue record for this book is available from the National Library of Australia
www.librariesaustralia.nla.gov.au

Printed and bound in Australia by McPherson's Printing Group

For the Romance Writers of Australia – without you I would not be where I am today

Chapter One

Adeline Walsh woke to the bright sun streaming through her bedroom window. No, hang on, it wasn't *her* window. It wasn't even her *bedroom*.

And she was naked. In the most enormous bed she'd ever slept in.

The sheets were silky soft, the pillows fluffy, and the sound of running water was coming from an ensuite off to the side of the room. She'd always loved the sound of water—waves at the beach, ripples down a creek, dogs splashing in the dam—but nothing could hold a candle to the deep throaty voice accompanying it.

'Country girls, shake it for the ones that lost you and the ones about to have you. Like aged whiskey … fine wine … darlin' you can have me anytime.'

She knew those beautiful lyrics off by heart. They'd been on repeat in her four-wheel drive ever since Ryder O'Connell—that's right, *the* hottest country music star in the country—had agreed to come sing at the annual Walsh Agricultural Show.

All *her* doing. And she was damn proud of it. There'd been so much community anxiety regarding the diminishing numbers attending the show the last few years, but scoring Ryder for the closing concert had done exactly what she'd intended—it had put Walsh back on the map. People had flocked not only from the surrounding towns, but from Perth and further afield as well. She'd been stoked with this result, but that wasn't even the highlight of the weekend.

As the events of the night before came rushing back, she couldn't curb her smile.

She'd slept with Ryder O'Connell.

It didn't matter that it turned out he'd had an ulterior motive in agreeing to sing at the show—to get back together with up-herself Tabitha Cooper-Jones—because everyone had ended up with the right people. Ryder might have thought himself in love with Tab, but *she'd* fallen for Fergus McWilliams, the new teacher, and didn't want a bar of her ex. Honestly, who in their right mind would choose a small-town teacher over a freaking celebrity?

Thankfully, Adeline had been there to soothe Ryder's hurt pride and make him forget that any other girl existed.

It might not have been the most amazing bonk of all time, but he'd seemed to enjoy it. The noise he'd made when he'd climaxed had been music to her ears. It made her feel powerful and sexy—and there was plenty of time for him to repay the favour.

His voice came to a crescendo as he sang the chorus about second chances and finding love on a country road. Her body thrummed along to the tune and she decided that now was as good a time as ever to claim that orgasm.

Throwing back the covers, she headed into the bathroom.

Ryder's eyes were closed as he rubbed soap all over his beautiful body. She took a moment to simply appreciate the view before stepping into the massive shower.

'Holy shit.' He jumped and almost slipped on the tiles as she placed her hand on his chest. 'What the hell?'

He was looking at her like she was a stranger who'd snuck into his space unwanted.

Trying not to feel hurt—maybe he just wasn't a morning person—she hit him with her most seductive smile. 'We're all about saving water in the country, so I thought I'd join you. Would you like me to soap your back? Or maybe …' She flicked her long hair over her shoulders, exposing her breasts, shivering at the thought of his hands and mouth upon them. 'Maybe you'd like to scrub me?'

'Look sweetheart,' Ryder said, turning off the taps, barely glancing at her chest, 'last night was fun, but it was a one-time thing. I've got a car waiting outside to take me back to Perth to catch my plane.'

Adeline blinked as he stepped out of the shower and wrapped a fluffy white towel around his waist. Was he for real? A one-off?

She wasn't naive enough to think that he'd propose marriage or anything (at least not straight away), but sometime in the night they'd spent together, she'd decided that he was her ticket out of here. She'd been all but ready to pack her bags—and her dogs, of course—and drive across the Nullarbor to join him in Sydney. Maybe she'd work for his PR team, helping write better copy than the stuff he currently had. They could be partners in business and in bed. The thought of leaving Gran, Sally and her gorgeous nephews didn't appeal, but with a bank account like Ryder's at her disposal, she'd be able to fly back to visit whenever she wanted.

Her fantasy even included the possibility of having her grandmother moved to a private nursing home on the other side of the country. Not that there was anything wrong with the residential care wing of Walsh Hospital—the nurses did their best—but Penelope Walsh deserved better than they could give.

Yet now the dream burst like one of the soap bubbles on the glass wall of the shower.

Ryder sprayed an expensive smelling cologne liberally over his naked body, ran some gel through his damp hair and then picked up his toothbrush.

'Don't mind me.' He didn't even look at her in the mirror as he spoke. 'Have a shower, take as long as you like, just be out of this shack by two. I promised the owners I'd be gone by then.'

Gone?

Adeline stepped out of the shower and plucked another fluffy white towel from the rack. 'Ryder,' she began, 'I had a wonderful time last night and I was hoping we could see each other—'

He cut her off with his hand in her face. 'Look sweetheart, it's not pretty to beg. Let's not make this more than it was.'

'B-beg?' Adeline spluttered. Saying she hoped to see him again was hardly grovelling.

He nodded as he brushed his teeth, then spat into the sink, not even bothering to rinse it. She guessed he was used to having people for that! He dropped the towel in a puddle at his feet, then strode into the bedroom. Adeline followed to find him pulling snug jeans onto his muscular thighs and realised that aside from the clothes he clearly planned to wear today, everything else was already packed and waiting by the front door.

A knock sounded on said door.

'That'll be my driver,' he explained, tugging a designer brand black t-shirt over his head. She followed him out into the open-plan living area. 'Don't forget, out by two.'

And then he left. No thanking her for organising the gig, no goodbye, not even a kiss on the bloody cheek. As the door of the cottage shut behind him, she glanced down at her clothes. Discarded in the height of passion the night before, her bra, knickers, boots, blouse, denim skirt and jacket formed a trail leading from the front door to the bedroom.

She snatched up a boot—caked in cow dung from traipsing around the showgrounds—and hurled it at the door, wishing she'd had the forethought to throw it at his head.

'Arsehole,' she screamed, and then began to gather the rest of her things.

Why did she keep doing this? Going after guys who were unavailable—either because they were heartless pricks or because they favoured someone else. What was wrong with *her*? She knew she was pretty. She had a good body. She wasn't stupid. She could sew, knit and cook, yet also knew her way around the milking shed and how to balance the farm books.

She was a bloody catch, yet none of the local men she'd ever had a crush on were smart enough to realise it.

The sound of a ringing phone pierced her suddenly throbbing head.

Her heart tripped. Could it be him? She'd given her number to his manager in case he needed to contact her directly before the big night. Maybe he was calling to apologise for his brusqueness and to tell her if she was ever in Sydney they should hook up.

He'd better hope he was good at grovelling!

But the caller wasn't Ryder O'Connell.

All hopes sank as the name Jane Walsh flashed up from the screen.

The last thing she felt like doing right now was talking to her mother. It would probably already be all around town that she'd gone home with the megastar—news had a way of getting out in small communities—and she didn't want to have to explain that she'd made yet another monumental stuff-up when it came to men.

The phone went silent, but she'd barely expelled her sigh of relief when it started blaring again. Her headache compounded. She needed water and Panadol pronto.

'What is it, Mum?' she spat as she answered. 'Has someone died?'

'Yes, Adeline,' her mother replied. 'Your grandmother.'

'What?' Her knees buckled and she sank to the floor. 'No … Are you … But …'

'There's no point falling apart over this. Penelope hasn't been long for this world for years. It's a miracle she lasted this long after her stroke.'

Adeline blinked back tears. 'Can I see her?'

'Why would you want to do that?'

Why? *Why?!*

Because she wanted to say goodbye, and needed to see for herself that the one person who'd always made her feel unconditionally loved was truly gone. Her grandmother might have had a stroke four years ago, but visiting her in the high-care facility attached to their local hospital had been the highlight of Adeline's days. Even though Gran was unable to talk anymore, they had so much history that they didn't need words to communicate. Gran always listened, squeezed her hand, and gave her a look that made her feel better, whatever the disappointment.

Adeline had never confided in her mother about her man and career problems—theirs wasn't that kind of relationship—but Gran had been there for every heartache and disappointment for as long as she could remember. Without her, she didn't know how she'd ever have crawled out of the dark hole she'd found herself in eight years ago when her dream of being a big city newspaper journalist had been cruelly pulled out from under her. It was Gran who'd plied her with ice cream, comforted her with soft words and encouraged her to volunteer for the *Walsh Whisperer* rather than give up writing entirely.

'Adeline? Are you still there? I know you and Penelope were close, but at least now she's in a better place and with her beloved Henry.'

She sniffed, mumbled 'Yeah, I guess,' and thought of the grandfather she only really remembered through her grandmother's stories. He'd died when she was five, but Henry and Penelope's love was legendary, the kind Adeline longed to have one day. Unlike that of her parents, who could barely stand the sight of each other most of the time. She'd only ever seen them hold hands or kiss— cheek only—when they were in public, keeping up appearances.

Why they hadn't just divorced she had no clue.

'I need to make more phone calls,' said Jane, 'but I'll see you when you get home. Drive safely. And, please God, tell me you used protection. Who knows where else that singer fellow has been!'

They disconnected at the same time—neither of them with anything else to say to the other—and that was when Adeline realised her other problem. Last night, drunk on Bundy Rum and the feel of Ryder's lips on her neck, she'd gone willingly with him into his chauffeured car, assuming he'd give her a lift back to the showgrounds to collect her Prado in the morning. She glanced out the window and saw nothing but empty paddocks.

'Dammit.'

The owners of this 'shack' no longer lived in the region, and the nearest farmhouse was miles away, not that she wanted to ask a local for help anyway. She'd be the laughing-stock of Walsh when they heard that Ryder O'Connell had abandoned her after having his wicked way.

She didn't have any close friends, and asking her parents or brother to come get her would be too humiliating, so there was really only one person she could call. Her ex-sister-in-law.

'Hey, Ads. I'm so sorry,' said Sally. 'I just heard about Penelope. Are you okay?'

See how fast news travelled in the country?

'I think I'm still in shock, but I need a favour.'

'Course. Even though I'm no longer married to your cheating scum of a brother, you're Levi and Tate's favourite aunt, and I meant it when I said we'll be family forever.'

Sally's words went a small fraction towards lifting Adeline's spirits. 'And you know my loyalties lie with you,' she said.

From the first time James brought Sally home to meet the relatives, Adeline had adored her. She was so warm and carefree—exactly the opposite of almost everyone else in their family. She'd become like the older sister Adeline had always wanted.

'Anyway, this is kind of embarrassing, but I need you to pick me up. Please,' she added. 'I'm at the shack on the Sattlers' farm and … my Prado is still at the showgrounds.'

'Say no more,' Sally said. 'The boys and I will be there in fifteen.'

Adeline dressed and tried to make herself presentable while she waited for her rescuer to arrive. Well, as presentable as was possible without make-up or a change of clothes. No wonder Ryder had run like the wind—her hair looked like she'd been rolling in hay and her hot pink lipstick and so-called waterproof mascara were smudged all over her face.

Exactly fifteen minutes later, Sally and her sons pulled up to the front door in her Jeep. Adeline climbed in and could have kissed her ex-sister-in-law when she presented her with a bacon sandwich, a cold bottle of water and a packet of Panadol. 'How'd you organise this so quickly?'

'I may have broken the speed limit getting here.'

'She almost ran into a cow that had escaped onto the road,' piped up Levi from the back seat.

Tate glowered at his younger brother. 'It wasn't a cow; it was a bull.'

'Geez, are you okay?' Adeline asked, her gloom momentarily forgotten. Escaped cattle had caused a few car accidents in these parts over the years, and hitting a bull was like slamming head-on into another car.

'Yeah, I swerved. It was Macca's, I think. He was already there trying to catch it.'

Adeline popped a couple of pills and took a bite of the sandwich. Bacon might not be able to fix her heartache, but it wouldn't make it any worse.

'So, your night? Did you *dance* with the handsome singer?' The way Sally said 'dance' made it clear she was speaking in code so as not to alert the boys to why they were rescuing her aunt from a strange place on a Sunday morning. 'And where is he now?'

Adeline sighed. 'Do you mind if we don't talk about it?'

'Course not.' Sally gave her a sympathetic smile, then whispered, 'I'm so sorry about Penelope.' She nodded towards the back seat where the boys were now concentrating on iPads. 'They don't know yet. Thought I should let James tell them.'

'Good idea.' Adeline sniffed, still not able to believe Gran was gone. She knew one day they'd meet each other again—and that Mum was right, her grandparents were finally together again. In heaven.

In time, maybe that thought would bring her comfort. But it didn't yet.

It wasn't long before Sally pulled up at the showgrounds, next to Adeline's white four-wheel drive.

'Thanks,' Adeline said, reaching for the door.

'Always here for you, girlfriend.' She turned to look at the boys in the back. 'Say goodbye to your aunty.'

'Bye Aunty A,' they chorused, not even glancing up from their screens.

Sally sighed. 'Call me if you need anything. I'll bring the boys round this afternoon before milking.'

Adeline climbed into her Prado and drove on autopilot out to the farm, parking in front of the homestead that had been in the Walsh family since before the town—named after them—was officially a town.

It was already abuzz. She recognised her brother's ute, her aunt and uncle's four-wheel drive and the vehicles of the neighbours from the farms on either side. The moment she stepped out of the car, Bella bounded towards her from where she'd been resting under a tree with her dad's two kelpies and her other dog, Ariel, who preferred to hang with the farm dogs.

She ruffled Bella's fur, taking comfort from its softness and the smile the animal always greeted her with—yes, maremma sheep-dogs actually grinned—and then snuck inside.

'It's for the best,' she heard her mother say as she snuck past the formal lounge room with Bella, hoping not to be noticed. 'Penelope's had no quality of life for years. I for one will be happy if I never have to set foot inside that nursing home again.'

Adeline scowled—she could count on one hand the number of times her mum had visited her mother-in-law the last year—and continued into the kitchen. Judging by the cakes piled up on the counter, baked sympathy had already begun to arrive.

She snuck a bottle of Margaret River's finest from the wine fridge, swiped a plate of chocolate cupcakes, and escaped to her bedroom. She needed a shower but didn't think she could find the energy to do anything except flop onto her bed, pour herself a (large) glass and stuff cake into her mouth. Bella climbed up beside her and rested her fluffy white head on Adeline's legs.

'Darling girl,' she said, sinking her fingers into Bella's soft, white fur. 'It's just you, me and Ariel now.'

With each gulp of wine, her tears came harder and faster. She'd never felt so alone. The thought of never seeing Gran again, of never being able to hold her hand, to talk to her—there were so many things she suddenly wished she'd said or asked—made her want to crawl under her covers and never wake up.

Chapter Two

After a couple of glasses of wine and more cupcakes than she could count, Adeline was exhausted but her mind wouldn't switch off. She grabbed her phone, collapsed back into her pillows, and started aimlessly scrolling Facebook.

What did people do to numb their thoughts before technology and social media?

It shouldn't have surprised her that there were already hundreds of posts about Penelope Walsh's death clogging her feed. As a stalwart of the CWA and someone who'd lived in their small community her whole life, she was well known. As Adeline scrolled through posts from locals, friends and family further afield, her throat clogged, and tears blurred her vision. She'd also received a few private messages from people who rarely gave her the time of day.

Even Meg Cooper-Jones had sent her sympathies.

This is what happened when someone died—folks who would normally bitch about you behind your back suddenly showered you with kind words and pity. Adeline knew she herself wasn't very well-liked, yet even if *she* died, everyone would probably be singing her praises. People could be so fake.

But genuine or not, no amount of sympathy or pity would bring Gran back.

As if sensing she needed comfort, Bella licked Adeline's hand and snuggled further into her side.

'The only good thing about Gran's death,' she told the dog, 'is that I'm more upset about that than Ryder's rejection. Bastard.'

She had a good mind to post something on social media about how he'd been a less-than-satisfying shag, but that would be poor form even if her grandmother hadn't just died and would also attract unwanted attention. It was bad enough that everyone in Walsh would know what had happened. She didn't want the rest of Australia privy to her humiliation as well.

'You're lucky you only have to deal with boys twice a year, Bella,' she said, thinking of the puppies she bred with her dogs. 'Sometimes I think I should just give up on men!'

Not that she'd ever had much luck with female friendships either. Except for Sally, but their relationship had been forged by a shared irritation with her mother. Jane Walsh had never thought Sally good enough for her darling son, even after she'd given her grandchildren. Adeline could relate because she'd never been able to please her either.

'Adeline! Are you in there? It's time to stop moping. There's work to be done.'

She startled at the sound of her mother's piercing voice coming from the other side of her bedroom door—as if thinking of her had summoned her.

Groaning, she hugged Bella close as she checked the time on her phone. Hours had passed since she'd retreated from the world. She'd hoped her family had forgotten her existence as she still wasn't ready to face any of them, but no such luck.

It might be different if they were a normal family—spending time together, sharing their grief and stories of Gran—but the Walshes didn't show emotion. It was a sign of weakness.

Before she could reply, the door opened to reveal Jane Walsh, hands perched on her trim hips. She looked immaculate as always—as if Adeline had opened the pages of *Australian Country* and her mother, in muted stone-coloured trousers, carefully curated chambray blouse and glistening pearls, had stepped into the room in her RM Williams boots. Polished. Worn casually, but deliberately.

Her eyes immediately went to the near-empty bottle on the bedside table. 'Have you been drinking?' she hissed, leaning down to sniff Adeline's breath.

Adeline pulled back but didn't dignify the question with a reply.

'And when did you last shower?' Jane asked, grimacing as she reared back. 'You look like Frankenstein's sister. Pull yourself together and hurry up about it. Father Phillip is here, and we have things to discuss before the boys head out for evening milking.'

Without another word, Jane stormed out in much the same manner she'd arrived, not bothering to close the door behind her.

Adeline supposed she should be grateful that her mum was even including her in the funeral preparations, and she owed it to Gran to make sure her wishes were respected, so she dragged herself out of bed, shut the door and then headed into her ensuite bathroom to transform herself.

Half an hour later, she emerged into the formal living room where her parents, James and Father Phillip sat, the good china teacups empty on the coffee table between them.

'Nice of you to finally join us,' tsked Jane.

'Hi Father Phillip,' Adeline said as he stood to greet her. She went over to give him a hug—she'd probably hugged the parish priest more than she had her parents in the last decade.

'I'm so sorry for your loss. Penelope was an extraordinary woman and I know you will miss her dearly. We all will.'

'Thank you.' Adeline retreated to the couch next to James, who was dressed similarly to their mother but in clothes that actually got a daily workout. 'Have you told the boys yet?'

'Yeah, I called them about an hour ago.'

'How'd they take the news?'

James shrugged. 'They're tough kids. They've grown up on a farm. They know death's a part of life. Besides, they weren't that close to her.'

Adeline had to concede that was true—although Penelope had been very involved when Levi and Tate were born, she'd been unable to be a hands-on great-grandmother since the stroke.

Jane cleared her throat. 'Enough of the chitchat thank you. We don't want to keep Father Phillip waiting any longer than we already have.'

'I'm fine,' the priest said, smiling. 'There's no rush.'

'Maybe for you, Father,' piped up Adeline's dad, 'but the cows don't wait for anyone.'

Adeline's cheeks burned at her father's words—sometimes she swore he cared more about the farm than he did about his own family. As a dairy farmer's wife, Gran would have understood that the milking must go on, but that didn't mean this felt right. She thought she saw slight disapproval in Father Phillip's expression as well, but he covered it quickly.

As soon as they started discussing the various options for the funeral mass, Jane took over the conversation—deciding on the prayers, arranging the order of service, even selecting the hymns.

As hard as Adeline found it to focus, she made sure to interject whenever Jane suggested something that she knew Gran wouldn't have wanted.

'What hymns do you think Penelope would prefer?' Father Phillip turned to her, trying to keep the peace.

'Gran's favourite was "Morning has broken".'

Jane shook her head. 'I don't think so. It's far too chirpy for a funeral. No, let's go with—'

'No,' Adeline interrupted, tears springing to her eyes once again. 'This is Gran's funeral, not yours, and I won't let you make it otherwise.' Until now, she'd only felt bereft, but now she felt furious as well. 'Why did you even drag me out here if you weren't going to listen to any of my suggestions? I knew her better than all of you!'

'Adeline,' warned her father, his tone sharp. 'Don't be rude to your mother.' Then he turned to Father Phillip. 'I'm sorry, but James and I need to head off to the dairy. Thanks for all your help.'

James shot to his feet and Father Phillip followed suit. 'Of course. Please call me any time over the next few days if you need.'

Her father cleared his throat. 'Thanks. But I'll leave all the arrangements to the ladies.'

When her dad and brother had left, Adeline turned back to Father Phillip. 'I'll choose the hymns and the Bible verses and email you the list. Thanks for everything.' She stood as well, feeling unable to be in the room with her heartless mother a moment longer.

'Where are you going?' called Jane as she started towards the door.

'Has anyone collected Gran's things from the hospital?'

Jane shook her head. 'The nurses said we could have until tomorrow.'

'I'll do it,' Adeline volunteered. It was a good excuse to get away, and she didn't want to leave her grandmother's precious things to people who didn't seem remotely affected by her passing. Left to her mother, they'd all likely end up in the big skip bin beside the hospital, whereas Adeline would lovingly pack them up, keep them safe and treat them with the dignity her grand-mother deserved.

After giving the dogs an early dinner, she climbed into her four-wheel drive and headed into town. Her heart squeezed as she drove past the shire office and saw the flag out front at half-mast as always happened when a local died. For the last few years with Gran in care, Adeline had often been the one to tell her when the flag was down and who had died. Gran hadn't been able to respond but Adeline knew she liked hearing about what was hap-pening in her beloved town.

A lump formed in her throat at the thought that she'd never have such a conversation again.

Inside the hospital, like on the farm, life was cruelly going on as usual. The two nurses on duty greeted Adeline with sympa-thetic noises and then left her to clear out Penelope's room. Beds in the residential care section were in high demand and she knew that by tomorrow, somebody else would likely have moved into her grandmother's room.

As she slipped inside the now cold and empty room, she closed the door behind her and inhaled deeply, trying to catch a familiar scent. When Adeline was a little girl, Penelope had always smelled of Pond's hand cream and Loulou perfume, and when she could no longer apply these two things herself, Adeline had helped. She picked up the tub of hand cream from the bedside table, opened it and rubbed some over her skin, then sprayed a few puffs of Loulou onto her wrists, before popping both items into her hand-bag. Next, she collected the photo frames—pausing to sigh at the photo of Penelope and Henry on their wedding day, both of them glowing and looking head-over-heels in love—and put them into a big recycling bag. It seemed heartbreaking that Penelope had so little when she died, but most of her and Henry's worldly possessions had been sold or given to charity when she'd moved out of her unit in town and taken up residence in the high-care, long-term wing of the hospital.

Miraculously, Adeline had managed to save Gran's collection of Folio Society editions of classic books, a few china ornaments—which she hoped to display one day in her own house—and letters between Penelope and Henry from when they were first 'courting', as well as the hundreds of journals she'd filled over the years. And she planned on keeping everything she found here as well. If she couldn't have Gran, the next best thing would be keeping the things near and dear to her.

The bed had already been stripped, so there were really only the clothes left. She removed the Sunday best that hadn't been worn in years and then smiled sadly at the huge stack of issues of the *Walsh Whisperer* at the bottom of the wardrobe.

Gran had collected every edition of the local paper since Adeline had been involved in its publication. When she'd first moved in here, a nurse had tried to throw the papers out, and although Gran couldn't vocalise her desire to keep them, she got so distressed that it soon became clear why. From then on, all the nurses and hospital staff knew never to get rid of them.

As Adeline piled the issues into more canvas recycling bags, a thought struck. The funeral might be massive and it would definitely have Jane's stamp on it, but it would be over quickly and then everyone would move on, whereas she could do something far more special to honour Gran's memory. She knew people laughed behind her back about how seriously she took her role as editor of the *Walsh Whisperer*, but even though it was only a small-town rag with local news, she enjoyed it, and no one could deny it played an important role in community engagement. Now she was even more grateful for her position because it meant she could give her grandmother the memorial she deserved.

The next edition would be dedicated to Penelope Walsh and all she'd done for this town, and it would be the best obituary that had ever been published.

Feeling slightly better now she had a mission, she packed up the rest of the stuff and then started taking it out to her four-wheel drive. On her way out, she bumped into Tabitha Cooper-Jones. Her chocolate brown hair was tied up in a practical ponytail, her full arm rested on her small baby bump and her amputated one hung limply at her side.

'Oh, hi Adeline,' said Tabitha with a cool smile. 'You must be here to collect Mrs Walsh's things?'

She nodded. Tabitha would be here to visit her own grandmother, and although Adeline and Tab had never been friends, didn't she know the protocol was to offer sympathy when someone's loved one had passed?

But the other woman offered no such thing—maybe she was still dark about Adeline and Ryder—instead gesturing to the bags in Adeline's hands. 'Can I help you with those?'

'No thanks,' Adeline replied, not willing to accept help from someone so rude.

Although Tab and Adeline were almost the same age and had grown up together, they'd never been close; she'd been far more interested in Tab's gorgeous older brother, Lawson. Sadly, he'd fallen in love with someone else, married young and had a child. When he'd lost his wife in tragic circumstances, she'd thought it was finally her chance, but then the mysterious Meg arrived in Rose Hill, and it wasn't long before she realised Lawson was a lost cause once again.

What did it say about Adeline that he'd rather hook up with an ex-crim than her?

'I'll be fine,' Adeline said, continuing with the bags. Tab probably only wanted to help so she could grill her about Ryder and then snigger about her misfortunes with Meg and the other members of their knitting circle, aka Stitch'n'Bitch.

No, thank you.

She made two more trips from Penelope's room to her Prado and then finally headed home. Once there, she packed Gran's precious things onto a shelf in her walk-in robe, next to the rest of the things she'd been keeping safe, then poured herself another glass of wine, opened her laptop and set to work writing the obituary.

But the words refused to come. Or rather they did, but each sentence she wrote, she read back and then deleted. It should have been easy to put her love and admiration for her grandmother into words, to write about all the wonderful things she'd achieved in her century on the planet, but nothing sounded good enough.

Argh. Adeline banged her fist on the desk. Maybe it was too soon. Maybe she needed to give herself time. Or maybe she simply wasn't a good enough writer to achieve what she wanted to. If only she could talk to Gran, to ask what *she* wanted the community to know about her life. How she wanted to be remembered. Adeline was about head into the kitchen for a snack—she hadn't eaten anything since the cupcakes—when she remembered she had Penelope's journals. When the notebooks had first come into her possession, she'd been tempted to read a few pages, but guilt had stopped her doing so. It had felt wrong to be reading someone else's innermost thoughts without their permission.

But now that Gran was dead, she'd do anything to hear her voice again, and as Penelope had been a committed diarist, the pages might also give Adeline inspiration for the obituary.

Feeling slightly less desolate, she grabbed the box of journals and took them to the bed where Ariel and Bella were already fast asleep. She sat down between them, picked up the first and started reading.

Penelope's scribbles about growing up on a farm and—as she got older—going to dances at the town hall, were not only comforting but hilarious. She could have written novels. If Adeline did have any talent when it came to writing, it was clear where it came from. As enjoyable as it was, she blushed a little when she got to the part about the crush young Penelope Elverd had on a nearby farmer's son, Henry Walsh. It sounded like something out of Jane Austen, only the setting was rural Australia rather than an English village. Gran had realised her feelings for her childhood friend Henry when she was only eleven, and had been ecstatic when four years later, he'd been her first kiss behind the cattle sheds at the Walsh Agricultural Show.

Their courtship became official after that—both sets of parents approved.

Henry had been an eligible bachelor like Charles Bingley, and Penelope clearly pictured herself in the role of Jane Bennet. There were many smug sentences about how he'd chosen her above all the other girls in town whose hearts also fluttered whenever he was near, but he only had eyes for her.

How romantic! Adeline swooned and sipped delightedly on her wine, still hoping—despite her latest romantic disaster—that one day she'd have a similar love story of her own.

She couldn't turn the pages fast enough, desperate to get to the part where Henry proposed. This was a story she'd heard numerous times from Gran, and she knew reading it would make her feel like she was sitting with her grandmother again, listening as the older woman reminisced.

But there was quite a shock before she got to the proposal.

A horrifying chapter of her grandparents' story that she'd never been told.

A terrible secret that Gran had taken to the grave.

Chapter Three

It was a beautiful spring morning when they gathered to farewell Penelope Walsh, the sun shining high in the cloudless sky and the local Catholic church packed to the rafters. Country people loved a funeral, almost as much as they loved a wedding. They were willing to sit through the long Requiem Mass due to the promise of the feast and wake—read *party*—that would follow. Normally Adeline enjoyed such occasions as much as the next person, but today she felt bereft.

In less than a week, everything she'd known about her grandmother, herself and her family had been turned upside down.

Was anything Gran had ever told her true? Who even was she? How had she been able to walk around town, to attend *church*, knowing what she'd done?

As the organist began to play and the congregation stood for Adeline's dad, brothers and three male cousins to carry the coffin down the aisle, she shuddered, the memory of what she'd read in the pages of Penelope's journal now forever imprinted on her mind.

I'm heartbroken. My life is over. I can't believe I'm even writing this. It doesn't make sense. Henry has ended things. Just when I thought we would soon be planning our wedding—I already had a dress picked out from the McCall's *magazine—he's told me it's over. That he's fallen in love with someone else.*

The music stopped as the pallbearers stepped back from where they'd laid the coffin on the raised platform at the front. Father Phillip approached the pulpit to welcome everyone, but Adeline couldn't stop thinking about the journal.

It's the most ridiculous thing I've ever heard. At first, I thought maybe she'd tricked him into sleeping with her—the two of us haven't even made love yet, we were waiting till we're married— and that she'd gotten into trouble, but he vows it's no such thing. He says they're soulmates and that he feels things for her he knew he never could for me. He was dreadfully contrite, but I didn't want to hear his apologies.

On autopilot, Adeline stood alongside everyone else as the organist began to play 'Guide me, O thou great redeemer' but she couldn't bring herself to sing. The hymn was not one of Penelope's favourites—after Adeline had read the journals, she'd told her mother she could choose the music and verses after all.

How could he do this to me? Our parents weren't the only ones hearing wedding bells—the whole town expected them—and instead he tells me he's going to marry her.

In the pew alongside Adeline sat her brother James, her nephews Levi and Tate, and James's new girlfriend, Zara. Her parents and her other brother, Max, who'd come from Perth with his fiancée, were in the other front row, across the aisle, with Dad's brother Tony and his wife, Louise.

Over my dead body.

After the welcome and first hymn, there were Bible readings—
mostly Psalms—by members of the family and Ivy Wellington,
Penelope's closest friend, who was still fighting fit. Did Ivy have
any idea what her old mate had done? Adeline would have said no;
Ivy was a god-fearing woman—always baking for church cake
stalls, leader of the prayer chain, an ex-Sunday school teacher and
much more. Then again, Gran had also done all these things at
various times.

Did anyone truly ever know what anyone else was capable of?

*I honestly don't know what he sees in that floozy. Her parents
don't even have land. The way she carries on, you'd think she was
raised in a barn. She plays cards at the pub with the men and last
week she was caught riding in a horse race, dressed up as a man.
Can you believe it? If we get married, the joining of our two farms
will make us the biggest landowners in the region, whereas if he
marries her ...*

Adeline's dad did the eulogy and her brothers both said a few
words as well. By the time they'd finished, the only dry eye in the
church was Adeline's.

*No. There has to be a way to stop them because I'll be damned if
I let that trollop steal what is rightfully mine right out from under
my nose.*

Even now, Adeline still flinched remembering Gran's use of the
word 'damned'. She'd never once heard Penelope say anything
closely resembling a swear word, but really, that paled in comparison to what came next.

*Thankfully, I've convinced Henry to give me some time to grieve
before he makes his little thing with Eliza Abbott public.*

Chills had rippled over Adeline's skin when she'd read that line. The name Eliza had become famous in these parts this last year or so. But surely Penelope couldn't be referring to *that* Eliza! The Eliza who the new tearooms in nearby Rose Hill had been named after. The Eliza who had died tragically young at her parents' general store, and who Meg Cooper-Jones believed now haunted the building.

> *As much as I loathe the idea of them continuing their sordid, clandestine affair, this gives me the chance to right things before she ruins his life. And mine.*

According to official records, Eliza Abbott had taken her own life when she jumped from the first floor and broke her neck falling down the stairs, but Meg and Tabitha—who ran the tearooms together—loved to tell visitors that Eliza had been pushed. Even after Adeline had experienced a very weird situation there herself—where a lightbulb had dropped from the ceiling and shattered against her mug—she'd wanted to believe it was a stupid story, but she had to admit that building did give her the heebie-jeebies.

Could Meg and Tabitha be right? No wonder they'd been even colder to her lately. No wonder Tab wasn't here and hadn't offered sympathy at the hospital. But no, even if they were right about Eliza, they couldn't know who pushed her!

… the chance to right things …

Even without what was as good as a confession in her grandmother's beautiful handwriting a few pages later, the timing was spot on. She'd looked up Eliza's death date online just to be sure, and hairs had stood up on the back of her neck. Eliza had 'taken her own life' mere days after Henry had ended things with Penelope.

Father Phillip had asked Adeline if she'd like to do a reading or say a few words during the service, but she'd refused. Everyone assumed this was due to grief, but how could she stand up in front of more than half the town knowing what she did?

That her sweet, beloved Gran—the woman she'd always looked up to, the woman who couldn't even bring herself to kill flies, the woman who'd taken Adeline to church since she was a little girl—was a murderer.

Was it any surprise that her family was so dysfunctional with this woman as their matriarch? Is that why her dad didn't feel guilty about fiddling the farm books to avoid paying tax? Is that why James had no qualms about sleeping with another woman when he was married to Sally? And maybe why Adeline had a mean streak she sometimes couldn't hold in?

Apples didn't fall far from the tree after all. And they were all descended from a killer.

Then another thought struck. Was this why her parents were miserable and why neither she nor her brothers were capable of having a healthy relationship? Why she'd never held onto a boy-friend for longer than a few months?

Were they all still being punished for Penelope's sins?

If only she hadn't read those journals, she'd still be blissfully unaware. She could focus on her grief, rather than the shame and anger battling within her. All her life she'd wanted a love like her grandparents had shared—but it was nothing but a farce.

Now, whenever she looked at the photo of her grandparents on their wedding day, she saw a whole different picture to the one she'd admired for years. Penelope didn't look glowing exactly, but rather smug. And what Adeline had always thought a dreamy expression on Henry appeared almost vacant, as if he were simply going through the motions expected of him.

Poor Grandpa. How could she have done that to him?

'You coming, Ads?' James whispered, nudging her as he nod-ded towards the front, his boys and Zara filing out ahead of him.

Adeline looked up to see that the rest of her family were lining up for communion. Mass was almost at an end, and she couldn't recall a word of it.

She shook her head—no way she could get up there and eat of the Lord's flesh, drink of his blood, knowing what she did. The shame was almost as bad as if she'd murdered Eliza herself.

'I'm not feeling well.'

Heads turned and people whispered as she fled from the church, but she didn't look back.

* * *

She didn't see her grandmother put into the ground, nor did she attend the wake at the local bowling club, and thankfully, if anyone noticed, they didn't come after her.

It hadn't really been a lie—she'd felt sick ever since her discovery. No, that was not a strong enough word.

She was disgusted. Ashamed of who she came from.

She needed to get out of the church, out of town, and back home to her dogs. And she didn't care what anyone thought of her leaving Penelope's funeral before it had finished.

But even with Bella and Ariel lying beside her on her bed, home didn't feel far enough away. It didn't even feel like home. Ryder screwing her over, Gran dying and then the horrible discovery in her journals felt like a wake-up call.

She was in a rut.

When she'd been growing up, she couldn't wait to head to the city and become a journalist, but when that had failed, she'd had nowhere else to go but here. She'd only meant to stay long enough to work out what to do next, but days had turned to weeks, then weeks to months and before she realised, she'd been back for years. Then Gran had her stroke and there was no way she could abandon her after that.

She'd stayed because of her grandmother, but she'd never really felt like this was her place.

Perhaps it was time to leave Walsh again, once and for all. But where would she go and what would she do?

Looking up to the ceiling, Adeline clasped her hands together and prayed, 'Please God, give me a sign. Help me work out what to do now.'

Chapter Four

Four months later

'Got turned down for another grant today,' Holden Campbell said to Ford and Bronte as they sat outside on the verandah after dinner, all three of them nursing cans of Coke. 'That's the third knockback this month.'

Sam and Toovs, two of Holden's foster kids, were inside washing up the dinner dishes. The most recent addition to the family was across the yard, and was supposed to be locking the chickens in for the night.

Bronte reached out to pat his knee. 'That's sucks. I'm sorry.'

He sighed and squeezed her fingers in thanks, but what was the point in having grand ideas if you couldn't fund them? Why couldn't he get the people with big dollars to see the importance of his proposal? What was more important than keeping young people off the streets?

His frustration had him desperate for a beer, but he didn't drink in front of the boys, and alcohol was a luxury they couldn't afford anyway. The income from Ford's barbershop covered the bills and food for the dogs, and kept their small holding going. As carers, the brothers also got a payment for fostering, but it was barely enough for the boys' food and clothes, and recently, Holden had to reduce his hours at the tattoo parlour, meaning their household income had also diminished.

'What reason did they give this time?' asked Ford, taking a sip of his drink.

Holden crushed his empty can in his hand. 'They didn't bother with one.'

Bronte sighed. 'If only one of us were good at writing grants.'

'You have plenty of other talents.' Holden winked at her, trying to lighten the mood. She wriggled her eyebrows in reply and her brow ring jiggled.

'Is *anyone* good at writing grants?' asked Ford with a chuckle.

'I reckon there must be a trick to it,' Bronte mused.

'Hey Holden!

He looked up as Rocky—his youngest charge, a thirteen-year-old redhead who'd arrived a couple of weeks ago after running away from countless foster homes—called his name.

'Look what just showed up!' Rocky was patting a dog, a large white beast that looked completely out of place alongside the other dogs. The interloper was a purebred, and judging by its glossy, knot-free coat, someone took very good care of it.

Holden pushed out of his deckchair, tossed his can in the bin, and went down the ramp to meet boy and dog.

'Hey girl,' he said, reaching his hand out for the dog to sniff. He could immediately tell she was female from the way she looked at him, slightly cautious, rather than defensive. 'What do you mean she just showed up?'

'I was hanging out near the chicken coop and she just ran up. I thought she was gunna try to eat them.' Clearly, Rocky hadn't yet put the hens away as he'd been tasked to do. 'But she just went and stood by them as if they were old mates or somethin'.'

Holden grinned—this was the most Rocky had said to him since he'd got here, and the first time he'd *ever* seen the boy smile. 'That's 'cos she's a maremma. You ever seen that movie *Oddball*?'

Rocky screwed up his face. 'Isn't that a fucking kids' show?'

'Hey, just because the target audience is young, doesn't mean it's … stupid. It's a great film. Anyway, maremmas are dogs specially bred to guard livestock. She wouldn't hurt the chickens, but she might stop the foxes eating them.'

'Can we keep her, then?' asked Rocky, bouncing on his toes.

Whenever a new foster kid arrived, Holden took them to the local dog shelter in Colac to choose a pup. This was something he'd initiated with their very first charge, because he knew firsthand the healing powers of a dog. In his experience, even the toughest kids went a little gaga over the opportunity to choose a pet for themselves. Holden, who'd picked up a few dog-handling skills when he'd been working around Australia, taught the boys how to train the dogs. Full of pent-up energy that needed to be channelled into good rather than destruction, the dogs and the boys made perfect companions. Through teaching the dogs obedience tricks, the boys learned the value of hard work and discipline and all sorts of other things about themselves.

Rocky, however, hadn't showed the slightest interest when they'd visited the shelter, and for the first time ever Holden had left without adopting anything.

Perhaps this stray was meant to be. Not that she looked like a runaway.

He glanced at his watch. It was late to call the ranger, but he didn't want to get Rocky's hopes up.

'Take her over to meet Vlad and Merlin.' Both Sam's and Toovs' dogs were bitzas—Merlin, a kelpie crossed with a cattle dog, crossed with an alsatian, and maybe a little border collie, and Vlad, a bull arab staffy cross who had the ugliest face you'd ever seen but the softest personality. 'She can stay the night, and we'll see if we can find out who she belongs to in the morning. Don't get too attached.'

He wasn't sure Rocky heard the last bit. Boy and dog were already running off to play together. As Holden turned back towards the verandah, movement in his peripheral vision made him look to the entrance of their five-acre property.

Well, hello there.

Jogging towards him was a woman who looked like she'd just stepped off the cover of a country music album—at least from the neck up. The kind of pretty that would make anyone look twice in the street, the kind of pretty that stole your breath, but … what the hell was she wearing?

'I'm sorry, I didn't mean to intrude,' she said breathlessly as she came up to him and looked frantically around. 'I'm looking for my dog; I think she ran this way.'

'Intrude?' Holden couldn't help giving her the once-over. Close-up she looked like that English actress, what was her name? The one in the steampunk show he and Ford had binged last year. Cara something. Long honey-blonde hair tied back in a high pony-tail with wisps escaping round her face, a cute nose, pretty, smoky eyes. 'You're not intruding at all. Everyone's welcome here.'

Her face relaxed into a smile. 'Thank you. So have you seen her?'

'Does she happen to be large, white and hairy?'

'I'd say fluffy rather than hairy, but yes, that sounds like Bella.'

Bella. Of course someone like her would have a dog called Bella. He gestured over to where a blur of white was tearing around with Rocky and the other dogs.

'Naughty girl.' The pretty blonde sounded so happy she might cry.

He held out his hand. 'I'm Holden Campbell. Nice to meet you.'

'Oh.' She stared at his tattooed forearms and the letters he had punched across his knuckles, then slipped her tiny hand in his. It was as soft and silky as her hair looked. 'After *The Catcher in the Rye*?'

He laughed. For that to be true, one of his parents would have to have known how to read, and he'd never seen his mother so much as look at a book until she'd found the Bible. 'I was named after the cars. My dad was a revhead.'

'Was?'

'Yeah.' He was not about to get into his messy family history with a stranger. 'And you are?'

'Oh,' she said again. 'I'm Adeline Walsh.'

'Pretty name. You're new around here.' It wasn't a question. Smallton wasn't a big place and there was no way he'd forget that face if he'd seen it before.

She nodded.

'And what brought you to our backwater?' he asked.

Fiddling with her golden blonde ponytail, Adeline said, 'I've come to live at the Smallton convent.'

The convent? He couldn't have been more shocked if she'd told him she was an alien sent from some far-off planet, but suddenly he realised why her colourless outfit looked familiar. It was the uniform of the religious nuts who lived just down the road. 'You're a *nun*?'

'Yes. Well, no. Not yet.' She sounded flustered. 'I'm a postulant.'

'A postu-what?!'

'It's someone who's thinking about becoming a sister, so they move into a religious community to learn about the way of life—whether you want to be in active service or dedicate your life to contemplative prayer. Only the second type are called nuns. Most people who join a convent are called sisters.'

'And you're going to become one?' he clarified.

Her pink tongue darted out and licked her upper lip as she nodded. 'Yes. I am.'

Jesus Christ. He had no words. Why would someone as young and pretty as Adeline Walsh take a vow of chastity? What a waste!

'Aren't nuns supposed to wear black and white from head to toe?' he asked as he rolled his gaze over her very demure outfit of navy trousers, white shirt, and a beige cardigan that looked like it belonged on someone twice her age. 'What's that called?'

'A habit,' she provided, as if he were a dimwit.

'Yes, that's it.' Despite her tone, he couldn't help imagining her in the full caboodle. She could probably wear a hessian sack and still look like a model.

'Some orders do still wear habits, but mostly these days sisters wear ordinary clothes.'

Ordinary? He almost snorted. Boring more like.

'You shouldn't believe everything you see in the movies, you know.' She folded her arms over her chest. 'Real life of service and prayer is very different.'

This time he couldn't withhold his snort as he thought of *Sister Act*, and all the disruption Whoopi Goldberg caused. 'Yeah, I'm guessing it's a lot less fun. You need your head read.'

She blinked. 'Excuse me?'

'The Catholic church is corrupt. All religion is. If you look at any of the trouble and conflict in the world, religion is usually at the core. I don't know who conned you into—'

'Conned me? No one *conned* me. I came willingly. Just as now I would like to leave here, willingly, as I have to get back to evening prayer.' She turned away from him and cupped her hands around her mouth, yelling, 'Bella!'

The beautiful white bitch looked over at the sound of her voice, then immediately went back to playing with Rocky, the other dogs and Toovs and Sam, who'd now finished cleaning up.

Holden stifled a smirk.

'Bella,' she screamed again as she started marching her pretty little behind towards the group.

The boys snickered while she danced around her dog, trying to grab its collar. Bella looked to be having the time of her life, Adeline not so much.

Eventually, amusement turned to pain, and he couldn't watch a second longer.

'Do you want some help?' he asked and then whistled loudly. His dogs immediately froze, and Bella followed suit a moment or so later. He took the lead from Adeline, attached it to the runaway dog's collar and then handed it back to her, their fingers brushing in the exchange.

Adeline pulled her hand away quickly. 'Thank you,' she said, sounding anything but grateful. 'Good night.'

'Bye,' he replied, still smirking as she jogged away looking as if she might break her arm in her efforts to wrangle the dog.

'Who was she?' Ford asked from his wheelchair as Holden returned to the verandah. 'You could have introduced us.'

'Forget about hitting on her,' Holden told his brother. 'She's a postulant.'

Ford frowned. 'A what?'

'Isn't that a someone who wants to become a nun?' said Bronte from where she was scrolling her phone.

'That's what she said.' Holden shook his head, still not really comprehending it.

Ford whistled long and slow. 'Serious? What a waste. Thankfully there are plenty more fish in the sea.'

'You're such a tart,' laughed Bronte.

'Like you can talk,' Ford shot back. 'Don't think I don't know about Holden and your *arrangement*.'

'Can you two take your heads out of the gutter so we can get back to business,' Holden snapped. 'Besides, little ears have big range and we're supposed to be role models.'

Bronte raised an eyebrow. 'Pretty sure those boys have heard far worse.'

'Maybe so,' Holden grunted, 'but they don't need to hear it from us.'

He sank back into his chair, determined to put the hot nun out of his head.

Chapter Five

Adeline hurried down the road, dragging Bella behind her, desperately hoping she wasn't going to be late for evening prayer. She breathed a sigh of relief as the convent came into view.

The Sisters of Grace lived in a large, beautiful, two-storey stone building that had been built in the late 1800s to house many more women than it did today. Located just beyond the outskirts of the town, it wasn't next to the church like many convents were, but it had a churchy look to it with a steepled roof and arched windows. Designed to withstand the Aussie summer, it also boasted a balcony up top and a verandah along the bottom. From a distance, Adeline thought it looked more like a painting than a real place.

She let herself in through the big iron gates at the front, ushered Bella around into the backyard, and then slipped inside and headed straight for the altar room. Her grandmother's rosary beads clasped tightly in her hand, Adeline entered for evening prayer to find the sisters and other postulants already kneeling, their heads bowed.

The women here were all at different stages of their commitment—while most of the sisters were fully committed and had been for years, there were two others not quite there yet. Michelle Elliot was a twenty-one-year-old postulant from Melbourne with black hair and an eternal grin, who'd taken her temporary vows just before Adeline had arrived and whose fun-loving, bouncy personality reminded her of a labrador. And then there was Lola Chen, a Chinese Australian who was almost ready to take her first vows after seven long years of training. Lola was warm and smart, a human beagle.

Mother Catherine—their Superior—looked up as Adeline tip-toed across to her place between Michelle and Lola. Like families at a dinner table, they all had unofficial places in the prayer room.

'I'm so sorry,' she mouthed.

The sister in charge gave no indication of her thoughts as she gestured for Adeline to take her place.

Adeline felt chastised, like Maria from *The Sound of Music* after losing track of time on the mountains, but this wasn't her fault. It was her dog's.

Bella must have smelled those other animals from a mile off and had been so delighted to find them. Although the convent had chickens, goats, cats, alpacas, and even a cow, she guessed Bella was missing Ariel and her dad's kelpies. It had nearly broken her heart leaving Ariel behind with her parents, but Ariel loved farm life, and Mother Catherine had said she could bring one dog but two would be too much. You were supposed to give up your worldly possessions when you committed to this life. Adeline had willingly left behind her phone, her expensive wardrobe, her massive collection of make-up, even her prized knee-high silver snakeskin Gucci boots, but if she'd had to give up Bella, she didn't think she'd have been able to take this massive step.

No matter that the dog was a terror, she was Adeline's heart, her whole world.

Taking a deep breath and literally praying she didn't stink after the exertion of trying to get Bella to hurry home from their late afternoon walk, Adeline focused on the words that were being uttered as she moved her fingers along her beads.

'Holy Lord, we thank you most heartily for all the graces we have received from You today. Take us under your protection tonight. Have pity on all poor sinners. Be with us as we ...'

Slowly, the anxiety she'd felt when Bella had run off and her shame at being late to prayer began to wash away. It was weird and wonderful the peace she found being with these women who lived their lives with such grace and faith. They were so different from the religious people she knew back in Walsh; people like her grandmother who attended church regularly, believing them-selves to be better than those who only came at Christmas and Easter, never mind the total heathens who never went at all and were doomed to hell.

Those types were always quick to judge and to gossip about others, and Adeline was ashamed to admit, she'd been one of them.

★ ★ ★

'So why were you late to prayer?' Michelle asked as they retreated to their shared bedroom following a supper of tea and homemade Anzac biscuits.

'I stupidly let Bella off her lead when we were on our walk and she sprinted ahead of me,' Adeline said, closing the door behind them. She glared down at her beloved dog who was slumped down onto the floor between their two beds, exhausted after her evening adventure. 'I followed her down this dirt track and found her on someone's property.'

Adeline kicked off her shoes and flopped onto her bed. The early wake-ups for morning prayer were catching up with her.

Even though she came from dairy country, the milking of the cows had been Dad and James's domain, so she'd rarely risen before the sun.

'It's only about a kilometre away, hidden off the road. I talked to a guy, but there were a couple of other adults on the verandah, three teenage boys and some dogs, which obviously attracted Bella.'

She'd only seen one female sitting on the verandah, a woman with reddish-brown hair cut in a jagged bob, wearing an oversized purple shirt, multiple face piercings and a wary expression as she watched Adeline talking to Holden.

'Sounds like you found Holden and Ford's place,' Michelle said, starting to plait her hair into two braids as she did every night. 'They're a couple of brothers who foster delinquent teens.'

'Is Ford the guy in the wheelchair?'

'Yep. Good eye candy those two.'

Adeline blinked, then widened her eyes in shock.

'What?' Michelle shrugged. 'Just because I've pledged to take a vow of chastity, doesn't mean I can't appreciate the male form, and you can't deny those brothers are hot.'

'Really?' Adeline kind of thought that's exactly what a vow of chastity meant, and she was fine with it. Besides, she wasn't sure the man she'd met tonight was hot. Maybe, if bearded, bushy-haired giants covered in tattoos were your thing. Luckily, even before she'd made the decision to live this life, lumberjack lookalikes were not at *all* her type. She'd always preferred her men clean-cut, clean-shaven and without visible tattoos—good solid men like Tabitha's brother Lawson Cooper-Jones. She'd mourned heavily the day he'd started going out with Meg McCormick.

'Well.' Michelle bit her lip and smiled coyly. 'Maybe it does. Would you mind not mentioning this conversation to Mother Catherine?'

'Of course not.' Adeline smiled through a yawn, then asked, 'So how do you know Holden and his brother?'

Michelle shrugged. 'I've seen them both around town. Everyone knows everyone round here.'

'Walsh—where I come from—is the same. You can't change your nail polish without someone having an opinion about it.'

Michelle chuckled and glanced at her nails, which—like Adeline's—were devoid of colour. 'Holden can be a bit of a grump, but Ford's really nice.'

'What kind of parents call their kids Holden and Ford?' Adeline shook her head. Had they been having a laugh? Setting them up for competition? Most car fanatics she knew were firmly in one camp or the other, so it seemed odd that a Holden lover also had a kid called Ford.

'Yeah, it's pretty funny, isn't it,' Michelle said, climbing into bed and reaching for her novel.

'Do you know why he's in a wheelchair?'

'No idea. Doesn't seem to let it get him down though.' Michelle opened her book and began to read as she did every night before private prayer.

Adeline sat on her bed a few moments, trying to work up the motivation to go brush her teeth and wash her face. She'd finally stood to go when Michelle said, 'Can I ask you a question?'

She sat back down. 'Of course.'

'Are you a virgin?'

Wow—that was not the question she'd been expecting.

'No,' she admitted eventually. She'd wondered if this fact would prevent her from becoming a sister, but Mother Catherine had told her that whatever she'd done before pledging her commitment to God and the church didn't matter. As long as she stayed true to her vows once she'd taken them.

'What's it like? Making love?'

Adeline grimaced at what she'd always thought a stupid, misleading term. 'You really want to know?'

Michelle nodded, hugging her book to her chest. 'I know I probably shouldn't be, but I'm curious.'

'To be honest, it's hugely overrated,' Adeline said, thinking back to her encounter with Ryder O'Connell. 'And quite frankly messy. It's not at all like you read about in romance novels. Trust me, you're not missing anything.'

Like fashion, make-up and her boots, sex was something she hadn't had any qualms about giving up—it had been the thought that she was permanently closing the door to the possibility of having kids that had given her pause. Her nephews were one of her greatest joys in life and she'd always assumed that one day she'd give them cousins. But even though she'd only been here a week, already she felt like it was the best decision she'd ever made. Michelle felt like the best friend Adeline had always wanted. And it wasn't only Michelle. The Sisters of Grace had welcomed her with open arms, love, friendship and food, and made her feel more part of a family than her own ever had.

They were all so joyous and optimistic. The convent was nothing like she'd imagined. The sisters saw the good in each other and celebrated life on a day-to-day basis. They took delight in every new flower blooming in their garden, but also in acts of service to those less fortunate than them.

'Well, you've made me feel better,' Michelle said. 'When I joined up my parents were worried I'd be lonely, and all my friends were like, what about sex? How can you give that up? Well, I figured you couldn't miss what you didn't know, but the way you speak, it doesn't sound like I'm missing much at all.'

Adeline agreed, warmth filling her chest at the possibilities that lay ahead. Back home, when she'd asked God for a sign of what to do next, the last thing she'd expected him to tell her was to join a convent, but after much consideration and more prayer, she'd chosen to give it a go. It wasn't like coming to live here was irreversible—the whole point of being a postulant was to experience a taste of religious life to decide if it was something you wanted to commit to—but already she knew this was what she wanted. That this was the right path for her. She wasn't silly enough to think that there wouldn't be tough times, times where she'd perhaps doubt her decision, but prayer and the support of her sisters would get her through.

Revived, she went into the communal bathroom down the corridor, readied herself for bed, then took Bella outside to relieve herself. As she waited for the dog to do her business, she looked up at the stars above, so clear and sharp in the night sky. She thought of Walsh, far away in the Great Southern Region of Western Australia, where the stars also shone in the same way. It was hard to believe she'd been gone less than two weeks—a few days on the road as she and Bella drove across the country and then a week in her new life—because she already felt so at home here.

The only people she really missed from Walsh were Sally and her nephews, whose photos were in frames on her bedside table. She'd been so busy since she arrived—getting to know the sisters and other postulants, learning the day-to-day routine of religious life, studying, praying and doing her bit to keep the household running—that she'd not had time to send Sally a proper update. Her sister-in-law probably thought she'd been eaten by wild dingoes on the Nullarbor.

When she and Bella returned to their bedroom, Michelle was snuggled under her covers, still reading, so Adeline decided to take the opportunity to write a letter home. She was allowed to send emails through the communal computer, but somehow a letter felt more personal. She imagined the joy Sally would feel when she saw the envelope sitting in their rural mail box alongside the usual bills and clothing catalogues.

Dear Sally,

You're probably wondering if I've fallen off the face of the earth, so this is to let you know I'm alive and living my best life and content in what I know you (and everyone else) thinks was a crazy decision.

Things have been busier than I imagined since arriving in Smallton, which by the way is such a cute little town. Well, when I say little, it's more than twice the size of Walsh but the buildings are quainter, and you can tell it was established during the Gold Rush. The post office, the two pubs and the Masonic Hall look like something from the set of an early Australian film. There's even this little old cinema that plays only Aussie movies. I haven't been yet, but my roomie (more on her later) says it's as cute inside as out.

Anyway, you're probably dying to know what life is like for me now. Living at the convent is a little like I imagined living in a dormitory at college might be, only with a more varied age range of housemates and less booze, sex and parties. Oh, and a lot more early mornings.

We get up at 5:30 every morning and head to the prayer room where we pray together for an hour. I can see you rolling your eyes, wondering what on earth we could find to pray about for so long, but the time goes fast. I always thought prayer was just asking for things, and yes, we do ask for things—peace in the world, food, and shelter for those in need, wisdom, and direction in our service—but it's also a lot about being thankful, about taking stock of what we already have. I'm telling you, it's better than yoga for clearing the mind.

Next is breakfast, which we eat in silence at long tables. Probably not something you can imagine with kids! The first few days the quiet felt strange, but now I'm used to it. It actually feels good to have permission to be together but not always talking.

There are thirteen of us here and we all pitch in with the cleaning, cooking, gardening, shopping etc, but on top of that each sister has an individual calling. Many of the sisters work outside the convent. Sister Josey works in the prison the next town over and although she's tiny and ancient, she apparently takes no nonsense from the inmates. You should hear some of her stories. Sister Mary works with the children at the local Catholic school, which she says is fun but sounds exhausting. And Sister Rita is a nurse.

The sisters remind me a bit of the CWA. Don't laugh! What I mean is they're a bunch of women passionate about Smallton and its people, who aren't afraid to get involved and do the hard work for their community. They bake for charity cake stalls, help raise money for women's shelters, volunteer at the soup kitchen, and Michelle (another postulant, and also my roomie) and Sister Lola have been giving English lessons to refugees. I'd quite like to help with that, but I guess we'll see what God has in mind.

Adeline wrote three full pages to Sally, spilling out her journey so far, and asking her to pass on hugs for the boys and say hi to her parents if she saw them. It felt good to be writing again.

'Goodnight,' she said to Michelle as she folded up the letter.

'Do you mind if I read a few more pages before switching off my lamp? I'll never be able to sleep if I close the book before I know who the killer is.'

'Not at all,' said Adeline with a chuckle. 'Enjoy.'

Chapter Six

The mattress shifted beside him, and Holden opened his eyes to see Bronte's silhouette as she climbed out of bed. She usually snuck out early, before the boys surfaced, but he got the feeling it wasn't anywhere close to daylight yet.

'What're you doing?' he asked, reaching for his mobile.

3:57 am.

'I can't sleep with you tossing and turning like you have worms or something,' she said, stumbling around the room, looking for the clothes she'd discarded last night.

He switched on his bedside lamp and sat up, leaning back against the headboard. 'Sorry.'

She shrugged, stooping to pick up her bra from the floor. 'It's fine.'

But he knew all too well that when a woman said she was fine, it meant the opposite, and that she wasn't just referring to his restlessness.

'Bronte, please, don't be like that. I've just got a lot on my mind. I'm ... distracted.'

'I understand. But sex is supposed to help you de-stress—and it's also supposed to be a two-person thing. Last night I may as well have been on my own.'

He was ashamed that she was right. After the boys had gone to their bedrooms and Ford to the kitchen to prepare a few things for the morning, he and Bronte had retreated to his bedroom, but he'd been too distracted to give her the attention she deserved.

'I'm sorry.'

'Stop apologising.' She sank back onto the bed and clutched his hand. 'We all have off nights, and we're cool, but you can't go on like this. I know you're focused on getting the tiny houses project off the ground and I get that you're stressed about Rocky, but you need to relax or you'll make yourself ill, and that won't be good for any of the boys.'

'I know.' But Rocky reminded him so much of himself at that age. Let down by his parents, hurt beyond belief yet bottling it all up inside, desperate for love and attention but refusing to let anyone close enough to give it to him. When that dog arrived last night, Holden had seen a glimpse of who the boy was deep inside, but he'd retreated right back into himself when the nun had come and taken Bella away.

Bronte started to yank on her boots.

'Don't go. Come back to bed and let me make it up to you,' he whispered, running his hand down her back.

Despite the thin cotton of her t-shirt, she shivered beneath his touch. 'Oh God,' she groaned. 'You better make this good, Holden Campbell.'

He pulled her back into the bed, boots and all, murmuring, 'Your wish is my command.' And this time, he refused to let thoughts of another woman creep into his head.

When they were done, Bronte rolled over, pulled the blankets up to her chin and succumbed to slumber again.

Holden, still unable to sleep, crept out of bed and then into the kitchen—not wanting to wake his brother or the boys—and made himself a coffee, pouncing at the kettle the moment it started to whistle. He was tempted to go outside and enjoy the peaceful time before sunrise, but he headed into the office instead. Ignoring the pile of unpaid bills on his desk, he switched on the computer. He'd get some money for his project if it meant applying for every grant available in this bloody country.

Rocky had a few years of foster care left before he'd be on his own, and hopefully by then Holden would have got through to him, but Sam was seventeen and in six months he'd age out of the system. Although he was basically a good kid, Sam had shown he had a wild streak and if he got in with the wrong crowd or fell on hard times again, Holden worried what might happen to him. His goal—to build several tiny houses on his property that he could rent at low-cost to ex-foster kids—seemed like a perfect solution, but the materials for just one house would cost at least twenty grand, and finding that kind of money was proving to be a problem.

By the time everyone woke a couple of hours later—teenage footsteps thundering down the hallway outside his office, loud arguments over the bathroom, the sounds of Ford cooking up a storm in the kitchen, and the dogs scrambling outside on the verandah as they were given their breakfast—Holden had applied for two more different types of funding.

'Morning bro,' Ford said as Holden entered the kitchen and dumped his empty mug in the dishwasher.

'Hey.' His brother was sitting at the large table in the middle of the room making sandwiches for lunches. Ford's wheelchair squeaked as he reached across to grab another loaf of bread. It killed Holden every time he heard that sound—he'd never get used to the idea that his brother would spend the rest of his life trapped in that chair because of him.

Shaking that thought from his head, he summoned a smile for Toovs and Sam, who were currently frying bacon and scrambling eggs respectively. Learning to feed yourself and others was one of the many skills Holden and Ford tried to give the boys in their care.

'Hmm …. That's good,' he said as he stole a rasher of bacon and then helped get everything else ready for breakfast. Rocky ambled in just as they were sitting down.

At seven o'clock every morning, Holden, Ford and the kids came together around the table to eat and discuss the day ahead.

'Anyone got any concerns?' Holden asked when the plates were filled and everyone except Rocky tucked in as if it might be their final meal.

'My only concern is going to school,' laughed Toovs. 'I should get myself suspended like Sam.'

Sam had recently stolen the school credit card and ordered pizzas to be delivered for his whole year group—the principal hadn't found it as amusing as everyone else—and he'd be doing jobs around the property for months to pay off what Holden had had to fork out to cover it.

'Don't even think about it,' Holden warned and saw Ford stifling a smirk. 'Sam's going to wish he was at school after I've finished with him today.'

The seventeen-year-old groaned and reached for another rasher of bacon, picking it up with his fingers, rather than the tongs. 'Better eat up then.'

Chapter Seven

Adeline sat on a wooden bench outside Mother Catherine's office and fiddled with the rosary beads in her pocket as she waited to be invited inside. She felt like a naughty schoolgirl waiting for a grilling from the principal. *Damn Bella.* As much as she loved her dog, the animal was already getting them into scrapes.

Shit. She wasn't supposed to say things like 'damn' or 'shit', but old habits were hard to break.

She jumped as the door creaked open and Mother Catherine appeared, her long salt-and-pepper hair tied up in a thick plait that hung over one shoulder. 'Adeline, you may come in now.'

'Thank you,' she managed as she pushed up from the stool and followed the tall, slender woman into her office. It was only the second time she'd been in there. The first had been on her day of arrival, but she'd been even more nervous then and taken in little of her surroundings.

Just like Mother Catherine, who reminded her of an old English sheepdog—fun but strong-willed—the office was nothing like she expected, but then she only had the one in *The Sound of Music* to compare it to. Sure, there was similar dark, wooden furniture—a desk, a couple of buffets that were very nearly identical to the one in her dining room back home—but the room was anything but dull. Sunlight shone in through the open windows, highlighting the pink painted walls and the inspirational quotes and Bible verses hanging on them. There was a floral couch opposite the desk, making the room feel much more like the office of a therapist than the head of a convent.

'Please, take a seat.' Mother Catherine gestured to the couch as she lowered herself into a matching armchair. 'Can I offer you a biscuit?'

She nodded towards a large tin on the coffee table. It was a bit of a joke between the sisters that their superior had a sweet tooth and the best treats were always to be found in her office.

'Um … no thank you.' Adeline could never eat when she was nervous.

'Are you okay, my child? You seem a little on edge.'

She swallowed and wiped the palms of her hands on her brown trousers. 'I just wanted to apologise for coming late to prayer last night. I don't want you to think I don't know its importance and I'll definitely not make a habit of it. It's just that Bella ran away from me while I was walking her, and I couldn't just leave her out there alone. But I promise—'

'Dear child.' Mother Catherine held up her hand and smiled warmly, the lines around her eyes crinkling. 'Please do not stress. I understand … sometimes these things happen, but in future, perhaps you should keep Bella on a leash when you walk her.'

'Yes. Of course.' Adeline nodded, imagining exactly what her dog would think about that. Back in Walsh, she'd had free run of the farm on their daily walks. Had it been selfish to bring her all the way here? Should she have left her at home with Ariel and the farm dogs?

'She's a lovely animal,' added Mother Catherine, her smile lines deepening. 'And she seems to be making herself not only at home but also useful. We haven't lost a chicken to foxes since her arrival and the alpacas appear to be quite smitten with her as well.'

Adeline beamed. 'Maremmas are wonderful dogs. They're extremely loyal, although not always the most obedient.'

'I've found the best people in life are often similar.' Mother Catherine winked. 'But I didn't ask you here today to talk about dogs.'

'Oh?' Adeline's stomach twisted as she realised this might not be a reprimand. Could it instead be the meeting about what her role would be at the convent? She hoped she wouldn't be asked to join Sister Rita, visiting the sick and elderly in hospital. She'd spent so much time visiting Gran these last few years, and hospitals were such depressing places.

'You've been here almost a week now and I wanted to touch base to see how you're settling in. I know convent life can take some getting used to—the early mornings, the communal eating, our various routines.'

'Oh, I'm loving it,' Adeline gushed, and then wondered if she should be so effusive. Wasn't living a religious life about making sacrifices for the greater good? 'I mean … I'm settling in fine. Everyone has been very welcoming and there's never a dull moment. I like being busy and there's always something to do around here.'

'That there is.' Mother Catherine smiled. 'But you need to remember that sometimes not being busy is just as important. It is in those quiet moments of solitude, when we push all else but God from our hearts and minds, that we feel closest to him.'

Adeline didn't trust herself to do anything but nod. She was going to learn to listen first and speak later. Her big mouth had got her into trouble many times in the past and it was just one of many things she wanted to fix.

'*Are* you feeling close to him?'

Adeline blinked—it was as if Mother Catherine could see right through her. 'I'm trying. I want to feel that way, but I'm scared.'

'Of what?'

'Of failure,' she admitted. 'Everyone here is so good and kind and caring and I want to be like that, but I just don't know if I'm good enough.'

'It is not about being good enough—none of us will ever be perfect. I think you're being too harsh on yourself. The other sisters speak very highly of you; however, you need to *want* to be close to God, not just feel like you should.'

'Oh, I do, I promise.' Tears rushed to Adeline's eyes. 'I've never wanted anything more. I felt so unsettled before I got here, unsure of what my purpose in life was.' Perhaps she should mention the discovery of Gran's confession and how it had rocked her to her core, but she felt too ashamed. It wasn't her sin, but the fact that she'd never suspected her grandmother of having such a black soul made her feel somehow accountable. 'From the moment I walked into the convent, I felt peace in my heart. I feel like I belong here more than anywhere I've ever been.'

'I'm glad.' Mother Catherine smiled again and leaned forward to pick a box of tissues off the coffee table, which she offered to Adeline. 'This is not always an easy path to follow—nothing worth doing is ever easy—but it is a fulfilling one for those who choose it. I can see your willingness and I think it's time for you to make another contribution to convent life.'

Excitement pricked Adeline's heart. She wiped her eyes, then sat forward on the edge of the couch. 'That's wonderful. I've been thinking a lot about what I have to offer, and I was wondering if I could help Michelle and Lola teach the refugee families English.

English was my best subject at school, and I think I'd be good at it.' When Mother Catherine's brow furrowed slightly, Adeline changed tack. 'Or I could work in the store? I've really enjoyed making the candles and rosaries.'

In Smallton, the convent was almost like a tourist destination. While they didn't offer tours, they did have a shopfront where they sold craft items made by the sisters—things like candles, religious jewellery, knitted toys, inspirational quotes in artistic calligraphy, honey from the bees they kept—and people often took selfies in front of the entrance to the main building.

'I must admit, I've never been much of a people person, so I think witnessing to those who come into the shop would be a good challenge for me.'

Please God, just not the hospital.

'You are a journalist, are you not?'

'Um … yes.' Adeline wondered at Mother Catherine's question. What did that have to do with her life here? 'Well, that's what my degree is in, but my career never really got off the ground. I … I had to leave my job at the city newspaper …' For reasons she'd tried her best to forget. 'So I went back to the farm, where I worked on the small local paper.'

She knew people had joked about her treating it like *The New York Times*—but was it a sin to take pride in your work?

'The *Walsh Whisperer*,' confirmed Mother Catherine. When Adeline showed surprise, she added, 'I took the liberty of doing a little background research and it sounds like you did more than work on the paper. The way people speak, you *were* the paper.'

'You spoke to people from Walsh?' *Oh God.* She could only imagine what some of them would say.

'Yes. The gentleman who took over from you said yours were big stilettos to fill and that you'd be greatly missed.'

Stilettos? That sounded just like old Trevor Norrish, who thought himself a bit of a comedian, but what did this have to do with her role here? 'I'm sorry … I'm not sure of the relevance of my journalism?'

'Have you seen Sister Mary's NunTalk column in the *Smallton Gazette*?'

Adeline nodded. In addition to the column, there was also a Dear Sister section where locals sent in their problems and Sister Josey offered highly amusing wisdom and advice. 'I've been reading all the back issues to get a feel for what goes on here.'

'Good idea. Well,' Mother Catherine clasped her hands together in her lap, 'Sister Mary is feeling a little burnt out and we both think it would be a good idea for someone new to take over.'

'Me? But I haven't been here long enough. I don't know enough about … *anything*!'

Mother Catherine chuckled. 'Writing about our life and work here will help you get better acquainted with the other sisters and our ways.'

Adeline couldn't help feeling a little disappointed—she wanted to do something that would help those less fortunate than her. But if this was what Mother Catherine wanted—if this was what *God* wanted—then she would do it. 'Okay, when do I start?'

'I've asked Sister Mary to meet with you this afternoon, before evening prayer, to go over everything. We both thought it would be good if her last column introduces you to the readers and she'll also be there to offer you any guidance while you get used to the role.'

'Thank you,' Adeline said. 'I promise I'll do my very best.'

'I know you will.'

Adeline thought she'd be dismissed after that and was looking forward to heading out into the garden to tend the veggie patch and talk to Bella while she digested all this, but Mother

Catherine leaned back into her armchair as if she was only just getting started.

'Now, what do you know about TikTok?'

'What?' She couldn't have been more surprised if Mother Catherine had asked her what she knew about quantum physics.

'TikTok. It's a social media platform.'

'Oh, I know. I'm just ... surprised you know about it.'

'I make it my business to know about a lot of things,' declared Mother Catherine. She paused a moment before asking, 'What is our purpose as sisters?'

Adeline took her time to answer, not wanting to make a mistake. 'To serve God. To love him and obey him. To belong to him and to share his message with others?'

'And that means doing our best to stay relevant in the modern world.' Mother Catherine retrieved a smartphone from her pocket and handed it to Adeline. 'I want you to get us going on NunTok.'

'NunTok?'

'Yes. It's the nun section of TikTok—you know, like BookTok and FarmTok?'

Adeline stared down at the phone as if it were a baby alien. Was this a joke?

'This was kindly donated by the Smallton Co-op,' Mother Catherine continued. 'When I mentioned what I hoped to do, the director gifted it to us.'

'Wow. And you want me to run a TikTok account for the convent?'

The older woman nodded as if Adeline had asked a very stupid question. 'If you think you're up to the task?'

'I ... Yes. I guess I am.'

'Good. It's settled then. I've already downloaded the app onto the phone and set up an account. The username is SistersOfSmallton, but now it's over to you.'

This was a lot to take in. She leaned forward and retrieved a biscuit from the tin.

'Um ... to be on TikTok, I'll need to do a little scrolling of other accounts. TikTok is all about following the trends.'

'That's fine,' said Mother Catherine. 'Just don't spend all day dillydallying on there.'

'So, what sorts of things to you want me to post? Bible verses? Prayers?' It all seemed a little odd to Adeline. Weren't prayers meant to be sacred?

'Oh, I'll leave that up to you. The goal is to show the world that we are real people who can have fun and enjoy life while also living our Godly purpose.'

Before Adeline could ask anything else, there was a knock on the door. She took the opportunity to take a bite of her biscuit, relishing the sugar hit.

'Come in,' called Mother Catherine.

Michelle appeared a second later. 'Am I too early?' she asked, grinning as usual and almost dancing on the spot.

'No, your timing is perfect.' Mother Catherine looked back to Adeline. 'I've asked Michelle to take you into town to introduce you to Mike, the editor of the *Smallton Gazette*, while she does the weekly grocery shop, and also to give you a proper tour. You never know, you might find some inspiration for TikTok.'

Chapter Eight

Once breakfast was done, it was chore time at Holden and Ford's place. Morning was for inside duties, and they had a roster system for keeping the house in order. Whoever was on clean-up washed the breakfast dishes, someone else collected the dirty washing from the various baskets around the old house to put the first load into the machine, and someone gave the dogs their breakfast and let out the chickens. Although the boys groaned and grumbled about the jobs they were expected to do, they very rarely refused. They might never voice it, but they knew that a room here was better than the alternative. They liked the camaraderie they'd found here and the security of knowing that no matter what they did, Holden and Ford would be there for them.

Most of the boys they'd fostered came from broken homes or abusive families. Their parents either didn't give a damn or were lost to substance abuse, and some of the boys had even been kicked out of home. A lot of them had even been tossed out of foster care homes after their (multiple) carers had been unable to control them. They came here because they didn't have anywhere else to go. When they first arrived, they often pushed boundaries, trying to see if Holden and Ford would also give up on them, but they soon learned that no matter how much they swore, talked back, fought with each other, or refused to do what they were told, that wasn't going to happen.

Generally, it took anywhere from a few days to a week for this realisation to dawn and then they did whatever morning chores were expected of them because it left their afternoons free to make stuff in the shed or work with the dogs, which was everyone's favourite activity. It was much easier to get the boys to work with their hands or the animals than it was to get them to do any reading or schoolwork, but Holden knew there was value in all types of learning. It was life skills they were teaching here, staying-off-the-streets-and-out-of-jail skills. And he didn't just abandon his charges when they aged out of foster care, or at least he tried not to. If possible, he helped the boys get housing and work in the area, and most Friday nights they still came around for a 'family' get-together. Often at least one or two spent the weekend, camping on his couches.

While Ford got ready for work, Holden did the rounds, supervising the chores and making sure the boys were ready for the day. Sam and Toovs were (miraculously) doing what they were supposed to be doing, but he found Rocky in the living room, watching cartoons on TV.

'Hey Rocky,' he said going over and sitting next to him on the couch. 'What ya doing?'

The boy didn't even turn his head. 'What the fuck's it look like I'm doing?'

Holden didn't flinch at the bad language. Rocky didn't know it yet, but no matter how hard he pushed, he wasn't going to give up on him. 'It looks like you're watching TV when you haven't done your chores yet,' he said, reaching for the remote and muting the sound.

Rocky finally looked at him, or rather glared. 'I didn't eat any breakfast so I shouldn't have to clean up, and my clothes aren't dirty.'

Holden made a mental note to make sure Rocky ate something soon, even if it meant bribing him with junk food when they did the grocery shopping. As for the clothes ... that battle could come next. Maslow's hierarchy of needs and everything. 'Okay then, why don't you go outside and help feed the dogs? You could even throw a ball around and give them some morning exercise.'

'They're not my dogs.'

Rocky was one of the kids rebelling against the system. He kept running away from wherever he was placed. Holden had heard of him on the grapevine and insisted on meeting the boy and petitioning the authorities to let him have a go. He'd been here almost three weeks and although Holden had tried all his usual tricks, Rocky had so far rejected all his attempts at connection, but at least he hadn't run yet.

'You know, we can go back to the shelter and try to find you a dog again,' he said, thinking that after meeting Bella, Rocky might be more responsive.

The kid just shook his head.

'Okay,' Holden said, trying not to feel frustrated, 'you can watch the rest of your show, but when everyone's gone, I'm gunna need you to come and work on the fences and help build a new chook pen with me and Sam.'

'Whatever.'

'Thanks.' Holden stood, unmuted the TV and then handed the remote back to Rocky. Sam and Toovs would likely grumble about him getting special treatment, but if it meant he was more amenable to coming outside and working later, so be it. Baby steps.

As he turned to go, Rocky said, 'Do I get paid like Sam?'

'Sam's not getting paid. He's working to pay me back for his, uh, misdemeanours.'

'What am I working for then?' The boy shrugged. 'I've done nothin' wrong.'

To get you out of the house and to learn some skills, which will hopefully help you develop purpose and self-worth.

He'd found that kids were much more likely to talk, to open up, when they were doing something productive with their hands. He could sit here all day next to Rocky on the couch and get nowhere, but get him outside and he'd have a chance.

'How about we make a deal?' he tried.

Rocky looked at him warily. 'What kind of deal?'

'You help me and Sam this morning and then when we go shopping, you can pick some snacks for the weekend.'

'What kind of snacks?'

'That's up to you—lollies, chocolate, chips—within reason of course.'

'Okay, fine.'

Holden's heart lifted when Rocky held his hand out to seal the deal, but he made sure not to show any of this hope as they shook.

'I'll be back to get you in half an hour,' he said and then, leaving Rocky to his cartoons, he headed back out into the kitchen.

Soon Toovs would hop on his bike and ride into town to the local high school, and Ford would drive to the barbershop in their minibus that had been modified specially for him. Later, Holden, Sam and Rocky would ride in on bicycles he'd found at the tip and fixed up so they were almost like new again. After they did the shopping, they'd trek the groceries across the road to the barbershop for Ford to bring home after work.

Holden didn't drive. It wasn't that he didn't know how, more that he didn't trust himself.

Chapter Nine

'I can't believe you've got a phone,' Michelle said as she settled behind the wheel of the convent's ancient Toyota Tarago.

Adeline clicked her seatbelt into place. 'It's not *my* phone. I'm not allowed to use it for anything but TikTok.'

'It's still exciting. I wonder why Mother Catherine didn't ask me to do it. Social media is the one thing I miss from my old life. It's so much harder to stalk people I used to know without it.'

Adeline shook her head at Michelle's confession—perhaps she'd just answered her own question.

While Michelle drove the short distance into Smallton, Adeline searched #NunTok and started following some other accounts. She was surprised to see how many sisters were on the platform, and by the time they arrived in town, her mind was exploding with ideas for how to bring the Sisters of Smallton to the world. And, if she succeeded at this, maybe Mother Catherine would consider her for other work as well.

As they passed the giant water tower on the edge of town that was featured on all the shire's tourism information, she wondered how she could feature it in a video. One of her favourite things she'd seen so far in the region, the round tower was painted with the most magical mural. Sister Rita had explained that it had been done by an Indigenous artist to pay tribute to the local Gulidjan and Gadubanud peoples. There was a portrait on each side, of a beloved female elder from the past.

'This area is known as women's country,' Sister Rita had told her, 'because the Gulidjan and Gadubanud people are a matrilineal society.'

Adeline thought it fitting that the town also housed the sisters, another group of wise and wonderful women.

Despite its name, Smallton was practically a metropolis compared to Walsh; there was even a Woolworths and a McDonald's. The main street was lined with the usual four-wheel drives and dusty dual-cab utes that you saw in any country town. As she slowed the Tarago, Michelle sang, 'Hail Mary, full of grace, please find us a parking space.'

Adeline laughed. In their short time as roomies, she'd frequently found herself giggling at Michelle's unique prayers, and was surprised how often they worked.

Sure enough, mere seconds after she'd uttered the request, a car pulled away from right outside the post office, which happened to be next door to the *Smallton Gazette*.

'Hey, can you say that again?' Adeline asked as Michelle began reversing into the spot.

'Say what?'

'The prayer about finding us a parking space. It'll make the perfect TikTok.' She was going to have to get better at filming things on the spur of the moment.

'Sure.' Michelle was delighted to be asked and did it with flair.

'I predict we're going to make you a TikTok star,' laughed Adeline as they climbed out of the van.

A bell pinged above the door as they entered the *Smallton Gazette*, and a man looked up from where he was on the phone behind a desk. He raised a finger as if to say he'd be with them in a minute.

'That's Mike,' Michelle explained as Adeline glanced around. The office wasn't much bigger than the tiny office in the community resource centre where she'd put together the *Whisperer*, but the set-up looked much more professional, and Mike surprised her.

She'd been the youngest on the paper back home—all the other volunteers were senior citizens—so when Mother Catherine had mentioned the editor, she'd been expecting an elderly man with grey hair or none, wiry whiskers on his chin and narrow spectacles he peered over when talking to people. But Mike was young— maybe early thirties—and *gorgeous*, in a golden retriever kind of way. He even had shoulder-length, wavy caramel-blonde hair.

'Hi there.' He stood as he put down his phone and walked around the desk to offer his hand. 'You must be Adeline. Sister Mary let me know you'd be popping in for a visit. Hello Michelle, how are you doing?'

'Hello, I'm great,' Michelle all but simpered.

'That's awesome. I must come down to the convent and grab some more of your honey. Used up the last bit on my toast this morning.'

Michelle grinned. 'I'll tell Sister Mary, she'll be stoked, and we'll drop round another jar for you next time we're in town, won't we, Adeline?'

She nodded.

Mike made them coffee and they sat in the small kitchen discussing the paper, which was distributed far more widely than the *Whisperer*.

'About a decade ago, when regional newspapers were being shut down all over the place, the Smallton Shire decided the *Gazette* was something worth saving, so they bought it and now it's entirely local.'

Mike explained that he was on salary but did his job with the help of a few enthusiastic volunteers. The paper went to print every Wednesday, for distribution on Thursday, and Adeline's column would be due each Monday. He was a typical journo and asked her a lot of questions about her own background, her writing experience and why she'd decided to become a postulant.

'I've always gone to church, but when my grandmother died recently, I did some soul-searching and the Lord led me here.'

Mike laughed. 'Love led me here.'

'Oh?'

He beamed and then turned around a frame on his desk to reveal a photo of him, his arms draped over a slightly older man with dark hair and dark glasses, but a bright smile similar to Mike's own. 'This is my husband, Reeve. Isn't he dishy?'

Adeline nodded—it seemed the polite thing to do—while feeling silently relieved that Mike was taken and therefore not going to become a temptation.

'We met at ComicCon a few years ago and fell instantly in love.' He winked. 'Just like the movies. We did the long-distance thing for about six months, but when this job came up where Reeve already lived, we took it as a sign.'

'Reeve works at the library,' Michelle said, 'so you'll meet him next.'

Although Adeline had been unsure about taking on the column, Mike's enthusiasm for his paper reminded her of how she'd felt about the *Whisperer*, and by the time they left the office, she was excited about having the chance to be involved in a community paper again, even if only in a small way.

After a quick trip to the library, where Michelle checked out ten new novels and Adeline met Reeve, who helped her find a copy of *TikTok for Dummies*, they visited the post office, the medical centre, the café, the op shop, the chemist and even the pub. Adeline was feeling overloaded and overpeopled, but they still had to do the grocery shopping.

'You grab a trolley too,' ordered Michelle as they entered the supermarket. 'We've got a long list.'

'Do you usually do the shopping?' Adeline asked.

Michelle was already throwing in items like a woman on a mission. It reminded Adeline of that TV show she'd loved when she was little—*Supermarket Sweep* or something.

'No, the sisters take turns. Whenever Sister Josey does it, she brings home way too much ice cream, but that woman is an ice-cream fiend. She'll eat two litres in one night if we don't hide it.'

Adeline laughed as they progressed down the aisle, then baulked when Michelle hauled a giant carton of Diet Coke cans into her trolley.

'What?' Michelle shrugged. 'Rita is a nightmare if she doesn't get her daily fix.'

Shopping with Michelle was more fun than any grocery shopping Adeline had ever done before and suddenly she realised she should be filming this—showing the world that just because a woman had decided to take vows of poverty, chastity and obedience didn't mean she couldn't have fun and the odd vice.

She whipped the phone out of her bag and started taking photos to create a montage on TikTok later. Once Michelle's trolley was loaded with food, they started on Adeline's, heading down the cleaning aisle and then to the toiletries. Her eyes boggled as she watched Michelle almost clear the shelves of sanitary pads and tampons.

'Next week is Aunty Flo's visit.'

It took a second for Adeline to work out what she meant. 'For everyone?'

'Yep, well, everyone who hasn't gone through The Change yet. Haven't you heard that when a group of women live together, their cycles sync? It's not a myth. That's why we also stocked up on chocolate and Panadol.'

Adeline nodded. 'The same thing happened when I was at boarding school.'

'Was your boarding school anything like Harry Potter's?'

'It was a lot less fun.'

'Oh.' Michelle halted on their way to the checkout. 'I forgot curry powder. You head to the front and start unloading. I'll be there in a mo.'

As Adeline rounded the end of the aisle, she almost collided with two teenagers who appeared to be having a trolley race.

'Rocky! Sam!' came a gruff voice from a few feet away. 'Quit dicking around and go get the pasta like I asked.'

Adeline looked up to confirm what she'd already guessed—the voice belonged to none other than Holden Campbell. He was wearing faded jeans and a red flannelette shirt, its sleeves pushed up to the elbows drawing her attention to his muscular, inked arms.

'Afternoon, Maria.'

'My name is Adeline,' she said before noticing the twinkle in his dark eyes. 'Is Maria the only nun you know?'

In response, he smirked and then glanced into her trolley.

Of course she had to run into him while pushing a trolley that was almost overflowing with feminine hygiene products. 'What? You don't think sisters bleed like other women?'

'Touché.' He ran a hand through his thick, dark, long locks, treating her to a close-up of the tattoos on his upper right arm. She made out a dog—or was it a wolf—and some kind of Celtic symbols before he dropped his hand back to his side. Holden himself reminded her a bit of a wolf, or maybe a dingo.

They stared at each other for a few moments in awkward silence. Something about this man made Adeline uncomfortable, and when she was uncomfortable, she turned to small talk.

'Why aren't the boys at school?'

'Rocky's on sabbatical and Sam's suspended,' Holden explained.

Sabbatical? Adeline wanted to ask him what exactly that meant, but Michelle appeared with the curry powder.

'I thought you were heading for the checkouts,' she said, looking between Adeline and Holden.

'Sorry, I distracted her.'

'I'll bet.' Michelle raised her eyebrows, making Adeline feel like a chastised child, even though the other woman was quite a few years younger than her.

What? *She* was allowed to talk about how hot Holden was, but Adeline wasn't allowed to have a conversation with the guy?

'How's your dog?' the shortest kid asked, and Adeline was grateful for the question.

'Bella? She's good. Naughty, but good.'

'Can you bring her to visit again?'

'Um … I don't know.' She got the feeling neither Michelle nor Holden would approve. 'I'm pretty busy.'

The boy's shoulders slumped, and she realised as she looked into his downcast eyes that Rocky looked more dejected than a boy of his age should, like a dog who'd been mistreated by its owners.

'Come on, mate.' When Holden put his hand on Rocky's shoulder, he flinched. 'We better finish our shop.' Then, as he and his two charges turned to go, he looked back and winked at Adeline. 'See ya round, Maria.'

A most unwelcome heat flushed through her body. 'It's Adeline,' she retorted, and heard him chuckle as he swaggered away.

'You should be careful of him,' Michelle warned as they began loading their groceries onto the checkout.

'What do you mean?'

'It's obvious he's got a thing for you. And I get the feeling he's the kind of guy who gets what he wants.'

He has a thing for me?

For a second, something in Adeline's belly fluttered at the thought, but she quickly banished it. 'Thanks for the warning, but I'm sure he was just being polite.'

'Is that what they call it these days?' Michelle teased.

Adeline rolled her eyes. 'I doubt we'll be seeing much of each other anyway, but even if we were, I've chosen my path and I don't plan on straying from it.'

Especially not for some redneck covered in ink, who didn't appear to have heard of haircuts or shaving.

Chapter Ten

'There.' Adeline smiled proudly at the screen as she put the full stop on the final sentence of her first ever NunTalk column. She looked at the time and saw that it was quite late, but while she was at the computer, she took the chance to shoot off a quick email to Sally and Mum, who would read it to Dad.

Hi everyone!

Hope you're all well and happy. I'm still loving life with the sisters. Mother Catherine has allocated me the job of writing a weekly column in the local paper and for a bit of fun, I've written it from Bella's point-of-view. I'm getting 'Bella' to interview the other sisters—asking them why they chose this life and to explain a little bit about what they do here.

All the sisters have such interesting stories. Sister Josey is almost ninety, but she has almost as much energy as Bella. She grew up around bikers and spent much of her adulthood on the streets, in and out of prison. When she was homeless at sixty-five, she met a sister at a shelter and found God. Now she visits prisoners herself, hoping she can help save others.

*Then there's Sister Mary, who wrote NunTalk before I did.
She's forty-two and calls herself a cradle Catholic, but that doesn't
mean she always wanted to be a sister. She's got a degree in political
science, but disillusion with life led her here. Sister Rita is a hoot
and has been a sister since she was fifteen. She even did her nursing
degree while at the convent. Like my roomie Michelle—this life is
something they both felt called to from a young age.*

*And Bella loves it here as much as I do. Although that's probably
because the other sisters spoil her rotten. Michelle keeps sneaking her
treats when she thinks I'm not looking. I tell her it's not good for
Bella, but they're almost as hard to control as each other.*

Speaking of Bella …

Adeline glanced around. Where was she? Her dog wasn't usually far from her side, but the only company she had right now
were the convent's two black cats—Benno and Barnabas—who
were watching her from on top of a nearby side table. In theory,
the cats were supposed to keep rodents under control, but they
seemed to spend most of their time sleeping or demanding cud-
dles. The two Bs were not fans of Bella, even though she'd been
doing her best to make friends since arriving.

Now that Adeline thought about it, she hadn't seen Bella since
the dog had gone outside with Sister Lola a couple of hours ago
to put the chickens in their coop for the night. As they went in to
evening prayer, Lola had told Adeline that Bella refused to come
back inside. She'd made a mental note to go get her afterwards,
but instead she'd been sidetracked by finishing her column. It was
weird that Bella hadn't whined to come in at the back door or
barked at a possum or something outside. Back home Bella and
Ariel were constantly going off at the slightest noise, always on
guard for intruders.

She quickly finished her email, then stood and stretched her arms above her head, trying to rid her back of the cricks caused from sitting so long. The convent was dead silent—all the other sisters having retreated to their rooms for private prayer and relaxation before bed. Even the noise of the computer shutting down sounded loud. She crept quietly through the big old building, the floorboards creaking under her feet, and headed outside to fetch Bella.

Shivering in the cool evening air, Adeline softly called the dog's name so as not to disturb anyone else. When there was no response, she sighed, then set off towards the chicken pen on the other side of the yard, thankful for the light of the moon showing her the way. The beloved chickens, who the sisters treated more like pets than providers, ran free during the day, which caused Bella great anxiety as she tried to keep an eye on all of them, but at night they were locked away to protect them from foxes. Adeline had been almost certain she'd find Bella by the coop, standing guard, so panic gripped her when the dog was nowhere to be seen.

Could Bella be hurt? Maybe bitten by a snake?

Although it was late autumn, Michelle had seen an Eastern Brown in the garden only yesterday. Her pulse starting to race, she hurried back inside to grab a torch.

This time when she went outside, she wasn't so quiet. She stomped along the path, hoping to scare off any snakes as she called 'Bella' over and over again. The convent stood on about two acres, which included the main building, some sheds, the gardens and a couple of paddocks. During the day, the garden made Adeline think of the Garden of Eden—full of luscious fruit trees, vegetables and beautiful blooms that the sisters made into bouquets to give to patients in hospital. There were also several large eucalypts providing shade that they sat under to read or pray. But at night, silent, cold and shadowy, it felt a little sinister.

'Come on, Bella, where are you?' she called as she headed for the paddocks, which housed the larger animals. There was a goat called Giles who had to be confined because every time he escaped, he ate whatever was in his path. Adeline still wasn't exactly sure of his purpose, but he was almost as beloved as the chickens. The sisters also had a cow named Juniper—after St Juniper, a follower of St Francis—which they milked every morning and night, and half a dozen alpacas.

Juniper looked up as she approached, but when Adeline scanned the paddock, she saw no blur of white among the other animals.

'Dammit, Bella,' she said under her breath. 'Where the hell—I mean *heck*—are you?'

She was about to go inside and ask Michelle to come help her look, when her torchlight shone upon a large hole under one of the fences.

A large, dog-sized hole.

Freshly dug if the upturned soil was anything to go by.

'No! Little devil.' This was the last thing she needed tonight when she'd been dreaming of bed and a nice long sleep before early morning prayer, but she now had a good idea where Bella might have gone.

She cursed under her breath. Without a phone number for Holden, she had only one choice. After collecting Bella's leash and donning a puffer jacket and beanie to keep her warm, she started down the road, walking the short distance to his place.

It wasn't long before she turned down the gravel driveway that had led her and Bella there at the beginning of the week.

She prayed she'd find her outside. She didn't fancy knocking on the door to ask for assistance. She could just imagine Holden's smug response when she admitted she'd lost track of Bella again. As Adeline got nearer to the house, she came upon what looked to be some kind of party. A bonfire lit up the sky and around it sat half a dozen boys on old milk crates roasting sausages, toasting marshmallows and generally larking around.

There were almost as many dogs as people—some stretched out between the boys, lazing in the warmth of the fire, and others play fighting with each other off to the side. And there was her blur of white, wrestling on the ground with the young boy from the supermarket.

It was going to be impossible to retrieve Bella without making a scene.

Adeline took a quick breath, her nerves jangling with determination as she strode out of the darkness and into the circle of mutts and unruly teens.

Holden looked up from where he was sitting on a crate, nursing a mug. 'Well, well, well, if it isn't Maria?' he said, smirking in that irritating fashion of his. 'I was wondering when you were going to turn up.'

'For the last time, my name's Adeline,' she snapped. 'And were you planning on keeping Bella *all* night?'

'Hey.' He shrugged. 'Not my responsibility to return your dog if you can't keep her under control.'

Adeline seethed. 'I *can* keep her under control. She was outside in the yard and when I went to get her in, I discovered she'd dug a hole, but I assure you, I won't be letting this happen again. Why didn't you call me?'

'One, I don't have your number.' He rubbed a hand over his scruffy beard. 'And two, seems like you guessed where she was anyway.'

'That's beside the point.' Turning away from him in a huff, she glared into the circle of boys and dogs, faces aglow as they peered into the flames at the centre. She'd have to scrub Bella for hours to get the smoke out of her beautiful fur.

'Bella come!' she shouted.

The white beast turned her head but didn't make a move to leave the young boy's side.

Holden chuckled and Adeline got a feeling of déjà vu from that first day they'd met.

Fingers curling into fists, she called the dog again, her frustration growing when Bella refused to budge. She felt the boys' eyes boring into her as if she was a TV show they couldn't get enough of. Some of them were trying to hide their snickering, others not even bothering. She suddenly felt very aware that she was the only girl present (dogs not included).

Where was the woman from the other night?

Her pulse raced as a shadow fell over her. She didn't need to look to know that Holden had come right up behind her. Could she feel the heat emanating from his body and blooming in her cheeks, or was it simply the fire?

'Anyone ever tell you you're super-hot when you're angry?' His voice was low so only she could hear.

Hot? Was he *flirting* with her? 'I'm not angry, I'm frustrated,' she said under her breath.

'Well, you're hot when you're frustrated as well.' This time his warm breath tickled the back of her neck.

Nope, definitely not the fire; suddenly her puffer jacket felt redundant.

She spun around and glared at him. 'Has anyone ever told you how annoying you are?'

'Once or twice. Want some help?'

As much as she wanted to tell him where he could shove his assistance, the way Bella was behaving didn't leave her much choice.

'Yes, that would be lovely,' she said, swallowing her pride and flashing Holden a saccharine smile.

As he whistled, all the dogs froze and looked towards him. 'Bella,' he barked. 'Come!'

The dog looked to the young boy, then back to Holden and reluctantly made her way towards them.

'Thank you,' Adeline said begrudgingly as she clipped the leash on Bella's collar.

'Not a problem.'

Bella started to whine and tug the leash back towards the circle.

'Seems like she wants to stay a while,' Holden said. 'Why don't you sit? Have a drink. Roast a marshmallow with us.'

Adeline's fingers went to the rosary buried in her pocket. Not only did she *not* want to stay, but she also shouldn't—she had an early start in the morning and could only imagine what Mother Catherine might say if anyone noticed she was missing.

'Or do you nuns have a curfew?' he added.

'I told you, we're not nuns,' she snapped, and too late realised he was only saying so to rile her up.

His smirk confirmed it. 'Sisters. I know. I know.' He pointed towards the bonfire. 'Please accept my sincere apologies and a cup of Milo.'

She could tell he was expecting her to turn him down, to run away as fast as she possibly could. Well, she'd show him. She wasn't afraid of a pack of boys and a few wild dogs, and she most certainly wasn't scared of their cocky, unkempt leader.

'One drink,' she said—half to Bella, half to Holden—'and then we're going.'

She unclipped Bella's leash and the dog immediately went back to the boy. Adeline followed. 'I think she likes you,' she told him.

The boy shrugged, ruffling the fur around Bella's neck. Adeline wasn't sure who was more in love, boy or dog.

'What's your name?'

'Rocky.'

'I'm Adeline. This is Bella, but I guess you already know that.'

'How old is she?'

'She's five. How old are you?'

'Almost fourteen,' he said, in a semi-aggressive tone.

'Cool.' She wasn't sure what else to say and started to back away.

'Come on.' Holden placed his hand gently on her arm and she tried to ignore the way her insides shivered at his touch.

What the heck was she playing at by staying here? She only hoped all the sisters had retired to bed by now and Michelle was too wrapped up in her latest thriller to notice Adeline was still 'working'.

'I'll introduce you to the rest of the gang.'

He got her another milk crate and sat her down between himself and Ford.

'Ford, this is Maria—the *nun* who can't seem to control her dog—and Maria, this is my annoying little brother, Ford.'

'I think he means his better looking, smarter, funnier, more gentlemanly brother,' Ford said, offering her his hand. 'Nice to meet you, *Adeline*.'

She laughed as she took his hand, but he wasn't wrong, at least not on the better-looking part. Whereas Holden had the look of a mongrel—as if he never gave a second thought to personal grooming—Ford's dark hair was cut in a fashionable style, closely shaved at the back and sides with a quiff at the top slicked with gel. He too had a beard but not a big bushy one like his brother's. His was close-shaven and his eyebrows looked as if he gave them proper attention as well. He wore a diamond stud in one ear and although she wasn't usually one for men with jewellery, it suited him. If he were a dog, he'd be a well-groomed cocker spaniel.

'Nice to meet you.'

Holden quickly went around the circle and got the boys to say their names.

'Sam,' said the other one from the supermarket, narrowing his eyes a little before taking a drag of a cigarette.

Pitbull, she thought.

The boy next to him had a dark-haired mullet. 'Thaddeus, but you can call me Toovs like everyone else.' *Rottweiler.*

She frowned. 'Why do they call you that?'

''Cos my surname's Toovy.'

'I see,' she said and looked to the next boy, who was older than the ones she'd met before. Maybe nineteen or twenty. He looked of Italian or Greek descent. Perhaps a cane corso. 'And you are?'

He lifted his hand in a quick wave. 'Luka.'

No way was she going to remember all these names, although her mnemonic habit of associating people with dog breeds often helped.

The last guy—Great Dane to a tee with his large size and shaved head—introduced himself as Mitch.

Rocky was definitely the youngest of the lot. He gave off the vibe of a chihuahua, as if he had small-dog syndrome. His voice hadn't even broken yet, whereas some of the others were even bigger and bulkier than Holden.

'And do you all live here?' she asked.

'Not anymore,' Holden said, grabbing a mug from a crate off to one side, filling it with liquid from an actual billy can, then adding Milo and a splash of milk. 'Here you go.'

She took the drink, mindful not to touch his fingers in the process. 'Thanks.'

'Careful, it's hot.'

'You don't say,' she said with a roll of her eyes.

'You know,' he said, nodding over towards Bella, 'you really need to train your dog. You're supposed to be in charge of her, not the other way around.'

And there she'd been starting to warm to Holden Campbell. Resisting the urge to throw the Milo back in his face, she said, 'I'll have you know that maremmas are notoriously difficult to train.' She wasn't about to tell him she ran a puppy kindy back in Walsh, because he'd only say she was clearly unqualified.

'Haven't met a dog *I* couldn't train yet.'

'Well, good for you,' she retorted. 'Do they call you the dog whisperer?'

Holden snorted.

'Stop taunting our guest,' Ford said, from where he was sitting in his wheelchair next to Adeline's crate. He offered her a bag of marshmallows. 'Find yourself a stick and please excuse my brother's behaviour; he's almost as difficult to train as a maremma.'

'Hah!' She grinned her thanks at Ford as she took a marshmallow.

'Here, you can have my stick,' offered the rottweiler—Toovs if she recalled—as he handed her a long, skinny one that was already dirty and globby on one end.

Adeline hesitated, but, unlike Holden, she didn't want to be rude. 'Thanks.' She put her marshmallow on the other end and followed as Ford wheeled himself towards the bonfire.

He shoved a very long stick—marshmallow on the end—into the flames. 'I can't get too close, or my chair gets hot and burns me bum.'

Adeline laughed as she angled her stick into the heat.

One marshmallow turned into two, turned into ten and the Milo cooled enough for her to drink it. Holden remained almost silent during her visit, and she got the feeling he was regretting his invitation. Ignoring his resting bitch face, she made conversation with Ford, who it turned out was the local barber—which accounted for his stylish do—and the boys, who were much more eager to talk about themselves than most teenage boys she'd met.

Mitch (the Great Dane) worked at the local co-op; Luka was waiting tables at a café while waiting for his big acting break.

'He's gunna go places,' Ford said proudly. 'You should have seen him play Tin Man in last year's theatrical society production. And he's going for an even bigger part this year.'

Luka looked down into his mug and even in the firelight, she saw him blush a little. 'I'm trying to save money so I can move to Melbourne or Sydney and audition for some proper productions.'

Adeline asked the others what they wanted to do when they grew up, but they were more interested in asking her a zillion questions about her life choices. So much for teenagers being sullen and silent, these ones were like a pack of journalists at a press conference.

'Where'd you come from?'

'What'd you do before becoming a nun?'

'What's it like living in a convent?'

She answered them as best she could. 'I'm from a small town in Western Australia called Walsh. It's actually named after my great-great-grandfather.'

'Wow.' Rocky sounded more than impressed. 'You have a town named after your family.'

'Like *Schitt's Creek*,' shouted Mitch.

'Yeah … I guess.' Adeline couldn't help but smile as she imagined exactly what her mother would think about being compared to the Schitt family. 'Although Walsh is quite different. It's dairy farming country and the town is very well kept. Last year we even won the Tidy Towns award.'

'Were you a farmer then?' asked Ford, popping a marshmallow in his mouth, not bothering to toast it.

'No.' She shook her head. 'My parents and brother work the farm. No room for me, not that I ever wanted to be that involved. I ran the local newspaper and bred maremmas, like Bella, which kept me pretty busy.'

'So she isn't your only dog?' asked Rocky, his eyes lighting up.

'She wasn't. I had a few but I rehomed my boys, and Ariel, Bella's sister, stayed on the farm. She's much more active than Bella, who is *usually* happy to stay by my side. I know you're not supposed to have favourites, but Bella's my best friend—I couldn't have left her behind.'

'Do you miss home?' This from Sam, who was onto another cigarette. It surprised her that Holden and Ford let their charges—if that's what these boys were—smoke.

'Not really.' She didn't say that although her family had lived there for generations, she'd never felt particularly at home in Walsh. 'I haven't had time to miss it. Life at the convent is surprisingly busy and it's impossible to be lonely with all the other sisters.'

They listened eagerly as she explained what each day was like.

'Don't you get bored doing so much praying?' asked Rocky, screwing his face up.

She chuckled. 'No. It's actually very peaceful. It forces me to slow down and take stock and has really helped me remember what's important in life.'

All of them looked sceptical at this reply, but it was the truth. Each day she spent with the other sisters, she felt more and more confident that she'd found her calling. Prayer gave her time to reflect, to realise that all her life she'd been seeking things that would enhance her status and popularity, when what she should have been doing was looking for how she could serve others.

'Have you ever had a boyfriend?'

Lost in her thoughts, she blinked at the question from the cane corso.

'Or a girlfriend?' said Mitch before she could reply that she'd never had a serious one. Not for want of trying.

Sam snorted. 'As if nuns can be lesbians.'

'Nuns can't have sex with men *or* women,' the Great Dane reminded him, giving him a look that said he was stupid.

'But she only just became a nun,' retorted Sam, throwing a stick at him.

'I don't get it,' said Mitch. 'Why the fuck would you willingly give up sex and booze and all the fun stuff in life?'

Adeline felt her cheeks flush. The last thing she wanted to do was talk about sex with a bunch of teenage boys, especially with Holden's intent gaze trained on her. Someone really ought to tell him it was rude to stare.

'Um …' She swallowed, searching for an answer.

'That's enough,' Holden said gruffly. 'Stop interrogating our guest.'

So, he hadn't lost the ability to speak. She shot him a grateful smile and then picked the leash up off the ground and pushed to her feet. 'It's probably time Bella and I were heading back anyway.'

She shouldn't have allowed herself to stay out so long, but she had to admit she'd had a good time. There wasn't much better than a good old-fashioned bonfire on a cold night, and the boys had been surprisingly good company. 'Thanks for having us.'

'Anytime,' Ford said, waving his hand from his wheelchair. 'It's always nice to have a bit of female company.'

'What do you call Bronte?' Holden asked.

Ford gestured around them. 'Do you see her here? Besides, she's not the only girl in the world, you know?'

Adeline wondered if Bronte was the woman who'd been here the other night. Whoever she was, Adeline sensed tension between the brothers, and didn't want to be a part of it. This time, instead of calling Bella, she marched straight over and clipped the leash on her collar before the dog could realise what was happening. She didn't want to give Holden yet another opportunity to critique her dog ownership.

'Come on, girl,' she said firmly. 'Time to go.'

'I'll walk you,' Holden offered.

'You don't have to do that,' she said, horrified at the prospect. He'd barely said a word to her all night, and she did not want to be anyone's obligation. 'I'll be fine. I'm a big girl, and Bella won't let anything happen to me.'

'I won't be able to sleep tonight unless I know you're safely tucked up in bed.'

Adeline swallowed at the thought of *him* thinking about *her* in bed, but something told her Holden would not be dissuaded.

'Okay, whatever,' she said, feeling way less nonchalant than she sounded. 'Let's go.'

Chapter Eleven

The last thing Holden wanted to do was walk the nun home, but it was late and no matter how much she protested, he wasn't going to let her wander down the deserted road alone. Who knew what kind of psychos might be waiting in the dark to take advantage? Rocky wanted to come with them, but Holden told him he needed to help pack up and then go to bed.

Halfway down the gravel drive, he regretted this decision. If the boy was with them, the silence wouldn't feel so awkward.

Normally he was okay with quiet, but tonight—aware of Adeline's arm swishing only a ruler's breadth from his—he felt an urge to make small talk. He'd been watching her all night, her cheeks glowing in the warmth of the embers as she talked and laughed with the boys and his brother, trying to work out what the hell her deal was. He couldn't wrap his head around why she'd made such a nonsensical decision.

'What *really* made you decide to become a nun?' he asked as they reached the entrance to his property. No matter how many times she told him they were called sisters, not nuns, he refused to play along.

'Well …' she began, tugging on Bella's leash as the dog tried to turn back around. 'My grandmother had just died, and she was really the only reason I was still living in Walsh.'

'I'm sorry,' he said, although he had no idea what it felt like to have grandparents.

'Thanks.'

'Were you close?'

'Incredibly. And I couldn't imagine staying in Walsh without her.' She gave an almost inaudible sigh. 'Anyway, I felt it was time to make some major life changes, so I prayed and asked God to show me what he wanted me to do with my life, then I switched on the TV and *Sister Act* was on.'

'What?' He spluttered so hard he almost swallowed his own tongue. 'You're kidding right?'

She shook her head.

'You can't seriously believe that God sent you the message to become a nun. You ever thought maybe he was telling you to become a lounge singer or something?' Now that he *could* imagine. If Adeline looked this good in the most boring clothes on the planet, she'd have punters throwing money at her if she got all dressed up in a shimmery gown and serenaded them.

'I may have considered that,' she agreed, 'if I didn't switch channels and stumble upon a documentary about old Aussie miniseries. Guess what show they were discussing at that very moment?'

He wracked his mind for something about nuns but came up blank. 'No idea.'

'*Brides of Christ.*'

Holden stopped walking and gaped at her. She had to be joking. This could not be the reason she'd made such a life-changing decision. 'Do you base all your major life choices on TV shows? Are nuns even *allowed* to watch TV?'

'We have a communal television at the convent, but obviously it was before I arrived that I saw those shows, and I didn't make the decision because of TV. I'd specifically asked God for a sign, and I got one. Two actually. But obviously I did my research about what was involved before signing myself up.'

'Obviously.'

'What's that supposed to mean?'

He held up his hands. 'Nothing. I just ... To be honest, I call bullshit.'

'Excuse me?' She perched her hands on her hips and her breasts thrust upwards, despite the thick puffer jacket covering them.

Tearing his gaze from her chest, he looked straight into her deep brown eyes. 'You don't join a fucking convent because you watched a couple of TV shows. How do you know it wasn't just a coincidence that these shows were on when you prayed? What if *Beverly Hills Cop* had been on—would you have joined the police force?'

'Maybe,' she said, a slight quiver in her voice. 'But ... but anyway, I don't need to justify my life choices to you.'

'Fair.' He nodded. 'I'm sorry,' he said, although he wasn't and to be honest, she sounded a bit defensive.

'Apology accepted,' she said, yanking Bella's leash hard as the wind whipped around them and she picked up her pace.

'So what Netflix series are the nuns—sorry, *sisters*—currently binging? Any recommendations?'

'We don't actually have any streaming services, but I don't miss them,' she added. 'The sisters are really fun, they're great company. We make our own entertainment.'

'Whatever you say, Maria. I'm still surprised they let you have a dog in there.'

'It's not a prison you know. My rights haven't been taken away.'

Yep, she definitely sounded defensive. 'Sure sounds like prison to me.' He'd been listening to her tell the boys about religious living—about getting up at the same time each day, praying together, eating in silence, making stuff to sell but not getting any of the profit. 'Or a cult.'

'Are you always this judgemental?' she spat.

'Me? Judgemental? I'll have you know, I'm the least judgemental person there is. I take everyone as they are.'

'Except nuns?' she retorted, reaching up and twisting her ponytail in her free hand. 'Is it God you have something against? Or just religion?' Before he could get started on exactly what his problem was with both, she added, 'Or is it because we're a bunch of women working together for the greater good?'

'What? Now you're calling me *sexist*?'

She shrugged and her soulful, deep brown eyes flashed with fury. Or was it amusement? 'If the shoe fits.'

Bella stopped again to sniff something, and he took the opportunity to set Adeline straight. 'I'm telling you, it doesn't.' He stared down into her gorgeous face. 'I *love* women.'

He loved burrowing his face between their breasts. He loved licking their pussies until they shrieked like cats. He *loved* being inside them. And right now, the thought of being inside Adeline had him burning up like he had a fever.

As if she could read his mind, he saw her cheeks tinge with pink beneath the moonlight and it was all he could do not to land his mouth on her luscious lips and kiss her until she could no longer breathe. His tongue went dry as he imagined exactly what she'd taste like—marshmallow, Milo, and something uniquely her. Sweet, with a hint of spice.

Holy hell. He was getting a hard on for a freaking nun!

If there was a God, the bloke was taking the piss.

Adeline blinked and then shook her head. 'Bella, come on,' she barked, turning in her boots and striding towards the convent.

Holden exhaled, realising he'd been holding his breath. There wasn't that much further to go but he'd said he'd see her home and that's what he intended to do. He wasn't an animal—unlike some of his dogs he could have desires and not act on them—so he shoved his hands in his pockets for safekeeping and followed her.

They walked a little further before Adeline spoke again. 'So do you and Ford foster the boys?'

'Yeah. That's right.'

'Bet they love living with you two rather than some stuffy old carers.'

'Eventually, I think they do. Most of them have been in trouble with the law, or have issues with substance abuse with they arrive. Sometimes they've been in the foster system for years, or they've been living on the streets because their parents don't want to deal with them anymore. Either way, by the time they get to us they're usually hating on the world and everyone in it.'

'They all seemed pretty happy tonight,' she said.

Holden felt a rare jolt of pride at her words. In the day-to-day struggles of trying to make ends meet and work out how to ready the boys for adulthood, sometimes he felt more like a failure than a success.

'Well, deep down they're good kids. Ford and I try to show them they have value and worth by channelling their energy into activities that will give their lives meaning and purpose, and also teach them life skills to help them go forward. We want to enable them to earn a living, eventually put a roof over their own heads, but our main goal is to keep them off the street—to give them the confidence and self-esteem not to fall away again—and continue to support them as best we can even after they age out of care.'

That made him sound like a saint, which he was anything but.

'How many kids do you look after? You must have a lot of bedrooms.'

He chuckled. 'We're only allowed to take three foster kids at a time. The extra boys there tonight were in our care before they turned eighteen. Those few still live in the area, so we're still a big part of their lives and make sure we get together regularly.'

'That's so great. Do you also foster dogs or something?' asked Adeline. 'You seem to have a lot of them.'

'We've only got two at the moment. The others there tonight belong to the older boys. But yeah, they're an important part of what we do. Probably even more vital than me and Ford. We get to the heart of the kids through the dogs. When they first arrive, many of them are so damaged, they're not prepared to get close to us. But it's almost impossible not to soften around a dog. The boys can talk to the dogs, play rough with the dogs, feed them or not feed them, love them or hate them, and the dogs will still be there.'

'Where do they come from? You have quite the assortment.'

'Same place as the boys really. We take in strays or those that have been abandoned and the boys help us train them, get them back on track. A few arvos a week, I get the dogs out doing circle work and obedience training. It's while doing these things that the boys open up with me and each other. These kids aren't the type to sit in a room with a therapist and talk about their feelings, although we do encourage that as well.'

Adeline chuckled and the sound almost knocked Holden side-ways. It was the sweetest thing he'd ever heard. 'I gotta agree with you on the value of dogs,' she said. 'Growing up, whenever I felt alone, our farm dogs always made me feel better.'

He wanted to ask her why she'd felt alone, but that would be skating too close to the personal. 'When did you get into breeding maremmas? They don't seem like the type of breed most dairy farmers have.'

'They're not. A few years ago I saw a documentary about Middle Island and was fascinated by the way they used maremmas there to watch over the penguins. To protect them from predators. Although we didn't have a big fox problem on our dairy farm, I knew that many sheep and chicken farmers did, and I wondered why more of them weren't using maremmas to protect their stock. I decided there was an untapped market in Western Australia, so I got a couple of puppies and started breeding them to sell to farmers in need of fox protection. My parents thought it was ridiculous but I've done okay out of it.'

'*Another* decision made because of a TV show?'

'Yeah, got a problem with that?' But this time she sounded amused rather than annoyed.

'Nope. You probably believe in astrology and all that shit as well.'

'I definitely do not. I believe in God. I look for his signs.'

Total nutbag. This should be making him want to steer clear of her, but instead, he found it weirdly adorable.

'Anyway,' she said, as the convent came into sight, 'I fell in love with the breed as well, and Bella has always been more of a pet than a protector.'

Holden slowed his steps—against his better judgement, he found himself wanting to prolong their time together. 'She's a gorgeous dog. Rocky has taken a shine to her.'

'Is the dog on your arm someone special?' Adeline asked, pointing to the sleeve of his jacket.

He raised an eyebrow—although they were covered tonight, she'd clearly noticed his tattoos before. He felt a little buzz inside at the thought that maybe she'd been checking him out.

'Yeah, he is. His name was Guru—he was an Alsatian cattle dog cross and as loyal as they come. I found him abandoned on the side of the road. He was skin and bones—nearly starved to death, but I saved him and ...' *He saved me.* 'Anyway, one of my colleagues did the tat for me just after he died.'

He'd bawled his eyes out the whole time.

'One of your colleagues?' she asked as they slowed in front of the convent's big iron gates. 'You're a tattoo artist?'

'Yep.'

'Wow.' She sounded impressed. 'So, where d'you work? I haven't seen a tattoo parlour in Smallton.'

'I'm not working much at the moment, but I take the odd shift in Colac. Ford owns the barbershop here in town and he's busy there a lot of the time, so I take on most of the home load. You got any tattoos?'

'No.' She snorted. 'No offence but I think they're repulsive.'

So *not* impressed then. 'Is that right?' he asked, half amused, half insulted. She didn't like it when *he* mocked *her* career choice.

'I'm sorry.' Her shoulders slumped and she looked genuinely gutted. 'That was rude. It's just, I've never really seen the appeal. But yours don't look bad ... not that I've seen them all, well, I don't think I have.'

Not yet, he thought, and then kicked himself. The fact that she found tattoos repulsive was just another reason why he needed to get her out of his head.

A light went on inside the otherwise dark convent and Adeline glanced towards it. 'Anyway, thanks for walking me home, but now I'm worried about *your* safety getting back.'

'Don't you worry about me, Maria. I'm big enough and ugly enough to look after myself.' He tipped his head. 'You have a good night.'

She rolled her eyes, presumably at his using the wrong name. 'Thank you, you too. And I'll try to keep Bella from bothering you again. I think she misses the company of the other dogs back home. She loves the animals here, but I guess it's not the same as hanging with her own kind.'

'That's understandable.' He shoved his hands in his pockets. 'If you want … maybe you could bring her to visit sometimes? Might tame her escape-artist tendencies.'

'Really?' She looked surprised by the offer, and he almost rescinded it.

What was he doing asking a *nun* if she wanted to hang out at his place? Still, he thought of Rocky and Bella; he was offering this for them.

It had nothing to do with the ridiculous attraction he felt. Adeline was fucking beautiful, literally one of the hottest women he'd ever met—but she was strictly off limits. Even if he didn't have any respect for the church, did he really think he could woo her away from her calling? And what if he did? It wasn't like he'd be offering her a relationship.

When it came to women, all Holden had to offer was a good time between the sheets.

'Sure,' he said eventually. 'The boys love her.'

'Wow—thank you, that's very kind.' She reached down to touch Bella's head. 'Maybe you can help me teach her a few manners while we're there?'

'Maybe,' he said. 'But you gotta promise me one thing.'

She eyed him warily, gold flecks in her dark eyes glinting in the moonlight. 'What?'

'Don't start preaching to us. And absolutely no praying. The boys and I do not need to be saved by you.'

'Okay. You got yourself a deal,' she said, offering him her hand.

'Great.' He wrapped his hand around hers and silently cursed at the jolt that went through his body, like he was a car and she a set of jump leads.

Adeline took her hand back and smiled. 'Goodnight, Jack. We'll see you soon.'

Jack? Holden shook his head as he watched her slip through the gate into the grounds of the convent.

What the hell did Jack mean?

Chapter Twelve

The morning after Adeline returned from the bonfire, she'd filled in the hole Bella had dug under the fence and gone around the garden checking for any other escape routes. In the week since, she hadn't once let the dog out of her sight. Every day she took Bella out into the garden first thing to do her business, then locked her in the laundry with her breakfast while she joined the other sisters for morning prayer. Then, before she got into her chores for the day, she and Bella went out on a mammoth walk to try and tire her out.

Despite Bella's insistent tugging in the direction of Holden's place, they always went the opposite way. Because *despite* what he might think, Adeline *was* the boss. She walked Bella through the town, often stopping in to chat to Mike at the *Gazette* and meeting other locals as she wandered the streets and admired the gardens. Some of them had complimented her on her first Nun-Talk column, which had been published two days ago. They all went crazy over the famous Bella; a few younger ones had even asked to take selfies with her. The dog was becoming quite the favourite on the sisters' TikTok account as well.

It was such a lovely change to be appreciated for her efforts. Even though she'd put her heart and soul into running the *Walsh Whisperer*, nobody ever took her seriously, never mind telling her what a good job she was doing. The other wonderful thing about being here was that no one had any preconceived ideas about her. No one knew her history. It was like her life was a blank canvas and she could paint a whole new beautiful picture on it.

Sometimes one or more of the other sisters would accompany them on their walks; once she, Bella and Lola even went as far as Lake Corangamite, a massive salt lake which was a good half an hour by foot from Smallton. They'd spotted all sorts of birdlife and even a lizard. She'd never felt so healthy in her life. So alive. Or so full of possibility.

Which was why she was determined to do nothing to jeopardise it all.

Every evening before final prayer, she took Bella on another long walk, once again avoiding Holden's place. She'd meant it when she told him she'd visit, but the more Adeline thought about his offer—and she thought about it more often than she should—the more she believed it wouldn't be a good idea to accept. It would be okay if she was going there simply for Bella's sake, but she'd be lying if she pretended that was the case.

Michelle had been right—Holden *was* dangerous. That walk home with him in the dark had planted all sorts of inappropriate thoughts into her head. The kind of thoughts someone who'd pledged to take a vow of chastity should *not* be having. Hot thoughts. Kissing thoughts. Thoughts about running her hands over his tattoos, through his messy hair and …

Geez. She wiped a hand against her brow, getting dirt on her face from where she was weeding the veggie patch.

When he'd told her he loved women, she'd almost melted on the spot—stupid hormones—and she got the feeling he'd been thinking about kissing her as well.

But even if she wasn't committed to a life here in the convent, the way he'd said those three words, 'I *love* women'—with heat and cocky insinuation—told her he was exactly the kind of man she should steer clear of. One might be fooled by the fact that he took care of all those delinquent boys, but you only needed to look at Holden Campbell to know he was a player. What kind of man flirted with a woman who'd just joined a convent? One with no scruples, that's what. He probably had the words 'Bad Boy' inked into his skin somewhere. And Adeline had had her fill of those kind of men—men who wanted her for nothing more than her body. Men who'd sleep with her a couple of times and then disappear into the ether, or worse, snub her when she saw them at the local football game.

No siree, she was never making that kind of mistake again.

Bella leading her to Holden had to be the devil's doing—he was testing her resolve. Or maybe … Holden was the devil himself in human form. Not only would that explain the heat that radiated from him, but it would also account for the way her body reacted whenever he was close. His insulting remarks turned her on almost as much as they infuriated her, and she didn't need that kind of temptation in her new life.

Hopefully, sooner or later Bella would forget her escapades at his place, and they could both get on with living their best lives.

That was Adeline's plan, which meant that when she wasn't trying to distract Bella, she threw herself into life at the convent. If there was a job that Mother Catherine needed done, she volunteered. She doubled her Bible study and prayer time, devoting a good chunk of each session to asking God to keep her from straying off the path he'd chosen for her. She relished her time in the garden—tending the veggie patch when it wasn't bucketing down with rain, and when the weather forced everyone inside, she interviewed her fellow sisters for NunTalk, played pool with Sister Rita and Lola, wrote letters to Sally, and worked on building up the Sisters of Smallton profile on TikTok.

That was a fun distraction indeed and every time they got a new follow, comment or like she felt a buzz at the knowledge that she was doing God's work.

At first some of the older sisters had been reluctant to get involved. Sister Josey made lots of mutterings about the world going to the dogs but after only a few days of watching the younger women learn dances out in the garden, she decided she needed to teach them a few moves.

'Adeline,' she called now from across the garden where she'd been sitting under a tree knitting beanies for the convent shop. 'How many views have we had on our last dance?'

Her knees and hands getting sore from the weeding, Adeline pushed to her feet and went over to join the older woman. 'I'll have to go check.'

When she came back with the mobile phone, Josey said, 'I was thinking since the sun is out, we should do something now.'

'Good idea.' Adeline was always happy to have content in her drafts folder for a rainy day—a literal *or* metaphorical one. 'I'll go see if I can drag anyone else into the shenanigans.'

'Okay, while you do that, give me the phone and I'll have a look for something fun to do.' She held out her hand for the device and Adeline chuckled silently as she went to solicit some of the others. If she wasn't careful, Josey would be taking over her job.

Five minutes later, she returned with Michelle and Sister Rita, who'd been busy baking muffins and cookies in the kitchen.

'I've found the perfect dance,' announced Sister Josey excitedly. 'And a great song.'

The other three peered over her shoulder to watch.

Barely two seconds of the video had played before Adeline shrieked. 'No!' She would dance to almost anything in the name of spreading the word of God, but she drew the line at shaking her tush along to Ryder Bloody—*whoops*—O'Connell. 'Absolutely not.'

'What? Why?' Michelle looked crestfallen. 'I love his music.'

'And when have you heard it?' Adeline snapped. Michelle always had music playing when she was working in the kitchen or in the garden, but she'd only ever heard gospel tunes.

'I listen to the radio when I'm in the van alone. I love the way his songs tell a story. He must be really sweet to be able to write from the heart like that.'

'Well, I'm telling you he's not—he's a total up-himself jerk, and I'm not going to sully our account with him!'

'Geez,' said Sister Rita. The other three also looked slightly terrified by Adeline's reaction. 'Do you know the guy or something?'

She took a quick breath. 'Unfortunately, I had the misfortune of … um …'

Why on earth did she react like this? Now she was going to have to give them some explanation. She couldn't lie but nor did she want to admit exactly how intimately she'd known him. Even though it was pre-life at the convent, the fact that she'd slept with a guy she barely knew simply because he was hot and famous didn't put her in the best light.

'He used to date someone from home,' she said eventually.

'Really?' Michelle's eyes widened. 'Have you met him?'

'Uh-huh. Briefly.' Not exactly a lie. Maybe not the whole truth. But not a lie. 'I know we're not supposed to talk badly about others, but Ryder is not a nice guy.'

TikTok forgotten, Josey said, 'I take it he's famous?'

Adeline and Michelle nodded.

'And it ended badly with your friend?' Rita asked.

Adeline didn't correct her on the friend thing. 'Yes. He and Tabitha used to go out together when they were young, and they also had a band. They were both on the road to stardom but then she got cancer and lost her arm—could no longer play the guitar—and he dumped her.'

'That's awful,' Michelle and Rita said in unison.

'The poor girl.' Josey pressed a hand against her chest. 'How's she doing now?'

Adeline thought of Tab, who'd had a baby girl just over a month ago. 'She's doing wonderfully. She's married to a lovely man, runs her own business, and just had a baby.'

The other women smiled their relief.

'Sounds like your friend is better off without this Ryder fellow,' Josey said, refocusing on the phone. 'Is there any way we can block him on here?'

'I don't think so,' Adeline said, wishing she could block her bad decisions from her memory. She still couldn't believe how stupid she'd been to fall for his fake charm and fame.

'Never mind. Plenty of other songs. What about we try and start our own trend?' Josey suggested.

'Look at you all up on the lingo,' Michelle teased their oldest sister.

Josey beamed at the compliment.

'I'm sorry,' Adeline began, 'but I'm not really feeling up to dancing right now. Maybe later?'

Before anyone could reply, she took the phone—Bella trotting along behind her—and headed into the house to pray. Talking about Ryder had brought up too many bad memories. The others may have been horrified about how he'd treated her so-called friend, but the truth was that Adeline had never been any better. She shuddered to think about how she'd behaved towards Tabitha, not to mention Meg, all because she'd seen them as competition in the husband game.

If she'd been a better person, she'd never have slept with Tab's ex-boyfriend or tried to dig up dirt on Meg. She'd always lamented her lack of friends, yet every single thing she ever thought and did pushed them away. Ryder's rejection had been just deserts.

After a solid hour of praying, asking God to forgive her for keeping the truth from her fellow sister and to help her to do better in the future, Adeline felt much better. She went to find the others so she could apologise for her weird behaviour. Sister Josey had the sign on her door that indicated she was having her daily pre-dinner power nap, but she found Michelle and Rita coming out of the kitchen, their arms laden with plastic containers. Delicious scents of apple, cinnamon and chocolate wafted from inside.

'Oh hello, princess,' Michelle said to Bella, somehow juggling the containers while at the same time reaching into her pocket to give the dog a little something.

'I told you to stop feeding her,' Adeline scolded. 'You're going to make her fat.'

Michelle beamed down at Bella. 'There's worse things than fat, you know?'

'Yeah, like being unhealthy,' Adeline retorted. 'What's all this for anyway? Looks like you're feeding an army.'

'It's for the soup kitchen,' Rita explained.

'Want to come with me tonight?' Michelle asked. Adeline could barely see her behind the stack of containers. 'Rita usually comes but she's not feeling great. Aunty Flo's giving her grief this month.'

Rita grimaced as she nodded. 'Oh yes, you'd be doing me a massive favour. I'm craving bed and a hot water bottle.'

'What about dinner? And prayer?' Adeline asked.

'I've left a lasagne in the oven for everyone else,' Michelle said, 'and we'll eat at the soup kitchen. As for prayer, we get a free pass when we're doing God's work.'

Adeline looked down at Bella, who'd swallowed her bit of biscuit and was sitting obediently in the hopes of getting another. While she'd love to get out for the evening—even if it was just an hour or so—she couldn't leave the dog alone in case she dug another hole and found her way back to Holden's place. 'Can we take Bella?'

Michelle and Rita exchanged a look of horror. After Bella had chased Barnabas and Benno around the convent yesterday and knocked over a statue of St Cecilia—the patron saint of music—in the process, they were clearly imagining the terror she might unleash in town with a bunch of strangers and food.

'I'll babysit our girl,' Rita offered.

'Okay. Thanks,' Adeline said, grateful that the sisters had fallen in love with Bella almost as much as she was. 'If you're sure. But you can't let her out of your sight. I don't want her to escape again.'

Rita chuckled. 'I know, I know. She can come hang out in my room and when I take her outside for a pee, I'll be her shadow, I promise.'

After clearing it with Mother Catherine—who thought it a splendid idea for Adeline to meet more of the locals—she went and got her beanie and jacket and then climbed into the old Tarago next to Michelle. They drove the short distance to the supermarket car park where a shipping container off to one side had been converted into a canteen of sorts. There were plastic chairs set up in small circles beneath temporary shelters, a stereo playing music and a surprising number of people already milling about. She saw pregnant women, others with small babies, old men in scruffy clothes and lanky teenagers who looked in dire need of a good meal.

Surely there weren't this many homeless people in Smallton.

As if reading her mind, Michelle said, 'There are lots of families doing it tough at the moment. Just because they've got a roof over their heads, doesn't mean they can afford to eat properly. Everyone's welcome here on Wednesday nights. That's why I bake a whole load of extra muffins and biscuits. Come on, I'll introduce you to the other volunteers.'

No sooner had she said this than a van pulled up alongside them. Ford was at the wheel, but he didn't make a move to get out as Holden climbed out the passenger side and two of his boys—the pitbull and the rottweiler—emerged from the back. Holden carried what looked like a slow cooker and the boys each held a crate of bread with the local bakery's logo on the side.

'See you in a few hours,' Ford called through the open window and then reversed the van, waving to Adeline and Michelle as he did so.

Suddenly Holden was in her line of sight, the sleeves of his flannelette shirt pushed up to his elbows, once again showcasing his tattoos. 'Hello,' she managed, her mouth suddenly dry.

'Michelle. Maria.' He dipped his head as if doffing a cap and then continued on, swaggering towards the shipping container, the boys following closely behind.

'Her name's Adeline,' Michelle called after him.

The side door of the container opened as he approached, and Adeline saw the woman who'd been at his place that day Bella first got away from her. Said woman grinned at Holden as she took the slow cooker from him and spoke to the two boys, who then placed the bread crates down on the trestle tables outside.

'Earth to Adeline!'

'What?'

'I said, do you want to help serve or do you want to make sure everyone's comfortable out here? Hand out the muffins and biscuits?'

'Um ...' No way she wanted to be in the confined space of the shipping container with Holden, even if there were two other women in there as well—the one she recognised and a middle-aged woman wearing a hijab. The latter caught her staring and lifted her hand in a friendly wave.

Adeline smiled and waved back. 'I'll circulate with the muffins.'

'Righto.' Michelle nodded. 'Have fun.'

Taking a deep breath, Adeline grabbed a container of apple and cinnamon muffins and then went over to introduce herself to an elderly gentleman. She tried to listen as he told her his life story—he'd been in the Vietnam war and married the nurse who cared for him after he was shot—but her eyes kept drifting towards the shipping container.

Despite the steady flow of traffic collecting steaming bowls of soup, the four volunteers inside looked to be having a lot of fun with each other. Holden kept laughing at something his friend was saying and his deep throaty chuckle carried over to Adeline, making her wonder what was so funny.

'Hey Maria, how you doing?' asked one of Holden's boys— Toovs! He had a crate in his hand and was collecting empty plates.

'I'm great, thanks, but my name's actually Adeline. Good job you're doing here.'

'Yeah, Holden brings us down here every Wednesday night. Keeps us out of mischief.' He winked. 'It's not that bad, but don't tell him I said that.'

'Your secret's safe with me.' Then, unable to help herself, she added, 'Who's that woman next to him?'

'Who? Takishah?'

Guessing that was the woman wearing the hijab, Adeline shook her head. 'No, the other one. I recognise her from that first time Bella escaped to your place.'

'Oh, Bronte.' He sniggered. 'That's Holden's girlfriend. He says they're just friends, but we know better.'

She forced a smile. 'I see.'

'Want me to introduce you?'

'No, thanks. I'll say hi some other time. Don't want to get in the way.'

'No probs. Well, better keep going before slave driver sees me and says I'm slacking off.'

His girlfriend, she thought as the boy walked away. Well. That *was* good news.

And to think she'd thought Holden had the hots for her. Talk about vanity. She'd probably just imagined his flirtation; it wouldn't be the first time she'd been wrong about a man's feelings. So much for thinking he was a bad boy—it was clear from the way he was interacting with Bronte that he adored her. And he was here, wasn't he? Helping feed people less fortunate than him. Obviously when he'd walked Adeline home the other night in the name of safety, that had been exactly his purpose.

She felt as if a weight had been lifted from her shoulders.

It shouldn't matter whether Holden was with someone else because she'd chosen her path—and planned to stick to it—but she was ashamed to admit that her heart had fluttered at the mere sight of him tonight. Knowing he and Bronte were an item would make it much easier to dismiss her awareness of him.

Thank you, Jesus.

Feeling more relaxed now, she gave Bert another muffin and moved on to a woman resting on the seat of a walker. This lady, Denise, turned out to be a hoot—telling her stories of her time working on the famous Hay Street in Kalgoorlie.

Adeline laughed. 'And what brought you to Smallton?'

'Well, when they lifted containment in Kalgoorlie—effectively killing Hay Street—it wasn't so safe doing my kind of work, so I hitchhiked back to Victoria where I grew up. My grandparents were from Smallton and when they died, they left me their small cottage.'

Yet Denise was here. Maybe she was one of those who had a roof over their heads but couldn't afford food, or maybe she just wanted company.

Either way, Adeline was having much more fun than she thought she probably should be at such an event. Back home, she may have organised a fundraiser for homeless people, but she'd never have allowed herself to get this close to them. If she were honest, she'd assumed they were all druggies or alcoholics who more or less deserved the lives they were leading. Tonight, she'd learned that many of them were simply everyday people who'd run out of luck.

'Good evening, ladies.'

Her insides—still not quite caught up—tensed at Holden's greeting.

'Hello handsome,' Denise said, wriggling her eyebrows at him.

'Hi Denise.' Holden grinned down at her. 'How you doin' tonight?'

'All the better for seeing you. Where's that delicious brother of yours?'

Holden chuckled as he rubbed his hand over his beard. 'He's back home with one of our boys tonight, but I'll tell him you said hi.'

Then he grabbed hold of Adeline's arm and pulled her away.

Chapter Thirteen

Holden had been watching Adeline all night, aware of every move she made as she did the rounds, introducing herself to the regulars. Tonight, her honey-blonde hair was tied up in a high ponytail that jiggled when she laughed. Every time she smiled, he found himself smiling too. Once when she'd bent down to pick up a spoon that old Bert had dropped, her boring brown pants had tightened over her butt, and he'd almost poured soup onto his hand instead of into a bowl. What kind of exercise must she do to get buttocks like that?

Perhaps the nuns did communal aerobics as well as communal prayer and communal TV watching.

'Excuse me,' she snapped as he inched her away from Dangerous Denise. 'I was in the middle of a conversation.'

'Don't get your knickers in a knot, Maria. You don't want to spend too long with the likes of Denise. She's a bad influence. Ford's terrified of her. She's been trying to get him to go on a date with her forever.' He plucked a muffin from her container and took a bite. 'Once she even chased him round the car park trying to get him to say yes. Luckily, even in his chair, Ford's faster than Denise with her walker.'

Adeline looked incredulous. 'That's not true.'

'It is. She's not homeless, she just comes here to pick up men. Swear to God,' he said, doing the sign of the cross.

'I didn't think you believed in God,' she retorted.

He shrugged. 'No more than I believe in Father Christmas, but that doesn't mean I don't like stuffing myself with ham and pavlova on December twenty-fifth.'

She smirked. 'You've got an answer for everything, don't you, Jack?'

He didn't bother with an answer and although he desperately wanted to ask her why she'd started calling him that, he wasn't going to give her the satisfaction. 'You haven't brought Bella to visit yet,' he said instead.

'I've …' She blinked a couple of times. 'I've been … busy.'

'Writing?' Man, those muffins were delicious. He had to give it to the nuns—they knew how to bake almost as good as the CWA ladies.

'A little.' The tiny space between her eyebrows creased a little. 'How'd you know?'

'I'm psychic.'

'What?'

He could tell she wasn't sure if he was joking. 'I read your article in the local rag.'

'Oh.' She bit her lip and he tried to ignore the sparks such a simple action ignited within him. 'I suppose you think it was stupid.'

He shook his head. Although he always read the *Smallton Gazette* to keep up to date with what was happening in town, he'd never bothered with the NunTalk column before. He was surprised to find it wasn't at all preachy, but instead consisted of funny anecdotes about life in the convent from Bella the dog's point of view. 'It was good. Content notwithstanding, you have a way with words.'

'Why, is that a compliment, Jack?'

'Yep. I give credit where credit's due.'

'Well, thank you.' She smiled, and her cheeks glowed with pride.

He felt a jolt of pleasure that he'd caused that reaction. 'You're welcome.'

'Mike liked it too,' she added. 'He asked if I'd like to do a few more community articles for the paper.'

'You're allowed to do that?'

'Most of the other sisters have jobs or volunteer work. We don't just sit around praying all day, you know.'

He smirked. 'Good to know. But if the whole nun thing doesn't work out, you should be a writer. I reckon you could make a shopping list interesting.'

Again, she blushed. 'I actually did journalism at university.'

'What? Why?' He shook his head. Stumped for words. He didn't know why but he hadn't considered the possibility that she'd had a proper job before now. She'd only mentioned breeding dogs and living on a dairy farm. She had a posh kind of aura around her, and he imagined she'd been a lady of leisure, sponging off rich parents or something.

'Well, it was a toss-up between journalism and law, but I liked writing—and my hair would be totally ruined by a barrister's wig anyway.'

He snorted a laugh. She was funny. 'No, I meant, why aren't you doing that now? You're wasted at the convent.'

'Dedicating my life to God is not a waste,' she said defensively.

'No offense to Mike—he's a good bloke—but you should be running the *Smallton Gazette*, or something bigger and better.

Why aren't you writing for *The Australian* or *The Sydney Morning Herald*? Hell, why aren't you writing for *The New York Times*?'

She half-laughed, but there was sadness in her eyes. 'I tried it in the big smoke—that's if Perth counts—but … it wasn't for me. I did run our local paper back home though.'

Something didn't fit. You didn't need to be an expert to tell she had the kind of talent that was wasted on small-town newspapers, and he got the feeling she wasn't telling him the whole story. 'Why wasn't it for you?'

'It just wasn't, okay.'

'Fine. Whatever.' He held up his hands in surrender. 'So, when are you bringing Bella round?'

'Um … I don't know.'

'Look, if you're too busy, do you reckon I could borrow her?'

Her eyes narrowed suspiciously. 'You want to borrow my dog? I thought you said she was a trainwreck.'

'Not the dog's fault.' When she scowled, he grinned. 'But it's not for me, it's for Rocky.'

'Oh? He's the small one, right?'

Holden nodded. 'He's having a bit of a tough time of it and the first time I've ever seen him show a bit of enthusiasm for anything was when he met your dog. He's like a different kid when she's around and I was thinking I could try and get Rocky to work with her. Teach her a few tricks. Make it sound like he'd be doing you a favour, not that we're doing this for him.'

A couple of kids came up to get muffins and when they ran off, their hands and mouths full, Adeline turned back to Holden. 'What's Rocky's story? You said he doesn't go to school. Why?'

Holden hesitated a moment, not wanting to break any confidences, but considering he was requesting Adeline's—or rather her dog's—assistance, he figured she deserved the basics. 'His dad killed his mum,' he said in a hushed voice.

'What?' Her face went pale beneath the carpark's lights, and he noticed her grip tighten on the box of muffins.

No matter how many statistics they saw in the media about deaths from domestic violence, it always seemed to shock people when they knew someone involved. 'Yeah. No surprises the poor kid's messed up.'

'That's awful.' Adeline twisted her ponytail between her fingers. 'I take it his dad is in jail?'

'Yep. It was gruesome. He got life.'

'Is he violent as well?'

'Who? Rocky?' Holden shook his head. 'I don't think so. Just withdrawn; I can see the anger there but he's pretty good at containing it.'

'Is he having therapy?'

'Yeah. And hopefully he's making some progress, although it's hard to tell.' Holden had tried to talk to him about his own experience growing up in not one, but two abusive households, but *his* mother was still alive, so no matter what he said, Rocky didn't see any correlation. 'This is the longest he's stayed in one place since his mum died so that's a good sign, I guess.'

'That's heartbreaking.' Adeline looked like she was going to cry, and Holden had to fight the urge to wrap his arm around her to offer comfort. Until she said, 'I'll pray for him.'

His fingers balled into fists. 'He needs connection, not prayer,' he said, and then he forced a calming breath before adding, 'and I really think Bella could be the answer. In my experience, dogs can work wonders even when therapists fail.'

'Okay, then. I can probably bring her tomorrow. About four o'clock, but I'll have to be back at the convent by five-thirty. Would that work?'

'Yes, perfect. Rocky will be thrilled, and you never know, he might just be able to teach Bella a thing or two.'

'I'll believe that when I see it.'

Holden chuckled. 'So, are you going to be a regular here at soup kitchen?'

'I hope so,' she said, but her tone didn't match her words.

'You don't sound so happy about that.'

'Oh, no, I am. I want to help, but ...' She glanced around. 'I wish there was more I could do. I can't imagine having to come out in the freezing cold just so you can get a decent meal. Is someone providing blankets for those on the streets? And what about health care? Bert doesn't look like he's brushed his teeth in years.'

So, she had a kind heart as well as a sexy butt.

'There are services, yes. Of course, there's always room for more, but don't underestimate what you gave some of these people tonight.'

'What do you mean?' She lifted the container, which now only held one lone muffin. 'I'm pretty sure these muffins don't have any magical powers.'

He couldn't help but smile. 'I'm not talking about the muffins. A lot of these people come here because they're lonely. Take Denise and Bert for example. Neither of them has any family or close friends. They're oddballs who tend to repel rather than attract, but I saw you with them. You gave them the time of day. You listened, and that meets a need that isn't as easy to provide as food.'

'Is that why you bring the boys here? Back home, the local primary school takes the kids to the nursing home to sing songs and read books with the old people. It's the highlight of their week.'

He nodded. 'And I bet the kids get just as much out of it as the residents. Sure, that's part of it. But I mostly bring the boys here so they can learn about being part of a community and giving as well as receiving. It's good for them to see that the world doesn't revolve around them and to be reminded that there are others even less fortunate than they are. It also gives them a glimpse of what their futures might be like if they don't work hard and avoid temptations such as drugs, alcohol, crime.'

Adeline smiled at someone over his shoulder. 'Hello,' she said, sounding slightly shy.

He turned to see Bronte approaching, Sam and Toovs behind her.

'I don't think we've officially met,' she said, holding out her hand to Adeline. 'I'm Bronte.'

She shook it. 'Nice to meet you.'

'Yeah, you too,' Bronte looked to Holden. 'I'm heading off— you and the boys need a lift?'

'Nah. Ford's coming to collect us. He should be here soon.' He could probably call his brother and tell him Bronte was driving them, but she wasn't planning on staying over tonight and he wouldn't mind another few minutes with Adeline.

'Okay, then. I'll probably see you tomorrow.'

Sadly, mere moments after Bronte leaned in and kissed him on the cheek, Michelle came up beside them. 'Time to head home to my book,' she announced.

'What about the other containers?' Adeline asked.

'While you were busy yakking with Holden here, the rest of us cleaned up and I loaded the *containers* into the van.' Michelle sounded narkier than he thought a nun should.

'Oh, okay, sorry,' Adeline replied. 'You should have come and got me.'

But Michelle was already heading towards the van. 'Night, Holden. Night boys,' she called over her shoulder.

Adeline held out her plastic container. 'Any of you want the last muffin?'

Toovs and Sam fought over it and were just agreeing to go halves when Michelle beeped the horn, startling the four of them.

'She's terrifying,' Toovs said.

'Yeah,' Adeline chuckled. 'And I have to share a room with her. I'd better go.'

'See you tomorrow, Maria,' Holden said.

'Bye Jack,' she replied with a wink.

It probably wasn't a good thing that he was so excited by the prospect of her visiting, but he figured there were two possible outcomes of having her there regularly.

Either the ridiculous chemistry he felt whenever she was within his sight would wane or … His whole body tightened. If she was any other woman, he'd probably seduce her and get her out of his system, but she wasn't just any other woman.

She was a damn nun!

'Did you see the tits on that chick?' Sam said to Toovs through a mouthful of muffin as Adeline hurried after Michelle.

Holden leaned right into Sam's face. 'What the hell did you say?'

'I just said she was hot. Geez, Holden—what the fuck? You got the hots for her or something?'

Holden grabbed him hard round the collar. 'You don't talk about women that way. Ever. You got me? If I *ever* hear you speak about Adeline or any other woman with such disrespect, I'll make you wish you were never born.'

Wide-eyed, Sam shook him off. 'I'm sorry, okay. It was just a compliment. And I thought her name was Maria.'

He took a deep breath. *Keep calm. He's just a kid.*

'A compliment,' he said, 'is telling someone they look good, or their dress is nice. It's not speaking disrespectfully about them to someone else.'

'Okay, I'm sorry,' Sam said, looking as if he was struggling not to cry.

Toovs also took a step back and was glaring at Holden like he'd lost the plot.

Fuck! He'd been making such good progress with these kids, and he couldn't believe he might just have blown it all because of a woman. It wasn't like he hadn't heard the boys say stuff about girls before, and it wouldn't be the last time either. He always reprimanded them, always tried to teach them respect for the opposite sex and for each other, but he was always level-headed in his discipline.

He'd never—not once—got physical with a boy, and he blamed Adeline for it.

What was it about her that made him almost lose his shit?

'Just watch your mouth, okay?' he said and then stalked off to the edge of the car park to wait for Ford.

He'd make it up to Sam later when he'd calmed the fuck down.

Chapter Fourteen

'Promise me you'll be on your best behaviour,' Adeline ordered Bella as they approached the gate at the entrance to Holden's property the next day.

Knowing he had a girlfriend meant she no longer felt anxious about being around him. Instead—still on a high from the night before at the soup kitchen—she was excited by the prospect of helping with Rocky. The buzz she got from helping people had been surprising—better than she'd ever had from gossiping and judging, which she now had to admit had been her two main pastimes back in Walsh.

Her grandmother and her mother had excelled at both, so Adeline had grown up thinking that was the norm. She'd grown up thinking she and her family were better than the other locals because they'd founded the town, because it was named after them, and because they were the wealthiest farmers in the region. Slowly, she was learning that wealth and status meant nothing if you lorded them over others rather than using them to do good.

The way Bella was tugging on her lead, she'd guessed where they were going.

'You're here to work, not play,' she told the dog, who only tugged harder.

Adeline sighed. Rocky would have his work cut out, but she guessed participation was more important than performance. Hopefully just being here would help.

That morning Adeline had asked Mother Catherine's permission to take Bella to visit Rocky. She'd explained that Holden had asked for Bella's help with one of the boys and Mother Catherine—usually so stoic—had a tear in her eye as she listened to Rocky's story.

'That poor dear boy,' she'd said. 'If Mr Campbell thinks Bella might be able to help him then you must go.'

Adeline felt buoyed by the prospect of making a difference in the kid's life. Maybe Bella running away had been in God's plan all along. Maybe it had been a sign that this was her purpose here—helping errant boys get back on track felt more meaningful than writing articles for the paper and playing on TikTok. Not that she wasn't enjoying both.

At the end of the gravel drive, they were greeted by Vlad and Merlin, their tails wagging as they tried to sniff her crotch. So much for these dogs being better behaved than hers! Adeline looked towards the house to see one of the older boys from the bonfire night—the Great Dane—on the verandah and Toovs and Sam kicking a football out the front. Holden was already over in the yard, looking all hot and rugged and dangerously delicious in his uniform of faded jeans and flannelette shirt with the sleeves rolled up to his elbows.

Bella danced around with the other dogs as if all her Christmases had come at once.

'Hi Adeline,' Rocky said, appearing as if from nowhere. 'Is it really true you want me to try and teach Bella some tricks?'

She smiled at him. 'How about we start with some manners?'

'You're on.' He beamed back at her and then turned his attentions to Bella.

Moments later, Holden whistled loudly, and the boys and dogs hurried over to the yards.

Adeline looked around. What was she supposed to do with herself while they trained?

Ford was nowhere to be seen, likely still at work. She looked around for the van she'd seen him drive last night but the only transport she could see were a few bicycles and a massive motorbike all lined up in the carport off to one side of the house.

Not knowing what else to do with herself, she headed over to the yards to watch. She had to admit Holden had a cool set-up. The paddock was like an obstacle course for dogs, filled with agility bars to hurdle over, poles to weave through, hoops to jump through, tunnels to run through and even some kind of seesaw thing. Although she'd bred dogs and even entered many of them into shows, she didn't know much about obedience trial training. After instructing the three boys to line the dogs up side-by-side ready to begin, Holden finally acknowledged her with an almost imperceptible nod. How rude!

Where were her thanks for giving up her own time to bring Bella here? She had a good mind to march into the fenced-off yard and drag her dog out of there.

The Lord's work isn't always easy.

The words which Mother Catherine—or was it wise old Sister Josey?—had told her soon after she'd arrived in Smallton came into her head. She wasn't here to feel comfortable; she was here to help Rocky and maybe the other boys too. Possibly even Holden. If anyone here was in need of God, it was him.

She perched herself on top of the wooden fence where she had a good view.

'You can't sit there,' Holden barked at her, addressing her properly for the first time that afternoon.

'Why not?' she retorted, embarrassed to be chastised in front of the boys.

'You'll distract the dogs.' He leaned down and picked up an errant milk crate from the other side of the fence and then all but shoved it at her. 'Sit over near that tree on this instead.'

'Thanks, *Jack*,' she said sarcastically as she took the crate and swung around to slither off the fence.

'You're welcome,' he replied in a similar tone, before turning away and ignoring her completely again.

Annoyed, Adeline sat on the crate but not under the tree where he'd told her to. If she was still a *distraction*, he'd have to come over and talk to her again, and this time she'd tell him that maybe it wasn't only her dog who needed training. *He* could do with learning a few basic manners as well.

After a while she grew self-conscious, so she pulled the phone from her pocket. It was funny how what was once so automatic— scrolling social media whenever she was bored or waiting somewhere—now felt like a last resort. Still, she may as well make the most of her time, interacting with other accounts and planning some content for the next few days.

In addition to helping her get to know her fellow sisters, managing the convent's TikTok account had given her access to sisters all over the world, and she'd learned so much from what they shared. She was commenting on a post from a sister in North Carolina when she heard the sound of a car rumbling up the gravel drive.

She turned to see a rusty, old, blue wagon with dozens of bumper stickers stuck on the back windscreen. Bronte climbed out— she wore a long denim skirt, a colourful, patterned shirt, green

Doc Martens boots, and multiple massive hoop earrings—and went round to the back of the car. Adeline had never seen the appeal of Doc Martens, but on this woman, they looked good.

Grateful for the distraction, she tucked the phone back in her pocket and walked towards Bronte.

'Hi. Can I help with those?' She gestured to the boot, which was full of boxes of groceries.

'Didn't expect to see you here again,' Bronte said, almost accusingly. She reminded Adeline of a Yorkshire terrier. Big personality, small but cute package.

'I brought Bella over so Rocky could have a go at training her,' Adeline replied. She didn't want Bronte to think she had any ulterior motives.

Bronte's expression relaxed. 'Ah, good idea.' She glanced across to the yards. 'Looks like they're both having fun.'

'I think so.'

'I don't suppose he's offered you a drink or anything?' Bronte jerked her head towards Holden and when Adeline shook her head, she rolled her eyes. 'He's a terrible host, but he has other qualities.'

Adeline's cheeks heated as she imagined what those other qualities might be.

'Anyway,' Bronte continued, 'they'll probably be a while yet. If you give me a hand with these, I'll get you a drink.'

'Thank you, that would be wonderful.' Adeline grabbed a box laden with fresh fruit and veg and then, with a quick glance back at Bella, followed the other woman into the house.

As they walked up the ramp onto the verandah, she noted rows and rows of shoe racks. 'Do you want me to take off my shoes before we go in?'

'Nah,' Bronte said, pushing open the screen door, a dozen bangles jangling on her wrists as she stepped inside. 'Those rules only apply to the boys. You should see the muck they bring in on their shoes.'

They headed down a short hallway and emerged into a massive open-plan kitchen. Bronte walked fast, not giving Adeline the chance to take much of the place in. But what she did see surprised her. The house was neat, the hallway walls painted a soft blue with framed posters of dogs, cars and rock bands. Someone seemed to be a massive fan of AC/DC and the Red Hot Chili Peppers.

It was very much a bloke's place, but it also felt warm and welcoming, and she wondered if that was due to Bronte's feminine touch.

The kitchen smelled spicy, and it was soon obvious that a slow cooker on one of the benches had been getting a workout that day. Curry or chilli, Adeline guessed as her stomach rumbled. The decor was rustic—like many of the farmyard kitchens back home—with exposed beams on the ceiling, a large island bench with a wooden counter, and pots and pans hanging from a rack on the ceiling. There were two fridges, two large ovens and a massive pantry that looked even more organised than her mother's. And that was saying something.

She noted a few things that you wouldn't normally see in a kitchen—the benches on either side of the room were at different heights and the kitchen sinks and hotplates had open space beneath them.

Bronte caught her staring and explained, 'That's so Ford's wheelchair fits underneath. The kitchen was the first thing he had modified when he bought this place.'

Now that Adeline realised it, there were all sorts of adjustments throughout the property to make it easier for wheelchair access and she guessed his van must have the same. 'Ford owns it?' She asked, intrigued. She'd assumed that Holden did.

'Yep.' Bronte nodded. 'He bought it with his insurance payout.'

'He hasn't always been in a wheelchair, then?'

'Nope,' Bronte said as she continued unloading the boxes.

Adeline guessed she wasn't going to elaborate and bit down on the impulse to push. She helped put the cold items away, but they left the pantry stuff for the boys to unpack. 'Holden and Ford make sure they are fully involved in every aspect of running the household,' Bronte said, moving around the kitchen like it was her own.

'Do you live here?' Adeline asked. It had sounded like Bronte was going back to her own place last night, but maybe she'd got the wrong end of the stick.

'Hell, no! I like my privacy and living with a bunch of stinky men is not my idea of peace, but I help out where I can. Now, what can I get you to drink? Tea? Coffee? Soft drink? I'm afraid this is an alcohol-free zone.'

'A tea would be great, thanks.' Adeline had once been a two or three glasses of wine a day girl, but the only alcohol she drank these days was communion wine.

With a nod, Bronte filled the kettle and grabbed two mugs from a low cupboard. When the drinks were made, they carried them out onto the verandah and sat in two comfy old armchairs, sipping and talking as they watched the boys and dogs from a distance. Bronte turned out to be great company, and they found many things in common. Both had a penchant for old musicals, and both had been sent away to boarding school and hated it. Bronte had been on a scholarship and looked down upon by the rich girls, whereas Adeline's relatives had been attending the same prestigious private school since it opened in the late 1800s.

'I was supposed to feel grateful to be getting such a swanky education paid for, but it actually sucked balls. Not to mention the fact that the only boys we ever got to associate with were the arrogant pricks from our brother school.'

Adeline nodded, totally able to relate to the arrogant pricks; sadly, Bronte would probably have put her in the same category had they met back then. 'Where did you meet Holden, then?'

'Back home when he was backpacking around Australia.'

'Where's home?' Adeline asked.

'A tiny little town about four hours south of Darwin, on the Explorer's Way. You probably haven't heard of it—Middle of Nowhere.'

Adeline frowned; she was pretty good at geography. 'What's it called?'

Bronte laughed. 'That's the name of the town—Middle of Nowhere. Some early settler called it that as a joke and it stuck. My folks own the roadhouse and pub—which is pretty much all there is in the town. Holden worked there for a bit and we became fast friends.'

'How long ago was that?' Adeline asked and then took another sip of tea.

'About nine years now. Or is it ten?' Bronte fiddled with one of her massive hoop earrings. 'Let's see, I'd just finished school, so actually it must be eleven. Time flies when you're having fun.'

Once again, Adeline felt a twinge of jealousy. That's what she'd always wanted in a man—someone she could have fun with as well as sexual and intellectual compatibility. She pushed the thought aside; the more she heard about Bronte and Holden's romance the better. 'And how'd you guys end up down here?'

'Well ...' Bronte held her mug close to her chest. 'When Holden moved on, we kept in touch. We emailed and called all the time, and then when he told me he'd finally settled in Smallton to help his brother, I came down to visit. And I fell in love with the area. At that stage I was living and working in Darwin and to be honest, I'm not one for the heat of the north—I much prefer the weather down here.'

Adeline nodded; she'd never been able to stand real heat either. 'Do you miss your family?'

A mistiness came into Bronte's eyes, but then she blinked it away. 'Course, but there's nothing for me where they are aside from them. Where're you from?'

'A small town as well. Just under two thousand people.'

Bronte threw back her head and laughed. 'Two thousand people? That's a metropolis compared to Middle of Nowhere.'

Adeline smiled and told her about Walsh—that it was dairy country and that her family had lived there for more than a hundred and fifty years.

'And do you miss *your* family?'

'Not really,' Adeline confessed. 'We're not that close. Although I do miss my nephews and my ex-sister-in-law.'

'Ex?'

Adeline explained the situation between James and Sally.

'No offence to your brother but it sounds like Sally is better off without him,' Bronte said, putting her empty mug down on the ground beside her. She sighed. 'Ah, I needed that.'

'Busy day?' Adeline asked.

'Something like that. Want a quick tour before the boys are done?'

Adeline's mug was still half full, but no way was she going to miss the opportunity for a legal snoop. 'Sure. That'd be great.'

Bronte walked her through the house, showing her into rooms she'd only briefly passed before—the dining and living areas, a big games room with table tennis and a pool table, not to mention a whole host of board games and video-game machines. One wall in the games room was covered in dozens of photos of teenage boys.

'These aren't all the kids Holden and Ford have fostered, are they?'

Bronte nodded. 'Some were only here a few days, others stay till they're eighteen, but no matter how long they're here, they get a photo on the wall. They're made to feel part of something.'

Next, they moved on to the bedrooms. Bronte didn't show Adeline inside Holden's or Ford's rooms but pointed out their doors before giving Adeline a quick glimpse into one of the boys' bedrooms, which had a single bed, a desk, a bookshelf and a set of drawers. 'Each of the foster kids has to have their own room,' she explained as she showed Adeline into another room that had two bunk beds, 'but Holden keeps this one for any of his previous boys who need a bed for a night or more. He has a vision to build these tiny houses out on the property so once the boys age out of care, they aren't just chucked out to fend for themselves but can transition to adult life.'

'What do you mean chucked out?'

Bronte explained that currently kids were only looked after in foster care until they were eighteen. 'Sadly, a lot then end up living on the streets, getting into drugs or worse because they don't yet have the means to properly take care of themselves. Sam's almost at that age, and Holden's terrified about what will happen to him then as he's not much for schoolwork or any work really.'

'Can't he just let him stay?'

'He could, but the funding for his care will stop. Besides, Holden doesn't want to stop them growing up, but he wants the boys to have the chance to become functioning adults without the pressure. In a safe environment. His tiny house idea will provide somewhere for kids who are no longer eligible for state care to live—kind of like a transition stage between foster care and real life.'

'That's a great idea.'

Bronte nodded, pride in her eyes. 'Yeah, he attended a course a year back about how to build them. Came back all excited and gung-ho about getting the boys to help with the building, so they develop their skills in the process. He's teaching them a bit of woodworking in the meantime but each one is expensive, even without the labour. And funding is an issue.'

'How expensive?' Adeline asked.

'Basic ones are anywhere from thirty to sixty grand.'

Adeline whistled.

As they moved outside, she couldn't help but feel amused at the similarities between here and the convent. Both places had large veggie patches and fruit trees, they both kept chickens and bees, and although she saw no sign of goats or a cow here, there was one lone alpaca out the back, not too far from a big shed.

'Bessie's another one of Holden's rescues,' Bronte said as she reached out and ruffled the alpaca's head. 'He found her abandoned on the side of the road when she was tiny. Hand-reared her himself.'

Adeline blinked at the idea of gruff, macho Holden hand-rearing anything, but it was also kinda cute. Perhaps that rough exterior was merely a mask.

Although she hadn't been feeling very affectionate towards him, it was almost impossible to hold onto that grudge as Bronte told her about everything he did here. The way he continually sacrificed himself to help the boys in his care, and even those no longer officially in it. Bronte's voice shone with love and pride as she spoke, but it was clear to see why Holden liked her as well. She was funny in a dry, sarcastic kind of way, and she was stunning, but had no airs and graces because of it. Adeline reckoned no matter what she thought of boarding school, Bronte would have been one of those girls who was effortlessly cool, and whom others secretly admired.

'So what kind of work do you do?' she asked Bronte as they circled back to where the boys and dogs had clearly just finished up.

'I'm a photographer. You know, engagements, weddings, baby showers, that sort of thing.'

Adeline wondered if Bronte was responsible for the wall of photos in the games room, but before she could ask, Rocky and Bella came up beside them.

'Hey gorgeous girl,' Adeline said, stooping to rub the dog's neck. 'Did you have fun?'

'She was so good.' Rocky was bouncing on his feet, grinning from ear to ear. 'Thanks so much for letting me train her.'

'You're welcome.' Adeline felt a lump in her throat that she was semi-responsible for Rocky's joy.

'Can she come again?'

'Of course.'

Footsteps sounded behind them and Adeline felt the evening chill as she turned to see Holden approaching.

'Hi Jack,' she said, and then immediately chastised herself for using the nickname in front of Bronte.

'Maria.' He nodded once. 'Bella did good. She and Rocky worked well together. Thanks for bringing her.'

Geez, it sounded like he had to work really hard to utter those words. What the hell did he have against her? She smiled widely to annoy him. 'You're welcome.'

'Do you want to stay for dinner?' Bronte asked. 'There's always plenty to go around.'

Adeline's stomach rumbled again at the prospect of that delicious smelling meal, but she glanced sideways to see Holden glowering.

'I can't. I've got to get back to the convent, but thank you for asking,' she said, and then made her goodbyes to Bronte and the boys.

She would have politely said the same to Holden, but he'd already gone ahead into the house. *So much for being friends.*

Chapter Fifteen

'Why are you being such an arsehole?'

'Excuse me?' Holden whirled around as Bronte stormed into the kitchen, where he'd just grabbed a sack of potatoes to start peeling them for dinner.

'To Adeline. You asked her here to help Rocky, but when I invited her for dinner, you were downright rude.'

'I asked *Bella* here.'

'And Bella's part of a package deal. If you want her to come back, you better be nicer to her owner.'

'I'm perfectly nice.'

Bronte snorted. 'Yeah, like a redback spider is nice. Like root canals are nice. Like soppy Valentine's Day cards are nice. Like—'

'Okay, okay, I get it.' Holden couldn't help but smile—Bronte always had that effect on him. 'I've got nothing against Adeline. You're totally reading into things.'

Bronte crossed her arms over her chest and raised her eyebrows. 'You forget I know you better than you know yourself.'

That's bullshit, he wanted to say, but the truth was, she did. She could read him even better than Ford could. And it was damn annoying. 'Fine. There's just something about her that gets my goat. Happy now?'

She grinned smugly. 'You're not attracted to her, are you?'

His instinct was to scoff—to deny such absurdity—but, as they'd just established, this was Bronte. 'What red-blooded male wouldn't be?'

'True,' Bronte conceded with a long sigh. 'If she wasn't a nun, I might go there myself.' Her sexual preferences had always been fluid. 'We could have a threesome.'

A *threesome?* His grip tightened on the potato peeler.

It wasn't that he was against such things per se, but he didn't want to share Adeline. Not with anybody. Not even with Bronte. Yet, if he admitted this, she'd never let him live it down. Thankfully, Toovs—who was rostered on dinner duty this week—entered the kitchen with Mitch, so the conversation ended.

'Hey,' Holden said, reaching for two aprons and throwing one to each of them. Even visitors had to help around here. 'I'm on mashed potatoes, one of you needs to make the meatballs and another a salad.'

'Do we always have to have vegetables?' groaned Toovs as he pulled the apron over his head.

Mitch laughed 'Yeah, they really know how to ruin a good meal.'

'If you don't eat your veggies,' Bronte said, 'you don't get any of the apple pie I picked up from the bakery today.'

That shut Toovs up, and he threw himself into his task wholeheartedly.

Holden smiled at Bronte. Sometimes it was good to have a woman around. It was good for the boys to have a female influence. Without her bringing a little femininity to the house, there'd be so much testosterone floating around, the place would likely explode with it.

'How was your day anyway?' he asked as Bronte pulled up a stool at the island bench.

She shrugged. 'Work wasn't bad. But I had some not-so-great news as I was driving home.'

'Oh?'

'Yeah.' She grabbed a banana from the fruit bowl and started to unpeel it. 'My dad's cancer's back. And it's bad. They've given him a month—two months tops—to live.'

'Fuck.' Holden dropped the potato and peeler, went over to her, wrapped his arms around her tiny body and pulled her close. 'Why didn't you say so before now?'

He'd been all het up about Adeline when his closest friend's heart was breaking, and he should have noticed something was up. Bronte adored her dad. They were close in a way Holden couldn't even imagine being close to a parent.

'Because you needed reprimanding first.' She sniffed and pulled out of his embrace. 'Anyway, I'm taking extended leave and going up there to stay, to help Mum with the pub so she can be in Darwin with Dad.'

'Of course. Is there anything I can do to help?'

She shrugged again. 'Go collect my mail every now and then? Check my pot plants aren't dying?'

'Consider it done.'

'What about your work?' he asked.

'I've contacted all my bookings for the next few weeks and managed to find other photographers for almost all of them. I know it's unprofessional to leave a couple in the lurch, but I have to put my family first.'

'Of course.' Holden nodded, as Ford, just back from work, wheeled into the kitchen.

'Has someone died?' he asked, glancing at their gloomy expressions.

Holden glared at him as Bronte replied, 'Not yet, but Dad's cancer's back.'

Ford's grin slipped from his face. 'Shit, I'm sorry.'

'Thanks.' She sighed, grabbed a knife and started chopping carrots like they'd done her a grave wrong.

There was a sombre mood over dinner. Bronte told the boys about her dad and that she was going to be away for a while. Although they didn't exactly say it, it was clear they were going to miss her like crazy. They weren't the only ones. How was Holden supposed to get through the highs and lows of each day without his best friend? Ford was a great support, but he could be too damn chirpy. His optimism and Pollyanna outlook about everything got annoying sometimes. When Holden vented, he didn't always want to be told to look on the bright side—to look at the good they were doing. He wanted someone to agree with him about how shit things could be.

Bronte was usually really good at that.

After the apple pie was devoured so there weren't even any crumbs left in the box, Bronte stooped down to hug Ford good-bye, and then Holden walked her outside to her car.

'Gunna miss you like crazy,' he said as he enveloped her in another hug.

'Don't.' She half-laughed, half-sobbed as she pushed him away. 'Or I'll start bawling.'

Bronte never cried. She was almost as hard as him. He wished he could go with her for support—and also to see her dad, who he adored too—but he couldn't leave Ford alone with the boys, even for a few days. Instead, he made do with squeezing her tight one more time and then let her go. 'Have a good flight and call me when you get there.'

'Will do.' She slid into her car, and he watched her head down the drive until her tail-lights disappeared, then turned back towards the house to find Toovs, Sam, Rocky and Mitch laughing on the verandah. Their heads were leaning close as if they were plotting mischief. 'What's going on?'

Toovs looked up. 'Holden, man, you gotta see this!'

He crossed over to the boys to see what had them so engrossed.

Oh Christ. His eyes boggled as he stared down at the video on Mitch's phone. A bunch of nuns were dancing and singing along to Taylor Swift's 'You belong with me', although they'd altered the words slightly, so they were singing about Jesus's love for all. If it weren't for the fact that he recognised half of them and for their boring uniform of brown and beige, he might not have been able to tell they were nuns. 'What the hell is that? Are they trying to give the cast of *Sister Act* a run for its money?'

'What's *Sister Act*?' asked Toovs. The others stared blankly.

He shook his head. 'Never mind. So, what *is* that?'

'NunTok,' explained Rocky, laughing. Holden was pleased to see him interacting with the other boys, but right now, he was distracted.

'Nun *what*?'

'It's TikTok,' explained Sam, 'but for nuns. These are the ones from down the road. See, there's Sister Michelle, Sister Rita and Sister Maria.'

'Her name's Adeline,' barked Holden. But *nuns on TikTok*? What the hell was the world coming to? 'Is this some kind of joke?'

'I don't think so,' Mitch said, 'but I think they're pretty hilarious.'

'Yeah, they're cool. Even the old chick,' said Sam, then grimaced. 'Sorry, I mean *woman*.'

'How'd you all find this?' Holden asked, still feeling guilty for losing his cool at Sam last night.

Toovs—who was possibly the smartest of the lot—lifted one shoulder. 'Something to do with the algorithm. It knows our location and shows us other accounts nearby that it thinks we might be interested in.'

'Right.' Holden nodded; Toovs may as well have been speaking in tongues. 'Anyway, you done your homework?'

'Yeah,' he chorused with Sam, who was back at school now.

'You better not be lying,' Holden said. 'I don't want any more phone calls from the school.'

The boys didn't reply, they were already back watching the phone. Holden was tempted to stay and see what else the nuns had been up to, but he forced himself inside to attend to other things.

That night, when the kids were finally in their rooms, Holden retreated to his own, climbed into bed and held his phone in his hand, his fingers twitching as he contemplated downloading TikTok.

Don't do it.

Until today, he'd never had any interest in social media; thought it a mind-numbing waste of time.

Swiping his screen unlocked, he opened the app store.

What the hell are you doing?

Shaking his head, Holden pitched his phone across the other side of the bedroom, took a deep breath, then lay back and closed his eyes. But once again, slumber evaded him. He tossed around and turned his pillow over multiple times, trying to get comfy, before giving in and throwing back the covers.

He'd download the app, take a quick look, and then delete it again. It would be like scratching an itch and once he'd looked, he could get on with his life, blissfully TikTok free.

His jaw clenched in impatience as he waited for what felt like an eternity for it to download, but then he quickly found the SistersOfSmallton.

Holy shit. There seemed to be dozens of videos and Adeline looked to be the ringleader of them all. Pretty soon, he'd lost an hour getting a glimpse into the secret life of nuns. In addition to the dances to popular songs, which they always put a religious twist on, there were day-in-the-life videos showing the nuns doing everything from praying and keeping bees, to quoting Bible verses and playing pool.

As fascinating as these insights were, it was the dances he kept coming back to. There was nothing overtly sexual about any of them, but his mouth went dry as his eyes zeroed in on Adeline in each one. He didn't know if she'd done dancing as a kid or something but the way she moved her body was a thing of beauty.

And all he could think about was her moving it in bed. With him.

Argh. Dammit. He hurled the phone across the room again.

So much for getting it out of his system.

Chapter Sixteen

Two days later, Adeline and Bella arrived for the next training session forty-five minutes early and carrying a box of freshly baked choc-chip cookies. The way to a man's heart and all. Although she wasn't trying to get to Holden's heart, she was determined to get through to his soul and figured this might work just as well. The boys looked up to him and if *he* didn't let her in then it would be much harder to witness to them.

Hence she was determined to catch him before he started the afternoon's obedience training. One thing left over from her past life was the irritation at the knowledge that somebody didn't like her. She could see that back home she may have given people reason not to, but she couldn't understand what Holden seemingly had against her and she was determined to chisel through his hard exterior.

The dogs greeted her as usual, but today the boys were nowhere in sight, and it suddenly occurred to her that they might still be on their way home from school. *Whoops.* She swallowed at the possibility of being alone with Holden but before she could second-guess her decision, Rocky called to her from over near one of the sheds. Or rather he called to Bella.

Relief washing through her, she followed the dog who was already darting towards the boy. 'Hey there.'

'Hi,' he said, barely looking up. 'You guys are early.'

'Um … yeah. Is Holden around?'

The words had hardly left her mouth when he came out of the shed. His eyes widened as they met hers. 'Maria. Hello. Wasn't expecting you for another half an hour.'

Her stomach did its usual gymnastics at the way he said her name—or rather his personal nickname for her. When had it become endearing rather than annoying? 'Hi Jack. I thought we could have a chat before things started.'

'A chat?' He looked as if he'd never heard of the concept.

'Come on, Bella.' Rocky ran off towards the house, the dog following closely behind.

Adeline turned back to Holden. 'I thought since I'm going to be spending time around here with Bella, we should get to know each other a bit.' When he raised an eyebrow, she opened the lid of her container and angled it towards him. 'Want one?'

He stared down at the cookies and for a moment she thought he might refuse her offer, but when he thanked her and took one, she let out a—hopefully inaudible—sigh of relief.

'These aren't bad,' he said after devouring it in two mouthfuls.

'Not bad?! I'll have you know those cookies won me first prize in the biscuit section at the Walsh Agricultural Show last year.'

'Is that right? So, you can write and bake. What *else* can you do, Maria?'

Convinced she must be imagining his flirtatious insinuation, she said, 'I play a pretty good game of tennis, and when I was sixteen, I was crowned Miss Golden Sausage.'

'What the … actual?' It sounded like he'd been about to swear but curbed his tongue for her. She appreciated it, considering she was trying super hard not to curse herself.

'Every year there's a sausage-making competition in Walsh because there were quite a few Italian settlers in the region, and they have this dinner dance to follow in the evening, where they award Miss Golden Sausage, Master Golden Sausage, and King and Queen of the Sausages.'

'As disturbing as that sounds, how can I not be impressed by such a title?' Holden said, swiping another cookie.

'Hey.' She snapped the lid of the container closed and held it against her chest. 'Don't be a pig. Save some for the boys.'

As if on cue, they heard voices coming down the drive and Adeline looked over to see Toovs, Sam and a couple of tag-alongs, all dressed in the uniform of Smallton High, appearing on bikes. Vlad and Merlin, who'd been standing close, their stares trained on the box of cookies, ran towards their owners.

'Come on then.' Holden jerked a thumb towards the house. 'Let's go get rid of those cookies. Also, remind me when we get inside to offer you a drink or something. If Bronte finds out I don't, she'll have my guts for garters.'

Adeline laughed. 'Bronte's great.'

'Yeah.' He nodded as they walked. 'She is.'

'We had a lovely chat on Wednesday. Will she be here today?'

'Nope. She's gone to stay with her family.'

'Oh. Will she be gone long?' Adeline felt less anxious being near Holden when Bronte was around.

He shrugged his broad, delicious shoulders. 'Dunno. Her dad's sick.'

Nerves were forgotten, replaced by concern. 'I'm sorry to hear that. Is it serious?'

'Yeah. Cancer. Terminal. He's got maybe a few weeks left.'

'That's awful.'

He nodded again. 'I think she'll likely stay until he passes.'

Adeline wished she had Bronte's phone number or email. They may have only just met but she really liked her and wanted to send her love and thoughts; then again, maybe Bronte didn't feel the same as her, maybe she'd just been being polite and would find such contact weird from a near stranger. She didn't want to come on too strong and scare her off.

It was loud inside the house as the boys thumped about, unloading schoolbags and discarding lunch boxes on the bench. Adeline pressed herself against the wall by the kitchen door so as not to get in the way. Before Holden allowed anyone to eat, he reminded them who was on washing up the lunch stuff and went through a roster of chores for the rest of the afternoon and evening. She wondered if he and Bronte planned to have kids of their own—he'd make such a great father. Firm but kind.

Then the boys and their friends pounced upon the cookies. The box was empty in a matter of seconds. Glasses of milk and juice were poured and guzzled. More food was sourced from the pantry and kids that didn't live there ate just as much as those that did. The thought of Holden and Ford's food bill terrified Adeline; she remembered how much her brothers used to eat when they were teenagers. Her mum was always going on about how they were going to eat them out of house and home, but there'd never been any real fear of that in the Walsh household, whereas here it seemed like a genuine possibility.

'What can I get you to drink?' Holden asked, jolting her from her thoughts. 'Tea, coffee, Milo, juice or water?'

'Do you have herbal?'

His eyes told her the answer.

She smirked. 'Just water thanks.'

He grabbed a glass—'Hope tap water's okay'—and started filling it before she could reply.

'Have you had any military training?' she asked, when the boys finally scattered to get changed and ready for dog training.

'No.' His eyebrows squished together. 'Why'd you think that?'

'You must have been a boy scout then.'

He snorted at this. 'Do I look like I was a boy scout?'

Her mouth went dry at his invitation to rake her eyes over his body—his muscular arms and his broad chest, which she guessed also to be inked, down to his narrow hips.

Nope. Definitely not.

She gulped down some water and thought of Bronte.

'Why d'you ask?'

'You run this place with such precision. It's impressive.'

'Only way not to live in mayhem. Ford does rib me a bit about it though.'

At the mention of his brother, Adeline said, 'I've been meaning to ask, what's the deal about your names?'

'What do you mean?'

'Well, it's just, Holden and Ford seem like an odd pair. Like, I know they're both cars and you said your dad was an enthusiast—'

'I think I said, "revhead".'

'Okay. *Revhead.*' She smiled at the interruption. 'But aren't most people loyal to one manufacturer or the other? You don't meet people with Holden *and* Ford t-shirts in their wardrobes. I think there was once even a brawl in the pub back home over which was best. People are as loyal to their car brands as they are to their football teams.'

'You're right.' He ran a hand through his thick, unruly mane—she was surprised his fingers didn't get caught. 'My father *was* a Holden man. When I was born, Mum wanted to call me Reginald—'

A burst of unladylike laughter shot from her mouth, and he gave her a stern look.

'But Dad insisted on Holden.'

'Is Reggie your middle name?' she asked, unable to resist teasing him.

'Look if you're gunna mock, I'm not going to tell you.' But his lips twisted upwards.

'Sorry. I promise I'll behave. Please, go on.'

He sighed. 'I was three when Mum got pregnant with Ford. I'm too young to remember, but the way she tells it, it was a near miracle that it happened because our father was rarely home, always out drinking with his mates, screwing around behind her back. Anyway, the night she went into labour he wasn't there, and she had to get the lady next door to take us to the hospital. I still remember the piercing screams she made while in labour. I was sitting out in the corridor waiting.'

'Wasn't there anyone else to look after you?'

He shook his head. 'Mum fell out with her family when she shacked up with Dad. They didn't approve of him. Smart folks.'

'What about the neighbour? She couldn't take you back to her place?'

'She didn't want to get any more involved than she already was.'

'Nice.' What kind of person left a three-year-old all alone in a hospital while his mum was in labour?

'Yeah, anyway, Dad never showed up, so when Mum was given the paperwork for the birth certificate and stuff in the hospital, she named him Ford out of spite. She knew he'd hate it. Thought it served him right for not being there.'

'Oh my goodness.' Adeline pressed her lips together to stop from laughing. Holden's mum sounded like a hoot. 'What did your dad do when he found out? I assume he turned up eventually?'

'Yeah.' Holden hesitated a moment. 'Two weeks later. He was furious she'd named him Ford without his consent. Started screaming at her. The neighbour who'd taken us to hospital called the police and when they came around, they found me hiding under my bed, holding the newborn and Mum cowering on the floor in the kitchen as he kicked the living shit out of her.'

Adeline gasped, all traces of amusement evaporating. 'Did he …?'

'No.' Holden shook his head. 'She survived.'

'Are your … your parents aren't still together, are they?' She recalled him speaking about his father in the past tense the day they met.

'Nah. Dad was arrested, went to prison a few months, got out and disappeared.'

'As in disappeared from your lives or *disappeared* disappeared?'

'The latter. He was listed as a missing person for a long time, but then when Mum wanted to get remarried and there'd been no sign of him on any public records or any sightings, the court declared him as presumed dead.'

'Wow. That's some story.' Her life was so normal in comparison. Sure, her parents fought, but never physically, and although she wasn't *close* close to either of them, they were both still around. 'So, how's your mum doing now?'

He snorted. 'She's fine.' But there was something bitter in his tone, and he immediately changed the subject. 'Anyway, better go gather the troops.'

Adeline followed him outside like a shadow, and as they headed towards the training paddocks, Toovs called out from where he seemed to be hanging upside down from a tree.

'Love your moves on TikTok, Maria.'

'Her name's Adeline,' Holden reprimanded.

What? She froze—her name the least of her worries—as she moved only her head to look up to Holden.

His smirk told her that Toovs wasn't the only one to have seen the Sisters of Smallton on TikTok. 'Did you learn to shake your booty like that when you were training for Miss Golden Sausage?'

Her cheeks flamed and her pulse started to race. 'You've seen my ... *our* account.'

He nodded, clearly amused.

'I'm surprised you're on TikTok,' she said, trying to regain her composure. 'You don't seem the type.'

'There's a lot you don't know about me, Maria,' he whispered, his breath hot against her skin as he breached the boundaries of her personal space, 'but you're right about that. The boys showed me.'

Oh Lord. She wanted the ground to split open and suck her down into the earth.

'You nuns continue to surprise me, that's for sure.'

She didn't bother correcting Holden on the whole nun/sister thing, she was too flustered at the thought of him watching her make a fool of herself on social media. No way she'd have posted some of their silly dances if she'd thought anyone she knew might watch.

'The boys think it's pretty cool,' he added.

She wondered what *he* thought, and then reminded herself that his opinion didn't matter—the sisters' TikTok platform was there to reach those in need of saving, and the fact that the boys had found her account meant they were reaching the right people. *That* was the important thing.

'I'm surprised they have phones,' she said. 'That must cost you a bit.'

'They were looking at Mitch's, but Toovs and Sam do each have a phone. I give them an allowance if they consistently do their chores without complaint, and they can spend it on whatever they want. Within reason. It's good for them to learn how to manage money.'

Adeline nodded. 'Bronte told me about some of the other things you do here and also about your tiny house idea. It sounds wonderful.'

'Thanks.' He shoved his hands in his jeans pockets as if slightly embarrassed by the compliment. 'But it won't be any good if we can't raise the funds to get it off the ground.'

'Have you thought of applying for a grant?'

'Nah, that's never crossed my mind.' It took her a couple of seconds to realise he was being sarcastic. 'I've lost count of how many bloody applications I've filled in, and not everyone in town is happy about us being here, so getting shire approvals and stuff will be another hurdle.'

'Smallton doesn't want you and Ford here?'

'Not me and Ford. The boys. Some people think that the teenagers we take in will wreak havoc. Whenever there's a break-in or graffiti in town, the police always come here first, and some local parents are scared our boys will be a bad influence on their kids.'

'And have they any reason to think this?'

He glanced back at the kids and lowered his voice. 'Look the boys aren't angels and when they first arrive, they can sometimes cause a bit of a stir. When Sam arrived, he stole a bit from local stores, but he wasn't good at it and always got caught. Thankfully that's back when he was underage—he's mostly been pretty good the last year or so—but he's got a juvie record and people don't forget. They're not willing to give outsiders a second chance.'

'That sucks,' she said, aware that she too had already had less than positive thoughts about them. She made a mental note to pray about her attitude later.

'It is what it is. Mostly we don't let the opinions of bigots bother us, but it's annoying when it causes financial obstacles. Anyway, enough chitchat.' Holden put two fingers in his mouth and whistled loudly, signalling it was time for training to start. 'You can sit on the fence today if it gives you a better vantage spot. The dogs know you now, so you won't be so distracting.'

'Thanks.'

As the boys and dogs bounded through the gate and into the paddock, Adeline made herself comfy to watch the action. She tried to focus on what they were doing, particularly Bella and Rocky, but Holden was like a magnet. Her eyes kept drifting to him, watching the way his legs moved in his jeans as he directed the kids. Funny how her view had totally shifted about him.

When she'd first seen his long scruffy hair, thick beard and tattoos, she'd written him off as some sort of vagabond, but now she saw him as a thing of beauty. She couldn't imagine him with short hair and bare skin, and for the first time in her life, she could see the appeal of tattoos and why it was often called body *art*. She'd heard what the dog tattoo meant to him, and now she wanted to learn the story of every other image inked into his skin. Those stories would form the story of his life, they'd give insight into his background, offer clues to what led him here, to dedicate his life—his time and his resources—to these boys who desperately needed love and a second chance.

Hearing about his father had given her a few more pieces of the puzzle, but she desperately wanted all of them. She probably shouldn't be so intrigued by this ruggedly sexy giant—he was taken and so was she—but if she concentrated on what he did and how she might help, rather than on his body and the way looking at it made her feel, then she should be fine.

'Afternoon, Adeline.'

'Oh my God.' She almost fell off the fence at the sound of Ford's voice just behind her.

He chuckled. 'Sorry. Didn't mean to scare you. Usually people hear me coming a mile away.'

'I ... I was ...' Her voice drifted off as her gaze turned back to the paddock. She'd been so lost in her thoughts that she hadn't heard Ford's van arriving, never mind him coming her way. 'I was praying.'

'Oh, in that case, I'll leave you be,' he said, putting his hands back on his wheels.

'No, please stay.' She climbed down off the fence. 'I'd love your company while I wait for Bella to finish.'

'In that case ...' She heard the click of his brakes as he locked the wheelchair into place, and she grabbed the crate she'd been sitting next to the other day and plonked herself down beside him.

'How was your day?'

'Good,' he said with a nod. 'Fridays are always busy in the shop. All the local blokes want to get their hair spiffy before heading to the pub to try to pick up.'

Although she laughed, Adeline couldn't help wondering how someone in his ... *position* managed to cut hair. She guessed that like he had at this property, he must have made adjustments at the barbershop so he could work. Not for the first time, she wondered what had happened to make him lose the function in his legs. Tabitha Cooper-Jones in Walsh had lost her arm to cancer in her late teens and always told people exactly what had happened when they first met. Adeline knew that Tab preferred people to be straightforward about her disability, rather than stare and talk behind her back.

Taking a deep breath, she hoped Ford was the same as she asked, 'How did you end up in a wheelchair?'

'Car accident when I was fourteen. Broke my back. Can't use my legs.'

'I'm sorry,' she said, even though it sounded so lame.

He shrugged. 'It could have been worse. And you'd be surprised how many perks there are—my shoes never wear out, and people part like the Red Sea when I'm coming, which means I never have to wait for a lift or anything. Also, I can always get a parking spot, even if there's no disabled parking. No one's gunna give a guy in a wheelchair a ticket.'

'That's true.' She smiled, admiring Ford's positive attitude, and feeling shame for all the times she'd felt hard done by. So many things she took for granted would be difficult for Ford, yet he didn't seem to let them get him down.

'And, yes,' he leaned forward and wriggled his eyebrows, 'I can have sex. Admit it, you were curious.'

Adeline felt her cheeks flush—would she be human if the thought hadn't crossed her mind?

'I'm happy to give you a demo if you want,' he added with a wink.

She laughed and shook her head—'You're terrible!'—but she didn't feel hot and bothered like she did when Holden said something flirtatious. Not that Ford wasn't attractive. If she looked at the brothers objectively, he was the better looking of the two, but she felt safe around him in a way she didn't feel around Holden.

'What are you two giggling about?' Holden started towards them, suddenly paying attention.

'Never you mind, Jack. How's Bella going?'

He glowered. 'Why do you call me Jack?'

'You'll never know.' This time she was the one who winked. 'By the way, I'm super impressed by the set-up you have here. Do you ever take the boys and dogs to actual trials?'

'I'd like to,' he said, resting his forearms on the fence. 'Eventually. I think it would be really good for them, but most of the trials are a fair drive away, so we'd need to sort accommodation as well as travel to and from competitions. Our van holds the boys, but not the dogs and everything else we'd need to take with us. Plus, we'd need to hire a driver for the extra vehicle. Just can't afford all that.'

'You don't drive?' She asked.

'Nope. I've got a motorbike.'

'Holden,' called Rocky. 'Come look at this.'

He lifted a hand to indicate to Rocky he'd be there in a moment. 'Don't listen to a word this bloke says about me,' he said to Adeline. 'He's a total bullshit artist.'

Then he swaggered back to join the boys and dogs, his fitted jeans accentuating his tight butt as he did so. Adeline's mouth went dry, and she cursed herself for her sinful thoughts. Michelle might be right that *looking* wasn't a sin, but according to the Ten Commandments, lusting after someone else's boyfriend was.

Sorry, Bronte.

'Why *do* you call him Jack?' Ford asked once Holden was out of earshot.

'Promise you won't tell?'

He pinched his thumb and index finger together and dragged it across his lips. 'I'll take it to the grave. Nothing makes me happier than knowing something my smart-arse older brother wants to, trust me.'

'Well ...' Adeline smiled; she too knew a few things about smart-arse older brothers. 'It's because he reminds me of a lumberjack.'

Ford frowned. 'He does?'

'Yeah. You know, he loves wearing those flannel shirts, he's got that big bushy beard, and does he even *own* a hairbrush?'

'Not last time I checked.' Ford threw back his head and cackled. 'I love it. It suits him perfectly.'

Chapter Seventeen

Sunday dinner was always a big event. Ford, who loved cooking, spent much of the afternoon in the kitchen preparing a roast with all the trimmings and the boys took turns on dessert duty. Just like Friday-night bonfires, it was something the kids looked forward to all week and they often had extras join them.

Holden was starving as he joined the others in the dining room just before six o'clock and took his place at the table, which was already laden with dishes full of meat, roast veggies, gravy and more. The first time Toovs had enjoyed Sunday dinner here he'd exclaimed it reminded him of a Hogwarts feast, only without the magic. Tonight, Mitch and Luka, and Mitch's new girlfriend, Tarryn—brave girl—had joined them, and they were all talking about the auditions for *Peter Pan,* which she and Luka were both doing, but there was still an empty chair.

'Where's Rocky?' Holden asked as the older boys picked up their cutlery like runners getting in position to race.

'We haven't seen him since just after lunch,' Sam said. 'Toovs and I asked if he wanted to play Fortnite with us, but he said he wanted to be alone.'

Alone? Holden's heart thudded. 'Did he sound upset?'

Both boys shrugged.

'You haven't seen him?' Holden asked Ford, his pulse quickening.

His brother shook his head.

Holden pushed back his chair. 'I'll go find him. You guys start but save Rocky and me a plate.'

'Want me to come help look?' Ford asked.

'Nah. You stay with this lot.' He didn't want an argument to break out over who got more potatoes—Ford's roasties were definitely fight-worthy—and hopefully he'd find Rocky fast.

He did a quick scan of the house, then called the boy's name as he walked through the yards towards the sheds. The dogs followed him as he searched the property, but Rocky wasn't anywhere to be found.

Shit. Holden tried to swallow the unease that rose like bile in his throat. How long had he been missing? And what kind of mental state was he in?

On the weekends the kids had more freedom, their routine was less structured than during the weeks, but Holden had let down his guard regarding Rocky. He'd spent most of the arvo working on another couple of grants in the office, messaging with Bronte and wasting a fair bit of time watching Adeline's videos on TikTok, when he should have been checking in on his most vulnerable charge. Cursing himself, he dragged his phone out of his pocket before remembering that Rocky didn't have a phone like the others.

Holden had told him he could work to get one, but he'd said he didn't care.

'What do I need a phone for? Who would I call?'

Dammit. He'd thought—thanks to Bella—they were finally making progress.

Bella! Could Rocky had gone to visit the dog? Maybe while Holden had been thinking of her owner, the kid had been missing Bella. He ordered Vlad and Merlin back to the house, then started jogging down the gravel drive, phoning Ford as he did so to tell him where he was going. If the kid wasn't at the convent, he'd have to expand his search, let the department know, maybe even call the police.

It wouldn't be the first time Rocky had run away from a foster home, but that wasn't something Holden was willing to accept just yet. He swore if he found the kid safe and well, he'd delete the bloody TikTok app and put all thoughts of Adeline Walsh out of his head. Being nice to her like Bronte had made him promise had only made things more difficult. Well, Bronte was gone now and what she didn't know wouldn't hurt her.

As he came to the road, he saw a small figure approaching from the direction of the town. Hope sparked in his heart as the figure walked beneath a streetlamp and he got a flash of Rocky's hard-to-miss bright red hair. *Thank fuck.*

'Well, you're a sight for sore eyes,' Holden said, resisting the urge to grab hold of the boy and pull him close.

'What's that mean?'

'It means I'm bloody happy to see you. When you didn't show for dinner, I was worried. Never known a teenage boy to be late for Sunday dinner.'

'Sorry.' Rocky stared at the ground, kicking a rock at his feet. 'I lost track of time.'

'Where've you been?'

Rocky shrugged one shoulder but didn't meet his gaze. 'Just walking round town. Thinking.'

His voice sounded choked, and Holden could tell he'd been crying.

'You know, if you ever wanna talk about anything, I'm all ears. And I get that sometimes we don't wanna talk, we just want to be alone, but do you think you could tell me next time you need some space? Just so I know you're safe.'

Rocky nodded, then said in a voice so quiet Holden only just heard, 'It's my mum's birthday today.'

'Oh shit, mate.' Holden reached out and patted him on the back. It was the first time Rocky hadn't flinched at any kind of touch, and, despite the boy's heartbreak, this felt like progress. 'I'm so sorry. I didn't know.'

He probably should have—it had to be in the paperwork he had on Rocky—but he'd never been much good at keeping track of dates.

Rocky wiped his eyes quickly, clearly embarrassed about being caught this way. ''Sokay.'

'Nah, it's not.' Holden vowed somehow to make it up to him. 'You shouldn't have had to deal with today alone. You don't have to deal with anything alone anymore, okay?'

Again, Rocky shrugged.

'And don't ever feel you have to lock your feelings up inside you. It's not weak to cry. Hell, I have a good bawl at least once a week.'

Rocky looked up and raised an eyebrow as if he didn't believe it.

'It's true.' Holden nodded. 'Just 'cos I look hard, doesn't mean I don't get sad or anxious. Ask Ford or Bronte; they're often the ones passing me the tissues.'

Rocky let out a short burst of laughter, then said, 'Do you believe there's more when we die? You know, heaven or something?'

Holden didn't believe in any such thing. He was more a life sucks and then you die kind of person. If God and heaven were real, then why the hell did the guy allow so much devastation and destruction on the place he supposedly created? Why was he so judgemental about people who weren't doing any harm to anyone else? And why did he allow bastards like their stepfather to hold themselves up as a face of the institution?

'Yeah, I reckon there is.' He forced the lie out of his mouth. 'I reckon your mum is looking down on you right now. Her soul will never leave you. She'll always be like a guardian angel watching over you.'

Guardian angel? Hopefully he hadn't taken things too far.

'You reckon they have birthday cake in heaven?' Rocky asked.

Holden nodded, relieved the kid seemed to have bought his story. 'Yep. Best birthday cake you've ever seen. All the icing, all the hundreds and thousands, lots of chocolate and lollies. Bet the birthday cake is the size of a house and never runs out.'

'Mum liked caramel mud cake the best,' Rocky said, finally meeting Holden's gaze, a hint of a smile on his face.

'Yum.' Holden smiled back. 'I don't mind a bit of a caramel myself.' All this talk of food was making him even hungrier, but he didn't want to rush Rocky back before he was ready. 'Is there anything you'd like to do to celebrate your mum's birthday? We could take a trip to visit her grave tomorrow or even make a cake for her tonight?'

He'd speak to Ford if Rocky wanted to do the latter. Holden was good at many things, but baking was not one of them. At the thought of baking, his mind—once again—went to Adeline. This time to those magic cookies she'd brought over. What was the secret ingredient that made them so much better than any other cookie he'd ever tried?

He shook his head free of Adeline and focused on what mattered. Rocky.

'Anything you want. You just say it and we'll do it.'

Rocky rubbed his lips together a few long moments, then said, 'I don't really like visiting her grave. She's not there, as you said. She's in heaven. And I think eating a cake without her would just make me sad. I want to do something more meaningful. Something that would make her proud.'

'Fair enough. Any ideas?'

'I'm thinking I might wanna try school again.'

'What? Really?' Holden failed to hide his surprise. He was doing his best at home-schooling and Rocky wasn't an idiot at all, but when he'd arrived, he'd been adamantly against formal education, promising he'd run away if anyone so much as tried to make him set foot inside the local high school.

'Yeah, I figure it might be better than hanging around here and being cheap labour for you all day.'

Holden chuckled. The boy had a good sense of humour.

'I don't want Mum's life to be a waste and I figure I'm all she had, so I need to make something of myself. I don't want to end up a loser alcoholic wife-beater like my dad. So I guess I need an education. And no offence, but a better one that you can give me.'

'No offence taken, mate. I think you've been teaching me more than I've been teaching you anyway.'

Rocky laughed. 'Your maths *is* pretty diabolical.'

'Hey, now you're just being mean,' Holden said, his tone light, 'but if you're sure, we can go down to the school tomorrow and chat to the principal.'

Rocky hesitated a moment as if he might have changed his mind but then said, 'Yeah, that'd be good. I think when I grow up, I want to work with animals, maybe even be a vet.' He glanced down at his feet. 'I'm probably not smart enough, but if I don't try …'

His voice drifted off and Holden's eyes watered. He was so proud of Rocky's mature decision and stoked at this evidence that they were making progress after all. Sniffing, he clapped his hand on his shoulder. 'I reckon you can do anything you put your mind to. And I'll help in any way I can.'

'Thanks,' Rocky said and then shivered. He was only wearing shorts and a thin t-shirt.

'Come on.' Holden risked ruffling the boy's hair and felt victorious when once again he didn't pull away. 'Let's go home and get some roast into ya.'

Chapter Eighteen

Adeline could not stop thinking about Holden's ideas for helping boys in need. Although she hadn't spent a lot of time at his and Ford's place, it was clear they made a difference to the kids in their care. It seemed preposterous that they'd been knocked back for grants and not supported by locals. People were always complaining about teenagers ending up on the streets, yet when someone like Holden had a vision for how to give their lives meaning and purpose, he was ignored or berated.

They probably saw his tattoos and bogan clothing and wrote him off as well.

It irked her that she'd been quick to judge those kids (and him) too, but now she'd seen the error of her ways, she wanted to do something to help. God had led her down that driveway for a reason, and maybe it wasn't only so Bella could help Rocky, and she could outreach to the boys, but also so she could be of practical assistance.

She'd prayed lots about this over the weekend and then, first thing Monday morning—following breakfast, communal prayer, and Bella's jaunt around the garden—had requested a meeting with Mother Catherine to discuss her idea.

'Come on in,' said the older woman, welcoming Adeline into her office, which smelled of fruity apple incense sticks.

Adeline smiled as she took a seat opposite the older woman on the floral couch, Bella flopping down on the floor at her feet. 'Thank you for making time for me.'

'I always have time for you. You seem to be settling in well?'

'Yes. I feel like I've been here forever.'

Mother Catherine nodded. 'You fit in well and I'm very impressed with your first two NunTalk columns. Sister Mary told me that yesterday when she was picking up a prescription at the chemist, the pharmacist couldn't stop singing your praises. I think some of them found her columns a little confronting.'

Adeline couldn't help but glow at these words—for so long she'd doubted whether she actually had any talent when it came to writing. She'd loved it but that didn't mean she was any good, but if this was indeed a God-given gift, then she wanted to use it.

'Don't keep me in suspense any longer,' said Mother Catherine, the lines around her eyes crinkling. 'You said you had an idea to discuss with me.'

'Yes.' Adeline sat up straight and held her chin high as she spoke. 'You know how I've been taking Bella down the road to train with that young boy?'

'Rocky? Isn't that what you said his name was?'

'That's right.'

'And how's he going? His story broke my heart.'

Adeline swallowed—whenever she thought about what Rocky had been through, she grew all emotional as well. 'He seems to be enjoying working with Bella, but I'm wondering if there's more I can do to help.'

'What exactly do you have in mind?' asked Mother Catherine, leaning forward to pluck a Mintie from the jar on the coffee table.

Adeline politely declined when Mother Catherine offered her one and instead explained the plans Holden had for the tiny houses.

'Apparently he's been knocked back for multiple grants and he's so busy keeping the place afloat and taking care of the boys that he probably doesn't have the time to organise fundraisers either. So ... I was thinking ... maybe I could help. I could look at his grant applications and see if I can offer any areas for improvement. Back home, I was successful at getting grant money for heaps of different local groups. There's a real skill to writing them and Holden might just need to tweak a few things.'

Mother Catherine leaned forward. 'And you believe God is calling you to do this? To help him with the grants?'

'I do.' Adeline nodded adamantly. 'I've prayed about it lots and asked the Lord's guidance and ideas keep coming, so I feel like that's his answer.'

'You have other ideas aside from the grants?'

'Yes. Holden told me the people of Smallton aren't always welcoming to the boys. They see them as a threat because they come from broken homes, and some have been in trouble with the law. But you should see the things he and his brother have helped them achieve. It's not just the dog training. Holden's teaching them woodworking and Ford's taught them to cook and even cut hair. They look after the kids really well, they're schooling them to be upstanding members of not only their household but also the community, and I think if people understood all this, they wouldn't be so averse.'

'So, what's your plan?'

'Well, I thought I could propose an article to Mike about them—showcasing the different things Holden and Ford do with the boys. Maybe interview Holden to get his backstory and his vision. And I was also thinking I could organise a fundraiser—something the kids can get involved with as well—to help raise some money for the first tiny house.'

'Sounds like you have quite the vision.'

Adeline wasn't sure of Mother Catherine's tone, so she added, 'I'm sure Michelle and Sister Rita can vouch for Holden and the boys. They've both met some of them at the soup kitchen.'

'Hmm.' Mother Catherine folded her papery hands in her lap and didn't say anything for quite some time.

Adeline couldn't tell if she was considering her ideas or if she'd fallen asleep. Finally, just as she was reaching for a Mintie to at least occupy her hands, her superior spoke again.

'I'm impressed by your drive and dedication to service, and if you believe the Lord is calling you to help these boys, then you must follow that call. Please keep me posted and, in addition to our prayers, let me know if the sisters can be of any practical help along the way.'

'Thank you.' Adeline felt a rush of gratitude and excitement. For first time in her life, she felt like she was doing something truly meaningful, something that could make a difference to others, and she couldn't wait to put her ideas to Holden.

After waving goodbye to Sister Josey and Lola, who were in the garden hanging a load of washing, she called for Bella, who'd been making small talk with the chickens. 'Want to come visit Rocky?'

As soon as she opened the convent's gate, Bella darted down the road towards Holden and Ford's place. Adeline had to jog to keep up with her, and despite the cool breeze, she worked up a little sweat and her pulse was racing by the time they turned down the gravel drive. As usual they were greeted by the other dogs, excited to have visitors, especially of the canine variety. After bestowing neck rubs and ear scratches upon Vlad and Merlin, she continued towards the house. A small hatchback parked out the front had her halting in her step. Holden must have a visitor.

Perhaps she should come back later? Talk to him next time she brought Bella for training.

Before she could retreat, an almighty thwack sounded from behind the house.

More thwacks quickly followed, and Adeline recognised them as the sounds of someone chopping wood. The dogs at her heels, she followed the noise to find a shirtless Holden wielding an axe as he annihilated a large tree branch, looking even more like a lumberjack than ever. An incredibly sexy one at that. She swallowed at the sight of his chest and arm tattoos in all their glory. Not to mention that little arrow of dark hair just above the waistband of his jeans.

Oh Lord. Have mercy.

'Maria?' He sounded surprised. 'What are you doing here?'

Besides standing here staring, my mouth open like a codfish?

She snapped it shut and averted her gaze, attempting to make eye contact. The way his dark brown pupils met hers had her going at weak at the knees like some vacuous heroine in a historical romance novel.

'Where's Rocky?' she asked, desperate for a chaperone.

Holden dropped the axe to the ground, straightened and ran a hand through his thick, unruly hair. 'In the house with his therapist.'

Ah, that would account for the strange car.

'Good news … he's decided he wants to go back to school. We're going to see the principal at the high school this arvo.'

'Wow.' Adeline tried to focus on what he was saying rather than imagining what it might be like to run her own fingers through that hair. 'That's wonderful.'

'It's a bloody miracle. Working with Bella has really helped, so thank you.'

'You're welcome.' She couldn't help it; once again, her gaze dropped to his chest, which really was a work of art. A magnificent dragon flowed over one shoulder, breathing fire towards his ribs.

Holden cleared his throat, and she snapped her eyes back to his.

'Please don't tell me you're here to withdraw the offer of Bella's assistance.'

'What? No. Of course not.' She rubbed her lips together, then said, 'I have a proposition for you.'

His brows caved towards each other, and he tilted his head to the side like a confused puppy. A German shepherd or pit bull or something like that. 'What kind of proposition?'

'Do you want to put your shirt on while we talk?'

He smirked. 'Why? Do nuns have a problem with bare skin?'

Only yours, she thought, as her traitorous ovaries quivered. 'I just thought you might get cold now you're not chopping wood.'

'I'm fine,' he replied, puffing out his chest a little. 'Feeling quite warm, actually.'

Bother. She couldn't help noticing his body glistening from the exertion. The old Adeline would have offered to lick the sweat from the crevices on his chest, but the new Adeline would do no such thing.

'What's the dragon for?' she asked.

He blinked as if shocked by her question, then pointed to it. 'This?'

She nodded. 'I was just wondering if there is a story behind *all* your tattoos?'

He took a moment, as if considering whether he wanted to share or not, then shrugged and started speaking. 'Most of them. But this one is because I was born in the year of the dragon.'

'That's cool.' She swallowed the moisture in her mouth.

'I thought you hated body art.'

'I do,' she lied, then silently cursed herself. Sisters weren't supposed to tell porkies. 'I mean … I thought I did, but I guess knowing they mean something changes my opinion a little.'

'I see.' He stared disconcertingly at her for what felt like forever. 'Anyway, you didn't come here to talk about my body art, did you? What's this proposition?'

'Um …' For a moment her mind went blank—or rather it was too full of thoughts of Holden's naked chest and tattoos, for anything else—but she managed to pull herself together. 'Well, I've been talking to Mother Catherine about what you've got going on here and the ideas you have that are hindered by lack of funding.'

He frowned. 'I don't remember mentioning our money issues to you.'

'Bronte and Ford both did,' she replied, undeterred by his gruff tone.

He folded his arms across his chest. 'And what exactly does this have to do with you?'

'I'm going to help you.' She offered him her warmest smile. 'As you know, I'm a journalist but I also happen to be an expert at writing grants. Back in Walsh, I was on several community committees, and I wrote hundreds of grants and almost all were successful. I can look at some of your old applications and help you see where you've been going wrong.'

'How do you know I have been going wrong?' he scowled, which sadly did nothing to taint his devilishly delicious looks.

'Have you been successful?'

'No,' he growled.

Adeline nodded. 'I don't mean any offence. What you're doing here and what you *want* to do is important. You just have to show that on your applications and you *will* get money. I know a few tricks that will really help, so together we can apply for some new grants. But I was also thinking about other ways to get funding and community support. Mike said he'd like me to write some other articles, so I thought I could pitch one about you and Ford, the boys, and why you foster.'

'Absolutely fucking not.' His expression grew even darker. 'Legally you can't write about the boys, but I wouldn't let you even if you could.'

'Okay, then.' Adeline refused to be deterred by his bad language or grouchiness. 'We don't have to start with the article. We could try a fundraiser instead. I also happen to be an expert at those. Quiz nights, cake stalls, bingo, car washes, you name it, I've organised it. I've already got the support of some of the other sisters, and everyone trusts us, so if we're seen to be helping, it might get more locals on your side. I'm thinking of one big fundraiser, but there are some little things we could do in the meantime. The boys could do a regular car wash—it would be good to get them involved. And I hear there's a monthly market in the square. You could use your artistic talents to offer face painting. I could help with a few basic hearts and rainbows, that sort of thing.'

'What's in it for you?' Holden asked, his arms crossed tautly.

'Nothing. I've pledged myself to a life of service and that's what I'm offering you.'

'I thought the vows were poverty, chastity and obedience?'

'I'm surprised you know that. Have you been doing research?' she teased.

When the straight line of his lips didn't so much as move, she added, 'The obedience aspect is to God. And he's spoken to me. I believe it's his will that I help you and Ford make this the kind of place that you envision.'

'Is that so?' He scoffed, then when she nodded, he spat, 'God can go to hell, Adeline. And you can take your charity back to the convent and shove it where the sun don't shine.'

His words were so harsh and unexpected he may as well have slapped her. Her eyes prickled with shock, sadness and anger. What kind of imbecile was he? Who turned down an offer like this?

'I ...' Adeline blinked. 'I don't understand. *Why?*'

'Because the last thing I need is a bunch of religious do-gooders trying to get their grips into my boys.'

'Religious do-gooders?' This time it was her turn to scoff. 'You know what? The sisters and I ... we're not that different to you and Ford. What you guys are doing here is very similar to what we do every day; help people in need and try to make the world a better place.'

In reply, Holden grabbed his shirt off the ground and yanked it back over his head.

Finally, thank God. Now she should be able to concentrate on the matter at hand.

'You can believe whatever the hell you like, Adeline, but I don't have to buy into your bullshit.'

Then, before she could respond—before she could tell him that it wasn't bullshit and ask him what his freaking problem was—he turned in his boots and marched off towards the big shed, the dogs starting after him.

Adeline acted fast, grabbing Bella's collar. 'Oh no you don't,' she said, fury burning through her body again. 'We're done here.'

How dare he treat her with such disdain! How dare he speak to her like that!

Who did Holden Campbell think he was?

Chapter Nineteen

Holden stormed into the large work shed and slammed the door behind him. He half expected Adeline to bluster in after him and call him out on his rejection, but it appeared she had the good sense to leave him be. Tension wracked his body, and his fingers were still curled into fists but if he were honest, he was disappointed as well as irritated by her proposition.

He'd been annoyingly chuffed when she'd arrived unexpectedly, and perhaps he was a dick, but when she'd told him she had a proposition for him, his dirty mind had taken a sharp dive into the gutter. He'd have to have been blind not to see the way her eyes kept drifting to his pecs, and he'd be a damn liar if he said he hadn't enjoyed it. It made him want to flex his muscles and bang on his chest like Tarzan. She'd made out like she was doing him a favour asking if he wanted to put on his shirt, but he could tell it was because his near nakedness distracted her. She'd been looking at him as if he were a piece of cake she wanted to gobble up.

Talking about his tattoos wasn't something he did often—they were personal, an artistic history of his life to date—but he would have told Adeline every little thing about himself if it meant she kept gawking at him like she had been. He hadn't been lying when he said he wasn't cold; her mere presence sent his body temperature soaring. If she'd told him right then and there that she wanted to make some magic between the sheets before she fully embraced a life of chastity, well … let's just say, *that* would have been a proposition he'd eagerly accept.

He'd enjoy taking off her boring brown and beige attire one ugly layer at a time and exploring every inch of her beautiful body before claiming her with hands and tongue. He started getting hard just thinking about it.

It was probably because his mind was so deep into this fantasy that her *actual* proposition had shocked him, but now as he stopped to think about it, it made much more sense.

Could he *be* more of a fool? Did he truly think he was so irresistible that one look at his bare-naked skin and Adeline would drop her knickers alongside all her morals and convictions?

Her belief that she could help him where he hadn't been able to help himself had annoyed him, but if it was just *her* making the offer, he might have accepted. Not the article—he didn't want to be the subject of some puff piece, or worse, a story that would require him to rip open his heart and spill his mistakes onto the page for all of Smallton to read—but the rest sounded good. Money sounded awesome.

And then she'd gone and blown it by talking about this being God's will and the other sisters being eager to help as well.

God's will? How many times in his teens had he heard about God's fucking will?! He knew what happened when the church got their clutches into a person. It was an excuse for all sorts of horrors, and only over his dead body would he or any of the boys in his care have anything to do with it.

What had he been thinking, inviting a nun into their lives?

Raging at himself, he dragged his phone out of his pocket and clicked on the TikTok app. He hadn't deleted it like he'd meant to, and he'd lost count of the hours he'd wasted watching videos of Adeline over and over again.

No more. His ridiculous infatuation with the nun ended now.

His finger was hovering over the screen, about to delete the app when his phone started ringing. Bronte's name flashed up at him. He was in no mood to chat and if it was anyone but her, he'd let the call go to voicemail, but what if her dad's condition had worsened? She was his best friend and no matter what was going on in his own head, he'd always be there for her.

'Hey Bron,' he answered. He leaned against a work bench and tried to inject warmth into his voice. 'How's things?'

'Yeah, okay. I'm just waiting for Mum and Dad—they're in with the doctor at the hospital—and I needed distraction.'

'How's Bill going?'

'Not fabulous. There's nothing more the doctors can do now than keep him comfortable, pump him with painkillers. He wants to—' her voice caught, '—to die at home, but we can't risk taking him all the way back to Middle of Nowhere. He's in good spirits considering, and we're trying to make the most of the time we have left. We're watching all Dad's favourite movies and he's telling us lots of stories from his childhood and adolescence. I'm so glad I came.'

'I bet he is too,' Holden said, her words sobering him. 'And who's taking care of Nowhere with Bill and Tricia and you in Darwin?'

'Their cook, Stan, and the other staff. They're amazing, all working way more hours than is legal … but anyway, enough about me.' Bronte sounded falsely upbeat. 'How are the boys? How's Ford? Any gossip from down there?'

'Rocky's decided to go back to school.'

'Seriously? What brought that on?'

He told her about Sunday evening—Rocky going missing, the chat about his mum's birthday. 'He wants to do her proud.'

'Aw.' Bronte sniffed. 'That's great. Anything else interesting happening?'

'Well, the nun offered to help me write some grants and do some fundraising.'

'Adeline?' Bronte sounded surprised. 'Is she good at writing grants?'

'She says she did a lot of them in her past life.'

'In that case, that's awesome. And I'm not surprised. Her articles in the *Gazette* are great, so she's clearly got a way with words. She could be just the support you need.'

'I turned her down.'

'What? Why?'

He pulled the phone away from his ear at Bronte's shriek. '*Why?* Because I don't need help from fucking nuns! I'd rather sell my soul to the devil.'

'Seems to me like you're cutting off your nose to spite your face,' Bronte said curtly. 'Besides, this isn't about you, it's about the boys.'

Shit. In all his rage at Adeline, he hadn't once thought about Rocky and how this might affect him. What if she stopped bringing Bella around because of how he'd spoken to her just now? What if she really could get him grants, meaning he could have a tiny house ready for Sam by the end of the year?

'I thought you'd agree with me on this. I thought you didn't like religion any more than I do.' He pushed off the work bench and started pacing. 'How many times have I heard you spouting off about the self-righteous, judgemental bigots who taught religion at your school?'

'Sure, they were annoying, but that doesn't mean I don't think you should accept help for building the tiny houses you want. It's not like you're going to give control of them over to the convent—you'd just be getting help from one of them.'

'There's no guarantees she'll be able to do any better than us,' Holden said, and that thought gave him an idea. Just because he didn't want her assistance, didn't mean he couldn't use some of her ideas. The boys weren't bad at washing cars—it was their job to vacuum, wash, polish and shine the van—and compared to tattooing demanding adults, drawing a few lions or Spiderman faces on kids would be a walk in the park.

How much could he charge for something like that?

'Holden!' Bronte's voice startled him. 'Are you still there?'

'Yeah, sorry, just … thinking. What did you say?'

'I *said*, why did you even invite her there if you hate her so much?'

'I don't hate her,' he countered. How much easier would it be if he did? 'I hate what she stands for. Anyway, I didn't invite her for me, I invited her for Rocky.'

'Well then, maybe you need to accept her help—for Rocky, for Toovs and Sam, *and* the others that will come after them.'

Bronte might have a point, but what she didn't know was that Adeline made him crazy. It wasn't like any other attraction he'd ever felt before. Maybe it was because he knew he'd never be able to have her, but he couldn't think straight when she was around, so spending more time with her wasn't a good idea, for either of them.

'Besides,' she added, 'I like Adeline—she's a cool chick—and I think it would be fun to get to know her better.'

'Nothing's stopping you,' Holden snapped.

Bronte let her disapproval be known in a long sigh down the phone line, but she had the good sense not to push the issue.

Chapter Twenty

Adeline reached for another weed in the veggie patch, yanking it hard as she imagined it was Holden Campbell's head.

Take that!

It had been a week since she'd offered to help him with his grants, and she needed something to take her frustration out on.

After their most uncomfortable conversation, in which he'd been rude beyond belief, she'd considered boycotting his place, no longer taking Bella there. That'd show Holden, but the problem was it would also affect Rocky, and after all that poor boy had been through, she refused to be the one to take something special away from him.

'Thought any more about my offer?' she'd asked Holden when she'd arrived for their next session. With any luck he'd had time to recover from his hissy fit and realise the error of his ways.

'The answer's still no,' he barked, then glanced over to where Bella was already waiting with Rocky in the training yard. 'But thanks for bringing her here. I was hoping you still would.'

'Of course,' she replied, tossing him her most saccharine smile, while inside her anger bubbled again. 'I wouldn't punish Rocky for your stubborn stupidity, Jack.'

The moment the words were out of her mouth she'd regretted them. Antagonising Holden wasn't going to win him over. What was that quote about killing someone with kindness? Mother Catherine had pretty much offered this exact advice when she'd spoken to her about his resistance.

Give him time. Be patient. Show him God's love and trust in the Lord to lead you both.

Unfortunately, patience wasn't one of Adeline's virtues.

'Thank you,' Holden replied, 'I appreciate that. Feel free to watch or go inside and make yourself a drink.'

Adeline noticed that he didn't call her Maria. The wall between them now might be invisible but it was as palpable as a thunderstorm, and beyond praying, she didn't know what else to do about it.

'Fuck!' She yanked her hand from the soil as her thumb throbbed with pain.

'Golly gosh, are you okay?' Michelle asked, jumping up from her own spot among the cauliflowers and rushing over to Adeline.

'I don't know.' Adeline bit her lip as blood dripped from her thumb. She hoped Michelle hadn't heard her bad language. 'Something sharp stabbed me. I think it was a nail or something.'

'Here, let me take a look at that.' Michelle yanked off her gloves and tossed them onto the ground. 'Why weren't you wearing gloves?'

'I forgot.' Which showed just how far she'd come—the old Adeline would never have forgotten something that would protect her precious hands. Then again, the old Adeline would never have been digging in the dirt either.

'This looks bad,' Michelle said. 'You might need stitches, but let's clean it up and see.'

With Bella at her feet and cradling her aching thumb against her chest, Adeline followed Michelle inside and into the laundry where they kept the first-aid kit, meeting Sister Lola on their way.

'What's going on?' asked Lola.

'Adeline stabbed her thumb on a nail. Is Sister Rita here?'

Lola shook her head. 'No, she's at the hospital. But I can take a look.' Although not a nurse like Rita, Lola had been in childcare before joining the convent and said she'd patched up numerous toddlers in her time.

'Youch, you did a good job,' she mused, once she'd cleaned the dirt from the wound and covered it in Dettol. 'I can bandage it and keep an eye on it here, but when was your last tetanus shot?'

Adeline shrugged. 'Can't remember but I'm sure it's fine.' She already felt embarrassed about dropping the f-bomb at the top of her lungs and didn't want to make any more fuss.

'You can't be too careful,' Michelle said, staring down at Adeline's thumb like it was a science experiment. 'Once my aunt Lauren got stabbed by a nail and her finger went all purple and almost fell off.'

Adeline shuddered—would the jab she'd had in high school still protect her?

Lola nodded. 'You should probably go get a shot just to be on the safe side.'

'Okay.' Adeline kinda liked her thumb and didn't want it falling off.

'Do you think you can drive yourself?' asked Lola.

Before Adeline could respond, Michelle said, 'I'll take her. I've got a few errands to run in town anyway. I'll go grab the keys and let Mother Catherine know what's happening.'

Five minutes later, with Lola promising to keep an eye on Bella, Michelle ushered Adeline outside and into the van, popping her seatbelt on for her like she was a small child.

'I'm sorry I swore,' Adeline said as Michelle turned out of the convent towards the town. 'It's just ...'

'Sometimes it feels necessary?'

'Exactly.'

'I understand. That's why I've come up with my own vocabulary for such occasions.'

'Oh?' Adeline's interest was piqued. 'Like what?'

'Well ...' Michelle flicked on the indictor. 'For the s-word, I just say "poop".'

Adeline screwed up her face; 'poop' simply didn't have the same ring to it. Even her little nephews wouldn't stoop to using such a word. 'You may as well not swear at all.'

Michelle was not deterred. 'And, instead of using God's name in vain, I say, "oh my goodness" or "golly gosh".'

This time Adeline had to bite her lip to stop from laughing. Michelle sounded so earnest, but there was no way you could take someone seriously when they used phrases like 'golly gosh'.

'If I'm cranky' Michelle continued, 'and want to call someone a bad word, I say they're a nincompoop. I try to refrain from thinking badly about anyone, but ...' She shrugged. 'I'm only human.'

'What about the ... the f-word?' Adeline asked. 'Do you have something for that?'

'Koala,' Michelle said matter-of-factly.

'What?!'

'If I need to use such a harsh word, I usually also need to calm down and check my own attitude, and so I say "koala". It's impossible to be angry when you plant an image of a cute, cuddly bear in your head.'

'I don't think koalas are actually bears,' Adeline said, but maybe Michelle had a point.

'Do you need me to come in with you?' Michelle asked as she parked the van in front of the medical centre.

'No. I'll be fine.' As much as Adeline loved the sisters, the only peace she got these days was during personal prayer time, so she happily accepted a few moments of solitude.

'Awesome.' Michelle beeped the van locked. 'I'm heading to the library. Come find me when you're done.'

As her roomie started in the other direction, Adeline went into the medical centre. It was her first time there, but she was already well known due to NunTalk, and, to the annoyance of a couple of elderly gentlemen who were waiting, she was whisked in to see the doctor immediately. While he checked Lola's handi-work and then gave her the injection, he waxed lyrical about her writing.

'Never bothered with NunTalk before, but my wife reads it religiously and she forced me to read your first few columns, and now I'm eagerly awaiting the next. Any hint about what it will be about?'

Adeline grinned, her pain finally starting to subside. 'You'll have to wait and see.'

He sent her on her way, refusing to let her pay, and as she headed towards the library where she guessed Michelle was perus-ing the shelves for her next gruesome crime novel, Adeline found herself passing Ford's barbershop. On previous trips to town, she'd always been with another sister and on a mission, so she'd never had the chance to take a look, but having got to know Ford a little over the past few weeks, she was curious and couldn't help cupping her hands around her eyes and peering in through the slightly tinted window.

Wow. It was nothing like she'd expected. Inside looked super modern and super funky with a back wall in white subway tiles, grey grout, a polished cement floor, and a huge leather chesterfield under the window. And was that an actual professional espresso machine down the back?

How she'd kill for a cup of proper coffee. They only had instant at the convent and if she had to make a list of things she missed from her old life, coffee would be right up there alongside Sally, her nephews and the other dogs. Her ex-sister-in-law wouldn't believe it when she told her she'd hurt her hand while gardening. Usually, it was Sally emailing Adeline about the scrapes the boys had gotten into.

A knock sounded on the window, startling her from her caffeine fantasy, and she refocused to see Ford on the other side of the glass, grinning widely. He lifted a hand to wave her inside.

A little bell tinkled above the door as she entered, inhaling the delicious aroma of cloves, coffee, leather and coiffed masculinity. There was a freshness to the shine on the leather seats and a touch of modernity in the huge industrial copper lights which hung over the mirrors. It was way more sophisticated than anything else she'd seen in Smallton. The rest of the shops on the main street— even Woolworths—looked like they were stuck in a time warp, somewhere in the late seventies or early eighties.

'Sorry,' she said sheepishly. 'I didn't mean to interrupt you.'

'Not at all. What can I do for you? 1980s perm? Purple rinse? Mullet? I usually only cut men's hair, but I'd be happy to make an exception for you.'

Adeline chuckled and absentmindedly reached for her ponytail. 'Thanks, but I'm good. I was admiring your espresso machine.'

'Ah.' Ford grinned. 'A girl after my own heart. Can I make you one?'

Adeline glanced at her watch. She'd been fast at the doctors and Michelle always took ages choosing new library books. 'If you're sure. I don't want to take you away from work.'

He gestured to the empty chairs. 'My next appointment isn't for another half an hour. My offsider needed a day off, so we didn't book many appointments.'

'In that case, I'd love one,' she said with a smile.

As Ford wheeled himself over to the machine and began to work his magic, Adeline admired his set-up. On a grey wall next to some classic brown barber chairs, vintage comic books were displayed in frames, celebrating the adventures of Superman, Wolverine and Spiderman—as if superheroes could be manufactured by a particularly good haircut or precise neck shave. It was the sort of place grandpas would hang out, if they were hipster grandpas who drank microbrewery beers and single-origin espressos. And who were universally loved by the ladies.

'This place is really cool,' she said.

Ford beamed. 'Thanks. It was my dream since I was a kid to own a barbershop. I used to do Holden and our mum's hair when I was little. I worked for other people getting experience, but when I saw this place on the market, something just felt right about it. I bought the house and the shop with the insurance payout that had been put in trust for me after the accident.'

Although Adeline was curious, she didn't ask for details.

'Take a seat.' He gestured to one of the leather chairs.

Adeline couldn't resist asking, 'How exactly do you …?'

She didn't have to finish her question. He reached for the sides of his wheelchair and, with the click of a few buttons, suddenly he was upright, and she could see how he'd be able to cut hair and move around his client. 'Ta dah! Magic.'

'Wow. That's clever.'

'It does the trick. After losing the use of your legs, you either get inventive or you give up. The latter was never an option for me; I refused to be told I couldn't fulfil my dream. With the help of my therapists, I found other paraplegic barbers and hairdressers around the world and worked out what I needed.'

'How long have you been in Smallton?'

He scratched his head. 'Let's see … must be coming up to ten years.'

'Where were you before?'

'The city, Melbourne. But I always had a hankering I'd prefer the pace of life in a small town,' he said, handing her the mug.

'Thanks,' she said.

He gestured towards the bandage wrapped around her hand. 'What did you do to yourself?'

She wanted to tell him it was all his brother's fault, but that would sound petty. 'Stabbed my thumb on a buried nail while I was weeding.'

'Youch!' He winced as if he could feel her pain.

'Yeah, it wasn't fun. I had to have a tetanus shot, just in case.' She lifted the drink to her mouth, but inhaled first, relishing the delicious aroma before taking a long, slow sip. 'Oh G … golly gosh. This is amazing.'

Ford's lips quirked upwards at one side. 'Did you just say, "golly gosh"?'

'Yes. I'm working hard on not using God's name in vain.'

'I see.' He nodded as if he approved. 'You weren't religious before you joined the sisters, then?'

'Oh, I was … technically. I believed in God and was raised going to church and stuff, but … having lived with the sisters, I can now see the way I lived wasn't godly at all. My heart wasn't in the right place.'

'And now it is?'

'Yes. I now think about serving God and what I can do for others, more than feeling like He and the world owe me, if that makes any sense.'

'It does.'

She took another delicious sip. 'So, did you and Holden live together in the city as well?'

'Nah. Holden was a bit of a drifter before I asked him to move here and become my carer.'

Adeline frowned. 'You don't seem like you need much of a carer.'

Ford smiled, and it was the first time she'd ever seen a tinge of sadness in his eyes. 'There are a few personal things I do need help with, but between you and me, I also missed him and thought it was about time he grew up and settled down.'

'Are you sure you and him are brothers?'

'What makes you ask that?' Ford said, his smile turning into an amused smirk.

'Well, you're as different as night and day. You're so sweet and happy, and he's ... such a ... such a nincompoop.'

Ford threw his head back and laughed. 'Nincompoop?! Now, I've heard Holden called a lot of things in my time but that one takes the cake.'

Adeline couldn't help but laugh as well.

'What's he done anyway?' he asked. 'I thought you two were getting along well, working together to help Rocky.'

'He hasn't mentioned my offer?'

Ford shook his head.

Adeline sighed, put down her mug and then recounted the conversation she'd had with Holden. 'He's barely looked at me since, never mind deigned to talk to me. You'd think I'd threatened to cut off his manhood, when all I want to do is help.'

Ford chuckled. 'Please, don't take it personally.' When she raised an eyebrow, he added, 'It's not you, it's—'

'My religion?' Adeline threw her hands up in their air. 'I gathered that much, but why? Has he got something against Catholics?'

'Not just Catholics,' Ford said almost apologetically as he ran a hand over his clean-shaven jaw. 'All church people. Because of our upbringing. Our stepdad was—*is*—a Pentecostal pastor. He's a religious fanatic and when he married Mum, he changed her, came between us. Long story short, there's a lot of bad blood and Garry's treatment of us has made Holden wary of anyone who believes in God. It's his problem, not yours, but I reckon we could definitely use your kind of assistance. And I don't want you to feel unwelcome here, or at our place. I'm always happy to see you.'

'Thank you.' Ford was so lovely—Adeline would much rather hang out with him than his stupid brother anyway. 'Why can't he be more like you?'

He snorted, then grinned. 'The world couldn't handle more than one of someone this awesome, but you know, he's not that bad beneath his rough exterior.'

Not that bad? Hah!

'Will you talk to him for me?' she asked, not willing to give up what she believed God wanted her to do. 'Try and convince him to give me a chance. I really think I can help you guys.'

After a couple of beats, Ford said, 'I would if I thought it'd do any good, but Holden's as stubborn as they come and if he thinks you and I are ganging up on him, he'll just dig his heels in even more.'

At that moment, the door of the shop was flung open, and Michelle flew in. 'There you are! I've been looking everywhere for you.'

'Sorry,' Adeline said, smiling at her friend. 'I got chatting to Ford, but I was just about to come find you.'

This conversation had run its course anyway—Ford may believe she could help them, but it was clear that his loyalties lay with his brother, and he wasn't going to upset the applecart for a near stranger.

Chapter Twenty-one

Thursday evening, after a hearty meal of braised beef pie with a side of broccoli and carrots that the boys ate because they'd been promised dessert, Holden went into the kitchen and returned with a large chocolate mud cake Ford had stayed up late the night before to make.

'Is it someone's birthday?' Toovs asked as their eyes widened at the sight of the massive cake. 'Where's the candles?'

'Nope.' Holden placed the cake down in front of Rocky and the boy looked up at him, confused. 'This is to celebrate your first week back at school. Ford made it last night. Well done, mate.'

'Thanks.' Rocky looked between Holden and Ford and then stared down at the cake as if he didn't know whether to smile or cry. 'If I'd known we'd get dessert I'd have started school weeks ago.'

The others laughed as Holden handed Rocky a knife. 'You do the honours, mate, and be sure to cut yourself the largest slice.'

'Aw,' whined Toovs and Sam good-naturedly, but they needn't have worried for Rocky made sure everyone got an equal share. And then another when they'd all devoured the first slice in what had to be record time.

'Do you mind if I FaceTime Bronte?' Holden asked Rocky. 'When I told her we were having cake for you, she felt sad she couldn't be here. I think seeing all our ugly mugs will cheer her up.'

'Okay,' Rocky said with a one-shouldered shrug.

Bronte was having dinner with her parents, but stepped outside to chat to Rocky.

'Hey buddy, how's school going?'

'Not bad. Some of the kids are dicks but some are okay and it's better than hanging around here with Holden all day.'

'Yeah, that would suck,' she laughed.

'Hey,' Holden objected, but couldn't help grinning as Bronte asked more questions about teachers and subjects and even what Rocky ate for lunch—and he gave more than one-word answers.

If he believed in miracles, he'd think one had happened in Rocky the last few weeks.

After a quick hello to Ford, Toovs and Sam, Bronte had to go back to her family and Holden promised to call her later for a proper chat.

'Since it's my special night, do I get out of the cleaning up?' Rocky asked, after they'd all had their fill of cake.

'Don't push your luck,' Ford and Holden said in unison, then they laughed.

With the usual grumbles, the boys pushed back their seats and cleared the table, leaving the brothers alone in the dining room.

'So proud of that kid,' Holden said, leaning back and resting his hands behind his head. 'Don't think I could be any prouder if he were my own flesh and blood.'

Every day for the past week, Rocky had been up early, chores done, uniform on and bag packed before the other two had even rolled out of bed. The first day Holden had ridden into town with him, bid him goodbye and lurked around the outskirts of the high school for a good hour in case anything went wrong, feeling hollow, as if Rocky had taken his heart into class with him. When he'd arrived home that arvo, he'd appeared entirely unscathed by the experience and Holden couldn't have felt more relieved. Both Toovs and Sam said they'd seen him in the yard between classes with other kids, and since then Rocky had even mentioned the names of a couple of boys who'd befriended him, asking if they could come over for a bonfire sometime.

And whereas Holden always had to nag the others to do their homework, Rocky so far hadn't needed to be reminded once.

'He's come on in leaps and bounds, hasn't he?'

Ford nodded, but Holden could tell he had something on his mind. 'You okay, bro?'

'I think maybe I should be asking you that.'

'Don't talk in riddles.'

Ford sighed, reached for the water jug, topped up his glass, took a sip, then said, 'I had a visitor at the shop today.'

Holden's heart went suddenly cold. Could it be their mother?

He knew Ford was still in touch with her and Garry, even though Holden had cut all ties. He wanted nothing to do with her while she was still with that man. Even if she left him, he wasn't sure he'd ever be able to forgive her for what her husband had put them through. He didn't understand how Ford—of all people—could.

'Who?' he asked reluctantly.

'Adeline.'

'Adeline?' Holden found himself torn between relief, irritation and—if he were honest—jealousy. 'What was she doing in the barbershop?'

'She hurt her finger and was at the doctor and—'

'How bad?' Holden interrupted. 'Is she okay?'

'She'll be fine. Got stabbed by a nail or something. Had to have a tetanus shot and happened to walk by. I wasn't busy so I invited her in for a chat and an espresso.'

'Sounds delightful,' Holden said sardonically.

'It was. She's a very delightful human.' He folded his arms across his chest. 'Why didn't you tell me she'd offered to help you with writing grants and fundraising?'

'I turned her down, so it didn't seem worth wasting breath.'

Ford sighed. 'Then perhaps the question should be *why* you turned her down?'

'You know why,' Holden snapped.

'You're like a broken record around here, grumbling about grant rejections and how you desperately need money to get the tiny houses built. Adeline sounds like she could help.'

'So she says, but she didn't give me any evidence or guarantees. Who's to say it's not just a ruse to wheedle her way into the boys' lives and start indoctrinating them with her church nonsense. You can't give these people an inch, or they'll take a mile.'

'These people!' Ford scoffed. 'She's not trying to take anything from you—from *us*. She's trying to help.'

'Did she ask you to talk to me? Is that why she came into your shop? Did she even hurt her finger?'

'God, Holden. Listen to yourself. Not all people who believe in God are like Garry. Most of them are genuinely good people.'

He shook his head, genuinely perplexed at how Ford could be so forgiving, so damn trusting of people. 'I'm not having this conversation with you. I've already had it with Bronte.'

'And let me guess … she agreed with me?' When Holden didn't reply, Ford said, 'Well maybe that's telling you something. Maybe it's time you stopped being such a bitter arsehole and started listening to the both of us.'

'Maybe you should both just butt out,' Holden growled. 'The tiny houses project is my idea, not yours.'

Ford raised his eyebrows as if to say 'Really? Are we really going to play this game?' and then said coolly, 'The last time I checked, the deeds for this property are in my name, not yours, so anything you build here *is* my business.'

Holden stared at the glass of water in front of him, wishing it was something stronger. He and Ford never used words to hurt each other. Sure, they didn't agree on everything, but their arguments were always logical, never personal, and Holden hated that the nun had caused a rift between them.

How dare she go behind his back to try to get Ford on her side.

He took a deep breath and forced his clenched fists to relax—it wasn't his brother who deserved his wrath. 'I'm sorry. I know you're as excited about the tiny houses project as me, but please, leave Adeline out of it.'

'Fine.' Ford sighed and shook his head. 'I won't say another word, but I want it on record that I think you're a stupid jerk.'

Holden laughed. 'Is that the worst insult you can come up with?'

Chapter Twenty-two

There was a lovely buzz in the air as Adeline climbed out of the van behind Lola and Rita at the monthly farmers' market. Country music was playing over the loudspeakers and the wafting scent of bacon and sausages made Adeline's stomach rumble even though she'd had a bowl of porridge not too long ago. There wasn't a cloud in the sky and despite the crisp temperature, the sun shone brightly. A good crowd was milling about already, the car park at the edge of the town square was full and the roads were lined with cars either side.

Sister Rita hurried to help Mother Catherine climb down from the passenger seat and then Michelle drove off, promising to find somewhere to park and see them all soon. It was her second trip of the day as earlier she'd delivered some of the other sisters to bring their wares and set up the convent's stall. Adeline was looking forward to a quick walk around the market before taking over from Mary and Josey for her shift. She planned on taking some footage for their TikTok account, as well as some photos for her next NunTalk column, which was going to be about all the different things the sisters made to sell.

'Hey Adeline,' called a young and familiar voice.

She turned to see Rocky waving at her from the edge of the car park where he, Toovs and Sam appeared to be washing cars.

What the?!

'You go ahead,' she said to the others. 'I'll find you in there.'

Sister Rita raised her can of Diet Coke— 'No worries'—and then continued on.

'Want us to wash the van for ya?' Sam asked as Adeline approached. They looked to be soaked through but having the time of their lives as they covered a red dual-cab ute in soap suds. 'We'll even do it for free on account of you being nuns and having no money of your own.'

Normally Adeline would find this comment amusing. 'Thanks. That's sweet,' she forced herself to say, then glanced around. 'Where's Holden?'

'He's in there, face painting,' Rocky said, pointing towards the village of tents selling everything from locally grown fruit and veg to handmade jewellery.

'Face painting?'

Adeline's blood began to boil. She couldn't believe he'd appropriated her ideas after rudely rejecting her offer of help.

Before any of the boys could reply, she turned in her boots and hurried towards the entrance of the square. She marched past the blokes from the local Men's Shed selling handmade wooden toys, the CWA with an array of cakes, and a couple of buskers. She stormed past a petting zoo overflowing with toddlers and young children who were squealing in delight over poor, long-suffering lambs, rabbits and a couple of joeys. Her eyes glossed over everything and everyone until, at the edge of the petting zoo, she saw a row of little kids lined up and at the front of them, there he was.

Just as she'd suspected. Sitting on a plastic chair, a crate with an array of tiny paint pots next to him, chatting to a tiny, dark-haired girl who was sitting on a stool in front of him. She and her mother looked to be hanging on his every word. The ... *koala-ing* nerve of him.

First the car wash and now this!

As she got closer, she saw the mum hand Holden a ten-dollar bill, watched as he shoved it into his hip pocket and then overheard him offering to do her next.

The woman giggled like a thirteen-year-old, tugging on her long beaded earrings. 'Oh, I better not. Don't want to keep these kids waiting.'

'Next time then,' he replied with a wink.

The bloody flirt!

Both still grinning, mother and child walked away—the kid's face now painted like an exquisite butterfly. Adeline wasted no time in striding over to Holden.

Ignoring the small boy who'd climbed onto the stool, she perched her hands on her hips.

'What do you think you're doing?'

'Morning, Maria.' He had the audacity to wink at her as well and she felt a flash of heat sweep through her. Rage, not attraction. There was nothing about this pompous, aggravating, ideastealing man that appealed. *Nothing at all.* He nodded towards her hand. 'How's your finger? I heard on the bush telegraph you had an altercation with a rusty nail.'

'Never you mind about my finger, Holden Campbell.' She had a good mind to poke him with it. 'What the fu—' She paused and took a quick breath. 'What the k—'

Nope, just no. The image of a cute, fluffy, native animal did nothing to calm her.

'What on *earth* do you think you're doing?'

'Two seconds, dude,' Holden said, patting the kid's knee as he stood and stepped away from the line. He nodded for Adeline to follow.

'What's the problem?'

Her body hot with rage, she gestured angrily at the line of children and parents now a few feet away. 'The problem?! The problem is it looks like you're raising money through face painting.'

His grin grew. 'No flies on you. I've already pocketed over two hundred bucks. Easiest cash I've ever made. And the boys seem to be doing well too. Great ideas you had.'

'So, you're not even going to pretend you didn't steal them from me?' she asked, her voice rapidly rising.

He smirked down at her and then leaned in close as if about to whisper something. She'd seen that look in his eyes before, the night of the bonfire. And it wasn't the kind of look someone in a relationship should be giving.

She jumped right back and shoved her hand in his face. 'Don't you dare tell me I'm hot when I'm angry!'

He lazily shrugged a shoulder and rocked back on his feet. 'If the shoe fits.'

Poor Bronte. It was one thing treating Adeline like her feelings didn't matter, but how dare he disrespect Bronte, with whom he was supposed to be in love. Especially while she was out of town visiting her *dying* father! She wanted to step right back into his personal space and slap that smug smile right off his face.

Then again, he probably wouldn't feel a thing because of that ridiculous beard.

'You can't just go stealing my ideas!'

'Sweetheart, I haven't stolen anything.' His voice was low and dangerous. 'As far as I know, you didn't invent the car wash or face painting. Also, I'd keep your voice down if I were you. People are watching and you're making a scene.'

Making a scene? Oh, she hadn't even got started yet.

'Don't you tell me what I'm making,' she yelled back, unable to calm herself, even though she knew he was right. A little voice in her head reminded her of the young audience waiting in line but she couldn't help herself. 'I don't know what your problem is, Holden Campbell, but—'

A firm but gentle hand on the small of her back had the words jamming in her throat. 'What's going on here?' asked Sister Rita.

'Adeline here is accusing me of stealing,' Holden replied, his voice as smug as a child dobbing in a sibling.

'What?' Rita looked from Adeline to Holden and back again.

Adeline felt close to tears. 'You know how I offered to help him raise some funds for his tiny houses project? Well, he basically told me where to go but now he's using my ideas as his own!'

'See? She's accusing me of stealing something that can't be stolen and she's scaring my potential customers.' Holden gave a friendly wave to the kids then looked back to Rita. 'You need to keep her under control.'

'Excuse me?' Adeline yelled. 'Don't talk about me like I'm some kind of wild animal.'

When he raised a self-satisfied eyebrow, she realised she was beginning to act exactly like that, but it was all Holden's fault. He made her crazy. How was she supposed to do good—to be a better person—if people like him kept getting in her way?

'Look,' she hissed, lowering her voice so only he and Rita could hear. 'I get that you've got some chip on your shoulder about religion, but don't take your stepdaddy issues out on me.'

His eyes narrowed and seemed to go even darker than their natural chocolate brown. 'What did you say?'

Adeline held her chin high. 'You heard me. I know you've got something against religion, and Ford said it's got a lot to do with your stepfather, but you can't let—'

'Don't tell me what I can and can't do, Adeline. You don't know anything about me, and this conversation is over.'

She opened her mouth to tell him it would be over when *she* said it was over—but Rita took a firm hold of her arm.

'Enough, Adeline,' she warned as she dragged her away. When they were out of earshot of Holden and the gathered crowd, she stopped. 'You looked like you were going to punch him.'

'I wanted to,' she admitted, and then immediately regretted it.

Although Adeline's pulse was still racing, she was already beginning to lament her inability to just let things go. What would Mother Catherine think if word got back to her that she'd been contemplating violence?

And then she looked up and saw the older woman hurrying towards them, a red toffee apple in her hand. The look on Mother Catherine's face said she'd either seen Adeline's actions firsthand or had already heard about them on the grapevine. *Koala!*

'What was that all about, child?' Although her words were kind, there was an edge in her voice, and Adeline felt awful, not only to have disappointed her fellow sisters but to have brought shame upon the convent. The last thing she wanted to do was make them look bad.

'I'm so sorry,' she said. 'I don't know what came over me, but I'm just so frustrated that Holden won't let me help him yet is happy to use *my* ideas.'

'Does it matter whose ideas they are as long as the end result is achieved?' Mother Catherine asked, laying a gentle hand on Adeline's arm.

'What do you mean?'

'You seem to be making this all about you, Adeline, but service to the Lord, service to others, should never be about us.'

Rita gave an encouraging nod.

'We need to give without an expectation of anything in return,' Mother Catherine continued. 'Your goal in offering to help Holden was so that he would raise money, to help the boys, right?'

Adeline nodded.

'And so, if that's what he's doing, it doesn't matter if you're not getting the credit.'

'That's not what I want,' she said testily. 'I just know he could make so much more if he let me help. Those ideas were only the beginning. Small fry compared to my others, which he didn't even let me finish telling him.'

But even as she argued, she knew there was a smidgeon of truth in her superior's words. When she'd accepted God's call to join the convent, she'd hoped it would help her feel better about herself and make others view her in a more positive light. While prayer and Bible study were all well and good, it didn't feel like they were *enough*.

She needed to *do* good to feel good.

'You can't force your help on anyone,' Rita said sympathetically.

Mother Catherine nodded. 'I know you felt this was your calling, and maybe it is, but you need to be patient and you need to seek wisdom and guidance from our Father. Ask Him what he wants of you. His plan is awesome. His timing perfect.'

'Thanks,' Adeline said, not only feeling chastised but also more than a little frustrated by what felt like platitudes. She *had* prayed and she *had* listened, and she felt in her waters, in her gut, that helping Holden was what she was supposed to do. 'Anyway, I'd better head over to our stall. My shift's just about to begin.'

Mother Catherine shook her head. 'The sisters can cover your shift. I think you should go and spend some quiet time alone with God, in prayer. You need a reset after today's … upset.'

Adeline's instinct was to object, but knowing it would be futile and rude, she bowed her head. 'Okay. And I really am sorry. I promise to do better in future.'

The older woman smiled and then held out the toffee apple. 'Here, have this. You could probably do with a bit of a sugar boost and Lord knows my teeth will thank me if I don't have it.'

'Thank you.' Adeline took the sugary treat and then, with her head down to avoid making eye contact with anyone, she made her way out of the markets.

Chapter Twenty-three

'Yeah, things are going pretty good,' Holden told Bronte after listening to her update about her father's torturous decline. She'd begged him to distract her and give her something to smile about. 'We made a couple of grand from the face painting and car wash on the weekend—much better than I could have imagined. It really pumped the boys up, made them feel like they're a part of something special.'

'That's great. And how's Ford?'

'Same as usual,' Holden said.

She didn't need to know that they were barely on speaking terms after Holden found out Ford had told Adeline about their tumultuous upbringing. Ford had sworn he'd barely said anything, but the fact that she'd been able to use his stepfather against him in their little tiff at the markets meant he'd revealed too much. Of course, Ford had argued that it was *his* past as much as it was Holden's, and while that was technically true, it still irked him that his brother and the nun had been talking about him behind his back.

'And is Rocky still going well at school?'

'Yeah, I think so. I'm trying not to count my chickens, but he seems to have settled in well. He's loving his classes and his teachers are shocked that he isn't that far behind. The maths and English ones are going to give him extra work to do over the holidays and he's actually keen. I wanted to make sure he was going to be okay before I took on any shifts at the tattoo parlour again but—' He paused as his phone made a noise telling him he had another call. He glanced at the screen and his stomach dropped. 'Sorry, Bron, gotta go. There's a call coming in from the school.'

It was rarely good news when the local high school phoned— either one of the boys wasn't feeling well or they'd gotten into some kind of scrape. It was probably about time for the latter; things had been … uneventful since the last call, which had been about Sam's pizza shenanigans.

He accepted the call. 'Hello, Holden speaking.'

'Good afternoon, Mr Campbell.' He recognised the principal's voice immediately, and calling him mister wasn't a good sign.

'How can I help you, Ms Hester?' he asked, telling himself not to panic yet.

'Has Jamie Rock come home yet?'

Holden frowned. 'Rocky? It's only eleven o'clock. He should be at school.'

'I'm afraid I have to inform you about an incident that occurred between Jamie and another student.'

Holden's grip tightened on the phone. 'Is Rocky okay?'

'Physically, he's fine. He punched the other boy during an English lesson, then immediately left school. I know his circumstances are extraordinary, but I'm sure you'll understand—'

'What do you mean "left"? How long ago was that?'

Ms Hester cleared her throat, obviously not happy about being interrupted. 'About half an hour ago. I'm sure you understand that getting medical help for the injured boy was our priority, but now

I need to talk to Rocky about how we're going to deal with his behaviour.'

'What did this other kid do to aggravate him?' Rocky might have had a hard life, he might have a violent father, but Holden had seen no signs of similar tendencies in the boy himself.

'He left before I could talk to him, but that's beside the point. He must learn that violence is never the answer, which is why I'd like you to bring him in to discuss it the moment he gets home.'

'If he left half an hour ago, he should have been back by now,' Holden said, unable to curb his anger. It was only a five-minute bike ride, twenty minutes on foot if he'd left in a hurry and forgotten his wheels. 'Why didn't you call me the minute he left? You know his history. You know he's vulnerable and—'

And he couldn't waste time yelling at Ms Hester. He scrambled so quickly out of where he'd been sitting at the kitchen table that the dogs at his feet jumped to attention and hurried outside after him.

'I've got to go,' he told the principal. 'Call me if he turns up there.' He made no promises to return the favour before disconnecting and shoving his phone into his pocket.

First, he checked the shed, in case Rocky had come home but was too scared to face him. It felt like a repeat of a couple of weeks ago and although Holden told himself he'd found him then and would find him now, he couldn't ignore the uneasy feeling in his gut.

This wasn't the same as a couple of weeks ago. This time he *knew* Rocky was upset.

After searching the sheds and the rest of their property, he called Ford.

'I'll have a drive around,' Ford promised immediately.

'Thanks. I'm going to check the convent.' Although the last thing he wanted to do was set foot in that place, perhaps Rocky had gone there to seek comfort from Bella.

He jumped on his motorbike and zoomed down the road to the large, two-storey, red-brick building he'd passed numerous times before and barely paid any attention to. Pot plants in baskets hung from the awnings and two black cats sat in rocking chairs on either side of the stained-glass door. He'd barely opened the iron gate when Bella bounded from around the back and over to him.

'Hello girl,' he said, not breaking stride as he headed for the front door. Surely if Rocky was here, he'd be with the dog, but maybe he was hiding? Maybe he was scared that Holden was going to be angry.

Taking the verandah steps in one go, he rapped loudly on the door with the iron knocker. About a minute later the door peeled back and Michelle appeared.

'Well, hello there. Isn't this a pleasant surprise. How may we help you, Mr Campbell?'

He ignored her cheeky tone. 'Is Adeline here?'

'I'm afraid she's in town having a meeting with Mike at the *Gazette*. Is there anything I can assist you with?'

'I'm looking for one of my boys. Rocky. He's about this high.' He gestured to just beneath his shoulders. 'Lots of red hair. Freckles.'

Michelle nodded. 'The one Adeline and Bella are helping, right? Shouldn't he be at school?'

'He ran away. I thought he might have come here because of Bella.'

'I'm sorry to hear that, but I haven't seen him. I'll check with the others and then we can help look if you like?'

It went against every grain in Holden's body to accept help from the church, but Rocky's safety was on the line so he was going to take any assistance he could get.

'Thanks. That'd be great.'

He left his mobile number with Michelle, retreated to his bike and called Ford again. 'Any luck?'

'No,' his brother said gravely. 'But he can't have gone far. We'll find him.'

'Dammit.' Holden kicked his tyre in frustration. 'Okay. I'll check back home again but if he's not there, we're going to have to report him missing.'

Chapter Twenty-four

'Thanks for the cuppa, Mike, and the chat. I'll email you my column tomorrow night.'

'Any time. And I can't wait to read it.'

Adeline hitched her bag onto her shoulder, pushed open the *Gazette* door and stepped out into the afternoon sunshine. Ever since the altercation with Holden at the markets, she'd been out of sorts. She felt like she needed to do something to make up for her behaviour but didn't know what. The sisters were all treating her as normal—having all forgiven if not forgotten what she'd done—but she couldn't forgive herself as easily. And she still had that gaping hole inside her, that urge to do something more than write articles and make TikToks.

She just didn't know what.

She'd been talking to Mike about this, asking him if he knew of any other local charities who might need assistance, and he'd given her a list of other organisations that might be happy to hear from her, but none of them gave her the same buzz that her decision to help Holden with his tiny houses had. Despite all evidence to the contrary, she still believed that God had led her and Bella down that drive for a reason and it was proving hard to let go.

She dawdled on her walk back to the convent, slowing as usual as she approached the water tower to look up and admire the mural that wrapped around the majestic structure. But today, it wasn't simply the artwork that took her breath away. There was someone up there. Aside from a few birds, that she guessed had nests on the roof, she'd never seen anyone on the tower, but then again, it was Smallton's pride and joy, so someone from the shire had to be maintaining it.

About a quarter way up the tower there was a ladder built into the wall, but to reach it you'd need a portable ladder and there was no sign of any such thing. Adeline frowned, suddenly realising that maintenance workers would certainly have bought the right equipment, so whoever was up there must be unsanctioned.

Before she'd finished this thought, she realised that she recognised the figure. And it wasn't a man but a boy, standing dangerously close to the edge.

Rocky!

Her heart shot to her throat. *Shit.* She didn't even berate herself for swearing. What was he doing up there? And why wasn't he at school?

Why do you think someone climbs up to such a height and peers over the edge?

No. She refused to listen to that voice in her head. Rocky was just a kid. And he'd been doing so well lately. But even as she tried to reason with herself, fear churned faster in her stomach.

She glanced madly up and down the road but there wasn't a car or person in sight. Did she have time to go back into town to one of the shops and ask for help?

Oh God, please don't let him jump.

Adeline's heart raced faster and sweat broke out on her palms. How the hell did Rocky get up there? If she didn't know better, she'd think he'd flown, but there really was only one possibility. He must have scaled the drainpipe and then jumped across to the ladder. She shuddered. It was a miracle he hadn't fallen.

'Rocky?' she screamed desperately. 'Are you okay?

He didn't answer and she wasn't sure whether he was ignoring her, or if the wind had carried her voice in the other direction. Either way it was a ridiculous question.

Of course he wasn't okay. An *okay* Rocky would be safely at school sitting behind a desk, not looking down over Smallton from its highest point.

She couldn't just stand here and watch disaster unfold. Holden would never forgive her if she didn't save the boy. Somehow, she needed to get up there and try to talk him down before it was too late.

Dumping her bag at the foot of the tower, Adeline pushed up her sleeves, took a deep breath and began to clamber up the pipe. It was a miracle she managed to gain any traction with the way her hands were sweating, but somehow, she pulled herself up inch by inch, using the cement against her feet for grip. Somewhere between the ground and the bottom of the ladder, her breath burning in her chest, she remembered the phone in her bag.

Koala! She could have called for help instead of attempting a one-woman rescue!

That was the problem when you basically broke up with technology—just like her phone was no longer the first thing she reached for when she woke up in the morning, it was also not something she relied on, even when she should.

Oh well, she was halfway up—the muscles in her arms and legs aching and her thighs chafing. It would be stupid to give up now and if she could stop Rocky jumping, all the pain would be worth it.

Her relief when she got to the bottom of the ladder was short-lived. From below, the distance between it and the drainpipe hadn't looked that bad, but now she wondered if Rocky was some kind of spider man, able to scale buildings.

If he can do it, you can do it, she told herself and held her breath as she stretched one hand towards the ladder.

It worked! Her fingers closed around the bottom rung and before she could chicken out, she launched herself across. For what felt like a year but was probably only five seconds, she hung precariously, feeling as if her arms might fail her at any moment. Then, somehow, she found a strength she didn't know she had to pull herself properly onto the ladder.

Although her arms felt like jelly, she finally got to the top and when she looked down, it seemed even higher than she'd imagined.

The sounds of Rocky pacing back and forth above spurred her on, and with a final deep breath to psych herself up, she used everything she had left to heave herself onto the roof.

'Oh my God!' Rocky shrieked as she slumped onto the top of the tower and tried to catch her breath. 'What are you doing up here?'

'I came up to see you.'

He laughed and shook his head. 'I can't believe you climbed all the way up here.'

'Well, *you* did,' she panted. 'Didn't you?'

'Yeah, but I'm ...'

Adeline didn't hear his reply as she rolled a little to peer over the edge—the paddocks on either side of the road and the town in the not-too-far distance swam beneath her eyes. 'Oh, my goodness, this is high.'

Rocky gave her a bemused look. 'Um … that's kinda the point.'

She shuddered—'I guess so'—then crawled away from the edge and sat up. 'I don't suppose you have any water up here?' She knew she was supposed to be talking him down, but conversation would be difficult when she was literally parched.

He shook his head—'Sorry'—then laughed.

'What's so funny?'

'Well, we're on a water tower but we have no water.'

She nodded, unable to find much amusement in any of this. 'Did something happen at school today?'

He looked sheepish. 'How'd you know?'

'Because you should be there but instead, you're up here.'

'It's nothin'.' Rocky shrugged, stepped right up to the edge again and stared down.

Adeline's pulse had started to slow but it spiked again. *Please don't jump.*

'You can tell me anything, you know. I promise I won't judge or tell anyone else if you don't want me to.'

He didn't say anything for a long while and then without turning, he muttered, 'Some boy was having a go and so I hit him.'

'I see. What was he saying?'

He glanced at her. 'Do you know about my dad?'

She swallowed, unsure whether to admit she did. Then again, the sisters weren't supposed to lie, so she nodded.

Rocky turned to face her fully. 'They were saying he's a pedo, which isn't true.' Adeline saw his fingers curl into fists at his sides. 'He's a fucking low-life but I don't think even he's that low.'

Her heart went out to the boy. As if he hadn't suffered enough. How dare some stupid kid make his life more difficult. 'Kids can be cruel,' she said sympathetically, feeling guilty that she'd been cruel plenty of times herself, and not just as a kid.

'I don't care what anyone says about my dad,' Rocky replied. 'I hate him too.'

'Then what did he say that upset you?'

'He said my mum was probably asking for what he did to her. That she was probably some whore who deserved exactly what she got.'

His voice cracked on the last word, and he squeezed his eyes shut.

Adeline could tell he was trying to be tough, not to cry. She found herself fighting emotion too—sadness and anger sparred as tears pooled beneath her eyelids. This poor boy had gone through more than any child should ever have to deal with. Growing up, she might have felt a lack of love at home, but there'd never been violence and she'd always felt safe.

'I can ignore the stuff people say about my dad,' continued Rocky, sniffing through his words, 'but when Gabe mentioned my mum, I couldn't let it go. It wasn't true. She was wonderful. She didn't deserve anything.'

'Of course she didn't,' Adeline agreed.

'I punched him right in the nose and told him if he ever so much as spoke about her again, I'd kill him. I might have done it right there and then if his dumb mate didn't pull me off.'

'I don't blame you,' she said. Rocky was only thirteen. It was hardly surprising he'd snapped.

'That's why I stopped going go to school,' he added. 'It wasn't because I didn't wanna learn or anything—I quite like writing essays and shit—it's because everyone knows about what happened to my mum. They're not supposed to but somehow, they always find out. And about my dad being in jail. And they never let me forget. Can't they see I wish he wasn't my dad?' Rocky kicked against the roof, dislodging a bit of loose cement. 'I know he's a motherfucking bastard! No one can hate him more than I do!'

With each shouted word, he stepped closer to the edge again, until he was standing right on the precipice staring down.

Adeline's stomach clenched. She fought the urge to lunge at him, to grab hold of his skinny body and pull him towards her, but any sudden movement might unnerve him and send them both plummeting.

'Um ... do you mind coming, uh ... a little closer?'

When he turned back to look at her, she patted the space beside her.

He shrugged, and then, with another fleeting glance at the ground far below, he closed the distance between them and sank down next to her.

Thank you, God. Relief whooshed through Adeline's body, loosening her limbs, which were still smarting from exertion.

'Anyway, I'll probably be suspended now,' Rocky said. 'If not expelled. And Holden's gunna be so disappointed.'

Adeline heard it in his voice—whether he'd admit it or not, Holden had become the father he'd never had. It was clear to see how much he loved and respected his foster carer and how devasted he was at the thought of letting him down.

'I'm sure Holden's made plenty of mistakes in his life. We all do.'

Rocky looked at her sceptically. 'Even nuns?'

'Yes, or at least this one,' she said with a smile. 'I've made many since joining the convent but none of us are perfect. Even Mother Catherine. She reminded me only recently that we all make mistakes, but if we learn from them and do better in the future, then they aren't in vain.'

'She sounds pretty wise.'

'She is. And Holden is going to understand why you did what you did when you explain the situation. Don't let these bullies ruin the good thing you've got going. It would be a tragedy for you to give up because of those losers.'

'You know what I hate even more than what they say about my mum?' Rocky said.

'What?'

'What it makes me do. She'd hate it. Even if I'm defending her honour, she'd say there's never any excuse for violence. But I just couldn't help myself, which makes me wonder …' His voice trailed off and he stared down at his hands.

'You're nothing like your dad,' she promised him.

He glared at her. 'How the fuck would you know? You didn't know him. You don't know me!'

Adeline tried not to panic at his angry outburst. 'I know enough,' she said gently. 'Tell me this; how was your dad with animals?'

'He hated them,' Rocky said without hesitation. 'Sometimes if there was a duck or a cat in the middle of the road, he'd actually speed up to try and hit them. I always wanted to get a pet but he never let me. Probably a good thing. He'd probably have killed it too.'

'There you go then.'

'What do you mean, *there you go*?'

She smiled. 'That's how I know you're not like your dad. I've seen the way you are with Bella. So gentle and loving and patient. She adores you and I know you'd never hurt her, which proves you're not like your father.'

'She's an awesome dog. I love her. Sometimes I feel like she's the only good thing in my life.'

'Well, you know …' Adeline couldn't believe she was about to offer this, but as much as doing so would break her heart, it couldn't be clearer that Rocky needed Bella more than she did. She had God and the other sisters to take care of her, to give her the love and family she craved. 'I was thinking maybe you could take care of her for me—on a more permanent basis?'

'What do you mean?'

'Life is really busy for me at the convent, and I don't have the time to give her all the love and attention she deserves,' she lied, hoping the Lord would forgive her just this once. 'But I think maybe you do.'

'Are you for real?' His eyes grew wide. 'You're giving me Bella?'

'Yes.' Adeline swallowed and willed herself not to cry. She'd still be able to visit her beautiful girl, and if giving her up helped give Rocky a reason not to end things, then it would be worth all the pain. 'If you want her.'

'If I *want* her?!' The boy beamed and then rushed forward and threw his arms around her, catching her off guard.

'Careful or we'll both go over the edge.' Her tone was light but her fear was real; she shivered as she imagined the drop. 'And then there'll be *no one* to take care of Bella.'

Rocky looked at her weirdly as she shuffled them further away from the edge, and then let out a deep sigh. Crisis averted. She wondered if Mother Catherine would allow her a glass of the communion wine this evening. Never had she felt more in need of a drink.

'Oh my God, are you scared of heights?' Rocky asked.

'I wouldn't say I'm scared, but I can't say I love them either.'

He snorted and then a laugh burst out. 'Heights are awesome. I love nothing better than being in high places. It makes me feel, I dunno … Safer somehow. Whenever I'm up here, I look down below and everything seems so small and—'

'Hang on …' Adeline sat up straighter. 'Are you telling me you've been up here before?'

Rocky nodded. 'Yeah, it's where I come whenever I need a bit of thinking time.'

'Oh my …' She closed her eyes a moment. 'So, you weren't about to jump?'

'What? No! Shit, did you think I was?' He shook his head and then hooted. 'If I killed myself because of what dad did that would be letting him win. And I'll never do that. I want to live; I want to make my mum proud.'

Adeline didn't know whether to laugh or cry. She'd just given away her beloved Bella under false pretences, but Rocky had been so excited she could hardly renege on the offer now.

'You will make her proud. I know you will,' she said. 'Now, please tell me getting down is easier than getting up?'

Chapter Twenty-five

Holden was frantic. He and Ford had searched every inch of road between school and home to no avail, and after checking the house and surrounds again he was heading back to town to talk to the police. He was beginning to wonder if Rocky had hitched a lift with someone. He couldn't have caught the bus to Colac as it only went early morning and evening. Why hadn't he asked Rocky where he'd gone that Sunday afternoon when he'd been late for dinner? He hadn't wanted to invade the boy's privacy but maybe that's where—

His thought died as he turned a corner too fast and the famous Smallton water tower came into view. He usually didn't even notice it but today his attention was caught by two figures climbing the ladder down from the top. Instinctively he slowed the bike.

Rocky. And *Adeline*? What the hell were they doing up there?

Having barely allowed himself to breathe the last forty minutes or so, Holden exhaled long and hard before killing the ignition. He climbed off the bike just as Rocky dropped to the ground.

'Holden?' the boy exclaimed.

Holden strode towards him and pulled Rocky's lanky body hard against his chest. 'Thank fuck. The school called; told me you'd run away. I've been worried sick about you.'

'Sorry,' Rocky said. 'I didn't mean to worry you. It's just—'

'It's okay, we'll talk about what happened later,' he said, relief overriding any anger. 'I'm just glad to see you. But don't *ever* scare me like that again, okay? If you need time alone to calm down or think, that's fine, but you gotta let me know where you are. My old heart can't take any more stress.'

'Deal,' Rocky said as Holden finally let him go.

The two of them turned back to the water tower to see Adeline frozen at the bottom of the ladder.

'Just jump,' Rocky shouted. 'It's not actually that far.'

'Not far my butt,' Adeline yelled. 'I don't want to break my neck.'

'Did you two go up there together?' Holden asked Rocky.

He shook his head. 'Adeline saw me. She thought I was gunna jump, so she climbed up to try and talk me down, I guess.'

Wow. Getting up to the first rung of the ladder couldn't have been an easy feat without assistance. He wasn't even sure he'd be able to do it. 'But you weren't planning on jumping?'

'Nah. If I were gunna top myself, I'd do it somewhere no one would ever find me.'

Holden clapped his hand on the boy's shoulder and squeezed.

'Do you reckon we should help her?' Rocky asked as Adeline tried some kind of gymnastics to get herself from the bottom of the ladder across to the drainpipe.

'Yeah.' Holden stepped closer to the edge of the tower. 'Maria,' he called. 'That's gunna be as dangerous as jumping. Trust me, if you jump, I'll catch you.'

'I wouldn't trust *you*,' she shouted, 'if you were the last man on earth. I climbed up, so I can climb down.' But she sounded more confident than she looked.

'Suit yourself.' He stifled a smile but didn't step back, poised to catch her if she fell.

Somehow, she managed to navigate the gap between the ladder and the drainpipe and Holden couldn't help cheering as she did so. 'Well done.'

'Shut up, Jack,' she retorted as she found her grip and then began to shimmy down.

He told himself he was watching in case she stumbled but the truth was he couldn't take his eyes off the way her practical pants stretched tight across her butt, and her legs squeezed the pipe.

And then, about a metre and a half from the ground, she lost her footing. His heart jolted as she slipped, and he rushed forward and put his hands on her hips to steady her.

'You're okay,' he whispered. 'I got ya.' And having her felt *so* good.

'Thanks,' she said in a begrudging tone as he lifted her to the ground. She quickly stepped out of his space and began to brush the dirt from the tower off her beige trousers.

'Hey guess what, Holden?' Rocky said.

'What?'

'Adeline said I could have Bella.'

He looked from Rocky to Adeline. 'Really?'

She nodded. 'I know I should have asked you first but ...'

Her voice trailed off and Holden could guess what had happened. Adeline had been using Bella as a bargaining chip when she thought Rocky was suicidal.

'It's fine, but are you sure?' He knew how much she adored that dog.

She took a moment, then smiled at Rocky and nodded. 'Yes, I know he'll take good care of her and she'll love being with other dogs again.'

Holden didn't know what to say. He felt bad about being such a jerk to her. He wanted to give her a hug, but he got the feeling that wouldn't go down well. Instead, he nodded, and turned back to Rocky. 'Well, we should get you home and have a bit of a chat before we go in and see Ms Hester.'

Rocky groaned. 'She's gunna suspend me, isn't she?'

'I don't know. But I wanna hear your side of the story first.'

'He was provoked,' Adeline said. 'And I'm not making excuses for violence, but that needs to be taken into account when the punishment is decided,'

Holden nodded. 'Noted. That's why I need the full story.'

'Can you give me a ride back on your bike?' Rocky asked, bouncing on his feet at the prospect.

'Nope. No one rides my bike but me. Start walking.'

'Okay,' Rocky said, but then looked to Adeline. 'When are you bringing Bella over, or do you want me to come get her?'

Holden's heart broke at the anguish in her beautiful eyes. 'How about we let them have one more night together?'

* * *

After a gruelling hour in Ms Hester's office negotiating Rocky's punishment, they arrived at an agreement. Gabe, now boasting a broken nose, would be made to formally apologise to Rocky, and both boys would receive a three-day suspension. Rocky would serve his in the principal's office at school because she didn't want him to fall behind any further, and this way, she'd be able to help him if need be. For all her bark, Holden could see that Ms Hester had Rocky's best interests at heart as well.

Once they were home and the boys were getting stuck into their afternoon chores, Holden headed back down the road to the convent and was greeted at the door by Michelle again. She was wearing an apron that said 'Love is spoken here, joy is chosen here, grace is given here' on the front and she had flour on her face and in her hair.

'Well, hello again. Glad to hear you found Rocky safe and sound.' She did the sign of the cross. 'Praise the Lord.'

'Indeed,' Holden said. 'Is Adeline around?'

'It's always Adeline, isn't it?' Michelle tsked. 'And here I was thinking maybe you'd come to visit me this time.'

Holden wasn't sure if she was joking or not, so he decided it was safer to say nothing.

She sighed. 'Come on. She's out the back with Bella.'

He followed Michelle into the vast entry hall and down the corridor out to the back. The convent wasn't much like he'd imagined—it was more modern and far homier inside. And the backyard was like some kind of botanic gardens. Looked like the nuns had green thumbs.

'She's over there.' Michelle pointed to where Adeline was sitting on a cast iron bench under a big eucalypt tree, Bella slumped at her feet. 'I'll leave you to it. The dinner won't make itself.'

'Thanks.' Holden walked quietly across to Adeline. Her eyes were closed, and she was fiddling with some beads on a long chain. The late-afternoon sunlight filtered through the foliage above, causing shadows to dance on her caramel skin. Man, she was gorgeous.

Sensing his approach, Bella looked up and then bounded over to greet him. 'Hey girl.' He stooped down and scratched her between her ears the way he knew she liked.

'What are you doing here?' Adeline demanded as her eyes snapped open and she shoved the beads into her pocket.

'I came to thank you for what you did today. For Rocky.'

'I did nothing,' she scoffed. 'I misread the situation. He was fine.'

'I wouldn't say he was *fine*, and he told me what you said to him—about not being like his dad and that. It really sunk in.' As Holden straightened, Bella ran off towards some chickens pecking in the dirt at the other side of the garden.

'I thought he was going to kill himself. I had to make him see that doing so would be a terrible mistake. And it's true anyway, it's clear to see he's nothing like his father and we all do make mistakes. His is relatively minor in the big picture. I'm sure Gabe's nose will recover, and he'll have a story to tell for years to come.'

'When we got home, he asked me about all the mistakes *I'd* ever made.' He gestured to the space beside her. 'May I sit?'

'If you must.'

Stifling a smile, he slowly lowered himself down next to her, not realising until his thighs brushed against hers how small the seat was. He sucked in a breath. 'I can't believe you climbed all the way up there. How?'

'I scaled the pipe, same way Rocky did.'

'Well, that's impressive.' He always gave credit where credit was due. 'Not sure I could have done that. Where'd you learn to do such a thing?'

'Pole dancing,' she replied, hitting him with a look that warned him not to mock.

Pole dancing. He swallowed. Mocking was the last thing on his mind. The image of Adeline pole dancing was not one he needed in his head. As if the TikTok dances weren't bad enough; he'd never get any sleep now.

'I took classes in Bunbury—a nearby town—a few years ago. Mum called me a "hussy" for participating in "such a reprehensible activity".' She made air quotes with her fingers. 'But it's not what most people think. And it was super fun. Much better than the team sports I had to play as a kid. Anyway,' she shrugged, 'without those classes there's no way I'd have had the skills or upper body strength for today.'

'Your mum was joking when she called you a hussy, right?' Although he knew firsthand about less-than-supportive parents, Adeline seemed so together that he'd just assumed she came from a happy family.

'My mother's not really the jokey type.'

Holden frowned. 'Does she have something to do with why you became a nun?'

'*Sister*,' she shot back. 'And no, not really. But she does think I've lost my mind. Anyway, are you going to tell me some of these mistakes you've made? The ones you told Rocky about?'

'Oh Maria.' He shifted a little in his seat, still far too aware of her proximity. 'How long have you got?'

She laughed, which was good because he wanted to lighten the mood.

'Well, my most recent mistake would have to be misjudging and rejecting you.'

He heard her quick intake of breath and then she turned to look at him properly for the first time since he'd arrived. 'What do you mean?'

He looked into her silvery-blue eyes, noticed how thick, dark, and long her lashes were and all he could think about was kissing her. He didn't think any man could think about anything else with her luscious lips mere inches from theirs. But somehow, he resisted. He'd come here to make a truce, not to make things even more complicated. Bronte and Ford were right. The tiny houses project wasn't about him; it was about helping young men stay off the streets, about giving them a proper chance to make a life for themselves.

And if Adeline could help him raise the funds needed to get it off the ground, then who was he to turn her down?

'Holden?' she prompted.

'Sorry.' He shook his head and ran a hand over his hair. 'If your offer to help me with grants and fundraisers is still open, then I'd like to accept. And also apologise for being a bit of a prick about it all.'

She raised one eyebrow. 'A bit?'

'Okay.' He half-laughed, half-sighed. 'I think the word Bronte used was "arsehole", and even that's probably not strong enough.'

'Bronte thinks you're an arsehole?'

'Yeah, she was furious when I told her I turned you down. Said I was being a bloody-minded idiot.'

Adeline smiled. 'I really like Bronte.'

'She likes you too. Anyway, *is* the offer still open?'

In lieu of an answer, she hit him with another question. 'Why did you turn me down? I know it's got something to do with religion and your stepfather, but what exactly did he do to make you so …'

Her voice drifted off, but he knew exactly what she was asking.

'It's a long story,' he said, glancing in Bella's direction. There was nothing like the comfort of a dog when you ripped open your heart.

'I've got as long as you need,' Adeline whispered, shifting her body slightly so she was fully turned towards him.

And maybe it was because of what she'd done today—risked her safety and then sacrificed her dog to help Rocky—or maybe it was because he didn't want her to think he was an arsehole for no reason, but he found himself opening up in a way he'd only ever done to Bronte and the boys. But it had taken years to tell Bronte the truth, and he only spoke about it to the boys when they needed to hear it. Like today, with Rocky.

'I told you my dad disappeared, right?' It was a rhetorical question. 'After that, things were pretty good for a few years. Well, when I say good, I guess they were tough for Mum. She worked two jobs to try and make ends meet, but we were a solid unit, just the three of us. We had fun together. Made the most of the little we had. Then, one day, the neighbour that took Mum and me to hospital when Ford was born, invited Mum to take us to Sunday school at her church. I was nine and I didn't wanna go, but I liked the drawing we got to do, and Ford and I both put up with having to learn Bible verses and shit for the mega morning tea that always followed. Those church ladies sure knew how to cook, and because Mum was a single mother, they often sent leftovers home with us.'

Adeline chuckled. 'That doesn't sound too bad to me.'

'It wasn't. After that, Mum got really involved in church and it was like we'd found the family we never had. Then one day, the old minister and his wife left and a new one arrived. He was single and set his sights on Mum the moment he arrived. Within weeks they were seeing each other, and because sex before marriage is strictly forbidden, a couple of months later they were married. We moved into a bigger house—the church house—with Garry, and almost immediately everything changed.'

Holden's jaw clenched at the memory. So much for lightening the mood.

'Mum said it was great we finally had a father who cared and wanted the best for us. What she couldn't see—but was blatantly obvious to me even at twelve—was that all Garry wanted was power and control. He didn't give a damn about me and Ford, but he liked to pretend we were this perfect happy family in public. He tried to force us to call him Dad. Ford's a people pleaser and so he went along with it. I never did, despite Mum begging me not to rock the boat.

'She changed under Garry's thumb. She became even more pious and super judgemental. The friends she'd had before, outside of church, completely fell away—or rather she rejected them because of their "ungodly ways"—and her life, our lives, revolved purely around the church. Around Garry. They even took Ford and me out of the local public schools—I was in high school by then, Ford still in primary—and sent us to this Christian one where we learned all about how sinful we were and how we'd go to hell if we so much as put a foot out of line. Garry very much believed in the man as the head of the household, and he inflicted his ideas and routines on us.'

'Was he abusive?' Adeline asked when Holden paused for breath. Talking about Garry always raised his heart rate.

'Not in such a way that anyone would ever believe it. He didn't hit Mum, but he *disciplined* us if we so much as rolled our eyes. The cane. That sort of thing. He was a firm believer in "spare the rod, spoil the child". I started to act up to see how far I could push him. I figured if he hurt me bad enough, Mum might realise what kind of person he was and leave him, but she always sided with him. It was always my fault for riling him up, for not toeing the line. So I just got angrier and more resentful. I hated him so much.'

'I don't blame you,' Adeline said. 'He sounds awful.'

'That doesn't even begin to describe him. Anyway, eventually I got expelled from the Christian school and I refused to go to church and listen to him preach. Instead, I spent my Sundays doing graffiti around town, honing my art.'

She laughed a little at that and he felt her gaze fall upon the tattoos on his arms. 'Well, doesn't look like that was entirely a waste of your time. What did Ford think of it all?'

Holden shrugged. 'As I said, he hates tension, so he was very much the good son, and I was the bad egg they didn't know what to do with. Until Ford started high school and developed a crush on another boy.'

'Ford's gay?' Adeline sounded surprised. Holden didn't blame her. After all, the man was an outrageous flirt.

'He's bi.'

'And your stepfather didn't like that?' she asked.

'Understatement of the millennium. He caught Ford and Tom getting a little too friendly in Ford's bedroom one day after school and lost the plot. He forbade them from seeing each other again and basically told Ford he couldn't leave the house except to go to school or church and that he couldn't have any friends over either. He told them both they were disgusting pieces of filth that needed to be fixed.'

'Poor Ford,' Adeline said, her voice full of emotion.

'Yeah. I was barely living at home by then, I was working at Macca's every shift I could get to try and save up money for a place of my own so I could get out the moment I was old enough. I stayed at mates' places as much as possible, but I heard about it on the grapevine.'

'About what he said to Ford?'

'No. Sorry. I'm jumping ahead.' Talking about this didn't come easy and it always brought his anger right up to the surface. He yanked at the collar on his shirt. He knew if he ever saw Garry again, he might not be able to control himself. 'Gay conversion therapy.'

Adeline gasped. 'What?'

Holden nodded. 'Garry called in some friend of his who'd supposedly had success in the area. I thought they were going to try to pray the gay out of him and I was so mad. How dare they make Ford feel like he was dirty and sinful, when he was a far better person than they could ever hope to be! I barged into the church, ready to give them a piece of my mind and found Ford throwing up.'

'They made him sick?'

'Uh-huh. They were doing a lot more than just praying. They gave him "medicine" to make him ill while showing him images of same-sex couples in erotic positions.' He swallowed, his whole chest tightening at the thought of what he'd seen that day. 'They were telling him he was vomiting because he had an illness. That his feelings for other boys were unnatural and unhealthy, and that they would help rid him of the "demons of homosexuality".'

'Oh, my goodness.' Adeline reached out and placed her hand on his knee. 'I can't even … that's just awful. And he was just a child. Poor Ford.'

He glanced down at her hand, not trusting himself to cover hers with his. 'Yeah. I know it's irrational to lump all religious people together with the likes of Garry, but …'

He couldn't bring himself to say any more.

'I understand, but I promise you, I'm not like that. I think Ford's fabulous and I don't think his sexual preferences are any-one's business but his own. And the sisters aren't like your step-father either. They're all good women, who want to share God's love, not hatred.'

'I know,' Holden said, although even the phrase "God's love" caused the hairs on the back of his neck to prickle. 'I can see that, but thanks for listening.'

She smiled as she withdrew her hand and rested it with her other one in her lap. He missed her touch immediately but knew if they were going to work together, he had to get over his attrac-tion and focus on what mattered. It wasn't going to be easy, but if he'd learned one thing in his life it was that nothing worth doing ever was.

'Dinner!' called one of the sisters from the back door.

Adeline jumped to attention. 'Sorry, I better go, but thanks for coming over and thanks for sharing. I feel like I understand you both a little better now.'

Holden stood, then shoved his hands awkwardly in his pockets. 'So, when can we get started?'

Adeline frowned. 'On what?'

'On the grants and fundraising and stuff.'

'*Oh*, that. You're serious about accepting my help?'

He nodded. 'If the offer's still open.'

She didn't respond immediately, and for a moment he thought he was going to have to beg. Then she smiled. 'I'll deliver Bella tomorrow after school and if you want, we can start then.'

He looked over to where the dog was still frolicking with the chickens. 'Are you sure you really want to give her to Rocky? I know you did it because—'

'I'm not going back on my word,' she said sharply. 'Besides, if we're going to be working together, I'll get to see her all the time.'

All the time. Holden was both excited and a little apprehensive at the prospect.

Chapter Twenty-six

Adeline was a puddle of emotions as she waved Holden goodbye, summoned Bella to her final supper in the convent, and then went inside to join the other sisters for dinner.

Tonight, it was one of her favourites—vegetarian lasagne and Greek salad with a special dressing that Michelle refused to share the secret ingredient of—but Adeline could barely manage one bite. She couldn't stop thinking about Holden. His vulnerability as he'd shared his story had broken her heart. It had been all she could do not to wrap her arms around him and hold him tightly. She knew he hadn't told her for pity or sympathy, but she couldn't help feeling it.

Poor him. Poor *Ford*.

The brothers had been through more than their fair share of trauma in their lives and now, more than ever, she believed she'd been led to them for a reason. And not just to help them fundraise. Perhaps her purpose was to help Holden see the light again. To help him rid his heart of all that bitterness and restore his belief in the basic goodness of humankind.

Do you really believe such a thing exists? scoffed a voice inside her, reminding her of her grandmother.

Yes, she retorted, *I do.*

There were bad people in the world, or at least people who did bad things—people like her grandmother and Holden's stepfather—but living with the sisters, she saw good at work every single day. She saw it in the big things and the little things they did for each other and the wider community. They had faith, not just in God, but in each other.

'Are you okay?' asked Sister Josey, noticing Adeline pushing the food around her plate.

She tried to offer a reassuring smile. 'Yes. I'm just processing a few things.'

Today had been the most emotional since she'd arrived at the convent. On the one hand, she was on a total high because Holden had agreed to let her help, but the scare with Rocky and then Holden's heart-wrenching story had left her drained. Not to mention the fact that tomorrow she'd have to hand Bella over to her new owner.

Usually she ate her feelings, but tonight she couldn't bring herself to eat a thing.

'What did Holden want this afternoon?' Michelle asked as she forked off another chunk of lasagne.

'Yes, you and he looked to be having quite the deep and meaningful when I called you inside,' Rita added, pouring some Diet Coke into a glass.

And they weren't the only sisters who looked intrigued. All eyes around the table were glued on Adeline.

'He came to thank me for helping with Rocky,' she explained, stabbing a cherry tomato with her fork. 'He also accepted my offer to help him and Ford with grants and fundraising.'

'Wow. That's great,' said Sister Josey, clapping her wrinkled hands together. 'What made him change his mind?'

'I think it was because I offered to give Bella to Rocky and—'

'Excuse me?' Michelle dropped her fork to the table as all the sisters stopped eating and stared open-mouthed at Adeline. 'You're giving our dog away?'

'I thought you'd all be relieved to see the back of her.' Adeline was only half joking. She was certain Barnabas and Benno wouldn't be upset. Yesterday, while the sisters were inside during evening prayer, Bella had dug a massive hole in the veggie patch before chasing Barnabas up a tree.

'But I love her,' Michelle said.

Adeline nodded. 'I know. I do too. And that's not going to change. We can visit, but Rocky needs her more than we do. He's been through so much and …' Emotion overcame her, even though she knew she'd done the right thing.

'Oh, Adeline.' Sister Rita shifted her chair closer and wrapped her arm around her shoulder. 'You're a good woman.'

'So, Holden feels like he owes you a favour?' asked Michelle, still sounding incredibly put out. 'Sounds like he's getting the better deal here. They get a dog *and* your assistance.'

'I want to help him,' Adeline said. 'I want to help *them*. And it's not just about the tiny houses or the money. Accepting our help is a huge step for Holden. I believe I've been called to help him, and if I have to let Bella go to do that, so be it.'

Mother Catherine beamed as she gave Adeline a nod of approval. 'Didn't I say the Lord works in mysterious ways?'

'Yes, you did,' Adeline replied, glowing inside at the knowledge she'd pleased their superior.

'I'm proud of you,' added the older woman. 'What you did today—first going after Rocky and then giving him Bella, shows true self-sacrifice. It shows true commitment to God.'

The others all murmured their agreement.

Adeline was too choked up with emotion to reply, but she managed a smile for her sisters instead. The sadness she felt about Bella was eased by the uplifting comments. Although she'd felt like this was where she wanted to be almost since the moment she arrived, today was the first day she'd truly felt she was living her purpose.

She finally felt that maybe—just maybe—there was a goodness inside her too.

The topic of conversation moved on to Lola's final vow ceremony, which was due to take place next month.

'Are you nervous?' Adeline asked, eager to learn as much as she could about the ceremony.

Lola's family were coming from various parts of Australia and her grandmother was coming all the way from China. Adeline wasn't sure if her family would make the trek from WA when she took her vows, but if her parents were there, she'd probably fumble her words worrying about what they were thinking.

'No.' Lola beamed as she shook her head. 'I'm excited. I was shaking the day I took my first vows, terrified of making a mistake, but I can't wait to take this final step into service.'

Happy to focus on something other than Bella for a while, Adeline listened eagerly to the plans for Lola's big day. In addition to the ceremony, there'd be a feast afterwards at the convent, which involved menu planning, flowers and entertaining Lola's family and important members of the Catholic church who would travel from Melbourne and nearby dioceses for the occasion.

After dinner, they cleared the dishes and sat around the dining-room table as Sister Josey read the latest emails to everyone. At first Adeline had found this evening ritual odd—shouldn't correspondence be private?—but the sisters had no secrets and she'd come to enjoy listening to everyone else's news from home almost as much as she enjoyed her regular updates from Sally.

'Here's one from your mum,' said Sister Josey, looking to Adeline.

Even before it was read out, she could almost guess what it would say. So far, all Jane's emails had been filled with benign gossip, grumbles about this and that, and they always ended with something along the lines of: *When are you going to come to your senses and come home?* Sure enough, today's was no different.

'Dear Adeline,' read Sister Josey. 'There's not much to tell from our end. I went to the school assembly the other day and saw Levi get an award. Ellie Winters had a fall and has moved into Penelope's room in the hospital. Richard Wellington got a vasectomy and everyone knows because Chloe has been telling the whole town how much of a sook he was about it.'

Michelle snorted and the other sisters tried hard to smother giggles.

'Trevor is doing a terrible job at the *Whisperer*. He tries to make every article funny, but his sense of humour is vulgar. When are you coming back to take over the reins again?

'Regards, Mum

'PS Dad says hello, which is more than he says to me most days!'

Michelle laughed. 'Your mum sounds like a hoot.'

'She's a character,' Adeline admitted, no longer embarrassed by these emails—the other sisters had told her that in the beginning, many of their family members had also found it hard to come to terms with their pledge to the church.

Tonight, there seemed to be more correspondence than usual, which frustrated her because she desperately wanted to slip away and spend some quality time with Bella while she still could. When the other sisters finally retreated to their bedrooms, she went outside to put away the chickens and then took Bella on a long walk into town and back. When they were both too exhausted to walk any further, Adeline led them back to the convent, where she got ready for bed.

'What time do you call this?' Michelle joked as she and Bella entered their bedroom. As usual her nose was in a book.

'Sorry, you didn't have to stay up. Bella and I just had a few words to say to each other before tomorrow.'

Michelle simply nodded, then closed her novel, switched off her bedside lamp and snuggled under her covers. Adeline climbed into bed as Bella slumped into her usual spot on the floor between the beds. She closed her eyes and silently said her evening prayers.

Dear Lord, thank you for everything you have blessed me with and thank you today for putting me in the right place at the right time for Rocky. I pray that you will guide him as you are guiding me and help us both to grow into good people. Thank you for cracking open Holden's heart. Please help me to help him raise the money needed to build the houses and give his foster boys the best chance of a future. Forgive me for taking for granted all the opportunities I had growing up. And please, give me strength tomorrow when I have to say goodbye to Bella ...

Her last dog.

She silently reached for a tissue, not wanting to disturb Michelle with her tears. She wondered if this was it for her and dogs. It would be strange not having a canine pal after years of dog breeding, but giving up Bella proved she was willing to serve and sacrifice.

And please Father, give me your comfort and take care of Bella in her new life with Rocky. In the name of the Father, the Son, and the Holy Spirit. Amen.

* * *

'Do you want one of us to come with you?' asked Sister Rita the following afternoon when it was time to take Bella down the road. All the sisters had gathered in the convent's front garden to say goodbye.

Adeline shook her head. 'Thanks. But I'm going to be fine, and I'm going to stay for a bit to start discussing my plans with Holden.'

Sister Josey stooped to ruffle Bella's neck fur—she didn't have far to go as she wasn't much taller than the dog. 'You be a good girl and make sure you come visit occasionally.'

Then Michelle took her turn. She dropped to the ground and wrapped her arms around Bella's big, fluffy neck. 'If they don't feed you properly there, you can always sneak back down the road to me.'

Perhaps it was a good thing Bella was leaving. The way her belly was growing, it looked like Michelle had been ignoring Adeline's pleas for her to stop spoiling her. She had to physically separate them, and Sister Josey wrapped an arm around Michelle as they waved them off down the road.

Rocky was waiting at the end of the driveway, still in his school uniform, and Bella picked up her pace, bolting ahead the moment she laid eyes on him.

'Hey Adeline,' Rocky yelled. 'This is the best day of my life. Come on, girl, let's go see your new bed. You're gunna sleep in my room, with me.'

Dog and boy raced up the gravel drive and Adeline followed at a much slower pace. She knew this was going to be hard, but she didn't expect the *physical* pain. Watching Rocky lead Bella away towards the house felt like someone had sliced a knife down her chest, reached inside and yanked out her heart.

'Hey. You okay?' She hadn't even noticed Holden sidle up beside her.

'Of course,' she lied, unable to meet his gaze. She was not going to cry. Not here. Not in front of Rocky. And definitely not in front of Holden.

'You're doing a good thing, Maria,' he said.

Adeline swallowed, nodded—'Thanks, Jack'—and *almost* managed to keep from crying.

'Hey,' he said again, reaching to wipe a tear from her cheek with the rough pad of his thumb.

His touch startled her from one emotion to an entirely different one.

'Sorry,' she whispered, swallowing hard as her nerve endings tingled.

He pulled her against him, wrapping his arms around her. 'You've got nothing to apologise for.'

Of course, at his delicious comfort, she started to sob. Hard and fast.

So much for not falling apart.

'I'm sorry,' she said again as she tried to pull away.

But Holden put one hand against her head and gently pressed it against his chest as his other arm tightened around her. 'Stop apologising. You're allowed to be upset. Take all the time you need.'

And so she did; staying there wrapped in his warm, strong embrace until her tears had soaked through his red flannelette shirt and finally subsided. Nothing had ever felt so good. And Adeline had never felt so safe and comforted in her life.

Pulling away, she looked up at him. 'You know, you give very good hugs.'

'So, I've been told.' He smiled down at her, warming her heart. 'It's actually listed on my resume.'

She coughed out a laugh and then sniffed again. 'Thank you.'

'No worries.' He took a tiny pouch of tissues out of his pocket and handed them to her. 'They're clean, I promise.'

'Are you sure you weren't a boy scout?'

'I was as much a boy scout as the pope is an atheist. I just had a feeling you might need one. Or two,' he added as she tore one out to wipe her eyes.

'Right … Now. Are you ready to work, Jack? I've got a lot to say.'

'Are you sure you're in the right frame of mind to talk business? We can take a raincheck if you're not feeling up to it today.'

Adeline shook her head. 'Nope, I'll be fine. As long as Bella's happy, which I know she will be, I can handle this.'

If she told herself this enough, maybe it would be true.

'In that case … After you.' He gestured for her to go ahead of him into the house.

'Have you ever thought about becoming a registered charity?' she asked as he held the door open.

'You think that would be a good idea?'

'Yes. I think it will help you get grants, and people are also more likely to donate money to a legal charity.'

'But I'm a foster carer, not a charity.'

'Of course, but I'm not talking about that aspect. I'm talking about your tiny houses project.' She pulled out her notebook. 'I took the liberty of going to the library and doing some research for you and—'

He held up his hands. 'Whoa, I need a drink before we get stuck into this. What can I get you? Coffee? Tea? Water?'

'A tea would be lovely, thanks.'

They found Toovs and Sam in the kitchen demolishing enormous bowls of Weetbix as if they were in some kind of contest. Both looked up when she and Holden entered.

'Afternoon, Adeline,' they said after quickly swallowing their mouthfuls.

'Hi boys, how was school?'

'We survived,' Sam replied with a roll of his eyes.

'You mean the school survived you,' Holden said as he crossed to the kettle.

Toovs stood and took his empty bowl to the sink. 'Rocky told us how you climbed up the water tower with him. Sounds unreal.'

'He's gunna take us up there soon,' Sam added, before lifting his bowl and draining the milk into his mouth.

'Not if I have anything to do with it,' Holden said.

Sam shook his head—'Such a killjoy'—but he was grinning.

'They're such great kids,' Adeline said when they left to do their afternoon chores. She knew they'd both come from sticky home situations—not quite as bad as Rocky's—but the way they were here with Holden, it was hard to imagine. They were a real credit to him. And Ford.

Holden tossed two soggy teabags into the bin, then picked up the mugs of tea he'd just made. 'Where do you want to sit? In here or outside?'

'It's such a beautiful arvo. Let's go outside.' Now that the boys had left, the massive kitchen felt a little cramped with just the two of them.

He nodded and Adeline followed him down the hallway, where they sat side by side on deckchairs, the afternoon sunlight spilling over them. Vlad and Merlin joined them on the verandah, sniffing around their feet for fallen goodies.

'Leave Maria alone,' Holden said, calling them off. They immediately dropped and rested their heads on their paws.

'Sorry I don't have anything else to offer you,' he said, handing her the tea. 'All the cookies you brought last time are gone.'

'Is that a hint?' she asked, before taking a sip of her drink.

He simply shrugged one shoulder and then lifted his own mug to his mouth. Adeline made a mental note to do some baking before her next visit.

'Okay.' Holden put his mug on the ground and then cleared his throat. '*Now* I'm ready. What were you saying about becoming a charity?'

Adeline smiled, put her own mug at her feet and opened her notebook. 'Okay, so I've been thinking about what you want to do and the best way to go about raising funds and getting the whole project off the ground and—'

The front screen door flew open and Rocky and Bella rushed out. 'Bella and I are gunna go practise her jumps,' the boy yelled as the two of them launched off the verandah.

'You were saying?' Holden prompted with a chuckle.

Adeline swallowed the lump in her throat as Bella grew smaller the further away she and Rocky got. 'My research tells me that although there are other tiny house charities overseas and in Australia, none focus on youth homelessness or housing for those exiting foster care like you plan to. I think you should launch a charity with the goal to do just this.'

'Whoa.' Holden let out a long breath and ran his hand through his thick mane. 'That sounds like a mammoth project. I was just thinking about building maybe four or five houses, so the boys I foster here would have some place to go when they turn eighteen.'

She grinned. 'I know ... but why think small when you can think big? Why help only a few kids, when you could help hundreds? You can encourage other people who have a bit of land to host a tiny house too.'

He nodded once. 'You've got a point, but I wouldn't even know where to start.'

'That's where I come in.' She pulled out a folder of pages which she'd printed from the Internet using the convent's computer, and set to explaining all the steps he'd need to take to register and get going.

Holden stared down at the paperwork. 'Looks like a lot of work.'

'Hey.' He looked over at her exclamation and she smiled at him. 'A wise woman once told me that nothing worth doing is ever easy.'

'That's true, but all this would take time. And I don't want to wait months or even years to get going.'

'You don't have to,' she said, unable to keep her excitement out of her voice. 'Why don't you start with the basics? Coming up with a name for your charity.'

The screen door flew open again and this time Toovs and Sam appeared. 'Hey Holden,' Sam said. 'Can we—'

'*Excuse me, Holden and Adeline,*' Holden reprimanded. 'I see you are in the middle of something, but do you mind if we ask you a quick question?'

Sam gave Adeline a slightly sheepish smile. 'Sorry to interrupt, but can we just ask Holden something?'

'Won't take long,' added Toovs.

Adeline nodded.

'We were wondering,' Sam began, 'if we can build another bonfire tonight.'

'There's heaps of wood.' This from Toovs. 'And we can gather it all ourselves.'

'Yeah, whatever. If you can find enough branches.' As it was Friday night, Mitch and Luka would be over soon and they were going to have sausages on the barbie, but they could cook them on the fire. 'But don't you dare light it before it's dark.'

'Yeah, yeah, we know the drill,' Sam said.

'Coming boys?' Toovs whistled to the dogs and they followed after them, leaving Adeline and Holden alone once again.

'Sorry,' Holden said, his tone bemused as he turned back to her. 'It's hard to have a conversation around here sometimes.'

'It's fine,' she smiled. 'The boys are the priority, after all. Perhaps you can get them involved in brainstorming a charity name.'

'Good idea.'

'And,' she continued, 'if you do decide to form one, it doesn't mean you have to delay your plans. We can do the paperwork for that, while also pursuing other avenues—I'll help you with applying for grants and we'll also organise a fundraiser.'

'More than the car washing and face painting?' he asked.

'Pfft. They're small fry. I'm thinking of a big event where we get all of Smallton and the surrounding communities involved. Not only will this raise money for supplies so you can start on another house, but it will help the locals feel a part of the project. And if they feel part of it, they'll want it to succeed, and they'll want to contribute.'

Holden picked up his mug and took another long sip. She hoped she hadn't hit him with too much too soon, but when she got excited about a project, she found it hard to think about anything else.

'Okay,' he said after a few long moments. 'So what are you thinking? A quiz night? Bogan bingo? Please don't suggest a cake stall. As much as I love cake, they've been—'

'Done to death,' she finished for him. 'Same goes for trivia and bingo. And besides, a bake sale isn't going to raise the kind of funds we need. We want something different so people pay attention, exciting so they want to get involved, and also something the boys would enjoy as they should be a part of this.'

'And do you have any idea of what that is?'

'Of course.' She smiled, then paused a moment for effect. 'I'm thinking we organise a human tractor pull competition. We get groups of people to register—'

'Hang on.' He held up a hand again. 'I know what a tractor pull is, but I've never heard of a *human* tractor pull. Is that what it sounds like?'

'It's where a bunch of people see how fast they can pull a tractor a certain distance. The school my brother went to in Perth does one at the end of every year. Theirs is a contest between teachers and the graduating year twelves, but I'm suggesting a contest where multiple teams enter and go against each other. We can get sporting and community groups involved, we can have different categories and ask local companies to donate the prizes. We won't just limit it to Smallton either. We'll promote the event to other surrounding towns and make a huge day of it. We'll sell tickets to come and watch as well as tickets to compete. There can be a sausage sizzle, popcorn stand. We can even get food trucks to come and pay a fee to be there.'

Adeline finally paused and Holden pressed the heel of his hand against his forehead. 'God, it sounds ace, but my head is gunna explode just thinking about all that organisation.'

She hugged her notebook to her chest, excitement building. 'Relax, this is what I do well. I was the fundraising queen back home. The trick is good planning. I'll do up a spreadsheet ...'

He made a face at the word.

'Spreadsheets not your thing?'

'I'd rather tattoo my own eyeball than do a spreadsheet.'

She laughed. 'Okay, well, let me handle the spreadsheet and how about you start by finding us a tractor?'

Holden leaned back in his seat and nodded once. 'That I can do. I reckon there are a couple of farmers I can sweet-talk into it, even if I have to get Ford to give them free haircuts for a year. How big does it need to be?'

Adeline grinned. 'The bigger the better, I reckon.'

Chapter Twenty-seven

Ford was frying bacon but paused to wolf-whistle as Holden walked into the kitchen on Monday morning. 'Got a hot date or something?'

'No,' Holden said, making a beeline for the kettle. He hadn't got much sleep last night and he needed a shot of caffeine before facing the day.

'Then why are you looking and smelling so fresh?' Ford stared up at Holden's head. 'Did you wash your hair?'

He shrugged. 'Yeah. So what?'

'It's just I can't remember the last time you did such a thing.'

Holden shot him a look. 'I didn't realise you were keeping track.'

Ford laughed. 'I'm a barber, I notice these things. And ...' He sniffed the air. 'Are you wearing *cologne*?'

Holden didn't bother with a reply, focusing instead on his coffee fix, which would hopefully calm his excitement. He couldn't wait to get stuck into the plans Adeline had outlined last week, but he was also looking forward to spending more time with her. She was smart, feisty and funny, not to mention selfless, and with

Bronte away in Darwin, this place was in dire need of a woman to even out the testosterone.

'You got a shift today?' Ford asked, turning his attentions back to the frying of bacon and eggs.

'Nah.' Holden shook his head. Since Rocky had gone back to school, he'd been able to accept some work again at the tattoo parlour in Colac. 'Adeline's coming around to look over my grant applications and try to work out where I can improve.'

After the constant interruptions they'd had during their first meeting, they'd decided to try again during the day, when the boys would be at school.

'*Ah*, I see.'

'What's that supposed to mean?' Holden asked as he added milk to his mug and glanced around the kitchen, making note of a few things he'd need to clean before she arrived.

'Suddenly the extra attention to personal hygiene makes sense.'

'I don't know what you're talking about,' Holden snapped. 'My hair's got nothing to do with Maria. It was just time for a wash.'

'Right.' Ford's tone said he wasn't buying it. 'But just remember ... she isn't *available*.'

'I know that. I'm not an idiot.'

But perhaps he was, because even though he knew it was wrong, ever since Holden had comforted Adeline about Bella, he hadn't been able to stop thinking about how it felt to hold her. She'd fit so perfectly into his arms, her head nestled against his chest. Selfishly, he'd wanted her to keep crying so he had an excuse not to let her go.

And he *had* washed his hair and put on cologne because of her.

Even though he knew nothing could ever happen between them, that didn't mean he couldn't make himself presentable. She always smelled nice, the least he could do was reciprocate.

'And anyway, you were the one who told me I should accept her help,' he reminded Ford.

Thankfully, Rocky entered the kitchen—Bella right behind him as she'd been all weekend—putting a stop to this ridiculous conversation. 'I think something's wrong with Bella. She didn't eat much of her breakfast and she just vomited.'

Frowning, Holden put down his mug and stretched out his hand to the dog. 'It's probably nothing. Here girl. You not feeling well?' She ambled over and he rubbed his hand over her neck. 'Maybe she ate something she shouldn't have.'

'You don't think she's missing Adeline, do you?' asked Rocky anxiously.

Holden moved his hands to her belly. *Holy shit.* 'Nope. Don't think that's it,' he said, looking to the boy. 'I reckon Miss Bella here is up the duff.'

'Up the *what*?'

'It means she's pregnant,' Ford said, raising his eyebrows as he wheeled the tray of bacon and fried eggs across to the table.

Rocky's eyes widened. 'She's gunna be a mum?'

'Who's gunna be a mum?' asked Toovs, coming into the kitchen, his hair still mussed from slumber.

'Bella. She's having puppies,' Rocky told him excitedly.

'Serious?! When? How many do you think she'll have? Can we keep them?'

'Hold your horses,' Holden said, straightening up and reaching for his coffee again, sobered by the thought of up to ten extra little mouths to feed. 'We'll have to take her to the vet to confirm it.' Which would cost more money. 'And we'll have to discuss the whole puppy situation with Adeline.'

Rocky looked horrified. 'You don't think she'll want her back do you?'

'I don't know,' Holden said honestly.

Ford snorted. 'Maybe that's why she gave the dog away. Perhaps she didn't want Bella getting pregnant out of wedlock to bring shame upon the convent.'

Holden shot him an amused grin, but could his brother be right? If she'd been a breeder, surely Adeline could see the signs earlier than most.

Sam came into the kitchen next and Toovs slapped him on the back. 'Congratulations, Grandad.'

'The fuck you talking about?' Sam asked, scratching his head sleepily.

'Merlin's gunna be a daddy.'

Sam blinked. 'Huh?'

They filled him in as they ate. None of the boys wanted to go to school, all of them too excited about the prospect of puppies. Rocky argued that he should stay to look after Bella, and Sam joked about taking Merlin out for a pint and a pipe to celebrate the good news.

'That usually happened once the babies are born,' Ford said as he buttered himself another slice of toast.

Toovs didn't see why he should have to go to school if the other two weren't going.

'Everyone's going to school,' Holden said, and then ushered them out of the kitchen. Miraculously, there were a few pieces of bacon left, and he slipped them to Bella as a treat. As far as he was concerned, pregnant women deserved a little pampering.

The kids finally headed off down the driveway on their bikes, and not long after, Ford followed them into town, leaving Holden alone to wait.

He glanced at his watch. Just over an hour until Adeline was due, which meant he had time to do a mad dash around the house and make sure no one had left any dirty socks (or worse, jocks) lying around. While he was at it, he cleaned the toilet and wiped

the dust from a few neglected surfaces. He could just imagine
the ribbing Ford would give him if he saw him doing this, but it
wasn't a sin to make the place presentable for the woman who was
kindly sacrificing her own time to help them.

When he was done, he went out into the yard to pull some
weeds while he waited for her to arrive.

It was Bella who sensed Adeline's arrival first. She lifted her
head from where she'd been lying nearby with Merlin and Vlad
and then shot off down the driveaway. Holden jogged after her,
just to be certain she wasn't making an escape, and then slowed as
he watched the reunion.

Even from a distance, he saw Adeline's face light up as the dog
ran towards her and his heart did a weird flippy thing in his chest
at the sight.

'Morning, Maria.' She was carrying a large bag and a big tin,
which he hoped contained the cookies he'd unashamedly hinted
at wanting. 'Can I take anything for you?'

'Jack.' She smiled at him as she handed him the tin. 'Thanks.'

'Are these what I hope they are?' he asked, lifting the lid, and
then grinning at the cookies nestled in tissue paper. *Yum*.

'Don't eat them all at once,' she said.

'I'll try my best,' he replied as they started towards the house.
'Did you know Bella was pregnant?'

She stopped in her stride. 'What? But … No! She can't be.'

'Well, I'm no vet but I've seen a few pregnant bitches in my
time, and I'm pretty sure she is.'

'Bella, sit,' Adeline ordered as she dropped to her haunches
and then moved her hands over the dog's belly. 'I can't believe it.
You're right.'

Holden glanced over to where Merlin was now sunning himself in the garden. 'Clearly Rocky wasn't the only one who took a
shine to Bella. How far along do you think she is?'

Adeline had another grope. 'I'd say she's about four or five weeks.'

Holden cackled. 'Merlin must have worked fast. The pups must have been conceived on one of your first visits.'

'You think Merlin's the father?' she asked, glaring at the kelpie crossed with something like a border collie or an alsatian, possibly other breeds as well.

'Well, unless it was an immaculate conception, then he's the only one of ours with his balls still intact.'

'How can you joke about this?' she exclaimed. 'Bella is a pure-bred maremma, and that dog is … is …'

He raised an eyebrow, waiting for her to finish her sentence. He could almost see her visualising the puppies that would be born of this union, and it was all he could do to keep a straight face.

'He's a mongrel!'

'True love doesn't care about things like that. Sometimes you just can't fight the chemistry,' he said. 'Haven't you ever seen *Lady and the Tramp*?'

She bit her lip, then blushed again. 'It's my favourite Disney movie.'

He grinned. 'Mine too. Though *101 Dalmatians* is a close second.'

Adeline looked at him like she wasn't sure whether he was joking or not, and he told himself to rein it in. He was veering far too close to flirting.

'I can't believe I didn't notice the signs. I thought she was just getting fat because Michelle kept giving her treats.'

When Holden chuckled, she shot him a glare.

'I also assumed your dogs were fixed. Why isn't he?' She pointed accusingly at the loveable scruff.

'Why isn't Bella?' he retorted.

'Because … because she used to be used for breeding and I didn't know if she might breed again one day.'

'Well, it looks like she is.'

Adeline scowled. 'I'd never have allowed her anywhere near Merlin if I'd known he'd take advantage!'

'Hey.' He pretended to be insulted. 'The way I remember it, you didn't *allow* her to come here, she came of her own accord and maybe that's 'cos she smelled Merlin's masculine scent and couldn't resist? Maybe she took advantage of *him*? Either way, don't be such a snob.'

'I'm not a snob, I'm just … shocked. Anyway,' she sighed. 'What's done is done. I'll understand if you want me to take her back.'

'Are you kidding? The boys would kill me. Unless *you* want to.'

'To kill you?' she asked, showing only a glimmer of a smile. 'I admit I've thought about it. But no, if you're sure you don't mind, Rocky can keep her. Mother Catherine made it very clear I could only have one dog with me at the convent. I think she'd have kittens if Bella had puppies there, but you better take good care of her *and* her babies.'

'I give you my word,' he said in all seriousness.

'Thank you.' She smiled back and they started up the drive. 'We should probably take her to the vet for a check-up.'

'I was gunna make an appointment. Do you wanna come with me?'

She hesitated a moment, then said, 'Sure.'

'Great. We can call this morning. By the way, I got us a tractor.'

Adeline glanced at him. 'Really? That was quick.'

'I don't muck around.' He pulled his phone out of his pocket, swiped through his messages, then angled it towards her to show her a photo. 'Will this do? I got it from Nola—she brings her boys in for haircuts with Ford.'

'Wow. That's … massive.'

'You said you wanted big.' He couldn't help wriggling his eyebrows suggestively.

She rolled her eyes. 'Well, that's the most important part taken care of. Next step is choosing a date and asking the shire if we can use the oval for the big day. Have you given any thought to the charity?'

He sighed. 'If you'll help, I think it's a great idea.'

'Excellent. And any name suggestions yet?'

'Toovs said Tiny Homes for the Not So Tiny.'

Adeline laughed. 'I like it but it could be a mouthful.'

'And Rocky came up with Home Sweet Tiny Homes.'

'Not bad. We can check just to make sure there's nothing too close to it, but first, grants.'

Holden nodded as they headed into the house, where he offered her a drink—Bronte would be so proud of his hosting skills—and this time she chose coffee. He gestured to the dining-room table where he'd set up his laptop and the paperwork. 'Take a seat. I printed out all my failed grant applications so you could take a look.'

'Thanks.' As Adeline sat, Bella snuck under the table and rested upon her feet.

'So why are you doing this?' Holden asked, grabbing mugs as he waited for the kettle to boil.

Her gaze didn't stray from where she'd already started reading the paperwork. 'I told you … I'm good at organising fundraisers and writing grants and I want to help.'

'But why?' he pressed, spooning coffee granules into mugs.

She looked up. 'Serving and helping others is part of what being a sister is about.'

'Maybe …' But that sounded like a line, and she'd been ridiculously cranky when he'd refused her help, like it was a personal affront. 'That might be part of it, but I get the feeling there's more.'

'Can't it just be out of the goodness of my heart? Because I believe in your vision?'

He raised an eyebrow. 'And that's *it*?'

'What more could there be?'

The fact that she wouldn't meet his gaze told him he was onto something. Something she didn't want to talk about.

Fine. He wouldn't push her. Not today.

'Okay then.' Holden delivered the coffees to the table and sat across from her.

'Thanks.' She picked up her mug and took a sip, her eyes returning to the grant forms in front of her.

He watched her flick through page after page, her teeth gnawing into her bottom lip as she read, occasionally pausing to scribble something in her notebook. She looked so earnest. A few strands of golden hair that had escaped her ponytail fell across her face and he resisted the urge to reach over and tuck them behind her ear. Even from this distance he could detect the tantalising sweet, floral scent wafting from her hair.

What shampoo did she use?

'Well?' He asked when he could no longer bear the suspense. 'Any clues where I'm going wrong?'

She sighed, looked up, then folded her hands together on top of the paper pile. 'Why do you care about this project?'

Huh? What kind of question was that?

'Because I don't like seeing kids throw their lives away after leaving foster care,' he said. 'It's a flaw in the system that we only look out for them until they hit eighteen and then we turf them out to fend for themselves.'

She clicked her fingers and grinned at him. 'That's where you're going wrong.'

'What? Giving a damn?'

'No.' Adeline took another sip of what had to be now-cold coffee, then said, 'The problem with all these submissions is that they aren't personal. You're presenting the facts and the problem but not with any *heart*. You asked me why I'm doing this, but that doesn't matter because this isn't *my* project. It's yours. And the people who hand out the money want to know why *you* care. Why doing this matters, to *you*.'

'That's it?' he asked. 'I need to make it more about me?'

'I think it'll help a lot. You need to stand out from other applications, and the way to do that is to make yours personal. Why'd you become a foster carer, Holden?'

His chest tightened. 'Because I was a foster kid too.'

'Oh.' She blinked. 'What happened to your mum and stepdad?'

He swallowed. 'They kicked me out.'

'What?' Confusion spilled across her gorgeous face. 'I ... I don't understand.'

Holden hated talking about his past. He still couldn't believe he'd told her all that shit about his stepdad, but telling her the rest? He may as well rip out his heart and hand it to her on a silver platter.

As if reading his mind, she said softly, 'You don't have to tell me, but if you want to start getting big money from places that can really help you move forward, then you're going to have to put it on the forms.'

He thought of the boys currently in his care, those that had been and those that would come. He thought of Sam, who was almost eighteen but by no means ready to do life alone. He thought of the desperate urge he had to make a difference. To do something that might go a fraction towards making amends for what he'd done. 'If I tell you, will you help me put it into words on the form? You're so much better at writing than I am.'

Adeline nodded.

'Okay then. But if I'm going to talk about this, I need something stronger than coffee.' He stood, walked across to the pantry and dug right into the back for his hidden bottle of whiskey. 'You want some?'

Chapter Twenty-eight

'You know how I told you about Garry trying to "fix" Ford?'

Adeline nodded.

'Well ...' He took an audible breath in and out. 'When I saw what the guy was doing to him, the images he was being shown, the tears pouring down his face, I lost my shit. Ford was a mess, and Garry was just standing there watching with this smug look on his face. I punched him hard and when he doubled over, his car keys fell out of his pocket. I snatched them up and ordered Ford to follow me. All I knew was that I had to get him out of there. Not just out of the church, but out of this life. Away from Mum and toxic Garry before they totally destroyed him. Although he was weak from vomiting, he managed to run outside and we jumped into the car.'

'He wasn't in a wheelchair then?'

Holden shook his head and the look that crossed his face told Adeline everything she needed to know.

Oh God. Her whole body went cold. No wonder he was so reluctant to talk about this.

Part of her wanted to tell him to stop. That she didn't need to hear it after all. But that would be a lie because although she might not *want* to hear it, she'd meant it when she said personal stories made the difference to grant applications. She needed to know this so she could help put it into words.

'I'd never driven a car in my life,' he continued, 'but I'd watched, and it wasn't actually that hard. Ford was laughing, egging me on. I guess we were both running on adrenaline, but I was just relieved to see him not as damaged as he could have been. We didn't have a plan beyond getting out of town, and I knew we had to be fast because someone would have called the police and they'd be onto us. So I was speeding and I guess not really concentrating because I was talking. I wanted Ford to know how wrong what had happened was.' Holden paused and took a breath. 'The last thing I remember telling him, before I lost control of the car, and everything went black, was that he wasn't dirty or sinful. That his feelings weren't wrong. And that anyone who tried to tell him otherwise was the evil one.'

Adeline didn't know what to say. Her heart broke at the anguish on his face.

'I woke up as the emergency services were trying to cut us out of the car. Ford was out of it … I remember screaming. I'd broken my arm and had glass from the windscreen buried in my forehead …' He pushed his hair back and she saw a diamond-shaped scar, normally covered by his scruffy fringe. 'But I wasn't screaming because of the physical pain. I was screaming 'cos I thought Ford was dead. I thought I'd killed him.'

'Oh Holden.' She couldn't help herself; she reached across the table and went to grab his hand, but he snatched it out of her reach.

'Don't,' he growled warningly. 'I'm not telling you this because I want your pity. I'm only telling you because you said it would help. *I* don't deserve your pity. I might not have killed my brother, but I ruined his life. Me and *Garry* ruined his life. If it wasn't for Garry and his fucking church, Ford would still be walking today. I made my favourite person in the entire world a paraplegic and all because Garry thinks he knows better than everyone else.'

Adeline slowly inched her hand back to her side, biting down on the urge to apologise.

'They kept me in the hospital overnight for observation, but when it came time for me to be discharged the next day, it wasn't Mum and Garry that came for me, but a social worker. She told me that my parents' priority now had to be taking care of Ford. She was the one who delivered the news that he was going to be a paraplegic.' He closed his eyes a long moment as if reliving that awful blow. 'She said I'd have to go into foster care as Mum and Garry couldn't look after us both now Ford had such high-care needs. But I knew the truth. Garry had convinced Mum that I was a lost cause and he'd made sure this wasn't temporary.'

Adeline was outraged. 'Surely they couldn't just abandon you?'

Holden shrugged. 'Who knows? But I wasn't going back anyway. I knew Mum would never truly forgive me and that Ford might not either. Hadn't I wanted out of that house anyway?'

She couldn't believe what she was hearing. How could parents turn a child away like that? He might not have been physically broken like Ford, but he was still a kid. She couldn't imagine the pain he must have been in. 'Did you get arrested for stealing the car or … anything?'

'Nah.' He grabbed a biscuit from the tin, and she thought maybe that was all he was going to say, but after scoffing it in two quick mouthfuls, he continued. 'Guess I was lucky that I hit a tree rather than another car. I found out later that Mum convinced Garry not to have me charged, and the policewoman said that paralysing my brother was punishment enough.'

'What was your experience of foster care like?' Adeline asked, her heart tensing with foreboding—everyone had heard horror stories about the system.

'Good actually.' Holden smiled briefly. 'I got given to two awesome people—Stella and Tim. We're still in contact today. They're like surrogate grandparents to the boys. They let me be me. They encouraged me to finish school and made me a part of their family, but at eighteen, they lost their funding for me, and the department needed them to take another kid. There wasn't room for me, so I hit the road. I didn't really know what I wanted to do, so I figured I'd hitchhike around the country, get whatever work I could while I worked out what to do with my life. But it wasn't as easy as I thought. The jobs I got were casual and it was hard to pay rent, never mind get a lease. I ended up on the streets and found myself in a pretty dark place. I got in with a bad crowd, was stealing to make ends meet and pay for drugs and alcohol. I was on a one-way path to self-destruction.'

'So that's why you do it.' Adeline snapped her fingers together. 'Because you've been there yourself. You understand the risks and want to save other kids from going through what you did.'

He nodded solemnly. 'Do you think telling my story will really help?'

'Yes. I do.' But she still had a few questions. 'What saved you? Did someone offer you a tiny house or something?'

'No.' He glanced down at Bella still slumbering on the floor. 'It was Guru.'

She frowned, thinking he'd met some kind of cult leader, and then remembered their earlier conversation. 'Your dog?' she asked, pointing to his tattoo.

'Yeah.' He rubbed his hand over it. 'Finding him gave me something to try for. Something to look after. Someone to be better for. All I can say is that needing to take care of him gave me the push I needed. I didn't care much about myself back then, but I wanted to give Guru the love and security he deserved, so I cleaned up my act and started working harder.'

'He sounds like a really special dog,' she said.

'He was.'

'So that's where the dogs come in around here too?' she asked, looking down to Bella and then into the hallway where Vlad and Merlin were sleeping.

He nodded. 'Guru saved me, and when I decided to start fostering, it just made sense that dogs were part of that.'

'Well, it seems to be working. Where'd the name Guru come from?'

'He was named after the Hoodoo Gurus—I was really into their music at the time. What's your favourite band?'

She could tell it was an attempt to redirect the conversation. He'd had enough of talking about himself. Although she still had so many questions—how had he and Ford reconnected? How had he kept going through all that trauma?—she had enough to get started on. Now that she'd heard his truth, she was willing to forgive him all the grouchiness and standoffishness, and more than ever, she wanted to help him succeed.

'Don't laugh,' she warned him. 'But it's Hanson.'

Of course, he laughed. So hard he almost choked on air.

She glared at him but soon found herself smiling too. It was good to see him relaxing again. 'There's nothing wrong with Hanson.'

'No, you're right. They're better than NSYNC or One Direction. But aren't you a little too young for them? You're what? Twenty-six, twenty-seven?'

'Don't you know it's impolite to ask a lady her age?'

'I'm not asking, I'm guessing.'

She rolled her eyes. 'I'm twenty-nine next Tuesday actually. And I found Hanson's album *Middle of Nowhere* in my mum's CD collection when I was in my teens. I couldn't tell you how many times I played "MMMBop".'

He dropped his head into his hands.

'What?' she demanded.

'This is bad. You're not only a Hanson fan, but their most annoying song is your favourite. It's one of the worst songs of all time.'

'We'll have to agree to disagree on that.' She smirked. 'Anyway, how old are *you*?'

He reached for yet another biscuit, then said, 'How old do you think?' before taking a bite.

She rolled her lips one over the other, pretending to be thinking. 'Fifty-two.'

'I'm thirty-four!' he exclaimed, clearly horrified.

It was her turn to laugh.

'You were having me on, weren't you?'

She winked. 'Maybe, although thirty-four *is* practically ancient. And that beard adds at least ten years.'

'Hey, insult me all you like, but leave the beard out of it.' He whacked her playfully on the arm, then gestured to her now empty mug. 'Can I get you another?'

'Yes, please.'

While he made more coffee, Adeline slipped off to use the bathroom. And wow, she couldn't help but be impressed. It was sparkling, even cleaner than the guest bathroom back home when her mother had visitors coming. When she returned to the table, she packed up the grant stuff and opened the timeline spreadsheet she'd done for the tractor pull. Later tonight, when the other sisters were in bed, she'd use the computer to type up everything he'd told her into a few concise paragraphs they could use for the grant applications, but for now it was on to the fundraiser.

It took them half an hour to divide up the organising jobs between herself, Holden, Ford and the boys.

'I'm going to ask Mike at the *Gazette* for thoughts on who we can approach for initial funding to pay for all the incidentals we need to get the fundraiser off the ground. Could you use your artistic talent to design a poster so we can start soliciting teams?'

'Since you asked me so nicely, of course. Do you really think we can do this in such a short time?' They'd set the date for seven weeks away in the middle of September, before the weather became too hot for the competitors.

'Easy-peasy.' It wasn't like she had other pressing things to do. Now that she'd done a few NunTalk columns she could write them quickly, and the other sisters had all got so involved in Nun-Tok that she could probably palm that off to Michelle, Rita or even Josey if need be. 'Don't underestimate me, Jack.'

He snorted. 'Never.' Then he leaned back in his seat. 'Can I ask you a question?'

She gave him an amused smile. 'Okay.'

'Why'd you *really* become a nun?'

'*That's* the question?' She sighed, annoyed. 'I … I already told you.'

'And I called bullshit, still do. You're young and gorgeous. You could do anything with your life.'

Gorgeous. Her hackles rose. All men ever cared about was her looks.

Adeline put down her pen. 'Why do you care so much what I do with my life?'

'I don't. You can do whatever the hell you like, I'm just trying to understand why someone like you would do *this*.'

'Someone like me?' She laughed bitterly. 'You don't *know* me … so you don't know what I'm like.'

'I know enough. I know that you love your dog more than life itself, but that you care enough about other people to give her up. That shows you're kind. All this—' He gestured to the paperwork spread out on the table, '—shows that you're smart and entrepreneurial.'

Smart? Entrepreneurial? She gulped. Those were two words no man had ever used to describe her.

'I guess it just seems like a waste,' he finished.

'Helping people is never a waste,' she said, still glowing from his compliments. She'd gone from furious to overjoyed in a matter of seconds. Talk about emotional whiplash. 'Isn't that what you're devoting your life to as well?'

'Yeah, I guess.'

Adeline smiled victoriously, thinking she'd won the point, until he added, 'Which proves you don't have to give up having a life, you don't have to give up sex.'

Sex. Whoa.

She gulped at the blasé way he'd dropped such a weighted word into the conversation, but she refused to let it fluster her. 'Why is everyone so hung up on the sex thing? To be honest, I wasn't that into it.'

'What?' Holden recoiled as if she'd hit him. 'You've *had* sex?'

She chuckled at the shock on his face. 'Of course. I'm almost twenty-nine and I only joined the convent this year.'

'How many people have you slept with?'

'Enough to know,' she said. 'It's supposed to be better than chocolate, but I'd choose chocolate over sex any day.'

His eyes bulged. 'You clearly weren't sleeping with the right people.'

'Oh, you'd be surprised by who I've slept with.'

'Someone I'd know?' he asked.

'Maybe,' she said, then immediately regretted it. What was she doing talking about sex with Holden Campbell?

'Someone famous?'

'None of your business,' she replied, but her cheeks burnt.

'Oh my God!' He grinned and slapped his hand against the table, startling all three dogs. 'Who was it?'

'I'm not telling *you*.'

'Prince Harry?'

She snorted and picked up a pen again, determined to get them back on track, but Holden was like a dog with a bone. He kept throwing names at her. 'The Pope?'

'No,' she laughed.

'Chris Hemsworth?'

'I wish.'

'Nick Kyrgios?'

'No thanks.'

He threw his hands up in the air. 'Scomo?'

'Don't be ridiculous. Give me *some* credit. And you may as well give up. I bet you haven't even heard of him.'

'Then what's the harm in telling me?'

She sighed. 'Fine. The last person I slept with was Ryder O'Connell.'

'You *know* Ryder O'Connell? You *slept* with Ryder O'Connell.' Okay, turned out he did know of him. 'He's just a person.'

'How'd you guys meet?'

She told him how Ryder had played at the Walsh Agricultural Show, which she'd helped organise. 'At the end of the night, we had a few drinks together, and one thing led to another. I went back to where he was staying and … we did it.'

'And it wasn't good?' Holden asked, leaning towards her. He was clearly more invested in this conversation than he should be, but perhaps men liked to hear about other men's failings in that department.

'I think he enjoyed it,' she said, 'but let's just say I'm fairly sure he hasn't ever heard of the concept of female pleasure. Maybe he thinks just having slept with *him* is enough of a coup.'

'So it was a one-off?'

She nodded, then reached for a biscuit herself. Turned out talking about sex was as exhausting as having it.

'Must have been bad,' Holden mused, 'if he turned you to celibacy.'

'He wasn't interested in anything more,' she admitted, unable to believe she was actually telling him this.

Holden shook his head and looked right into her eyes. 'Then he must be an idiot as well as a shit lover.'

Adeline's insides twisted. How on earth had they got around to talking about sex when she'd come here to work? *Pull yourself together.*

'Anyway, sleeping with him had nothing to do with becoming a sister.' Not really; it was part of it, but the decision to change her life had been a long time coming. 'Look, we should get back to business. I can't stay much longer.'

'Right. Of course.' Holden nodded as if she'd reprimanded him, and they turned their attentions back to planning.

When they were finished, they had a detailed list of every task that needed to be completed between now and the tractor pull. Adeline also gave him homework, to read the information she'd printed off about forming a legal charity.

'Next meeting Friday, then?' When he nodded, she added, 'I want to interview you for an article in the *Gazette*, but I promise we won't make it too personal. We'll stick to the purpose of the tiny houses and also promote the tractor pull. I'll make it sound so good, no one will want to miss out.'

He stood and saw her to the front door. 'Adeline,' he said as he opened it.

Her heart skipped. Whatever he wanted to say must be serious if he hadn't called her Maria. 'Yes?'

'Do you ...' He shoved his hands in his pockets and took a quick breath. 'Do you mind not talking about Ford's accident to the other nuns or anyone else in town? I know we've got to put it in the forms and such but—'

Without thinking she reached out and touched his forearm and immediately pulled back. Their eyes met. For a moment she forgot what she was going to say. Holden appeared to have lost his train of thought as well.

And then she remembered.

Swallowing, she said, 'I promise I won't tell a soul. And actually, we don't have to put it all on the forms either.' While the event had clearly shaped who he was, it wasn't what mattered here. 'The important part is why the tiny houses project means something to you, and that's because you were a foster kid who lost his way when you aged out of the system. We don't need to explain why you were in care.'

'Thank you, Maria.' The relief on his face was palpable.

She smiled; happy they were back on nickname terms. 'All good, Jack.'

Chapter Twenty-nine

'Morning, Maria,' Holden said as he opened the door on Friday morning. Wearing navy trousers and a black puffer jacket, with the addition of a pink beanie on her head, Adeline stood on the verandah, a smiling Bella already by her side. He hadn't witnessed their reunion this morning, wanting to give her some alone time with the dog.

She grinned at him and tapped her canvas bag, which looked to be bulging with paperwork. 'Morning, Jack. I hope you're ready for hard work.'

'Always.' He tipped an imaginary hat and let her in, Bella following behind.

'It's freaking freezing out there today,' she said as she pulled the beanie off her head.

He couldn't help staring as her hair fell around her face in long honey-gold waves. It was the first time he'd seen her without her hair caught back in a high ponytail, and with her cheeks pink from the cold, she looked even more beautiful—and less like a nun—than usual.

'At least the rain's stopped.' The last few days the weather had been unrelenting. More than once as he'd ridden into Colac to work, he'd almost skidded around a slippery corner.

'Praise God,' she said.

He rolled his eyes. 'Shall we sit in the living room? The fire's roaring in there.'

'Good idea.' She followed him into the room where she dumped her bag on the coffee table and made a beeline for the fireplace. 'Magic,' she said as she rubbed her hands together and then slowly removed each woollen glove, before moving on to her jacket.

Although he knew Adeline didn't mean it to be, it felt like a striptease, and he had to take a moment. 'Can I get you a drink? The usual?'

'Actually, can I have a Milo?' she asked, pausing in the act of undressing.

He nodded and fled into the kitchen, where he placed his hands on the bench and took a deep breath. Ever since she'd told him about her disappointing sex life, he'd barely been able to think about anything else. She couldn't *really* believe that chocolate was better than sex. He reckoned he could change her mind about that. But that wasn't what she was here for, and if he didn't want to ruin their potential friendship, he needed to get a grip.

His reaction to Adeline simply taking off her gloves and jacket was ridiculous.

What was he? *Fifteen?*

Resolving to be on his best behaviour, Holden whipped up two Milos, squeezed cream onto the top and then sprinkled the cream with extra Milo.

'Goodness that looks good,' Adeline exclaimed on his return. She moved away from the fire, took her mug from him and lowered herself onto the couch.

Holden sat diagonally across from her in one of the armchairs.

'I thought we'd divide our time into three sections,' she said after taking her first sip. 'To start with I'll show you what I've done on the grant and if you approve, we can submit a few applications. Then I'll fill you in on the progress I've made getting sponsorship for the tractor pull.'

'You've already got sponsors?'

'You didn't doubt me, did you?' She shook her head. 'Oh ye of little faith. Of course I've got sponsors, but I'll tell you about that when we get to the fundraising section of our meeting. And finally, you can tell me how you're feeling after reading all the charity information.'

He couldn't help smiling at her strict timetable.

'I hope you've done your homework,' she said, raising her eyebrows over the top of her mug.

He was glad to say he had.

'Excellent.' She put her mug down, retrieved a piece of paper, and handed it to him.

'What's this?'

'Read it.'

And so, he did.

'Wow. This is fu—freaking amazing,' he said when he'd finished. It was what she'd written to go in the section on grant applications about why he believed the project was important.

She made the tiny homes he was hoping to build—one-bedroom, single-storey structures, each with a micro kitchen and bathroom—sound like a lifeline for the boys, a halfway point between foster care and independence. During their discussion he'd told her that each one would be built on a small concrete slab and be fully self-contained. There was nothing new here; it was his story, his vision, yet the way she'd written it with such emotion—as if she'd experienced it herself—had him tearing up a little.

'Why aren't you a journalist anymore?' he asked, putting the paper down on the coffee table.

'That's what you have to say after reading that?'

He nodded. 'It's amazing. Thank you.'

She beamed.

'So, *why*?' he prompted.

Her smile dropped. 'It just wasn't for me.'

'I recall you saying that when we spoke at the soup kitchen, but why? What part of it wasn't for you? It obviously wasn't the writing.'

She blushed and looked down at her hands. 'It's stupid. *I* was stupid.'

He saw vulnerability in her eyes and lifted his foot, using it to nudge her knee. 'Hey, we might have only known each other a short time but the last thing you could ever be is stupid.'

She looked then and he saw her eyes were full of tears.

'Oh, Maria.' His heart cracked and he fought the urge to get up and go join her on the couch. 'What happened?'

'When I finished uni, I got a job at a major paper in Perth. I couldn't believe how lucky I was—lots of my classmates couldn't get related employment and ended up working at Coles or doing a DipEd. It was only later that I found out it wasn't my work that got me the job, but my looks.'

He frowned as she continued. 'The editor who hired me was very friendly. Only in hindsight I can see his familiarity for what it really was. He was grooming me. I'd only been there for a few months when he made a pass. When I refused to sleep with him, he fired me.'

'What?' Holden's exclamation was so loud that the dogs all looked up from their beds near the fire. 'That's unfair dismissal. I hope you took him to bloody court!'

She shrugged one shoulder. 'I had no proof. I was on a six-month probation, so he was within his rights. He claimed my work wasn't good enough for a major newspaper.'

'But that was clearly bullshit.'

'I wasn't sure. Maybe I *wasn't* good enough. Anyway, I had to go home because I could no longer afford rent. My grandmother convinced me not to give up journalism completely, but to volunteer at the *Walsh Whisperer,* and I ended up loving it.'

She might have loved it, but that didn't mean she wasn't capable of greater things.

Holden's jaw tensed. He wanted to fly to Perth right that instant and hunt that editor down. How dare he! Holden could only imagine where Adeline would be right now if that bastard hadn't tried to take advantage of her, then knocked her confidence enough to sabotage her career.

'Anyway, what's done is done,' she said firmly. 'I'm happy with my life now. I love being at the convent and if I hadn't come here, I wouldn't be helping you. Everything has turned out how it was meant to.'

Holden wasn't so sure about that, but he let it lie.

They spent the next couple of hours submitting grant applications and setting up a ticketing system online, so teams could start registering for the tractor pull.

When the tickets were live, he reached across and closed the laptop, which was resting on Adeline's knee. 'Lunchtime.'

'Hey,' she objected, 'we've still got heaps to do, and I can eat and work.'

But he shook his head. '*I* need a brain break. Come on.'

With a theatrical sigh, she followed him into the kitchen where he ordered her to sit at the table while he heated up some pea and ham soup and put butter and freshly baked bread on the table.

'Did you make this?' she asked, lifting her spoon.

'No. I have many talents, but cooking is not one of them. Thankfully, I have a Ford.'

She smiled as she tasted the first mouthful, then said, 'I was thinking ...'

'Is this fundraiser, charity or grant stuff?'

She nodded.

'Then ...' He pressed his finger against his lips. 'Hold that thought till after lunch. I told you, we're on a break.'

'Fine.' She stuck her spoon into the soup again.

They spent the next little while talking about silly things— arguing over whose most embarrassing moment was the worst, sharing memories from places they'd travelled, dreaming of places they'd like to—because that's what friends did. Holden figured if he got to know Adeline more as a person, he might be able to stop thinking of her as a woman.

'Do you have any allergies?' Adeline asked as she reached for another slice of bread.

'You mean aside from religion?' he joked.

'I think that's more of a phobia,' she replied dryly.

He nodded. 'I'm allergic to dogs.'

'What?' She glanced at the three canines who'd followed them into the kitchen and were lingering under the table looking for scraps. 'But you love dogs!'

'Yeah. Just because something's bad for you, doesn't mean you can't want it.' How true that felt right now.

'What about you? Are you allergic to anything?'

She shook her head. 'Okay ... phobias? *Aside* from religion.'

'I'm scared of injuring someone I love again,' he blurted, surprising even himself.

'I'm not sure that's a phobia,' she said, softly, 'but it's understandable. Is that why you don't drive?'

'Yep.' But he didn't want to dwell on that. This was supposed to be a fun, light-hearted, getting-to-know-each-other chat. Why couldn't he have just admitted that snakes gave him the heebie-jeebies? 'What do your friends and family think about you becoming a nun?'

'I told you, it's *sister*. Not nun.' She sighed. 'And I didn't really have any friends, but most of my family think I'm crazy. My mum is just waiting for me to come to my senses and my brothers think it's a joke.'

How could someone like her not have any friends? Perhaps the girls she'd known growing up had left town. 'What about your dad?'

'Oh, he doesn't care about anything but his precious cows. It's neither here nor there what I do with my life.'

Sounded like her parents were almost as shitty as his. 'Do your brothers work with him on the farm?'

'Only one of them. I've got two. They're both older and both total jerks. James is on the farm with Dad, and he was married to the most amazing woman—Sally. She's an artist and has done murals similar to the ones on the water tower. They've got two little boys—Levi and Tate—but he cheated on her and now they're getting divorced.'

'Are you and Sally close?'

She nodded. 'Yeah, she's my friend just as much as my sister-in-law.'

'So you *do* have friends,' he exclaimed.

She laughed. 'One. I had *one* friend, but now I have lots. The sisters at the convent have become my friends and family all rolled into one.'

'And you have me too,' he said seriously. 'And Ford. Anyway, why's your other brother a jerk?'

'Max?' She reached for some bread and broke it daintily, as if it had feelings and she didn't want to hurt them. 'Well, he's a defence lawyer—the farm and country life weren't good enough for him but defending murderers and rapists is right up his alley.'

There was so much he wanted to unpack in that sentence, but Adeline hit him with another question.

'You're so good with the boys. Do you think you'll ever have kids of your own?'

He didn't have to think about his answer. 'Nope. Never.'

'Why?'

'I'd rather help ones in need than bring more into it. What about you? Did you ever want a family?'

'Yes,' she admitted. 'I used to, but it was probably because that's just what I thought you did—grow up, get a career, get married, have kids. I'm not sure I'd have been a good mother anyway.'

'Why the hell do you think that?' he asked, reaching for his glass of water.

'My mother isn't very maternal, neither is her mum.'

'I thought you said you were close to your grandmother?' It surprised him how much detail he remembered about every conversation they'd ever had.

'My *dad's* mum. And I was, but ...' Her voice trailed off.

'But what?'

'Nothing,' she said firmly, reaching for her glass of water and downing half of it in one gulp.

Interesting. Now he knew why she'd given up her dreams of journalism, he wanted to know what the deal was with her grandmother. Because there was definitely something.

'Have you ever thought about formal training?' she asked, interrupting his thoughts.

He frowned. 'What do you mean?'

'As well as being a father figure, you're a teacher and a counsellor to these boys and although the way you've turned their lives around should speak for itself, sometimes the bureaucrats who are choosing where to distribute funding put more weight on pieces of paper. If you had a degree in social work, decision-makers might take what you want to do with the tiny houses more seriously.'

'I thought spilling my guts onto the grant form was going to be enough?'

She laughed. 'I think it'll help, but I also think you have a lot more to offer the world than tattoos.'

He raised an eyebrow. 'Art's important. It brings people joy. It connects people and helps them hold onto meaning in their lives. Don't underestimate the power of body art.'

'I love *art*,' she said firmly. 'Although I prefer it on inanimate objects. I told you my sister-in-law's an artist and I'm not saying you have to give up the tattoos; I just think you have more to give. You've been through so much yourself that you'd be perfect to counsel kids who are going through trauma.'

Could he? What if he told them the wrong thing? Then there were all the years of study to get the piece of paper. He'd barely managed to finish high school. He shook his head. 'Nah. I'm not good with books. Besides, a degree would take years, and we need money now.'

'Whatever you think,' Adeline said. 'I just believe you'd be good at it.'

'Thanks,' he replied, 'but this is veering too close to work— and we're supposed to be on a break.'

She glanced at her watch. 'I think our break has been long enough, don't you?' Then she stood and picked up her plate, bowl, glass and cutlery.

He sighed and did the same, joining her at the sink where she was already putting in the plug and starting to fill it with water. 'Leave all this. I'll do it later.'

'If we do it now, you won't have to do it later,' she said, pushing up her sleeves and plunging her hands into the water. 'You dry.'

He stifled a smile. 'Anyone ever told you, you're bossy?'

'You say that like it's a bad thing,' she retorted.

So they stood together at the sink, while Adeline washed their lunch things and Holden dried them, and it felt weirdly right, standing side-by-side doing something so mundane. He had a flash of them doing this often, day after day, night after night. *What the?* He rubbed the tea towel harder than necessary over a bowl. He wasn't planning on doing this forever with anyone. Least of all a nun!

It was her damn shampoo. The smell was going to his head, impinging on his senses. 'What shampoo do you use?'

'What?'

'It's very strong, so I was just wondering.'

She blinked and looked up at him. 'You don't like it?'

He swallowed. Oh, he liked it. He liked it *too* much. 'I didn't say that.'

'We make it at the convent. It's made with lavender and geraniums. We sell it at our store, and at the markets.' She winked up at him. 'I'll get you some if you want, Jack.'

Oh God. Her face was so close to his and all he could think about was kissing her. His chest grew tight, and the room felt claustrophobic as they stared at each other for a few long moments.

'Why'd you call me Jack?' he asked, trying to break the tension.

'Nice try,' she chuckled, but met his gaze head on. 'I told you … I'll never tell.'

'I'll get it out of you eventually,' he said gruffly, unable to tear his eyes from her lips. If she smelled like lavender and geraniums, he could only imagine what she'd taste like.

'Is that a challenge or a threat?'

If he didn't know better, he'd swear she was flirting with him. Could he be any more foolish?

Before he could reply, his phone started ringing.

Saved from insanity by the bell.

He put down the tea towel and then dug the mobile out of his pocket. 'It's Bronte. I better take it.'

'Of course. Go.' Adeline shooed him with her hands. 'I'll finish up here.'

Without another word, he went outside. Maybe the fresh air would clear the craziness from his head.

'Hey Bron,' he said as the screen door banged shut behind him.

'How's my main man?' she asked, and it was so good to hear her voice. She was safe, a comfort.

'I'm great. How's things with you? How's your dad?'

He spoke with Bronte for a good ten minutes and when he came back inside, he found that Adeline had moved their work into the dining room and was sitting at the table typing madly on his laptop.

She looked up as he entered. 'Everything okay?'

He shrugged. 'As good as it can be. Her dad's in a bad way but is refusing to let go. He's not eating and barely drinking anything, so it can't be much longer now. She just needed a distraction for a few minutes. I told her you were here, and she said to say hi. She's stoked I agreed to let you help.'

Adeline beamed. 'Tell her I said hi back next time you speak to her.'

'Will do,' he replied, then sat down to join her. 'Now … where were we?'

Chapter Thirty

'Happy birthday to you, happy birthday to you, happy birthday dear Adeline, happy birthday to you.'

Adeline awoke early Tuesday morning to Michelle singing at the top of her voice. 'Shush,' she said, laughing. 'You'll wake everyone up.'

Michelle shrugged as she picked up her towel and hurried out of the bedroom, no doubt to get one of the two showers before anyone else did.

Adeline smiled and then sighed, lying back in bed and staring up at the ceiling. She was twenty-nine today. When she was younger, she'd expected to be married and living in the city, working at a major newspaper, thinking about starting a family by this age. If anyone had told her she'd be spending her thirtieth year and beyond in a convent, having pledged herself to a life of chastity, obedience and poverty, she'd have laughed so hard her head would probably have fallen off.

But now ... here she was ... and she couldn't be happier.

Finally, her life had purpose, meaning and value. The convent felt more like home than anywhere ever had and the sisters more like family than most of her real family did.

When Michelle returned from the shower, Adeline slipped down the hallway into the bathroom and laughed at the words her friend had written in the steam on the mirror: *Many Happy Returns of the Day.* It was an old-fashioned expression and one her grandmother had favoured.

For a moment, that thought brought with it a nostalgic sadness. This was her first birthday without Penelope. As much as her gran's diary confession had shocked and upset her, they'd shared many special moments over the years, and she couldn't help missing her. Pretty much all her good childhood memories were of her grandmother. Her mum never made much of a fuss of birthdays, but Gran had always baked a special cake and decorated the dining room with streamers and balloons, until the last few years when she'd no longer been capable.

Adeline scrutinised herself for a moment, thinking about how much had changed since this time last year.

If it wasn't for the spiritual crisis brought on by Penelope's death, would she even be here? If she hadn't been so grief-stricken and in shock, feeling like she somehow needed to make amends for Eliza's murder, she'd never have asked God for direction and she'd probably still be living an unsatisfactory existence in Walsh.

The Lord worked in mysterious ways.

After showering and dressing, she returned her things to the bedroom and then she and Michelle hurried down the hallway to the prayer room, passing Benno and Barnabas lingering near the entrance of the kitchen. Mother Catherine and a few of the other sisters were already in the dimly lit room when they entered. No eye contact was made as they joined the others kneeling, and then silently awaited the arrival of Sister Josey and Sister Mary, who were always late.

'Dear Father ...' Mother Catherine began when everyone was present, their rosaries jangling between their fingers.

Although this part of their day was sacred, Adeline's mind kept drifting to other things. She thought about the NunTalk column she needed to write today—after Holden's question about her shampoo, she'd decided to write a feature about the products they made and sold at the convent.

She bit down on a smile at the thought of him. Funny how her first impressions had been totally off the mark. Yes, he could be gruff and grumpy—who wouldn't be a little wary of people after what he'd been through?—but Ford was right; once you got past his rough exterior, he was a really good guy. There was a depth to him she hadn't imagined when they'd first met and he was also heaps of fun to be around.

In addition to being partners on an amazing project, they were friends—he'd said as much on Friday—and knowing this made her heart sing.

'We thank you for bringing Adeline to us ...'

She started from her reverie at Mother Catherine's mention of her name.

'... and pray you will guide her in her journey towards her first vows. Help Adeline to grow closer to you and help us to nourish her on this path. We pray for a lovely birthday, a time where she can reflect on what you have given her thus far and how she can love and serve you every day for the rest of her life. In the name of the Father, the Son and the Holy Spirit, Amen.'

After prayer and breakfast, everyone went about their business— Sister Josey heading off to the prison, Sister Mary to the school, and Sister Rita to the hospital—and Adeline commandeered the computer to write her column. It was lunchtime by the time she'd emailed it to Mike, and then she and the remaining sisters ate soup at the outside table because the sun was shining briefly and they wanted to make the most of it before it disappeared again.

She spent the afternoon tending the garden and making Tik-Toks with Michelle. She was almost ready to go inside and clean up when a head full of messy red hair appeared over the fence.

'Adeline!'

'Hi Rocky. What are you doing here?' she said, pushing to her feet.

'It's … it's Bella,' he cried.

Her heart shot to her throat. 'Is something wrong? She's not in labour, is she?' There were still a few weeks until the puppies were due.

'Umm … don't know.' He shrugged, then looked down at his hands. 'Holden says you should probably come.'

'Go,' ordered Michelle. 'I can manage dinner by myself.'

'You sure?' Adeline asked. It was her turn to help.

Michelle nodded. 'The birthday girl shouldn't have to do the cooking anyway.'

'Thanks,' Adeline said. It would be the worst birthday ever if anything happened to Bella.

She tried to ask Rocky what exactly the problem was as they hurried down the road, but he barely said a word and she didn't press him too much because she knew he must be worried sick too.

When they got to Holden and Ford's place, it was almost eerily quiet. Even on the days when it was only her and Holden, there'd always been a dog or two to greet her in the front yard.

'Where is everyone?' she asked.

'Inside with Bella,' was Rocky's quick and solemn reply.

She quickened her already fast pace as she raced towards the house. It must be bad if *everyone* was with her. 'Has someone called the vet?'

Rocky didn't reply as he shucked off his boots at the front door.

Adeline pushed it open and went inside. The house was also deathly silent.

'They're in the dining room,' Rocky said, coming up behind her.

Even before she'd flung open the door, the room erupted with shouts of 'Surprise!' and 'Happy birthday!'

She froze in the doorway as tiny streamers rained down upon her from party poppers. Bella rushed over from the other side of the room where she'd been standing with Vlad and Merlin, and she looked as healthy as ever. As well as Holden, Ford, Rocky, Sam and Toovs, Mitch and Luka were also there. The guys were surrounded by balloons, and on the wall behind them hung a massive multicoloured Happy Birthday banner.

'Oh, my goodness,' Adeline shrieked and then promptly burst into tears.

'That's not the reaction we were hoping for,' said Ford from his wheelchair, a party blower in his hand.

She laughed through her tears. 'No. Sorry. This is ...' She sniffed, smiling so hard it hurt. 'This is such a wonderful surprise. Thank you.'

Holden stepped forward and reached out to pick the streamers from her hair. 'Happy birthday, Maria. I mentioned it was your birthday to Ford and the boys yesterday and we weren't sure if nuns celebrated, so we thought ... since you're helping us out, throwing you a party was the least we could do.'

'Thank you.' She smiled up at him, then looked to the table, which was overflowing with food. There were little red cock-tail sausages and tomato sauce, sausage rolls and pies, rainbow popcorn, jelly cups, honey joys, chocolate crackles and fairy bread. Adeline couldn't remember the last time she'd had fairy bread. 'You've thought of everything.'

'We each chose our favourite party food,' Rocky said, now beaming.

'Which is yours?' she asked.

'The red sausages. My mum used to call them little boys.'

They all laughed, then Adeline said, 'You should be an actor, Rocky. You looked so grave when you told me to come, I thought Bella was dying or something.'

He sighed and ran a hand through his unruly hair. 'It was awful. I'm such a shit liar, but Holden said you were more likely not to suspect me.'

Adeline smiled at Holden. 'He was right.'

Their eyes met for a few moments and her cheeks heated, then suddenly he cleared his throat. 'Enough chitchat. Let's eat.'

The boys stood back to let Adeline fill her plate first, then they all took their food out onto the verandah. Ford sat in his wheelchair, and she and Holden sat in the seats that he and Bronte had been sitting in the night she'd met them. The boys plonked themselves on old milk crates and the dogs weaved between them all, desperately hoping scraps would fall to the floor.

'So how old are ya, Adeline?' asked Sam, before shoving a sausage roll into his mouth.

'Don't you know it's impolite to ask a lady her age,' Holden scolded.

She laughed. 'I'm twenty-nine.'

While they ate, conversation turned to the tractor pull. The boys were super excited and eager to help. Toovs, Sam, Mitch and Luka were even planning on entering a team. As late afternoon became evening, the temperature dropped dramatically. Adeline shivered and rubbed her hands together to try and warm up.

'You cold?' Holden asked.

She shrugged. 'A little. I left home in such a hurry; I didn't think to bring my jacket.'

He went inside and returned a few moments later with a black puffer jacket. It was almost identical to her own, except that it was much, much bigger. 'Here.'

'Thanks,' she said as she took it, then slipped her arms inside, one after the other. It smelled of him—something earthy and a little spicy—and she had to resist the urge to turn her head and bury her nose in the shoulder.

When the food was gone, the boys started kicking a footy around out the front. Adeline glanced at her watch and realised it was nearing evening prayers, which meant she'd missed dinner, but Michelle would have told the others about Rocky and they'd be worried about Bella.

'I should probably be going,' she said, standing as she looked from Ford to Holden. 'Thanks so much for today.'

'We haven't had the cake yet,' Holden protested.

'Cake?' Adeline didn't know how she could possibly eat another thing. 'You made me a cake?'

Holden nodded. 'Well, Ford did but I decorated it.'

Now she was curious.

'Boys!' he yelled. 'Cake time.'

The ball was abandoned as they all hurried back inside and gathered around the dining table.

'Back in a sec,' Holden promised before heading to the kitchen.

'Don't forget the matches,' called Ford.

He returned with a large cake, shaped like a person, and decorated like a nun dressed in a traditional habit. The cake had an uncanny resemblance to Adeline.

'Wow. That's …' She laughed, unable to find the words. 'I told you you're wasted on tattoos. Perhaps you should take up cake decorating for a living.'

'I wouldn't do this for just anyone,' he said as he began to light the candles. 'Happy birthday to our favourite nun.'

'Sister,' she corrected as everyone echoed his sentiments.

'Whatever, Maria,' he said with a mischievous grin.

When the candles were lit, they sang 'Happy birthday'. Adeline couldn't remember a time when she'd felt so … so full. In her heart *and* stomach.

'I'll walk you to the gate,' Holden offered, when she insisted that she really must go.

She said goodbye to Ford and the boys. Rocky brought Bella over for a quick hug, but when Adeline and Holden left the house, boy and dog stayed inside.

'Do you miss her?' Holden asked as they started down the driveway.

'I do. But I know she's happy and I can see the change in Rocky, so my heartache is worth it.'

'You can have one of the puppies. The boys already want us to keep them all and that is *not* going to happen.'

She laughed at the image of up to ten puppies running riot around Holden's property. 'Maybe. I'll have to talk to Mother Catherine about it. Not sure what Benno and Barnabas will think though. They seem quite happy to see the back of Bella.'

'Benno and who?' he asked.

'They're the convent cats,' she explained. 'After St Benedict and St Barnabas. All our animals are named after Catholic saints.'

'Of course they are.'

She chuckled at his tone. Since starting to work together, they'd unofficially agreed not to talk religion.

'Well, thank you,' she said, pausing as they came to the end of the drive. 'You made this my best birthday ever.'

'Seriously?' Holden asked with a lift of an eyebrow.

She nodded. 'It was really special. Thank you.'

'You're welcome,' he said, staring intently down at her.

Oh, but he was gorgeous. She swallowed, cursing herself for thinking such wicked thoughts.

'Okay. Well, bye.' She started to take off his jacket, but he held up his hand and shook his head. 'Keep it for your walk home. You can bring it back next time.'

'Thank you.'

'It looks good on you,' he whispered, so softly she wasn't sure she hadn't imagined it.

And then, before she knew what was happening, Holden's lips were on hers.

His hands landed on her hips, drawing him against her as her own fingers moved from his shoulders up into his hair. Their mouths opened, their tongues danced, and she wasn't sure if the moan came from him or her, but the feeling of his body pressed against hers had her nerve endings buzzing and pleasure ricocheting through her.

His hair was surprisingly soft, much softer than she'd imagined in her fantasies.

A sudden cold flooded her. This *wasn't* a fantasy. She froze—it didn't matter that it was the most magical kiss of her life, it was wrong—and then tore her lips from his.

Chapter Thirty-one

'Oh my God,' Adeline cried. '*Shit!* I'm not supposed to use the Lord's name in vain. Or swear.' She slapped her palms against her cheeks, which had turned a delicious shade of crimson. 'Holy hell, I can't believe you did that. You had no right!'

Holden couldn't help smirking, even though she was accusing him of untoward behaviour. 'I think if we replay the footage, we'll find that *you* kissed *me*.'

'What?' She took a step back and her mouth dropped open.

He nodded as he recalled the way those lips had felt as she'd pressed them against his. She'd tasted better than he'd imagined in his wildest dreams.

Her eyes widened.

'Anyway, who cares who started it? I'm more concerned with why we're not still doing it,' he said, and reached out to pluck another errant bit of streamer from her hair.

Adeline flicked his hand away like he was a pesky blowfly.

'Don't touch me.' Her chest heaved as she pushed her hands against him to hold him back. 'And don't even think about kissing me!'

He couldn't help but pout. It was like tasting bacon for the first time and then being told you could never have it again. 'Why not?'

'Because I'm a nun!' she cried, throwing her hands into the air.

'I thought you were a sister. Actually, I thought you were a postulant, which means you haven't taken any vows yet. So don't get your knickers in a knot. You haven't done anything wrong.'

'Yes, I have!' She looked close to tears, but this time they weren't joyful ones.

'Hey, relax.' He put his hand on her shoulder. 'You look like you're about to have an aneurysm. Take a breath. It's not like I've seen you naked or anything.'

Although he could imagine.

'What about Bronte?' she shrieked. 'Not only have I gone against my beliefs, but now you've cheated on her with me. I *like* Bronte. She's a good person. And if I really *did* kiss you first, then it's my fault. Oh God ... I really am the most awful p—'

'Maria. Chill,' he ordered, starting to worry about the state she was working herself into. 'You can have your Catholic guilt if you must, but you don't need to worry about Bronte. We're not together.'

'What?' She shook her head. 'But ... Toovs said ... And before she went to see her dad, she was always here. Did you break up? Was it because of me?'

'No, she's always here because she's my best mate.'

Adeline blinked. 'So, you don't sleep together?'

He raised an eyebrow and gave her a sheepish grin.

'Actually, don't answer that,' she rushed. 'It's none of my business.'

But Holden had nothing to hide. 'We have been known to,' he said. 'On occasion. But it's not what you think. We're what I guess you'd call—'

'Fuck buddies?' she interrupted, her cute button nose crinkling.

He chuckled. 'I was actually going to say, "friends with benefits", and anyway, I thought you weren't supposed to swear.'

'Oh koala.' She slapped her hand over her mouth. 'I'm going to hell.'

He smirked. *'Koala?'*

Adeline looked close to tears as she explained. 'It's what I'm trying to say whenever I feel the need to curse, but right now, I don't think koala is strong enough.'

'Maria, I don't think koala is *ever* strong enough,' he said, thinking about how much he wanted to kiss her again.

Hell, he wanted to do a whole lot more with her, but … the bottom line was he liked her and he didn't want to play games.

Somehow, he was going to have to resist his carnal urges and respect her wishes.

'I've got to go,' she said, clutching her bag to her chest as if it was a shield for protection.

'Maria,' he said. 'I'm sorry things got a little heated.'

'A little?' She whimpered at his words and he couldn't recall any woman ever looking this desolate after locking lips with him.

'Yeah. A little,' he tried to reassure her. 'It was just a kiss.' Albeit a very good one.

'Whatever it was, it *can't* happen again. Even if you're not with Bronte, nothing can ever happen between us. You understand that, right?'

He nodded. 'Yep. Crystal clear. As long as *you* can control your wanton urges and don't kiss me like that again, I most definitely can, but do you think maybe this is a sign?'

'What do you mean?'

'Well, maybe you kissing me is a sign that you shouldn't be joining the convent. That it isn't the right fit for you.'

Her eyes widened in fury. 'This was *not* a sign, Holden. This was nothing but a temporary lapse in sanity. I promise you, I will never, *ever* kiss you again!'

He wasn't sure who she was trying to convince but she'd better mean it, because there was only so much he could take. It was bad enough when he'd thought the attraction was one-sided, but no matter what she said, now he knew that it wasn't.

You couldn't kiss someone like that if you weren't into them.

'Excellent,' he said, shoving his hands in his pockets. 'In that case, see you Friday for our next meeting?'

'Yes.' She licked her lips. 'See you then.'

And then she turned and hurried down the road as if she couldn't get away from him fast enough.

Fuck. Holden let out a long, deep sigh and ran his hands through his hair, his whole body tight with desire. He needed Adeline to help him with the fundraiser, but how the hell was he supposed to work with her after this?

He'd lied when he told her it was just a kiss.

Truth was it was the best damn kiss of his whole life.

Chapter Thirty-two

Adeline couldn't believe what had just happened. Had Holden been telling the truth? Had *she* really just kissed *him?*

And if so, was he right? Could her impulsive actions be a sign?

No. She refused to believe it.

Nothing had ever felt as right as being part of the Smallton convent.

Nothing except your lips on Holden's.

And if a simple kiss felt that good, imagine what a little bit more might feel like.

'Stop it,' she scolded the voices inside her head. No good could come from thinking those kinds of thoughts.

But it had been so much easier to ignore her feelings when she'd thought he was in a relationship with Bronte.

Now that she knew about their arrangement ...

No. She shook her head. Now *nothing*. This didn't change anything!

They could do what they liked, but she loved her life at the convent and was not going to throw it all away for what might be nothing but a brief fling or a one-night stand. She'd have to go to confession but then ... *Oh koala.*

What if Father told Mother Superior and she was asked to leave?

Bile rose in Adeline's throat. Could she have been any more foolish? Why did she keep making mistakes with men over and over again?

You don't have to tell anyone.

Once again that little voice tried to lure her to the dark side.

Shame filled her from her toes right up to the burning tips of her ears. Of course she had to tell Mother Catherine, but how could she sit through evening prayers with the older woman's disappointed gaze trained on her? That's if she wasn't sent packing immediately.

Thankfully, Sister Rita was in the garden putting away the chickens when Adeline got back.

'Well, well, well, look what the cat dragged in. Hope Bella's okay, but we missed you for your birthday dinner.'

'Sorry, Rita,' she said, hoping the tears she'd shed on her way home hadn't made her eyes bloodshot and her face puffy. 'Can you tell Mother Catherine I'm sorry, but I won't be coming to prayer? I'm not feeling well.'

She would speak to her in the morning once she'd had time to think.

Rita's face immediately morphed from her usual cheerful expression to one of concern. 'Are you okay?' she asked as she shut the gate of the pen. 'Is Bella okay?'

'Yes. Bella's fine. I ... It was a ruse. Holden ...' She could barely bring herself to say his name. 'He and the boys made me a birthday cake.'

'Oh, that's so sweet. They're clearly grateful for all you're doing for them.'

'Yeah …' Her chest tightened with guilt. She didn't deserve Rita's praise. 'Anyway, I'm not feeling very well now. Maybe I ate too much, but I think I might be sick.'

This wasn't a lie, although her nausea wasn't due to too much fairy bread, sausage rolls and cake.

Rita grimaced sympathetically. 'Oh, you poor darling. Go. I'll let everyone know and come and check on you later.'

'Thanks,' Adeline managed and then slunk into the house and into her bedroom where she fell to her knees on the edge of the bed and clasped her hands together in front of her.

'Father, forgive me for I have sinned. I know you know what I've done, but I just want to say I'm so sorry I succumbed to temptation.'

She couldn't loathe herself more if she'd kissed the devil himself.

She prayed for Mother Catherine's forgiveness and asked God to give her the words that showed how truly sorry she was for what she'd done. She considered telling Mother Catherine that Holden had been the one to initiate the kiss, because surely the older woman couldn't hold *his* actions against her! But … lying would only exacerbate her guilt. If she truly wanted forgiveness, then she needed to own her actions.

'Are you okay?'

Adeline jumped at the sound of Michelle's voice behind her. 'Haven't you heard of knocking?'

'Uh, it's my bedroom too—I don't have to knock. I just came to see how you were doing.' She peered down at Adeline and then made a face. 'Rita said you were sick, and you certainly look like it. Something you ate?'

'Something I kissed,' Adeline blurted before she could think better of it.

'What? Oh goodness.' Michelle pressed her hand against her chest and then lowered herself onto her bed as if her legs could no longer hold her. 'Who?'

'Holden.'

'Holden *Campbell*?'

'How many Holdens do you think I know?' Adeline snapped and then immediately regretted taking out her guilt on her friend. 'Sorry, but yes.'

'Wow.' Michelle blinked and then let out a long whistle. 'I told you he was dangerous.'

'Not helpful,' Adeline sobbed, pulling herself up onto her own bed and leaning against the wall. She hugged her knees to her chest.

'Well?' Michelle demanded.

'Well, what?'

'Was it any good?'

Was it good?! Good didn't even come close—it was the best kiss of her life—but she wasn't going to kiss and tell. 'That doesn't matter. I shouldn't have done it. We were just … it had been a lovely afternoon and he walked me down the driveway. He'd given me his jacket because I was cold, and he told me it looked good on me and … next thing I knew I was kissing him.'

'*You* kissed him, not the other way around?'

Adeline rubbed her lips together a few moments, her mind drifting to the kiss as she tried to replay it. But although this made her body temp soar again, she found no further clarity. 'I think so,' she admitted. 'It's kind of a blur, but he definitely kissed me back.'

'Of course he did,' Michelle scoffed. 'And you may have kissed him, but he had no right to tell you that you looked good in his jacket. What kind of man flirts with a sister?'

Adeline opened her mouth to defend him, but then realised how that might sound.

'Is that his jacket you're wearing?' asked Michelle, nodding towards it like it was a coat made from the fur of an endangered native animal.

'Yes.' She shrugged out of it, conscious again of the smell of him that wafted all around her.

Michelle stood, and Adeline could feel the disappointment radiating off her in waves. 'I'd better get to prayer. Hope you feel better soon.'

'What do you think Mother Catherine is going to say?' Adeline called anxiously as Michelle reached for the door handle.

The younger woman slowly turned back to look at her. 'Are you in love with him?'

Adeline recoiled, almost banging her head on the wall at the question. 'Of course not.'

She'd barely known him five minutes. How could she be in love with him?

'Do you want to kiss him again?'

Adeline deliberated only a moment. 'No.' Which was the truth, because although her hormones wouldn't mind another brush with his lips, her heart and head were one hundred percent in opposition to the idea.

Michelle nodded and then smiled. 'Good, because if you were planning another pash-fest, then perhaps you should reconsider whether this is really the life for you. We sisters can't go around kissing men willy-nilly, but if you're definitely not in love with him—if the kiss truly was an error of judgement, a mistake—then maybe it should stay between you and God.'

Adeline couldn't believe what she was hearing. 'Are you saying I shouldn't tell Mother Catherine? That *you* won't tell her?'

Michelle took a moment and Adeline's stomach twisted as she waited for her friend to change her mind, but then she shook her head. 'Ask the Lord for forgiveness, forgive yourself, and then move on. This can be our little secret, but if it happens again—'

'It won't,' Adeline cut in.

Although she wasn't usually much of a hugger, she leapt off the bed and threw her arms around her roomie, almost knocking her off her feet.

'You better not let me down,' Michelle warned, extracting herself.

'Thank you,' Adeline said as Michelle started towards the door. 'I promise I'll stay on the straight and narrow from now on.'

Chapter Thirty-three

It was fully dark; the older boys had gone home, and the younger ones were getting ready for bed by the time Holden finally returned. Sweat pouring off his forehead and his shirt soaked, he headed straight for the kitchen to grab a glass of cold water.

'You took your time,' Ford said, rolling into the room as Holden was gulping down the drink.

'Sorry. Decided to go for a run.' After the kiss, he'd needed to clear his head.

Ford raised his eyebrows but if he wanted any more information he was out of luck. As close as they were, Holden wasn't going to tell his brother what had happened, or he'd never hear the end of it. Ford would think him kissing a nun hilarious, or he'd try to make out like it meant more than it did.

Like it meant *something*.

'I've been trying to call you,' Ford said. 'I was about to send one of the boys out to look for you.'

'I'm a grown man. You don't need to worry about me if I disappear for a short while. I can look after myself.'

'I wasn't *worried* about you. Bronte's been trying to get hold of you.'

Holden's body turned to ice as he glanced over to his phone, still on the kitchen bench where he'd left it earlier. He knew what Ford was going to say even before he said it.

'Her father passed away a couple of hours ago.'

'Shit.' He put his now empty glass down on the bench and snatched up his phone. 'How'd she sound?'

'How'd you think? She's heartbroken. I tried to offer comfort but it's you she wants to talk to.'

Guilt swamped him. Even though she'd known her father's death was imminent, Bronte would be hurting. And he'd been out kissing Adeline while his best friend needed him. He took the phone onto the verandah and sank into his chair. The air was bitter cold, but he was still hot from his run. His pulse slowed as he waited for Bronte to pick up.

She did so after a few rings. 'Hey.'

'Oh, Bron.' His heart broke at the anguish and pain in her voice. 'I'm so sorry.'

She sniffed. 'I've been trying to call for ages. Where were you?'

He swallowed. Although he and Bronte weren't an item—he hadn't lied about that—it still felt like a betrayal. 'I just went for a run.'

'Since when do you go running?' she asked accusingly.

'Just decided to start. I'm not getting any younger, so thought I'd better do some proper exercise to ward off the middle-age spread.'

If this was a video call, Bronte would be able to tell he was lying, but instead she laughed loudly. 'That's the most hilarious thing I've ever heard. I didn't know you were so vain, Holden.'

'It's also a good de-stress at the end of a hard day.'

'Well, next time take your phone with you,' she ordered. 'Buy one of those armband thingies if you have to.'

'Good idea.' He waited a few moments for her to speak again, but when she didn't, he said, 'Were you with Bill when he passed?'

'Yeah; Mum too. It was really peaceful, actually. We were both holding his hands when he took his last breath.'

'That's good. How is Tricia?'

'Devastated. And in shock. I am too. Like, logically I know it's real … I know he's gone, but I can't really believe it. I just wish …' She paused and he could tell she was crying. 'I just wish I'd … visited more. But he wasn't old, and we thought he'd beat the cancer. I thought I had more time. I thought he'd live forever.'

Holden knew there were no words that would comfort her, and silently cursed the distance between them. 'Are you still at the hospital?'

'Uh-huh, but tomorrow we're going back to Middle of Nowhere until the funeral. The staff have been great, but we can't leave them on their lonesome forever.'

'Do you know when the funeral will be?'

'Not sure yet. Probably next week sometime.'

'And will it be in Darwin?'

'Yeah, I guess.'

'Well, keep me posted. I'll try to get there for it.'

'You're gunna come to the funeral?' she said, her tone surprised but hopeful.

'I'd like to.' If he could organise everything here so Ford and the boys would be okay. 'I want to give you and your mum a hug. I want to support you while you support her. That's if you want me to.'

'I'd love that.'

Holden could tell she was crying again, and he felt so helpless here, thousands of kilometres away, unable even to pass her tissues.

'And Mum will be stoked,' she added. 'Dad loved you like a son, and she does too, but I don't want you to feel guilty if you can't. I know it's not easy for you to just drop everything.'

'I'll be there,' he promised.

'Thanks, Holden. You're such a good friend, but I better go check on Mum now.'

'Give her my love.'

'I will,' she said. 'Love you.'

'Love you too, babe,' he told her, and then disconnected.

* * *

The next afternoon, his flights booked, his bag packed, and every-thing organised for the next week for Ford and the boys, Holden climbed on his motorbike to begin the ride to Melbourne airport, stopping via Smallton convent on his way out of town. He'd con-templated sending one of the boys down after school with a note, but that seemed like a cowardly thing to do. If there was any hope of things getting back to normal between him and Adeline, of them settling into any kind of friendship, then he needed to not make a big thing about talking to her.

It would be best for them both if they could just pretend the kiss never happened.

He chuckled awkwardly to himself as he lifted his hand to ring the bell on the convent's massive door. If you'd told him a month ago that he'd ever visit this place, he'd have laughed out loud, and now he'd been here three times in just over a week.

Once again, Michelle answered. He almost asked if she was their official butler, but her cool expression and the way she said 'Holden' told him she wasn't in the mood for jokes.

Had Adeline told her about the kiss? Did they all know?

He pushed that thought aside, feeling oddly nervous, which was ridiculous. He was a grown man—who cared who knew? Besides, he hadn't done anything wrong. 'I need to speak to Adeline.'

Michelle folded her arms across her chest. 'I'm not sure that's a good idea.'

He sighed—that answered his question then. 'Look, I'm not here to make trouble. I just need to talk to her quickly about the tractor pull.'

Michelle tapped her fingers against her lips as she deliberated, then said, 'Fine. Be right back,' before slamming the door in his face.

He took a step back. He wasn't the only one startled by the noise.

Two black cats who had been sleeping on the porch rockers jumped off the chairs and glared up at him with sharp, yellow eyes.

'Hey boys. You must be Benno and Barnabas,' he said, stooping down to stroke them.

One of them immediately stalked off, but the other rubbed himself against Holden's fingers for a few seconds before sinking his teeth into him.

'Ouch!' He yanked his hand back. This was why he preferred dogs. You always knew where you stood with them, whereas cats were more like women. Hot one moment, icy the next. He shook his finger and winced at the bite mark.

'What are you doing here?'

Distracted by the cats, he hadn't heard the door, but now he turned to see Adeline a couple of feet away. If possible, she looked even more gorgeous than usual. She literally took his breath away, until he saw Michelle standing directly behind her, glaring in much the same way as the cats had.

'I ... uh ... came to see how you were, after ...' He stammered under the younger woman's unnerving gaze. 'After yesterday.'

Adeline's whole face turned red, and her eyes narrowed. 'I don't want to talk about it,' she hissed. 'I'm fine.'

'Okay then.' Maybe he *should* have sent a note. 'I also came to let you know that I'll be away the next few days, maybe up to a week. If there's anything that needs to be done regarding the fundraiser, Ford and the boys can help.'

'Where are you going?'

'I'm heading to Middle of Nowhere. Bronte's dad passed away yesterday afternoon.'

Adeline's standoffish expression softened immediately. She indicated for Holden to follow her into the front garden. 'I'm sorry to hear that,' she said, once they were out of Michelle's ear-shot, but not her view. 'Is she okay? Are *you*?'

'She's as good as can be expected. And I'm sad, but more worried about her and her mum. They're a very close-knit family.'

Adeline nodded. 'Please give her my love.'

'I will,' he promised, trying not to stare at her lips. It was almost impossible to talk to her without thinking about their kiss.

'Will Ford and the boys be okay without you?'

'Yeah. Ford's got a full day of appointments today but he'll cut his hours back a bit after that to be there when the boys need him, to make sure they're pulling their weight around the house and so he can help with their homework.'

'But what about ...' Adeline rubbed her lips together a little, not at all helping his resolve. '*Him*?'

She placed great emphasis on this last word, making Holden realise she was talking about Ford's more private requirements.

'There's a local retired nurse who comes to help if I'm ever not available.'

'Okay, that's great.' Adeline fiddled with her ponytail, reminding him of when her hands were in his hair only yesterday afternoon. It seemed forever ago, yet he could still taste her like it had only just happened.

He wondered if she too was remembering their kiss. If he wasn't acutely aware of Michelle watching them like a hawk, he might not have been able to stop himself dipping his head and enacting a replay.

'Is there … anything else?' she asked eventually.

'No.' He shoved his hands in his pockets. 'I better be going. Don't wanna miss my plane.'

'Travel safe,' she said. 'I'll pop over to your place to visit Bella this afternoon and let Ford know that if he or the boys need anything they can call here.' She glanced briefly back to Michelle. 'The sisters and I would be happy to help out.'

'Thank you,' he said, swallowing the instinct to reject her offer. 'I really appreciate that.'

He turned to go but found he couldn't. Not without at least trying to clear the air between them. 'I really am sorry for yesterday,' he said in almost a whisper.

'You don't need to apologise.' Her mouth set in a hard line. 'It was entirely my fault.'

Holden wanted to ease her guilt—to tell her that technically she might have initiated the kiss but he'd been a willing participant and if she hadn't made the first move, he more than likely would have done so himself.

'Let's not play the blame game,' he said. 'I just hope it doesn't come between us.'

'I'm not going to let it affect the tractor pull,' she said sharply.

'That's not what I meant. I really enjoy spending time with you and I hoped we might be able to be friends.' He didn't know if that was possible, but he genuinely wanted to try. Now that she was in his life, he couldn't bear the thought of her not being in it.

'Oh. I see.' And then the corner of her mouth lifted, and she gave him a half smile. 'I guess we could give that a go.'

Chapter Thirty-four

The flight from Melbourne landed in Darwin just after midnight, and the place where Holden had rented a motorbike wasn't open until the morning, so he caught a taxi to the nearest motel and crashed the moment his head hit the pillow. He'd barely slept in the last forty-eight hours and when he woke the sun was blazing through the windows as he'd forgotten to close the curtains. He rolled over and saw the time flashing 10:05 on the ancient digital alarm clock on the bedside table. *No way.* He couldn't remember the last time he'd slept this late. No wonder he was starving.

After a quick shower, a phone call to Ford to check on the boys, and an apology to reception that he'd slept past checkout, he grabbed a big breakfast at a café on the way out of town and then hit the highway south. It was just over five hundred kilometres from Darwin to Middle of Nowhere, but he'd learned when he'd lived here that no one thought anything of distances like this in the Northern Territory. Aside from the annoyance of having to overtake road trains and enormous caravans towed by grey nomads in four-wheel drives, there was nothing quite like riding a motorbike in such a picturesque part of the country. The sky was a clearer blue than anywhere else in Australia, contrasting with the deep red of the earth and the crocodile-green native shrubbery on either side of the Stuart Highway.

But although he admired the scenery as he rode, he only stopped when he needed to pee, desperate to get to Bronte to comfort her and Tricia, and to help out behind the bar or in whatever capacity they needed. It wasn't right that they had to soldier on in the midst of such raw grief.

The journey gave Holden plenty of time to think. He thought about the boys, about the tiny houses project. He thought about Adeline and that one scorching kiss. He thought about Bronte and Tricia and about how Bill's death would leave not only a gaping hole in their hearts but also in the business. How would Tricia manage on her own?

He was starving again by the time he finally slowed on the outskirts of the tiny town that was Middle of Nowhere. If it wasn't for the tavern and roadhouse, it would be a blink-and-you-miss-it place. Aside from the main building and motel rooms behind it, the 'town' consisted of little more than a handful of mostly deserted old shacks.

It had been years since he'd last been here, but the old place looked the same from the outside—he chuckled as usual at the 'Macca's Drive Thru—557 km' sign and all the other 'junk' that gave this place unrivalled character.

Nothing much had changed on the inside of the tavern either. There were still massive water buffalo horns on the wall behind the bar and bras hanging from the ceiling, left by tourists since a barman had a bet with a backpacker way back in the eighties. And a whole heap of other memorabilia too. It was rare that anyone stopped in at the Nowhere Tavern without leaving a token of their appreciation, be it a cap, a business card pinned to the bar, postcards, stickers or a flag. Some even left number plates. Not a surface inside or outside was left bare.

It still looked like the place that had been Holden's home for a while long ago, but knowing Bill wasn't here made it feel almost like a foreign country. It also felt strange being here without Guru—when he'd lived and worked here, his dog had been like a shadow. He hovered in the doorway of the tavern, thinking of the man who'd been more of a father to him than his own dad or his stepdad could ever hope to be, and the dog who'd turned his life around, then headed inside.

It was just after four o'clock, yet a lot of travellers had already pulled over for the night—either to take a room out the back or to park their caravans—and most of them appeared to be inside enjoying Happy Hour, which he remembered was actually two hours from four to six every day. Behind the long bar were two blonde women who looked to be in their very early twenties. Sitting on the other side of it was someone who had to be a ghost, because he'd looked no less than a hundred when Holden worked here.

'Tony?' he asked hesitantly as he put a hand on the old bloke's shoulder.

The grey-haired, grey-bearded man turned his head to look at Holden and frowned a second before his eyes sparked and a smile moved his beard upwards. 'Holden?'

'You *remember* me?'

'Never forget a face. Guess you're here because of Bill.'

Holden nodded.

'Damn shame. Bill was like a son to me, and sons aren't supposed to go first.' Tony lifted his pint glass to his mouth.

One of the blonde bartenders greeted Holden with a 'Hey! Welcome to Nowhere. What can I get for you?' She had some kind of Scandinavian accent.

'Um … is Bronte around?' he asked.

'Holden used to work here,' supplied Tony gruffly, wiping froth from his beard with the back of his hand.

'Oh.' The bartender's eyes lit up. 'You're Holden? Bronte and Tricia talk about you all the time. Is she expecting you?'

Holden shook his head and the girl squealed, then turned and ran out the back.

Less than a minute later, Bronte appeared through the multi-coloured plastic strips that hung above the doorway between the bar and the back office. She froze, blinked, and then shook her head before racing around the bar and launching herself at him.

'Oh my God! What the hell are you doing here?' she yelled as he let his backpack fall to the floor so he could catch her in his arms.

'Told you I was coming.'

'But you said for the funeral. And that only just got finalised. I was about to give you a call.'

'Well, I'm here now so you don't have to, but tell me this,' he whispered low in her ear. 'How the hell is Tony still alive?'

She laughed through tears. 'He'll tell you that an apple a day might keep the doctor away but a pint a day keeps the Grim Reaper away.'

'The way I remember it, it was a fair few more than one pint.'

Bronte shrugged as she let him go. 'And people say beer's bad for you. Speaking of, would you like one?'

There was nothing he felt like more after the long ride, that and maybe a plate of Nowhere's famous BBQ beef and barra. 'Kill for one, but I'll get it myself,' he said, slipping behind the bar and leaning his backpack against the wall. 'Where's Tricia?'

'Having a lie down,' Bronte replied.

Holden could only imagine how lost Tricia must feel without Bill. Not only had they been best friends and lovers, but they'd worked together almost every day of their married life. Whereas Bill had always said he'd be like Tony—living in Middle of Nowhere till his last breath—Tricia had hoped that one day they could sell the business and retire. Do a road trip around Australia like so many of the seniors who visited this place. Now they'd never get to.

As Holden poured his pint and another for Tony, Bronte introduced him to the current Nowhere crew. This included Jake, a lanky young bloke from Brisbane with a mullet, and the blonde bartenders, Ingrid and Freja, identical twins from a small town called Trosa in Sweden—'Although not quite as small as Middle of Nowhere,' Ingrid explained, in a sing-song tone—as well as a grumpy bloke in his sixties who ran the kitchen. Bronte told him that Stan's bark was much worse than his bite. 'And wait till you taste his beef and barra. Think he's the best cook we've ever had.'

'I'll be the judge of that,' Holden said, rubbing his empty belly.

It always amazed him how few people it took to run the roadhouse, pub and motel rooms behind them, but that's because everyone worked their arses off—it wasn't like there was anything else to do in Middle of Nowhere. The workers became like family to each other and got their social life from the tourists and truckies who travelled up and down the Stuart Highway between South Australia and the Northern Territory.

He sat and ate next to Tony, talking about how the world could progress and change, but the Nowhere Roadhouse and Tavern never would.

'That's until Bill left,' Tony said, staring gloomily into yet another pint of beer. The man never seemed to get drunk and barely ate more than bar snacks.

Holden nodded. Bill's presence was noticeably absent. Although there was still laughter on both sides of the bar, it wasn't Bill's loud, booming guffaw that reverberated around the building, and the tourists suddenly seemed just that; passers-through. Whereas Bill had always made it seem as if they were part of the Nowhere family, even if they were only there a night. By the time someone who'd had a meal or a few drinks in the Tavern headed out to their caravan or motel room, Bill knew their life story and had often counselled them through their woes as well.

Tricia emerged to help with the dinner service about an hour after Holden arrived, and she looked almost as old as Tony. The grief had gone to her eyes, which were bloodshot and had large dark bags beneath them.

'Holden,' she said, her voice full of emotion.

As he'd done with her daughter, he wrapped her in his arms and held her close. 'I'm so sorry, Tricia.'

Those words weren't nearly enough but there were really no words that would provide comfort. The best thing he could do was offer practical support to her and Bronte in the days leading up to the funeral.

At about nine o'clock, Bronte called last drinks—9 pm equated to midnight in Middle of Nowhere—and half an hour after that everyone was gone.

Bronte grabbed a key off the rack and gave it to Holden, then said goodnight as he went to a motel room out the back, but they both knew it was only for show. The moment Tricia was in bed in the house, Bronte would sneak into his room.

While he waited for her, he took a shower to wash off the red dust he'd collected along the highway and then grabbed his phone. He'd only meant to text Ford and the boys, but somehow he found himself on TikTok, checking in on what Adeline and the nuns were up to. They'd uploaded a new dance sometime in the last twenty-four hours and he must have watched it a dozen times.

Did she know how provocative these videos were? Or was it only him who saw them this way? Surely no one else would be sick enough to fantasise about a nun in such unsexy clothing.

He started at the knock on his door, shoved his phone in the drawer of the bedside table like a teenage boy caught watching porn, then went to open it. Bronte stood there, a bottle of Jack Daniels in her hand. Her hair was wet, telling him she'd taken the time to shower as well. If she noticed the erection tenting his shorts, hopefully she'd assume it was because of her.

'Don't you have a key?' he asked.

She nodded. 'But it's against motel policy for an employee to let themselves into a guest's room without asking permission.'

Holden chuckled, grabbed her hand, and pulled her inside. 'Consider yourself permanently permitted.'

She slipped off her thongs, then grabbed two glasses from the shelf above the mini fridge before retrieving an icetray from the tiny freezer part of it. She made two drinks and handed one to him.

'I'm so glad you're here,' she said as they clinked glasses.

'Me too,' he replied, then added, 'To Bill.'

'To Dad,' she echoed.

They both took long sips and then settled onto the bed, nursing their drinks as they sat up against the headboard.

'Tell me something funny,' Bronte demanded. 'I'm shattered and I need a laugh.'

'The nun kissed me.'

'What?' She shrieked so loudly that Tricia probably heard her in the main house and the whiskey danced in her glass. 'Adeline?'

'Yeah. You know how I told you we made a birthday cake for her? Well, I walked her to the road when she left, and she said it was the best birthday she'd had in a long while.'

Bronte's eyebrows crept up her forehead.

'Then she said thanks, and stretched up on her toes. I thought she was going to kiss me on the cheek, and you could have bowled me over with a feather when she went for my mouth instead.'

'I'm … I'm speechless. Did you kiss her back?'

'Yeah, isn't it polite to reciprocate when someone lays one on you?'

'Ah, no. Not if you're not attracted to them.'

His fingers tightened around the glass. 'I've already told you I'm attracted to her. You yourself noticed how hot she is.'

'True,' she conceded with a nod. 'So why didn't you tell me when you rang?'

'It didn't mean anything. I wasn't keeping a secret, but you and I had other things on our minds.' He reached for the bottle to refill his glass and topped hers up as well. 'Besides, I'm telling you now, aren't I?'

She seemed to accept this. 'So, are you gunna kiss her again? Is she leaving Jesus for you?'

He snorted. 'Don't be ridiculous. We've both agreed to pretend it never happened. You can't say anything to her. She'll kill me if she knows I told you.'

Bronte stared down into her drink. 'I might not get the chance to tell her anyway.'

'What do you mean?'

She took another long gulp, then said, 'I think I'm gunna stay.'

'What? Here? Forever?'

'Maybe not forever, but indefinitely. Mum can't run this place by herself even with Stan and the staff to help. I don't see I have any option but to come home.'

Even though Holden had known this might be on the cards, it still shocked him to hear it. 'Do you think you might sell?'

She shrugged and pulled her knees up to her chest, hugging them close. 'It's too soon to make those kinds of decisions. I just want to be here with Mum and support her for the next little while. Once we've had time to grieve, then we'll have to talk about what to do next.'

'Well, for the next five days I'm here to help as well. I'll stay till after the funeral, and I'm here to be used and abused, okay? Whatever needs doing; hauling beer, peeling potatoes, cleaning toilets, changing sheets … You name it, I'm your man.'

Bronte smiled, then put her glass down on the bedside table, turned to him and cupped his face between her hands. 'What am I going to do without you, Holden Campbell?'

'You'll never be without me,' he said. 'There might be three-thousand-odd kilometres between us, but I'll always be with you in spirit. We'll talk all the time and maybe I'll even bring the boys up to visit. Reckon they'd love it up here.'

'That would be great.' Then she leaned in and kissed him.

Conversation was over. He'd made her laugh and now it was time to make her come. As Bronte climbed on top, straddling him, he tossed aside his own glass, reached over to switch off the bedside light, and then slipped his hands under her shirt. She moaned as he cupped her breasts and then she pressed her hips against his groin.

'Have you got a condom?' she whispered.

'Yeah,' he replied, digging it out of his pocket and passing it to her.

But that didn't turn out to be the problem.

He couldn't get it up. No matter what Bronte did to try and rouse him, his dick refused to play along.

'Fuck. I'm sorry,' he said, jamming his hands through his hair as embarrassment sat heavy in his gut.

This had never happened before. Since he'd discovered sex behind the sports shed with Laura Williams in grade nine, he'd never not been able to get it up. And he and Bronte had always been compatible in that way. He knew he wasn't the only person she slept with. She often dated other people and occasionally indulged in one-night stands. Both of them were sexual beings but didn't want the commitment that came with a 'relationship'.

And they were happy with their arrangement.

'It's because of the nun, isn't it?' she said, rolling over.

'What?!' Thank God the lights were off because his face was suddenly burning.

'I'm not an idiot. You've fallen for Adeline.'

'It's not fucking funny,' he said, offended by her amused tone.

'Yes, it is.' She laughed as she reached over to switch the lamp back on and search for her clothes, which they'd ripped off while trying to get in the mood. 'It's fucking hilarious. It's the funniest fucking thing I've ever heard. Holden Campbell, the man with a heart so hard he doesn't even get emotional over an RSPCA ad, has fallen in love.'

'I'm not in love,' he scoffed.

'That would be amusing itself,' Bronte continued, ignoring his protestations, 'but to have fallen for a woman who has taken a vow of chastity, now that takes the cake.'

'She hasn't taken vows. Not yet.'

'What?' Bronte looked momentarily surprised. 'Oh right, but she plans to.' Her expression turned sympathetic. 'Holden, I know plenty of women who would fall over their feet to get into your bed, but I really don't think she's one of them. And, quite frankly, she doesn't seem your type.'

Before he could say he didn't have a type, she added, 'Do you think this is a case of wanting what you can't have?'

He sighed; hadn't he wondered this too? 'Maybe, but I can't help thinking it's a fucking waste that someone like her is locking herself up in a convent for the rest of her life.'

'It's what she wants,' Bronte said with a shrug.

'It's what she *says* she wants,' he retorted, 'but I've got this gut feeling that it isn't what she wants deep down.'

Bronte reached for the Jack Daniels. 'What makes you think that?' She took a swig right from the bottle.

'Just a few things she's told me about her past,' he said, not wanting to break Adeline's confidence. Not that she'd told him the stuff about her crap relationships and abusive boss was secret, but it wouldn't feel right talking about all that with Bronte.

She looked at him with an expression he didn't recognise.

'What?' he asked.

'It sounds like you really care about her. And I'm worried about you getting hurt falling for someone who isn't available to love you back.'

He grabbed the bottle off her and took a gulp. 'I'm not gunna get hurt. And I told you; I think she's hot, but I'm not fucking in love.'

'Of course not,' she snapped, her voice raised. 'Because Holden Campbell doesn't *do* love, right?'

'Yeah, that's right. I don't. I wouldn't even be feeling like this if she hadn't fucking kissed me!'

He couldn't believe they were having this conversation. It was ridiculous. He probably couldn't get it up because he was tired. Bronte was making a mountain out of a molehill.

He put the bottle down again and reached for her, determined this time to follow through on what they'd started. 'Let's stop talking about this bullshit and—'

'Oh, no you don't.' She shook her head and held her hand out to warn him off. '*I'm* not in the mood anymore.'

'Shit. You're not jealous, are you?'

Bronte snorted. 'Me? Jealous? I don't want love any more than you do, but if I did, it wouldn't be with someone as messed up as you.'

'Hey! I'm not messed up,' he exclaimed, offended.

'Yeah.' She patted him on the head like she would one of the dogs. 'You just keep telling yourself that, sweetheart.'

And then she swung her legs off the bed, slipped on her thongs, leaned over and kissed him on forehead. 'Sleep well, my darling.'

'I'm sorry, Bron,' he called as she headed for the door.

She turned back to look at him. 'We're good, Holden. As much as I enjoy being your friend-with-benefits, it's the friend part that matters to me more than the benefits. And I'm not about to let your *little* issue come between us. Now, get some sleep and I'll see you in the morning.'

Messed up? Him?

Talk about pot-kettle-black. He might have made a conscious decision to never get into a committed-forever type relationship with anyone, but at least he had a good reason.

What was Bronte's excuse?

Whatever it was, he felt guilty that the evening had ended like this and vowed to make it up to her tomorrow. The day started early in the roadhouse and he planned to be there to do whatever was needed to make things easier for her and Tricia.

Once again, he switched off the lamp and closed his eyes, but immediately the vision of Adeline's new TikTok dance appeared in his head. How the hell did anyone look so sexy in that uniform? Maybe if he imagined her in a full nun's habit, it'd turn him off.

He tried, but it didn't work.

All he could think about when he pictured Adeline in a long black robe and veil, was sneaking his hands under the skirt and pushing it up around her waist and …

'Dammit!' He punched his hand into his pillow. This was insane!

So much for out of sight, out of mind.

Chapter Thirty-five

The little bell above the door of the *Smallton Gazette* office jingled as Adeline pushed it open on Saturday.

'Morning Adeline,' Mike said, looking up from the couch in the reception area, where he and Reeve were drinking coffee and reading the state and national newspapers.

'Hi boys. Thanks so much for coming in on the weekend.' She put down the container she'd brought, which was full of chocolate muffins, and shrugged out of her jacket. As usual, Mike had the heating cranked up to toasty levels.

'Our pleasure,' Reeve replied with the goofy grin Adeline had come to love.

'Yeah, beats doing housework or gardening,' Mike added, 'and we're always happy to help a good cause.' Not only were Mike and Reeve giving up their Saturday to help fold flyers for the tractor pull, but the *Gazette* had donated the paper and the printing, and free advertising space. 'What time will the boys be here?'

Adeline glanced at her watch. 'Should be any minute.'

'Awesome.' Mike pushed to his feet. 'Can I get you a drink before everyone arrives?'

'A coffee would be great, thanks.'

Mike looked to Reeve, who laughed. 'I'm onto it. You two go through and get organised.'

While Reeve cleared up the newspapers and went to make her drink, Adeline followed Mike into the back room, where he'd set the table up with a stack of flyers in front of every seat.

'Wow. These look better than I thought they would.' She picked up one of the flyers. 'Wait till Holden sees them.' He was still away, but Ford had told her Bronte's dad's funeral was on Monday and he'd be home late the following day.

Adeline had mixed feelings about his return.

While she'd meant what she said about wanting to be friends, she felt a lot safer knowing that he and his lips were thousands of kilometres away, not even in the same state as her. The last few days, the guilt had eased, and she'd felt like she could breathe again. As long as he wasn't here, she could almost pretend that the kiss hadn't actually happened. Except at night, when her mind wandered, and she found her fingers absentmindedly running along her jawline as she recalled the tantalising sensation of his beard against her skin.

It was then she'd force herself to imagine what he and Bronte might be up to in Middle of Nowhere, but that didn't bring her relief either.

'Yeah, they turned out alright,' Mike replied. 'By the way, I read your article. It's fabulous. You really got to the heart of what Holden wants to do and why. Hell, you almost made me want to build a tiny house of my own.'

She laughed. 'Thanks. So, it'll be in this week's edition?'

He nodded. 'Front page.'

Just then Reeve entered the room carrying three steaming mugs. 'Have you asked her yet?'

Adeline frowned. 'Asked me what?'

'Whoops. Guess that's my answer.' Reeve smiled sheepishly as he put the mugs down on the table.

'It's not common knowledge yet, but Reeve and I are moving back to Melbourne,' Mike said.

'What?!' she exclaimed. 'Why? When?'

'I've been offered a job at the *Melbourne Observer*.'

Adeline looked to Reeve. 'What are you going to do in the city?'

He smiled. 'I've started applying for jobs in the area, but I've always fancied writing a novel so if it takes a while to get one, maybe that'll give me the push I need.'

'Well, I … I guess congratulations are in order,' Adeline managed, yet inside she was gutted. She loved working with Mike. 'But I'm going to miss you guys.'

'Aw, sweet Adeline.' Mike wrapped one arm around her shoulder. 'We'll miss you too, but we'll keep in touch, and … I was hoping you might consider taking over from me here.'

It took her a few moments to understand what he was saying. 'You want me to be the editor of the *Gazette*?'

He and Reeve both nodded enthusiastically.

'It makes perfect sense,' Mike said. 'I know you can write, and I know you've had experience running a small-town newspaper.'

Adeline was flattered but admitted, 'The *Walsh Whisperer* was a lot smaller than the *Smallton Gazette*. And it was a volunteer position, so—'

'Don't doubt yourself,' Mike interrupted. 'In the short time you've been here, you've proved yourself to be an amazing writer and the way you're helping Holden shows you're also community-minded and good at organising things. The shire would prefer to hire someone who already lives in Smallton, and because you've joined the convent, you're also a safe bet. It's not like you're going to move away anytime soon.'

'Nope. Not planning to, but … wow. I don't know. I mean I'd love to …' It would give her something to really get her teeth stuck into once the tractor pull was over. 'But I'd have to talk it over with Mother Catherine.'

She wasn't sure being editor of the local paper would classify as the kind of work sisters were allowed to do outside the convent. The others all did more service-related work. Then again, the paper was a community service of sorts—it kept the locals connected.

Mike nodded. 'Of course. Have a chat to her and then let me know as soon as you can.'

'I will,' Adeline said, although her words were barely audible over the sound of the front door opening, the bell above it ringing, and noise erupting into the building.

'Sorry, we're late,' shouted Sam. 'Toovs had a bowel issue this morning and we had to wait for him doing number twos.'

'If you don't shut up, I'll fucking make you,' Toovs yelled.

'Boys, boys, settle down,' came Ford's calming voice. 'We're here now and that's what matters.'

Adeline, Mike and Reeve went out to greet them.

'Where's the snacks?' Rocky asked, looking around. 'Ford said there were gunna be snacks.'

Adeline laughed. 'There will be, but folding comes first. How about we see how many flyers we can fold in an hour and then take a morning-tea break?'

Rocky, Sam and Toovs exchanged a look and then all nodded.

'Deal,' Rocky agreed.

They went into the back room, the wheels on Ford's wheelchair squeaking as he pushed himself through. Adeline showed the boys how to fold the flyer with three folds so that the title would be on the top when someone lifted it out of their letterbox.

Of course, they made it a competition to see who could fold the most flyers in the shortest amount of time, and while Adeline, Ford, Reeve and Mike worked at a slightly slower pace, they enjoyed easy conversation. Adeline told them that the convent was busy getting ready for Lola's final vow ceremony in a few weeks.

'We've been spring cleaning every surface getting ready for the extra guests—Lola's friends, family and the bishop are coming from Melbourne—and also preparing decorations and the menu for the feast.'

'It sounds like a wedding,' Ford said.

'It's exactly like that,' she explained. 'Where do you think the phrase Brides of Christ comes from?'

'Do Lola's parents give her away like the father of a bride usually does?' asked Reeve.

'You know I'm not actually sure.' Each day Adeline learned something new about being a sister, but there was still so much to uncover.

'I hope you'll write about it in your NunTalk column,' said Mike as he started to stack the folded flyers into boxes.

'Oh, I will. Promise.'

'Have you heard from Holden?' Mike asked Ford, and Adeline sucked in a quick breath at the mention of his name. 'How's Bronte doing?'

'Yeah. She's okay,' Ford replied. 'Holden's trying to give her and her mum time to organise the funeral, so he's been busy helping as much as he can at the roadhouse and tavern, burning the candle at both ends. He sounds exhausted.'

Adeline couldn't help but wonder if he was exhausted from all the sex he and Bronte were likely having. Not that it was any of her business. Holden and Bronte could do the deed twenty-four hours a day, seven days a week, hanging from the ceiling fans for all she cared.

'Must be time for muffins,' she announced, pushing back her chair to stand.

The boys did not need to be asked twice.

Adeline retrieved the container and handed it to Toovs. 'Take these outside to eat.' She'd seen the way they devoured food and didn't want the crumbs ending up all over the office. It'd probably do them good to get some fresh air and stretch their legs before the final folding session.

Mike and Reeve opted for muffins and fresh air as well, but Ford and Adeline stayed inside, and each had another coffee.

'Do you mind me asking how you and Holden ended up living together?'

Ford frowned at her over the top of his mug. 'He's my brother.'

'Yeah, but he told me that after your accident, he—'

'He told *you* about my accident? Like how it happened?'

She nodded. 'Yes, and that he was behind the wheel.'

Ford's brow knitted. 'What else did he say?'

And so she told him what Holden had told her—about their stepfather trying to 'fix' him, about the stolen car, the accident, about Holden being put into foster care and then after that how he hit the road and travelled Australia.

'Wow,' Ford breathed. 'He rarely talks about any of that with anyone.'

'He only opened up because I told him he'd be more likely to get a grant if he made it personal, showed he has firsthand experience in the situation he wants to help the boys with. But he hasn't said anything about your relationship during those years. How'd you come to live here together?'

'As soon as I came round after the accident, I wanted to see Holden. I wanted to tell him I didn't blame him for what happened. Like him, I blamed Garry. Do you know what that wanker told me the first time I saw him after I woke up?'

Adeline held her breath.

'He told me my injuries were punishment for my sins. That God had taken the use of my legs so I could never "indulge in immoral sex".'

She gasped, horrified that anyone could say such a thing to a kid. 'He really said *that*?'

'Yep. Joke's on him anyway, because as I told you, I'm fine in that department.' Ford winked. 'Anyway, I didn't want to lose my brother as well as my legs, but Garry refused to let me see him. Mum said she couldn't go against her husband but that if I promised not to tell him, I could write letters to Holden, and she'd make sure they were posted. He didn't answer the first few, but I persisted and eventually we became kind of pen pals. When he went travelling, he'd send me postcards from various places. They came sporadically and didn't say much. We never spoke about the accident.

'Over time I learned to live without my legs and, as you know, I trained as barber. I had insurance money in a trust account, which I couldn't access until I was twenty-one. The moment I could, I bought the business and the property here, and I wrote to Holden inviting him to come live with me. I missed him and I wanted him back in my life. Besides, I needed a carer once I moved out of Mum and Garry's place. I think it was that that swung him.'

'And how long after that did you start fostering?'

Ford shrugged. 'About three or four years. Once we were settled, and the business was thriving, Holden told me what he felt compelled to do and I thought it was a good idea. Between me and the kids … we keep him too busy to beat himself up about what he thinks he did to me.' He paused a moment, then added, 'What he refuses to remember is that I willingly got in that car with him.'

The door to the office opened and their conversation was interrupted by the return of Mike, Reeve and the boys, but at least Adeline knew a little more. They worked solidly for another hour and then headed down to the café and had lunch—Ford's shout—before the afternoon work of putting up posters around town and distributing the flyers to letterboxes all over Smallton.

Adeline had church tomorrow but Ford was going to drive the boys into Colac so they could deliver some there as well. She felt a little guilty that she wouldn't be able to help, but it was probably just as well because by the time Ford dropped her at the convent, she was shattered, and her feet were aching from all the walking. A sneaky nap before dinner felt like a good idea.

Usually, at this time on a Saturday afternoon, the sisters could be found reading, playing board games or doing craft, but today the convent was unusually silent and empty, except for Benno and Barnabas lounging on the couch in the living room. Adeline frowned, wondering where they all were, then heard a squeal and cheering from the … *the garage?*

'What's going on?' she asked as she entered to find everyone gathered around some gym equipment, including two rusty old exercise bikes, a treadmill that looked ancient enough to be the first one ever invented, several dumbbells, barbells of various sizes, and a couple of benches for weightlifting. 'Where did all this stuff come from?'

'It was a donation from the high school,' Mother Catherine explained as Michelle lay on the bench lifting a barbell, Rita spotting her. 'They got new stuff a few years ago and all this was gathering dust in their storage shed.'

'Okay, then …' Adeline said, still confused as to why they'd all suddenly become fitness fanatics. Even tiny old Josey was swinging two small dumbbells from side to side, and Lola was working up a sweat on one of the bikes.

'Lola, Michelle, Josey and I are entering a team into the tractor pull,' Rita explained, taking the barbell from Michelle and putting it back into its resting spot.

'What?' Adeline couldn't help but laugh. While Rita, Lola and Michelle could possibly hold their own in the women's category, Sister Josey was surely going to hinder their chances of success. It was hard to imagine her pulling a child's wagon, never mind a great big tractor.

'Yeah, why not?' Lola asked, between pants. 'It'll be fun. And if it takes a good cause to get us fit, then so be it.'

'We heard the footy club team are going to be wearing nothing but tighty-whities, so we're going to do it in full habits,' Michelle added, wiping her brow with the back of her hand.

'Because that'll make it a whole lot easier,' Adeline said with a chuckle.

'Oh, ye of little faith. Remember, we've got God on our team,' Rita said, then tapped Michelle on the shoulder. 'Up you hop, it's my turn.'

Although Adeline had been ready for a nap, watching this 'training' was too amusing to give up. She sat down next to Mother Catherine to watch the show.

'I know the focus around here has been on Sister Lola's vow ceremony lately,' said the older woman, 'but I want you to know that your contribution to the convent and the greater community has not gone unnoticed. I'm impressed with what you've done with the NunTok account and your dedication to helping the Campbell brothers with boys in need has been outstanding.'

'Thank you, Mother Catherine,' Adeline said, guilt pricking her heart.

Would she be so glowing in her praise if she knew about the kiss? Her superior's belief in her only made her more determined to never let anything like that ever happen again.

'What will you do with all your time once the fundraiser is over?'

'Well, actually,' Adeline began, 'I had an interesting proposition from Mike at the *Gazette* today.'

'Oh?' Mother Catherine turned to properly look at Adeline.

'Yes, he's been offered a job back in Melbourne. And ... he wants to know if I'd like to be editor of the paper.'

'I see.'

Adeline couldn't tell how Mother Catherine felt from these two words, so she rushed to add, 'I told him I'd have to talk it over with you. And that I wasn't sure it would be appropriate for me to take on that role.'

'I don't see why not. We are all about using our individual skills to serve God and others. Your talents clearly lie in writing and community events. I think you'd be an asset to the paper.'

'So I can do it?' Adeline asked, unable to keep the excitement out of her voice. The *Smallton Gazette* might not be *The New York Times* but it would give her the chance to do some actual proper journalism again as well as lead the small team beneath her.

'I didn't say that,' said Mother Catherine, bursting Adeline's bubble. 'It is not my decision to make. You need to pray about it. You need to seek guidance from our Lord to see if this is what he wants for you.'

'Oh, of course.' She swallowed. 'I will. Thank you.'

Mother Catherine patted her knee. 'Now, since the others seem a little preoccupied, maybe you could go and get a start on dinner?'

Chapter Thirty-six

Two weeks had passed since Holden had returned, leaving Bronte to stay behind in Middle of Nowhere to help her mum. She'd asked him to clear out her unit in Smallton, send her clothes and a few personal belongings, and put all her furniture into storage. He'd taken the boys to help him with this task and after they'd boxed everything up, they'd deep cleaned the place. Holden had expected loud complaints at this unexpected chore, but they all loved Bronte and did the job in unusual silence.

He wasn't the only one who was going to miss her.

Luckily, they had much to focus on with the upcoming tractor pull and the impending arrival of Bella's puppies. She was getting fatter by the day and Rocky treated her like a queen, slipping her little bits of human dinner when he didn't think anyone was looking and making her comfy beds of pillows all around the house. Much to his frustration, she didn't seem interested in any of his nesting assistance.

'She'll have the pups where she wants to have the pups,' Holden said. 'When *she's* ready.'

He'd never had a dog have puppies before, so he didn't know what to expect, but Adeline had given him some idea. She visited Bella almost daily, and in addition to talk of grants, the formation of a charity and the tractor pull, she told them about Bella's previous litters and other stories from her time as a dog breeder.

There was no longer any joking around or flirtatious banter between them; their relationship was now purely professional.

Holden could almost see the wall she'd put up around herself. They'd run into each other at the soup kitchen and again in the supermarket, and both times it had been like they were strangers.

She was still the same around Ford, in fact sometimes when the three of them were sitting on the verandah or at the dining-room table working, he felt like the third wheel.

He'd never been jealous of his brother, but the way Ford and Adeline laughed and talked in such an easy, friendly manner made his chest tighten with envy. As wonderful as their kiss had been, he would do anything to turn back time and have things go back to how they were.

He missed her as much as he did Bronte. Maybe even more.

The dogs started barking and he started from his reverie, looking from where he was up on a ladder de-clogging the gutters—which had been overflowing during downpours they'd had the last couple of nights—towards the driveway.

Holy hell. Adeline. Usually, she didn't come until later in the day, when the boys were home, but—he glanced at his watch—it was only just past midday.

Wondering what she wanted, he climbed off the ladder, wiped his wet hands on his jeans and went to meet her. Of course, the dogs beat him to it; even Bella, who was much slower on her feet these days.

Stooping to stroke the dog's fluffy white fur, she looked nervously towards him as if she suddenly realised they were alone. 'Hi Holden.'

'Hello, Adeline,' he said. Since his return they'd stopped using their nicknames. Just further evidence of the chasm that now stretched between them. So much for being friends. 'What can I do for you?'

'I've got good news and … I couldn't wait till this afternoon to tell you.'

That sounded promising—on multiple levels. He smiled. 'Can I offer you a drink? Will you come inside?'

She shook her head. 'I can't stay. I just wanted to tell you that we've hit fifty teams signed up to the tractor pull.'

'Seriously?!' He couldn't believe it. When she'd suggested the idea, he'd thought they'd be lucky to get a handful of participants.

She nodded. 'One group is coming all the way from Sydney.'

'Wow. I'm … gobsmacked.'

'At a hundred dollars per team, that's already five-thousand dollars. And that's even before we take into account the ticket sales of everyone coming to watch and the fees the food carts are paying us to be there on the day. Also, I've got a couple of regional radio interviews lined up for you, which should get some more teams registering before registrations close.'

'My God.' Seriously, this woman! 'You're amazing, you know that? Thanks to you we might actually raise enough money from one fundraiser to build the first tiny house.' He'd allocated twenty-thousand dollars for the supplies and would use the boys and himself as labour.

'Only one? I'm hoping for at least two.' Her lips curved into a smile, and they beamed at each other.

He couldn't resist pulling her in for a quick, friendly hug. 'Thank you,' he whispered.

'My pleasure.'

'There, that wasn't too hard, was it?' he said as he let go.

She frowned. 'What wasn't?'

'We hugged but you managed to control your crazy urges and not kiss me.'

He'd been trying to make a joke—to get back that fun banter they used to share—but the moment her face fell he knew he'd made a grave error of judgement. 'You're not still beating yourself up about the kiss, are you?'

Her lack of reply, the way she simply stared at the ground as if someone close to her was buried there, told him she was.

'Hey,' he said, wishing he could reach out and try to comfort her with a touch. 'You need to stop. You made a mistake, but you're not a terrible person. Even nuns aren't perfect all of the time.'

'Stop saying that,' she cried. 'Stop saying that I'm not terrible. You know nothing about what kind of person I am! What kind of *family* I come from.'

'Huh? What's your family got to do with this?'

'My grandmother was a murderer.'

'What?' He wondered if his ears were playing tricks. Then again, hadn't he known there was something off, the way she spoke about her grandmother?

Adeline slapped a hand over her mouth as if she was almost as shocked as he was by her words. 'Never mind. Forget it.' She turned to go.

Instinctively, Holden reached out and grabbed her hand. 'Oh no, no, no, no, no.' She couldn't just say something like that and expect him to drop it.

Her eyes met his and he could tell she was close to tears. Her hand shook in his grip, and he suddenly realised her whole body was trembling.

'I'm making you a cup of tea,' he said, ushering her up onto the verandah and into one of the armchairs that had seen better days. He grabbed a crochet rug from the back of the other one and draped it over her shoulders. 'Stay there.'

Holden wasn't sure whether she'd do as he said, so he made the tea as quickly as the kettle would allow and grabbed his emergency bottle of whiskey from the back of the pantry as well. He didn't know whether nuns were allowed to drink anything other than communion wine, but Adeline looked as if she could do with something stiff.

He breathed a sigh of relief when he went back outside and she was still sitting where he'd left her, the crochet blanket wrapped around her shoulders, hugging her knees to her chest as she sobbed.

'Here.' Holden handed her the mug of tea and when she took it, he held up the bottle of whiskey. 'Want a drop of this in it as well?'

She shrugged one shoulder then held out the mug. 'Thank you,' she whispered once he'd spiked the drink.

He nodded, then took the armchair beside her. Although his head felt like it might explode with questions—What was her grandmother's name? Had he heard of her? Did she really murder someone? Who? *How*?—he felt it would be better to simply wait for her to talk. He knew better than anyone how difficult talking about family and the past could be.

'I don't know why I told you that,' she said after taking a few sips. 'I don't know why I'm determined to make you think I'm bad when I'm trying so hard to be good.'

He didn't know what to say to that. If it was true that her grandmother had killed someone, that didn't make her bad by association. Unless … 'You didn't help your gran with … uh, the … death, did you? You didn't bury the body?'

She shook her head, then sighed. 'I suppose there's no reason not to tell you. It all happened so many years ago. Gran's gone now and so are all her victim's relatives as far as I know.'

Holden held his breath, waiting for her to say more.

'I thought my gran and my grandfather were soulmates—that was the story she always told us. Knowing what I do now, I have a feeling he might have thought differently, but he died when I was young, so my memories of him come from my grandmother and my parents.' She took a quick breath. 'Anyway, while they were dating—"courting" as they called it back then—he fell in love with someone else, and when he broke it off with my grandmother to be with the other woman, she murdered her.'

'Seriously? Why didn't she go to jail?'

Adeline scoffed. 'You only go to jail if you get caught. Gran wasn't that stupid. She made it look like the woman took her own life.'

'Who was this other woman?'

'Her name was Eliza Abbott. She lived in the next town over with her parents who owned the general store there. The story goes that she died in a tragic accident when she fell down the stairs, although according to the local paper at the time, everyone believed it was suicide. A couple of years ago, this woman, Meg, bought the run-down building and did it up into a tearoom. But almost immediately she started experiencing weird goings-on. You know, the usual—cold drafts, doors opening and closing when they shouldn't.'

Holden raised an eyebrow—he did not believe in ghosts. 'So, typical old building things?'

It was almost as if Adeline didn't hear him. 'Anyway, Meg started doing research and discovered the story of Eliza dying in the building. She strongly believes that it's Eliza's ghost there and that she wasn't suicidal, and didn't accidentally fall, but was pushed.'

'So what makes you think your grandmother killed her? Couldn't your grandparents' break-up and the time of her death just be a coincidence?'

She shook her head. 'I don't *think*, Jack, I *know*.'

He managed not to smile at her use of his nickname. 'How?'

'She pushed Eliza down the stairs.'

Holden frowned and resisted the urge to take a swig of whiskey himself. 'I meant *how* do you know? Did she tell you?'

'No. After she died, I was going through her stuff trying to find some special anecdotes to put in her obituary. Instead, I found a confession.'

He couldn't hide his shock. 'If she was clever enough to get away with murder, surely she wasn't stupid enough to write it down.'

Adeline shrugged one shoulder. 'No, not that stupid, but I could read between the lines. She journaled her whole life. One week, she was blissfully in love, next Henry had ended things, telling her he was in love with Eliza. She asked him not to make it public for a while because she didn't want the town to be gossiping about how she'd been passed over for someone of much lower class. She says in her diary that she will do *whatever it takes* to get Henry back and then a few days later, she writes that all will be fine, that she has sorted the little issue that arose between them. I checked the timing, and the day she wrote that is the day Eliza died.'

'Maybe it's just a coincidence she died that day. Bad luck?' He winced when he realised how that sounded, but Adeline shook her head adamantly.

'No. I know it's true. And it explains why I always feel uncomfortable at the tearooms. People often tell me I look exactly like my grandmother did when she was young, so Eliza probably knows we're related.'

'Look, even if it is true, imagine the guilt your grandmother must have lived with her whole life.' It was bad enough living with the knowledge that because of him, his brother would never lead a normal life; how much worse would it be if he'd actually killed Ford?

'Her journal didn't make it sound like she felt much guilt,' Adeline scoffed. 'She made it her mission to comfort Henry and eventually they were married as originally expected. Later, months after the wedding, she wrote something about being sure she'd done the right thing. That sometimes men don't know what's good for them and have to be protected.' She shook her head. '*See* what kind of monster I'm related to? And all my life I looked up to her, idolised her, wanted to be just like her.'

'Even if what you think did happen, it doesn't make *you* a monster,' Holden said, unable to believe she really thought this. 'Don't you remember what you told Rocky about his dad? You are *not* your grandmother. You're an amazing person. You're kind, caring, giving and you shouldn't punish yourself for someone else's actions.'

'I'm horrible,' she shouted back. 'I've always been horrible. The person you know is not the person I've been all my life. You ask anyone in my hometown, and they'll tell you what an awful person I am.'

He opened his mouth to object, but she barrelled on right over the top of him.

'You want examples? I'll give you examples. When this woman Meg first came to town a couple of years ago, I was jealous that a guy I'd always liked suddenly started showing interest in her. So, you know what I did? I made it my mission to dig up dirt on her. I didn't care about what this might do to her, or how it might hurt Lawson; I only cared about myself. Because my grandmother raised her children and grandchildren to believe we were better than everyone else in town. She always told me I was more beautiful and smarter and that I deserved to have whatever I wanted, because the fact that we were Walshes—founding members of the town—meant we were superior to everyone else.

'No wonder I never had any friends. And it was all based on a lie anyway. If Henry had married Eliza like he'd wanted to, I wouldn't even be alive. None of us have any right to be here. I think my grandmother's sin poisoned us all. My parents ...'

Adeline was clearly trying to get him to think badly of her, but it wasn't working. Every self-loathing word she spat only made him think more highly of her.

And then suddenly it clicked.

'Is this the grandma you told me died just before you joined the convent?' he asked, interrupting the apparently never-ending list of grievances she held against herself.

She nodded.

'Oh Maria, is that why you became a nun?'

'I told you, we're called sisters,' she said, but didn't deny it.

Holy shit. He couldn't let her throw her life away trying to pay penance for someone else's sins.

'But that's ridiculous. You don't have to make good for something your grandmother did, what, seventy years ago or something? Sure, let go of the lies she told you and don't repeat her mistakes, but you can't change the past. Throwing your life away isn't going to bring Eliza back.'

She sniffed, then met his eyes with a sad smile. 'I know that. And you're right, maybe I did pledge as a postulant partly because I believed someone needed to pay their dues for what Penelope did, but I do have faith and I genuinely believe that God led me here—that it was His will for me to end up in Smallton. I don't expect you to understand, but I've found who I am here. I've learned so much about myself, who I *was*, and who I *want* to be, and I've never felt more like *me* than I do at the convent. I've finally found my life's purpose.'

'I'm glad,' he told her. 'I'm glad you're happy, but can you please promise me one thing?'

'What?' she asked, her tone cautious.

'Please stop feeling guilty for something that was out of your control. Please believe in yourself—in your good heart and kind soul—like the rest of us do.'

For a moment, she pursed her lips and Holden thought maybe she was going to start crying again, but then she sniffed. 'I'll try,' she promised. 'Oh, but I have other good news too.'

'Don't tell me, you've got the Hemsworth brothers to sign up to the tractor pull?'

She laughed. 'No, not that good. I've accepted the position of editor at the *Smallton Gazette*.'

'Seriously? I'd heard Mike and Reeve were moving back to Melbourne, but I hadn't heard that.'

'I only just said yes. I had to do a lot of thinking and praying about it first.'

'Well, congratulations,' he said. 'That's wonderful news. Sounds like you're going to be a very busy lady.'

'I am,' she replied with a smile. 'But don't think this lets you off the hook. I'll still have plenty of time to help you get Tiny Home Sweet Homes off the ground.'

Holden grinned. 'I'm glad to hear it.'

Chapter Thirty-seven

Five days later, Adeline woke in the night to the sound of tapping on her bedroom window. It was pitch black inside and at first, she wrote it off as the wind. People weren't kidding when they said that Victoria often experienced four seasons in one day. Early that morning it had been thunder-storming, then during the day it had been sunny and spring-like, which was just as well as they'd been busy doing final preparations for Lola's vow ceremony tomorrow. The afternoon had been overcast and windy, and then as night fell it brought with it a bitter chill that she'd hoped had been over until next winter.

Tap. Tap. Tap.

Adeline frowned. It didn't sound like the wind. Could it be one of Lola's guests? Maybe they'd locked themselves outside and needed help getting back in. But what would any of them be doing wandering around outside at eleven o'clock at night?

Tap. Tap. Tap.

Her heart froze. Perhaps it was an intruder. Then again, wouldn't they just break the window?

Deciding it could only be a wild animal sheltering on the windowsill, she pulled back the curtain to look and squealed at the sight of a big, burly, bearded man on the other side of the glass.

'Holden?' she hissed, her pulse racing.

He pressed his index finger against his lips, then gestured for her to open the window.

'Finally,' he said when she did. 'I thought I'd turn into a bloody ice statue before you answered.'

'How did you know this was my bedroom? Please tell me you haven't been just tapping random windows,' she whispered, shuddering at the thought of him waking Mother Catherine, or even sister Josey—she might have had a heart attack with the fright.

'I saw Michelle spying on us from this bedroom when we were out in the garden that time. I knew you shared with her so …' He shrugged as if to say, 'here I am.'

Yes, here he was. But …

'*Why* are you here?' Adeline hissed as glacial air whooshed in through the open window.

'Sexy PJs.' He smirked at the cute little puppies all over her Peter Alexander pyjamas. They'd been a gift from Sally last Christmas.

Her traitorous nipples hardened as he raked his gaze over them, and she hoped the flannelette was thick enough that he couldn't tell.

'Shut up,' was the lame retort she managed.

'How do you sleep with her making that racket all night?' Holden asked, nodding towards Michelle's prostrate, snoring form.

'She's nothing compared to Bella.' And then it suddenly hit her. 'Oh goodness. Is that why you're here?'

He nodded. 'Yep, I'm pretty sure she's in labour. Thought you might want to be with her.'

Oh goodness! If Mother Catherine found her sneaking out with a man in the middle of the night, she'd be sent packing immediately, but no way was Adeline missing the birth of Bella's puppies.

She'd just have to make sure she didn't get caught.

'I'll meet you on the road in two minutes.'

As Holden retreated, she closed the window, grabbed a pair of old yoga pants to pull on over her pyjamas, and then added a few more layers up top so she didn't freeze to death on the way. She contemplated leaving a note for Michelle but decided she'd be back long before morning prayer, then slipped out of the bedroom and crept quietly through the convent to the front door.

As far as she could tell, only Benno and Barnabas saw her leave, their beady yellow eyes glinting at her as she passed where they were lazing in the living room.

Outside, she saw Holden's dark silhouette waiting in the moonlight. The shrubs in the front garden were swaying in the wind.

'Come on,' he said, switching on a flashlight as she arrived beside him. He aimed it down the road and gestured for her to go in front of him. As they walked, the wind picked up and Adeline cursed the fact that she'd forgotten her beanie. Her hair whipped around her face, making it even more difficult to see in the dark.

And then, as if it could get any worse, it started to rain. Heavily.

They both began to run, but Adeline's foot caught in a pothole.

'Koala,' she yelled as she pitched forward.

But Holden was quick. He caught her before her hands hit the gravel, although not in time to save her from twisting her ankle. Couldn't Bella have chosen a better night to go into labour? And why hadn't Adeline thought to grab an umbrella? Why hadn't *he*? More to the point, why hadn't he brought his motorbike? They'd be there by now if he had.

'You okay?' he asked, his hand still steadying her.

'I'll be fine,' she said, shaking herself free, determined to ignore the spark where he'd touched her, but the moment she tried to walk, she winced.

He thrust the torch towards her. 'Hold this,' he said, turning his back. 'And get on.'

'What?' She stared at him; his shoulders were so ... so broad, but he couldn't be serious. 'You want to give me a piggyback?'

'Don't you think I'm strong enough?'

Oh no, that was not the problem at all. Adeline had no doubt that Holden could carry her to the ends of the earth if need be, but the thought of their bodies pressed closely together like that made her cheeks burn. And they weren't the only parts of her getting hot.

Since she'd told him about Gran, they'd been doing a very good job of pretending there was never any chemistry between them. They'd moved past awkwardness and into what she believed could be the foundations of a solid friendship.

But try as she might, those pesky feelings of attraction refused to die.

'I don't want to be an imposition,' she said.

He snorted and then hefted her onto his back before she could voice any further arguments. She tried to relax as she settled her arms around his neck and felt his hands hook together beneath her butt—*oh geez*—but that was near impossible when they were both sopping wet and her head was mere millimetres from his neck.

'Keep the light pointing ahead,' he growled, as he strode down the road through the howling storm.

By the time they got to his place, Adeline's ankle injury felt like a distant memory. What pain? The heat from his body and the intoxicating scent of his skin were like some magic analgesic. She tried to tell him she could take it from here, but he piggybacked her right into the shed, where she saw Bella lying on her side atop a massive pile of blankets by the back wall. He carried her over to the dog and as he gently put her down, Adeline gasped at the sight of a tiny black and white bundle of fur, the area around its nose a pale red, its eyes squeezed tightly shut, and its fur still damp. The first puppy!

She hobbled closer and peered down. 'Well done, girl.'

Bella looked up at her and smiled with pride as she began to push the next puppy out.

'Where's Rocky?' Adeline asked; she'd been expecting to find him—if not all the boys—here.

'I tried to wake him when I realised what was happening, but he was dead to the world. He's gunna kill me tomorrow.'

'I see,' she replied, trying not to freak out at the realisation that they were alone.

Holden picked up a towel from a pile and handed it to her. 'Here, take this and dry yourself off a bit. Might pay to take off your jacket and use a blanket to keep warm.'

She'd almost forgotten that her clothes were soaked. 'Thanks,' she said, taking the towel from him. 'You're very well prepared.'

In addition to the pile of clean towels, there were the blankets Bella was labouring on and another couple thrown over an old couch.

'The boys have been hoping she'd give birth in the house, but she kept sneaking out here and fussing around in this corner today, so I had a feeling. I thought these supplies might come in handy.'

Adeline nodded her approval as she attempted to dry her hair.

'Want a cup of tea?' he asked, gesturing towards a kettle on a table in the corner. 'Don't have any milk but I could go into the house and get some if you want.'

'Black tea will be fine, thank you.'

While he made the drinks, Adeline shrugged out of her jacket, wrapped a thick blanket around her and settled onto the couch just as another puppy was born—this one all white, except for one black ear.

'Two down, five to go,' Holden said as he handed her a mug of tea and then slid down onto the floor and leaned his back against the couch. They knew from Bella's ultrasound at the vet that she was having seven pups.

Adeline shifted to the very end of the couch. 'There's plenty of room up here for you.'

He looked up at her. 'You sure?'

She swallowed. She could tell he was checking that she was okay with being so close to him and while she wasn't exactly sure about that, it didn't feel right to make him sit on the cold, hard ground when the couch was big enough for at least three. 'Of course.'

Holden settled himself at the other end—leaving ample space between them—and, sipping their tea, they watched Bella as her two new puppies nuzzled at her teats.

'How long's it usually between births?' he asked.

'Anywhere from thirty minutes to an hour.'

'So we could be in for a long night?'

She nodded. 'Got much on tomorrow?'

'Nah. Just housework and making sure the boys do their homework and get outside a bit before playing video games. What about you?'

'It's Lola's final vow ceremony. Hopefully I don't fall asleep during the service.'

He laughed, then said, 'Feel free to lie down and get some rest between deliveries. I'll wake you when there's any action.'

It was a sensible idea, but there was no way she'd be able to nap with him watching her. And what would she use for a pillow? His lap? Her insides squeezed at the thought. No, she'd just have to stay awake. She wracked her mind for something to talk about, unable to bear the awkward silence, but Holden got in first.

'So did you always want to be a journo? Ever thought of writing fiction or anything?'

'No, never fiction. It was either journalism or law. I was interested in both, but as a kid I was always scribbling on scraps of paper. My brothers used to hate it when Dad put the news on the TV, but I ate it up. I was fascinated with what was going on in the world outside of Walsh. A career as a reporter seemed a good fit.'

He nodded.

'What about you?' she asked. 'I know you said you kind of fell into being a tattoo artist, but you're clearly creative. What did you want to be when you grew up?'

'I guess maybe something in art,' he admitted. 'I used to draw a lot as a kid, and art was my favourite subject, but my mum and stepdad always told me it wasn't something you could make a career out of.'

The more she heard about his parents, the less Adeline liked them. 'Well, I'm glad you showed them. Before tattooing, what did you do?'

'Bit of everything. Fruit picking, farm work, bar tending, bathroom cleaning. Followed the work around the country. You name it, I've probably done it.'

It was her turn to laugh. 'Sounds like you're a *jack* of all trades, then.'

His eyes widened. 'Is that why you call me "Jack"?'

She shook her head and smiled teasingly. 'Nope. I had that name for you long before I had any clue what you did.'

Holden frowned, then scratched his head, clearly trying to solve the puzzle.

'Hey.' He nodded towards the dogs. 'I think she's having another one.'

Teasing and conversation halted and they watched in awe as Bella welcomed a third puppy—this one all black—and began to lick it clean.

'This really is magic,' Holden mused. 'She's a natural, isn't she?'

Adeline smiled. 'Yeah, she's amazing.'

No matter how many births she'd witnessed, it still felt like a miracle every time. And tonight, with the rain pelting down on the tin roof, being here with someone who'd never seen it before somehow felt even more extraordinary. Holden couldn't take his eyes of the sight in front of him, and Adeline couldn't take her eyes off him. There was just something spellbinding about watching a grown man, with a thick beard and tattoos on almost every inch of his muscular body, misty-eyed over the birth of puppies.

'What are you looking at?' he asked, catching her staring.

She gulped—'Um, I was just wondering about your other tattoos'—and gestured towards the ink peeking out from beneath his sleeves. 'Is that a tail?'

He nodded, pushing up his sleeve to reveal a gorgeous picture of a lizard. It was so realistic and almost 3D; it looked like he had an actual frillneck lizard sitting on his arm. 'When I was a kid, I used to collect creatures from around the garden and keep them in containers as pets. The lizards were always my favourite.'

She laughed. It was difficult to imagine Holden as a little boy, before life had made him hard. 'How'd you become a tattoo artist?'

'Because of this lizard actually. I've always drawn,' he said. 'It was something I did to relieve stress when I was young. Anyway, not long after I moved here, I went into Colac to get this done. I showed the artist a picture I'd drawn and she asked if I'd ever thought of becoming a tattooist myself. I'd been helping Ford set up the barbershop, doing odd handyman jobs for people and the occasional shift at the pub, but when she offered to take me on as an apprentice, it was too good an opportunity to refuse. The rest, as they say, is history.'

'You drew that picture yourself?' she asked.

He nodded.

'You really can draw,' she said, staring down at it in admiration.

He laughed, then asked. 'What would you get if you got one?'

'I wouldn't. You know I think they're gross,' she lied, because she no longer thought any such thing. At least not on him.

'Humour me,' he said, meeting her gaze head on. 'Would you get Bella? A character from an old TV show? Book? What about a picture of a nun?'

It was her turn to laugh as she pictured the last one. 'Okay ... hypothetically, if I were to get a tattoo—'

'Which we both know you won't.'

She nodded faux-seriously. 'I'd probably get a typewriter. When I was little, I used to make up stories on this old typewriter of my grandmother's. I think it's what started my love of writing.'

Holden pulled a pen out of his pocket. 'Give me your arm.'

'What are you doing?' she asked, but she was already shrugging off the blanket, inching closer to him on the couch, and pushing up the sleeve of her jumper.

Chapter Thirty-eight

Holden looked down at Adeline's bare inner forearm in his rough hands. Her skin was almost as pale as a sheet of paper and so soft. Every cell in his body was on fire.

What kind of game was he playing, initiating a situation where he had to touch her like this?

He'd been so caught up in the magic of this moment that he'd dropped his guard. Ever since she'd told him about her grandmother, he'd been on his best behaviour. He'd be a liar if he said he no longer wanted her, but knowing that wasn't what she wanted had made restraint a lot easier. He'd hoped in time the lust would fade and their friendship would become enough, but here, alone in the dimly lit shed, the wind and rain howling outside, a pure miracle playing out in front of them, it was easy to forget *who* she was. Easy to forget they weren't just two people who had the undeniable hots for each other.

But you have to forget. That's what she wants.

The voice in his head might be right, but he couldn't back out now. He'd look like an idiot and in doing so, he'd also be admitting that he was affected by the situation. That he was affected by *her.* And he didn't want to make her uncomfortable, so instead, he swallowed hard and told himself to imagine she was just another client.

To focus on the art, not the canvas.

Not daring to look up and meet her gaze, he began to draw.

First, he sketched the outline of the typewriter, then the keys and the bit where the paper went at the top. Then he shaded in the detail, making the image 3D. Neither of them said a word while he drew, but he could feel Adeline's intense gaze, feel her warm breath punctuating the cool night air not far from his face. He could smell her minty toothpaste and that lavender and geranium shampoo that drove him insane. Her skin was so soft it was like drawing on silk.

So much for not noticing the canvas!

When the basic typewriter was finished, he should have lifted his pen and put the lid back on, but he didn't. He couldn't bring himself to stop touching her, so he added more detail in the form of flowers growing out from the edges and then a butterfly perched on the top of the paper as if the ancient typewriter had been abandoned in a secret garden years ago.

Oh God. Bronte was right. He was in serious danger of falling for Adeline Walsh.

It wasn't only that he was attracted to her beyond belief, but she'd cracked open his heart and got under his skin in a way no woman had before. He liked her as a friend, but he wanted her as something much, much more, and knowing he could never have her was a special type of torture.

He forced himself to lift the pen before things got ridiculous, before the drawing became as insane as his rapidly growing feelings.

'Tada,' he said, trying to sound nonchalant when he felt anything but.

'That's ... that's gorgeous,' Adeline whispered, running her fingers over the typewriter.

Of course, all he imagined was her running those fingers all over him.

'Don't sound so surprised.' He sounded crankier than he meant to.

'I'm not.' Adeline looked up into his eyes. 'I was just wondering about Mother Catherine's stance on tattoos.'

His heart sank at her mention of the convent, at the reminder that she was off limits. And he realised he was a lost cause.

He wasn't in *danger* of falling for her. He'd already fallen. Hard.

Shit. He turned to look at Bella, hoping to break the spell before Adeline might catch something in his expression that gave him away, and was just in time to see another miracle coming into the world.

'Puppy number four,' he said. Maybe he could make some excuse to leave her or send her packing after this one. Three more puppies meant at least another hour or two in her intoxicating presence, which would be absolute bloody torture.

'Oh, look.' Adeline grinned as the newest dog emerged. 'It's got a black love heart on its tummy.'

She was right. Puppy number four was almost all white, except for a few splotches of black on its face and a patch on its stomach that was undeniably heart shaped.

'Looks more like a slice of pizza to me,' Holden lied, in no mood for love hearts. But then he noticed the puppy didn't seem to be squirming the way the others had been, and his own anguish was forgotten. 'Hang on, is it okay?'

But Adeline was already on her feet, closing the distance between herself and Bella and dropping to her knees.

He watched helplessly—his heart in his throat—as she gently grabbed the tiny, wet, lifeless body and placed her finger against its chest.

'It's not breathing,' she whispered.

She sat cross-legged and placed it on her knee, angling it so its head was pointing downwards as she pried open its mouth and peered inside. Seconds later she moved positions again. Lying the puppy down on the blanket beside Bella, Adeline put two fingers back on its body and compressed a few times. Then inhaling loudly, she put her hands on its tiny mouth and lowered her own.

It looked like she was about to give the puppy the kiss of life when it spluttered a little and then gave a piercing whine.

Holden let out a breath he hadn't realised he'd been holding as Adeline whispered, 'Thank God.'

He stayed silent as she put the puppy right up against one of Bella's teats and encouraged it to nuzzle. Mum immediately began to lick baby clean as it took its first, tentative sucks.

'Is it going to be okay?' he asked, kneeling next to her.

She shrugged. 'I don't know, but ...'

'But it wouldn't have been if it wasn't for you,' he said, placing his hand on the small of her back. They stared at the dogs a few long moments, then Adeline finally pushed to her feet.

'Watch them while I wash my hands.'

He said he would, but it was her he couldn't take his eyes off as she walked over to the sink in the corner and began to scrub. He didn't know many women—hell, he didn't know many *people*—who'd be willing to put their mouth to a lifeless puppy to try and save it.

He'd never witnessed anything more astonishing in his life.

The smile she gave him as she dried her hands on a towel undid him.

'That was amazing,' he said, standing and walking over to her. '*You* are amazing.'

And then every ounce of resolve Holden had been clinging to crumbled.

He couldn't help himself. He ploughed his hands into her hair, cupped the back of her head and drew her lips to his.

But their mouths had barely touched before every part of him turned to ice. What the hell was he doing? *Fuck.*

He'd overstepped and she'd never forgive him.

'I'm so sorry,' he gushed, his hands curling into fists as he dropped them to his side. Why couldn't he control his damn urges?

'Don't be,' Adeline breathed, closing the distance he'd just put between them.

This time it was she who reached for him. She put her hands on either side of his face, pulled his mouth to hers and kissed him like her life depended on it.

Chapter Thirty-nine

Liquid heated flooded Adeline's body as she moved her hands up into Holden's hair and opened her mouth to deepen the kiss. A distant voice in her head told her this was wrong, but she couldn't resist the pull of lust. There was no doubt where this was leading. The feel of his pen tip etching her skin had been the most sensual thing she'd ever experienced. This had been inevitable from the moment he'd started drawing.

Or maybe much, much earlier.

If she were honest, there'd been something between them from almost the first time she'd laid eyes on him, but since their kiss— no matter how hard she fought against it, no matter how much she wished it weren't so—her feelings for him had been growing ever stronger.

Resisting the attraction had taken everything she had but she no longer had any fight left in her. Some things were impossible to ignore and the chemistry that charged between them was one of them.

She didn't *want* to fight it.

She wanted to touch, to taste, to feel the sensations that flooded her when his hands and mouth were upon her.

In that moment, nothing else mattered.

His hands still in her hair, Adeline sighed as Holden moved his hot mouth along her jawline, then kissed her neck. Her head fell back as pleasure rippled through her.

Unsure she could stand a minute longer, she gripped his shoulders, feeling the heat of his body seep into hers as he continued to work his magic.

'Are you sure you're okay with this?' Holden asked, his breath warm on her ear.

'Yes,' she hissed back, scrambling for the hem of his shirt. She was okay with this but not *only* this. She needed more. A lot more.

Seconds later, he was shirtless, and Adeline couldn't tell whether she'd been the one to remove his clothes or he had. Neither did she know who initiated their transition to the couch, but one moment they were upright and the next they were tumbling onto it. She lay on her back, Holden's long legs entwined with hers and his deliciously hard body stretched out on top of her as he kissed her again.

Deftly, his hand snuck under her pyjama top, and they both moaned when he discovered she wasn't wearing a bra. She trembled as the rough tips of his fingers skated across her nipples, which were already rock hard and aching for him. He cupped one breast and then the other as if he were memorising them with his touch, before pushing up on his knees.

'Can I take off your jumper?'

She nodded, sitting up slightly to assist him. Her pyjama top also went and then they were both topless. Desperate and no longer cold, she reached out to touch him, almost as if to check he were real. As if *this* were real. She ran her fingers along his collarbone. His skin was smooth and hot beneath her touch, and he sucked in a breath as she moved her hand down over his pecs and then ... lower.

'Don't touch that,' he said, pushing her back down, then gripping her wrists and bringing them up over her head. 'Not yet.'

Before she could object—not that she was planning to—he dipped his head and licked the underside of one breast, before swirling his tongue around the bud and sucking it deep into his mouth. She shrieked at the intensity of the pleasure that rocked her, her breath already fast and shallow.

'You like that?' he whispered.

'Uh-huh.'

'What about this?' he asked, kissing from her breast down her belly.

She was wound up too tight to reply, but guessed the whimper that escaped her mouth gave him the answer he was looking for. He dipped his fingers to the waistband of her pyjamas and skated teasingly along the top, before sliding his hand right into her knickers.

'Oh God!' she cried, totally forgetting her vow not to take the Lord's name in vain.

His fingers slipped easily inside her and her body rocked against the rhythm of his touch. She'd never been so wet in her life. Just when she thought she could handle it no longer, he let her go. 'Can I kiss you?'

Her eyes widened as she realised he didn't mean her top lips. Embarrassment overcame her for just a second, but then desire got the better of her and she nodded.

'Lift up,' he ordered and when she did as she was told, he pulled her pyjama pants and knickers right off her legs, so she was lying entirely naked beneath him. Perhaps it was the way he was looking at her—his eyes black with hunger as if she were a forbidden fruit—but she didn't feel one iota of self-consciousness as he dipped his head and teased his tongue right into her.

She could count on one hand the number of times a man had done this to her and it had always been after she'd taken care of him first, almost as if they'd felt obliged, but nothing about what Holden was doing felt like an obligation, which only turned Adeline on further.

'You taste so good,' he growled. 'I've wanted to do this from the moment I first saw you.'

'You're … very good … at it,' she managed, barely able to form words, never mind coherent sentences as he dipped his head back between her legs, his beard abrasive and delicious against her skin as he sucked the life out of her, bringing her to the kind of bone-shattering climax she'd only ever read about.

'Take off your jeans,' she ordered when he was done.

Her body was swollen with desire and although she felt like she'd just exploded, if she didn't have him right now, she would literally die. She didn't expect to orgasm again, but she wanted the connection that came with having Holden buried deep inside her.

'Yes, ma'am,' he said, still grinning as he stood to quickly do as he was told.

But when he was done, instead of joining her again like she wanted, he stood there in all his naked glory—and it really was glorious—and checked in with her once again. 'You sure you want to do this, sweetheart?'

Sweetheart. Her heart swooned at this term of endearment, whispered in his baritone voice. This was her chance to back out but the voices in her head telling her to keep going were louder than those telling her to stop.

'Yes,' she replied with the utmost conviction as she yanked him back down on top of her and gasped in utter ecstasy when he sank into her solidly and filled her completely. Her body surged against him, over and over and over again.

And nothing had ever felt so right.

This was it. *This* was what sex was supposed to feel like. This was what had been missing in all her other relationships.

'Oh, God!'

And then she couldn't think anymore. She took the Lord's name in vain again as Holden thrust one more time, pushing some button deep inside her and causing her to explode all over again.

He swore and breathed her name, his release following mere seconds after her own.

Afterwards, he collapsed atop her, and they clung to each other, their hot, naked bodies slick with sweat, their hearts pounding so hard that she could feel his thumping in time with her own. They both needed to catch their breath, and in that moment, all Adeline could think was that he'd destroyed her. Ruined her for anyone or anything else.

Suddenly she understood the term 'making love' because that was exactly what this was. She wasn't just attracted to Holden's body—if that was the case, she would have been able to resist him, resist this—she was attracted to everything about him. His wry humour, the way he teased her at every chance he got, his kindness, how he always put Ford and the boys, even the dogs, before himself.

What they'd just done felt like so much more than just the act of sex. With Holden inside her, she'd felt more alive and more *herself* than she ever had in her life.

This was why she'd never had success with any other guy before—she hadn't been waiting for God, she'd been waiting for *him*. And God or fate or whatever had led her here not because she was destined to be a nun, but because they were destined to meet.

It all made illuminating sense.

'I love you,' she blurted, unable to keep this wonderful truth inside her a second longer.

But Holden stilled above her. 'What did you say?'

'I love you,' she repeated.

She'd told others this before, but now she understood that she'd never meant it with any of them. This was different. This was all-consuming. Suddenly everything made perfect sense—why she couldn't stop thinking about him, why she wanted to help him, why she'd felt this weird pull towards his place ever since the first time Bella escaped here.

Nothing else mattered but them.

But Holden shook his head and rolled off her. 'You're just saying that 'cos of the sex,' he said gruffly.

'No, I'm not,' she objected, stung.

'Yes. You are.' He was already reaching for his jeans and now the cool air hit her like a shower of ice. 'You said yourself you'd never had good sex before. Well, now I've shown you how mind-blowing it can be when it's with someone who knows what they're doing, and it's gone to your head. Once you recover, you'll realise that great sex and love don't have to go hand in hand.'

'Damn, you're cocky,' she said, fighting tears. Not to mention condescending. How dare he tell her how she felt!

Holden shrugged one shoulder as if to say, 'it's not cocky when it's the truth' and then stooped to grab his shirt as casually as if he hadn't just ripped out her heart.

He might not feel anything more for her, but her heart had been involved just as much as the rest of her when they'd come together.

'I hope you're right,' she told him as she scrambled to gather her own clothes, not wanting to give him the undeserved perk of gazing at her naked body a second longer. While they'd been busy, another puppy had been born—now there were five—but no way could she stick around to welcome the next two. She yanked on her pyjama pants and threw the top and jumper—still mingled together—over her head. 'With any luck, I'll wake up tomorrow and see what a fucking bastard you are and feel nothing but remorse for what we just did.'

She couldn't believe they'd had sex right there in the shed where any of the boys could have walked in on them.

It was like a demon had taken control of her body.

They hadn't even used a condom. What the hell had she been thinking? What if she got an STD? Or worse. What if she got pregnant? She doubted Mother Catherine would buy the old immaculate conception story, even though it had worked well enough for the Virgin Mary. *Oh God.* Nausea welled in her stomach at the thought of the conversation she would have to have with her. Keeping secret about the kiss was one thing, but even Michelle would agree she needed to come clean about this. Even if she wasn't pregnant—*Please God don't let me get pregnant*—this was a sin too big to bury.

But first she had to get through tomorrow—or rather today— because she couldn't ruin Lola's big moment.

'Do you want me to walk you back to the convent?' Holden asked as Adeline shoved her feet into her sneakers.

She glared up at him, her fingers fumbling with the laces. 'Are you for real?'

Too full of shame, too full of sadness, she could barely stand to look at him, never mind walk the agonising kilometre or so up the road with him beside her trying to pretend that nothing had changed between them.

Everything had changed, and his rejection felt a million times worse than Ryder O'Connell's or any of the others that had come before.

'I'm sorry,' he called as she fled out into the stormy night.

'So am I,' she yelled back.

Sorry she'd ever met Holden Campbell.

Tears streamed down her face, blending with the rain as she hurried back to the convent and then quietly snuck inside. She needed to erase all evidence of her night-time excursion before anyone woke up. Her plan to sneak into her bedroom to collect dry clothes before heading to the bathroom faltered when she stubbed her already sore foot on the corner of her bed.

'Fuck.'

Of course, sleeps-like-the-dead Michelle sat upright in bed at the sound of her curse. 'Adeline? Is that you?' she asked, her voice croaky with sleep as she scrambled to switch on the bedside light.

'Yes, sorry, go back to sleep,' she replied, keeping her head down as she gathered her things. If Michelle saw her face, she'd see she'd been crying. 'I'm just going to have a shower.'

'At this time of the night?'

'It's morning.'

'Hang on …' Michelle narrowed her eyes. 'Why are you soaking wet? Have you been out?'

Adeline's stomach turned to rock, but she couldn't tell her roomie about her transgressions, at least not until she'd spoken to Mother Catherine. 'Yes, I was at Holden's—Bella had her puppies.'

'Wow, that's cool.' Michelle's eyes lit up, but then she frowned. 'How did you know?'

'I'm tired, wet and cold. I'll explain later,' Adeline said, rushing down the hall into the bathroom before Michelle could pry the whole dirty truth out of her.

Under the warm shards of water, she attempted to scrub the scent of him from her skin and the memories of what they'd done from her mind. She moved the soap to her arm to wash away the typewriter he'd drawn on her skin but couldn't bring herself to do so. It was so beautiful, and he'd been so tender and sweet while he'd been drawing it. Had that all been a ruse to knock down her defences?

Was his endgame always to get her into bed?

It was hard to imagine the man she'd grown to know—and love—over the last few weeks could do such a thing, but then again, the Holden who'd touched her like her body was a temple was hard to reconcile with the Holden who'd acted so cruelly afterwards.

One of them was a fraud. One of them was faking it.

Her heart wanted to believe it was the latter, but her head told her otherwise.

If only she'd listened to her head in the shed last night, she wouldn't have to give up the best thing that had ever happened to her. Leaving the convent—leaving the sisters, her *friends*—would be another kind of heartbreak.

How much more could she take?

But as the water started to go cold, Adeline began to wonder if maybe she didn't have to throw it all away. Maybe she didn't have to tell Mother Catherine after all. She hadn't told Michelle, and it was unlikely Holden would say anything to anyone. He'd made it quite clear he didn't feel the same way about her, so it wasn't like anything was ever going to happen between them again.

When she'd first arrived, Mother Catherine had told her that the fact that she'd had sex before entering the convent wouldn't prevent her from giving herself to this vocation, as long as she committed herself entirely to God from that moment forward. Well, she'd made a mistake, but she hadn't taken first vows yet— she was still a postulant—so maybe it wasn't an irreparable one.

And she knew she'd never break the chastity rule again because if she couldn't have Holden, she didn't want anyone else.

Chapter Forty

'You look like shit,' Ford said as Holden came into the kitchen the following morning and headed straight for the coffee.

'I've been up all night,' he replied, reaching for his favourite mug.

Ford frowned, the flipper in his hand halting over a hotplate of pancakes—their ritual Sunday-morning breakfast.

'Bella had her puppies,' he added just as Rocky entered.

'What?!' the boy shrieked. 'When?'

Holden spooned double his usual amount of coffee into the mug. 'Early hours of the morning. One had a bit of a rough start, but they all seem to be thriving now.'

After Adeline had left, he'd gone into the house and showered, then attempted a few hours of sleep before getting up just after dawn, checking on the dogs again, and making sure they hadn't left any evidence of their encounter.

'You promised you'd wake me,' Rocky yelled, but he was already halfway out of the house.

The other boys, also on their way into the kitchen for breakfast, wondered what the commotion was about and as soon as Holden told them, they hightailed it after Rocky.

'Damn, the eggs are gunna go cold,' Ford said, but he sounded excited rather than disappointed. He turned off the stove. 'Are the pups cute?'

'What do you think?'

Ford grinned. 'In that case, I better go have a look-see myself. Breakfast can wait.' He started wheeling himself towards the door. 'You coming?

Holden shook his head. 'I've had my dose of cuteness for now.'

He couldn't bring himself to go back yet again to that place where he'd had the best sex of his life. It was so much better with Adeline than it had ever been with anyone else, and the only explanation he could think of was that he felt more for her than he'd ever felt for anyone else. When she'd said she loved him, his heart had felt like it was shattering into a million pieces. The raw honesty and emotion in her voice told him she was telling the truth. She wasn't mistaking her feelings. It had taken all his self-control not to hold her close and tell her he felt exactly the same. That he loved her too. Had done since the moment she'd run chaotically into his life all those weeks, months, ago looking for Bella.

But he'd kept that secret firmly locked inside him and instead he'd tried to make Adeline hate him, because no matter how much it pained him to hurt her, he just didn't deserve the happiness that would come with accepting her love. It would be better for her—better for the both of them—if she got over him quickly.

He plucked one of the pancakes off the hotplate, taking it and his coffee to the table, but he was so filled with remorse that he couldn't stomach more than one mouthful.

When Ford returned from the barn he was still staring at the pancake in his hand, drowning in heartbreak and guilt.

'You should see the boys, oohing and aahing over the puppies like a bunch of old ladies.'

'Huh?' he said, blinking his brother into focus.

'I guess they'll come in when they're hungry.' Ford wheeled over to the stove and flipped the cold pancakes into the bin, before cleaning the hot plate, sizzling some butter onto it and then dropping on more lumps of batter. As he worked, he asked, 'You going to go tell Adeline?'

'She already knows,' Holden admitted, staring into his empty mug.

Ford turned from the pancakes to look at him. 'She was here overnight?'

He simply nodded.

'Hang on ... why do you look like someone died? You're more than just tired. What's going on?'

He hadn't planned on telling anyone—not Ford nor Bronte—what had happened between him and Adeline, but the words just came out as if he needed to get it off his chest. Confess his sins. 'We slept together.'

'You *what*?'

'Keep your voice down,' Holden hissed, glancing towards the back door. He didn't want the boys hearing this.

'I'm sorry, but when you say you slept together, you mean ...?'

'Yeah, we had sex.'

'Oh boy.' Ford's eyebrows shot up and then he wheeled himself over to peer out the window. 'No sign of the boys, tell me everything.'

First, Holden confessed the kiss they'd shared weeks ago; how they'd made a pact that it would never happen again and managed to get back to some kind of normal, even though he'd been unable to get her out of his head.

'I can't believe you didn't tell me this before now. Does Bronte know?'

Holden nodded. 'But I was trying to forget it.'

'And even knowing you had this crazy connection, you deliberately went to her bedroom in the middle of the night and lured her into the shed?' Ford asked.

'You make it sound like I'm some kind of predator. It wasn't like that. We both wanted it.' At least at the time.

Ford shook his head in disbelief. 'Is that why you didn't wake Rocky? You wanted to be alone with Adeline?'

'No. You know how the kids sleep—once they're out, they're dead to the world.' But even as he said this, he wondered if it was true. Perhaps he could have tried harder to rouse the boy.

Ford exhaled loudly and ran a hand over his closely cropped hair. 'What happens now?'

'What do you mean?'

'Are you two an item? Is she going to leave the convent for you?'

Holden's stomach twisted at the suggestion. He recalled the way she'd spoken about her life there when she'd told him about her grandmother. He knew how lost and alone she'd felt until she joined the sisters.

'I hope not,' he said.

Ford blinked. 'So it's not going to happen again?'

Holden swallowed. Oh boy, did he want that. He wanted to touch her and taste her again, he wanted to take her and hold her like she was the most precious thing in the world. He wanted to sleep with her. Not just have sex with her, but really sleep with her.

He wanted to wake up with her.

'No. The itch is scratched now.' He shrugged. 'At least on my part.'

'What do you mean?'

'She told me she loves me,' Holden admitted.

'And what did you tell her?' Ford asked, an edge to his voice.

'I told her she was crazy, that the sex had gone to her head. I told her she should go back to the convent and forget it ever happened.'

Ford stared at Holden, and for a moment he thought maybe his brother was going to throw something at him. In which case he'd welcome it. He'd told Ford because he wanted to be punished. He was furious with himself, but the self-loathing wasn't enough. He wanted real, physical pain.

'You're a fucking bastard, you know that?' Ford said.

He nodded. This wasn't news to him. He'd known that ever since he'd woken up in the hospital all those years ago only to be told he'd made his brother a cripple. Since then he'd called himself a lot worse than anything Ford ever could.

'What the hell were you thinking? Adeline isn't like Bronte. This would have been massive for her. She's training to become a *nun* for fuck's sake! You could have ruined her life.'

'I wasn't thinking, okay?!' That was the problem. He hadn't even used a bloody condom! But in that moment, he'd lost his head.

He'd forgotten who he was, who she was, and all the reasons why sleeping with her was a bad idea.

'So what's this mean for the tractor pull?' Ford asked.

'Huh?'

His brother repeated the question and Holden shrugged. After their first kiss, Adeline had been adamant that she'd continue to help with the fundraiser, but this might be where she drew the line.

But they couldn't just cancel it—not when it was only a few weeks away.

'I guess that's up to her. If she doesn't want to be involved any-more, I'll respect that and handle it all myself. But if she does ...'

What *would* he do?

Did he really think he could continue to work so closely with her after what they'd done? That he could just forget she'd told him she loved him and ignore the fact that he'd fallen in love with her as well?

Talk about a recipe for disaster.

'Maybe you could be the mouthpiece between us,' he asked Ford hopefully.

Ford looked at him like he was the scum of the earth, but then nodded.

'Thanks,' Holden said, relief washing over him.

'Don't thank me,' Ford snapped. 'I'm not doing this because I want to make things easy for you. I'm helping because I care about Adeline, and she doesn't deserve the way you've treated her.'

Holden agreed, but just to keep Ford angry at him like he deserved, he said, 'Chill. It's not like I killed someone. It was sex between two consenting adults.'

Ford opened his mouth as if to tell Holden exactly what he thought of this, but at that moment the back door flew open and Toovs and Sam thundered into the kitchen, effectively putting an end to the conversation.

'Those puppies are fucking unreal,' Toovs yelled, grinning harder than Holden had ever seen before.

'I can't believe Bella had that many inside her,' added Sam, reaching for one of the pancakes Ford had been adding to the pile while they were talking. 'I mean she was fat, but Jesus!'

Holden stood and went to put his mug in the dishwasher. Then he grabbed his keys off the hook on the wall. 'I'm going for a bike ride.'

'Where you going?' Toovs asked through a mouthful of pancake.

'Colac,' he replied, and then left the house before anyone could ask any further questions.

Chapter Forty-one

By the time Adeline emerged from the bathroom, the house was starting to rouse. She could hear the water running in the other shower, and some of Lola's guests were already nursing cups of tea in the living room. Although some things were going to be done differently today, the sisters still gathered as usual for morning prayer. Adeline was so tired she didn't know how she'd make it through this half hour, never mind the rest of the day. She tried to get into the celebratory mood as she helped Michelle and Rita prepare food for the reception and the other sisters assisted Lola to get ready—exactly like bridesmaids would a bride—but when the time came for her to get dressed for church, her stomach churned.

Mother Catherine and the sisters who had already taken perpetual vows were wearing their formal habits—black tunic with wooden rosary bead belt, black veil, white collar, a cross hanging around their neck and the plain silver ring on their left hands, a symbol of their union with Christ. Lola would now also wear this habit for sacred occasions, whereas Michelle, a novice, having only taken first vows, had a white headpiece instead of a black one. They all wore plain black shoes.

Adeline, having taken no official vows yet, dressed in a long black skirt and a smart white shirt with a tiny pin of a cross on her lapel.

Despite not being in full habit, she felt like a fraud.

The sisters were so pure, so full of joy, singing and laughing as they dressed for the ceremony and then piling into the Tarago and the other cars that took them the short distance into town to the Catholic church. As she entered the building—jam-packed with more people than she'd ever seen for the regular Sunday services—she tried to forget about the last twenty-four hours and focus on the proceedings. She sat a couple of rows back from the front next to Michelle, and the whole congregation rose when the procession entered. First came the local priest, then the bishop who had come all the way from Ballarat for the service, followed by the servers and altar boys, then Lola, Mother Catherine and the other fully professed sisters following behind.

Lola looked radiant as she headed down the aisle towards the crucifix hanging on the wall, exactly like a real bride walking towards her groom. She showed no signs of doubt—not a hint of cold feet—and Adeline remembered how she'd said that she'd been a bundle of nerves taking her first vows, scared she might do something wrong, but in the weeks leading up to these ones, she'd felt nothing but excitement and reverence. The service began with the proclamation of the gospel and prayers, and incense was wafted around the altar to represent the congregation's prayers rising up.

During the Rite of Calling, the bishop asked Lola if she were ready for this life, then came the reading of scripture and the homily, before the Litany of Saints where Lola lay prostrate on the floor in front of the altar while everyone prayed to the saints, asking them to help her in her journey. And then it was the moment of profession. Lola stood at the front, her hand on the Bible and Mother Catherine's hand on hers as she read the vows she'd written earlier, making her promises to God. Adeline knew from her studies that Mother's hand was a symbol both of reception of the vows and a promise from her and their community to support Lola throughout her religious life.

As Lola signed her vows on the altar, Adeline glanced sideways to see Michelle beaming as if this were the most magical thing she'd ever borne witness to, but it felt surreal to her. Although it was happening right in front of her eyes, she felt more like someone watching a show on TV. When Michelle pressed a tissue into Adeline's hand, she realised she was crying. Her eyes met those of her roommate, who gave her a wink, totally misunderstanding her emotion.

She wasn't crying because she was overwhelmed by the sanctity of this moment; she was crying because of Holden and the fact that she'd never get to walk up the aisle towards him.

Part of her thought it was ridiculous to have such intense feelings—to be in love—after such a short time, but the heart knew what the heart wanted.

And whether she could have him or not, Adeline's heart wanted Holden.

With this knowledge came the realisation that she couldn't sweep last night under the carpet—she had to tell Mother Catherine—but first she had to sit through the rest of Mass and then the celebratory feast with the bishop, the priest, the sisters, many of the congregation, and Lola's family and friends.

She'd never wanted to attend a party less.

★ ★ ★

Following the meal, which Adeline nibbled at like a mouse, she slipped out into the garden to get some much-needed fresh air.

Thankfully the rain had eased earlier that morning and the mid-afternoon air once again held the promise of spring.

Sitting on the bench under the big old eucalypt, a gentle wind swishing in the leaves above, she contemplated her future.

Would she have to leave the moment she told Mother Catherine? Or would she be allowed time to pack up her things and work out where to go from here? Would she go back to Walsh? The thought didn't bring much joy—she could imagine the whole town whispering over their trolleys in the IGA about her failure to become a nun—but perhaps it would have to be a stopgap while she worked out what to do next. She didn't even care about people talking behind her back anymore.

Gossip couldn't hurt as much as unrequited love, and others couldn't loathe her anywhere near as much as she loathed herself.

'May I sit?'

Adeline knew even before she turned towards the voice that it belonged to Mother Catherine. Her stomach twisted with nerves at the conversation they were about to have but she nodded, nevertheless.

Mother Catherine smiled—'Thank you'—and then sat beside her, smoothing her long black tunic over her knees. 'How did you find your first vow ceremony and celebrations?'

Adeline swallowed. 'It … it was …'

When she couldn't find the words, Mother Catherine took her hand. 'Something is bothering you, dear child.'

It wasn't a question. Adeline wondered how she'd ever thought she could try and pull the wool over her superior's eyes.

'I'm so sorry,' she said, tears springing to her eyes again.

'Has this got to do with Holden Campbell and why you snuck out in the middle of the night?'

'You *knew* about that?!'

Mother Catherine simply nodded. She was like God—she saw and *knew* everything.

'I ... I ...' Shame burned her cheeks, but she couldn't bring herself to tell her the sordid details, so instead she confessed, 'I'm in love with him.'

Mother Catherine smiled. 'Then why are you crying, my child?'

Adeline's tears froze in shock. 'Because I didn't come here to fall in love. I came here to learn to serve God. To be a sister. And instead, I'm nothing but a failure.'

'You came here to explore this way of life, to see if it was the right one for you. There's no shame in discovering it's not. There's no shame in love between two people. God's a big fan of that as well, you know.' Before Adeline could tell her that this love was one-sided, Mother Catherine added, 'I had my suspicions from the day you arrived that you were only destined to be with us for a short while.'

'You what?' Adeline couldn't believe what she was hearing. 'Why didn't you say something?'

Perhaps she could have been spared this heartbreak if she'd been told back then she wasn't a right fit for the convent. Then she might never have even met Holden.

Mother Catherine chuckled. 'I knew God had brought you to us for a reason. I think you came to us for healing, and I think God chose us because of our proximity to the Campbells. And just like you said, he sent Bella down the road for a reason—to lead you to Holden.'

Adeline couldn't hold back her anger. 'Well, if that's the case,' she spat, 'then God has made a monumental fu— *stuff up*, because he forgot to bring Holden into the plan. When I told him I loved him, he told me in no uncertain terms that he didn't feel the same way.'

Mother Catherine blinked. 'Are you sure? Maybe he just got scared by the l-word. Men sometimes need a little longer to realise their feelings.'

'Quite sure,' Adeline said, recalling the horror in his eyes. 'He couldn't have been clearer if he'd hired a plane and scrawled his *un*-feelings across the sky.'

'But I … I saw the way he looked at you at the markets—total adoration and devotion.'

'What?' Was Mother Catherine on drugs? 'We were furious with each other that day. We were arguing and hating on each other.'

'And the heat in that argument was as visible as if real fireworks were shooting between you,' said the older woman with a smile. 'There's a fine line between anger and passion.'

'Well, *you* might have seen passion,' Adeline admitted, her cheeks flaming again as she thought of the early hours of the morning, 'but I promise you that's all Holden feels towards me. That's all any man ever feels. It's like I have a big sign on my forehead saying I'm a girl to take to bed but never home to the parents. I shouldn't be surprised. I thought coming here and trying to live a better life would remove such problems from my life, but obviously I'm the problem. I'm too weak to resist temptation.'

'You're not weak, Adeline.' Mother Catherine's voice was more forceful than she'd ever heard it, almost cross. 'As I've told you before, none of us are perfect. We all make mistakes, but God is forgiveness, and you need to learn to forgive yourself. As long as you hold onto this idea that you are innately bad, you will never be able to live a full and happy life.'

'But what am I supposed to do now?' Adeline asked on another sob.

Mother Catherine smiled and gently took her hand. 'Listen to what God wants. He has a plan for you. You just have to trust him.'

'You don't think that plan is for me to be a sister? That I just took a diversion along the path?'

'What do you think?'

Adeline swallowed, then shook her head. Nothing had changed since her revelation in the church.

Mother Catherine nodded. 'All is not lost though. You have your job at the *Gazette*. Maybe you can rent a house in town and really throw your heart and soul into that. While you're looking, you can stay here as long as you need. We'll always be your family, even if you're not a sister.'

How could words both break her heart and fill it at the same time? 'Thank you,' she sniffed.

In reply, Mother Catherine took her in her arms and gave her a much-needed hug.

After this conversation, Adeline wasn't in the mood to head back to the celebrations, so she went to her bedroom instead and changed into some comfy old clothes. After a few months in the convent uniform of sensible navy trousers, white shirt and a cardigan to keep off the chill, it felt odd donning her old clothes, and besides she had little to choose from since she'd kept the bare minimum, giving the rest to the women's refuge when she'd arrived.

She'd only just lain down on the bed to try and get some rest when a knock sounded at her door, and although she was in no mood to talk to anyone, she called, 'Come in.'

Sister Rita appeared, her usual Diet Coke can in her hand, and a smile on her face. 'You've got a visitor.'

'Who is it?' Adeline asked.

'Holden Campbell. Guessing he wants to talk to you about the tractor pull?' Rita said, pretending to lift a fake weight in her arm.

Holden? Adeline's heart lurched. What was he doing here? Could he be here to apologise? Maybe he'd come to tell her he was wrong about last night and that he did have feelings for her.

'Please, tell him I'll be there in a moment,' Adeline said, throwing back the covers.

Two minutes later, after pinching her cheeks to give them some colour and checking that her eyes weren't too bloodshot from crying, she found him standing awkwardly on the porch, staring out towards the road, a tiny paper bag in his hand.

He turned as she cleared her throat, and then frowned slightly as he took in her outfit of black yoga pants and an oversized hoodie emblazoned with the logo of the Walsh Wanderers Football Club.

They spoke at the same time.

'What are you doing here?'

'Sorry about last night.'

She raised her eyebrows, all her dreams dashed in that one sentence, which didn't sound like the declaration of love she'd been hoping for. 'What exactly are you sorry about?'

His face went pale and despite his beard, Adeline saw his Adam's apple moving to indicate he was swallowing in discomfort. *Good.* Why should she be the only one suffering?

'I'm sorry for hurting you. I'm sorry I can't reciprocate your feelings.'

Ouch. She folded her arms across her chest. What did he want her to say to him? That she forgave him for sleeping with her and ditching her like pretty much every other guy she'd ever been with?

She knew the Sisters of Grace were supposed to be forgiving, but she wasn't going to stand there and ease his guilt. Rita was right, he was probably here because of the tractor pull.

'You don't need to worry about the fundraiser,' she said coolly. 'I'm not pulling out and I don't need your help anymore except for heavy lifting on the day. Everything is pretty much organised.'

'Thank you. I appreciate everything you've done. And I know you probably don't want to work with me anymore, although if you do need anything, please let Ford know and I'll do it, without getting in your way. But that's not why I'm here,' he said, offering the small white bag in his hand. 'I wanted to give you this.'

'What is it?' she asked, automatically taking it from him.

'It's the morning-after pill. Since the Smallton Pharmacy is closed on Sundays, I rode into Colac to get it for you. So our little mistake doesn't turn into an accident that stops you being a nun.'

She almost laughed at his stupidity—he couldn't honestly think her life could go on as normal after what they'd done—but his words hurt too much for laughter.

Our little mistake.

She wanted to throw his *gift* back in his face—to maybe even make him stew a little, let him think that if she was pregnant, maybe she'd keep it—but that would be cutting off her nose to spite her face. She didn't even have a place to live and couldn't sort out her own life; pity the poor baby that ended up with her as a mother! Besides, she was too sad for revenge.

But she didn't thank him. That would be taking things too far.

Instead, she swallowed all the words, all the heartache, and tucked the bag into the front pocket of her hoodie before heading back inside and closing the door behind her.

Chapter Forty-two

They couldn't have asked for a more perfect day for the tractor pull if they'd put in a request to God himself, which Adeline quite probably had. The sun was shining, the temperature was in the mid-twenties and there wasn't a cloud in the sky. Holden hoped that if today went well, it would help towards making her realise she wasn't a terrible person. A terrible person wouldn't have thrown her heart and soul into this event the way she had. A terrible person would have backed out after he'd rejected her, but she hadn't done any such thing.

The only terrible person around here was him.

Although they hadn't spoken since the afternoon at the convent, she'd been true to her word and hadn't let what had happened between them stop her from doing everything she could to make today a success. She talked to Ford at the barbershop when she had messages or requests for him to pass on to Holden, and Ford had also told her when Holden was working so she could visit Bella and the puppies, but he'd not seen so much as a glimpse of her.

He'd hoped her absence from his life would also free her from his mind, but that hadn't been the case at all. If anything, the sleepless nights had only grown more frequent.

The boys must have sensed that something had gone down between them, but they hadn't said a word. Maybe that was because he'd been a grump to live with and they didn't dare say anything to make it worse. His grumpiness was just another thing to feel guilty about. Ford had called him out on it more than once, but he simply couldn't help it. He'd never felt more dejected in his life.

They'd all arrived at the crack of dawn to set up and despite feeling like he'd prepared himself for seeing Adeline again, Holden struggled to breathe at the sight of her in denim shorts, silver sneakers and a fitted pink jumper. He had to use all his mental energies not to stare at her bare legs. It was weird to see her out of nun uniform again, but perhaps she'd thought shorts and sneakers more practical for the day's requirements. Still, with so much skin on view it was impossible not to remember holding her. Impossible not to think about how she'd felt when she'd been quivering beneath his touch. She was like a drug and as much as he knew he couldn't have her, that didn't stop him wanting another fix.

Swallowing his discomfort, he made his way across to say hello. They were, after all, joint organisers of this event, so they needed to be civil today at least. She was holding a clipboard and was surrounded by a posse of nuns.

'Holden,' she replied coolly to his 'Good morning'.

'Everything's looking good here. Pity it wasn't another month or so and we could have brought along the puppies to find new homes. Maybe auctioned them off.'

She raised an eyebrow. 'Ford gave you the order of events and everything I need you to do, right?'

He nodded.

'Well then, let's not waste time with idle chitchat. We've got a lot to achieve in the next couple of hours.'

The sisters surrounding Adeline glared at him—with a vitriol he didn't think Brides of Christ were supposed to harbour—which meant she must have confessed at least some of what happened between them. He didn't care what anyone else thought of him, but he didn't want to make things more difficult for her than he already had, so he stepped back, and headed back over to Sam, Toovs, Rocky and Mitch and Luka, who'd just arrived.

'Hey congrats, mate,' he said, shaking Luka's hand and clapping him on the shoulder. 'Heard you scored the star role.'

Holden could tell he was trying to suppress a grin and be cool about it. 'Yeah. Thanks.'

Rocky laughed. 'I can't wait to see Luka in a dress.'

'It's not a dress,' Luka argued.

'Anyway.' Holden cleared his throat. 'You boys ready?'

'Ready?' Mitch pumped his arm muscles theatrically as he looked to the others. 'We were born ready, right bros?'

Rocky punched the air. 'Yeah, we're gunna cream the other teams!'

Holden forced a laugh. 'I meant, are you ready to help set up?'

'Sure,' they agreed.

'But we don't want to over-exert ourselves,' Sam warned. 'We need to conserve some energy for the big event.'

Holden rolled his eyes—*any excuse*—but over the next hour, the kids threw themselves into setting up the barricades and shade tents. The event would take place in the middle of the oval—a straight stretch of twenty metres where the teams would compete to see how fast they could pull the donated tractor over the finish line. On either side of the track, they erected shade for spectators, leaving spaces in between for the food trucks and stalls to set up.

While the boys did the heavy lifting, Adeline, Ford, Michelle, Sister Lola, Sister Rita and a few other volunteers made sure everything else was in order. Mike and Reeve—who were moving to Melbourne next week—were also there, setting up a PA system for announcements. Somehow Adeline had managed to secure a professional horse racecaller to do the honours today. Was there anything she couldn't achieve?

At about eight-thirty, Nola arrived to deliver her vintage tractor and nab a good vantage spot for herself and her kids to enjoy the day. Her twin seven-year-old boys reminded Holden of the puppies as they jumped around her and begged for candy floss and lemonade.

Soon after, the teams began to arrive to collect their number bibs and the time of their event. The groups would go in order of age and gender, with the teenagers first, then the adult women, the men and finally the mixed teams. A number of families had registered just for the fun of it, and it seemed as if everyone who hadn't registered had come out to watch.

By ten o'clock the oval was brimming with people. Holden took the microphone and welcomed the crowd—participants and spectators.

'Thank you for coming today. I'm blown away by the support we've received over the last month or so for Home Sweet Tiny Homes, a project very close to my heart.'

He didn't want to drone on too long, but spent a few minutes explaining how he had been a foster kid with nowhere to go when he hit eighteen. He talked about his firsthand experience as a foster-carer, saying that the funds raised today would help house a foster child while he made the transition to independence. He didn't name Sam as the candidate for the first tiny house but said that he hoped to get his current foster kids involved in the building of the tiny houses on his property.

'If you haven't already read the wonderful article that Adeline Walsh wrote for the *Gazette*, then I strongly recommend you do, as it gives even more background on the need for a charity like ours.'

He found her in the crowd but when their eyes met, she quickly looked away and he swallowed his hurt to continue. She might not want to look at him but that didn't mean she didn't deserve praise. After her article had been published, they'd had an influx of donations from local business owners, and even some pledges from farmers to offer work to boys in need and put a tiny house or two on their own properties.

'And speaking of Adeline, please give her a mammoth round of applause. Today wouldn't be happening if it weren't for her. Not only has she done the majority of the work to organise the tractor pull, but she believes in my vision as much as I do and has helped me make it a reality in every way. Adeline's new to our community and some of you may not have met her yet, but make sure to go say hi, because I'm telling you all, we're damn lucky to have her.'

As the crowd applauded, Adeline still wouldn't look at him, but he could see her perfectly and she was scowling. His heart turned over in his chest as he realised that nothing he said would ever fix what he'd done. He could apologise until he was blue in the face, he could sing her praises to all and sundry, but it wouldn't change the situation.

'Right,' he shouted into the microphone with false cheerfulness. 'Time for the teenage teams to head to the starting line. Let's get this show on the road.'

The girls' groups went first—there were netball players, swimmers and even a string quartet who did surprisingly well—and then the boys. Sam, Toovs, Mitch and Luka had, like many of the other teams, decided to dress up for their race and the crowd was in hysterics as they tugged the tractor towards the finish line wearing pink ballerina outfits, which a woman from the local CWA had made for them. As teams consisted of four, Rocky couldn't join them, but his cheering from the sidelines rivalled that of an American football cheer squad.

'Well done,' the horse caller boomed over the PA, reading out their time. 'Brothers From Another Mother are now in the lead!'

At this news, Rocky ran towards the finish line and leapt at his foster brothers, who caught him and laughed as they paraded back down the track carrying him above their heads.

In the end, four boys from the school football team wearing superhero costumes beat them for top speed in their category, but they didn't care. They were having the time of their lives, as, it appeared, was everybody else.

Everyone except Holden that is. He stayed out of Adeline's way as best he could, but that didn't mean he wasn't aware of every move she made every moment of the day. Whenever he saw her laughing or chatting with someone, muscles tightened all over his body as he felt the kind of intense jealousy that he hadn't known he was capable of feeling.

As the day went on, the smell of popcorn, fairy floss and sizzling sausages combined with the sweat of the participants and scent of motor oil wafting from the old tractor, but even the less pleasant smells couldn't dampen the mood of the crowd.

The atmosphere was like a cross between a school sports carnival and a country show. In addition to the races happening centre-oval, there were teams warming up on the sidelines, shouting friendly taunts of rivalry to each other. Onlookers were smiling, laughing, and cheering loudly at the shenanigans on field. Kids were squealing as they ran up and down behind the barriers in their own races against the tractor pullers. The only negative sounds were the cries of toddlers overwhelmed by the crowds, fuelled up on sugar and heading towards nap time.

After lunch when the mixed teams took their turns, everyone watched in amusement as Michelle, Sister Lola, Sister Rita and tiny Sister Josey—all dressed in full habits—tugged and tugged, barely moving the tractor an inch. They didn't get within spitting distance of the finish line, never mind log a competitive time, but the sisters were the undisputed highlight of the day. When they finally admitted defeat, several locals threw in generous extra donations in their name.

When the last race had taken place, Ford and Adeline tallied the amount raised so they could make an announcement when they awarded the winning teams their trophies.

'I think maybe you should sit down,' Ford said when he found Holden.

'Why? Is it not as good as we'd hoped?'

Ford shrugged. 'I dunno, is thirty-five thousand dollars in the ballpark?'

Holden felt his knees go weak. 'You're kidding me.'

If they shopped around and bought some windows, doors and things second hand, that might be enough for *two* tiny houses.

'Nope.' Ford beamed. 'Well, done bro. I'm proud of you.'

Holden was shaking as he stepped up to the podium once again, this time to announce the winners and let everyone know what a success the day had been. Of course he thanked Adeline again, but a public acknowledgement wasn't enough. He couldn't let the sun go down without personally thanking her for everything she'd done; for helping with the grants (decision still pending), encouraging him to set up the charity (in the process) and—almost single-handedly—pulling together this fundraiser.

He wouldn't have achieved half of that without her.

'Adeline,' he called, jogging over to her as the crowd rapidly dispersed—some to the pub to continue the fun, others home to put whiny children to bed.

She turned slowly as he approached. 'What is it?'

He swallowed, suddenly second-guessing—hadn't she made it crystal clear she didn't want to speak to him? 'I just … I just wanted to say thanks for today and for everything you did in the lead-up. I really appreciate it. No way I could have achieved all this without you.'

'You've already thanked me enough. Besides, I did it for the kids,' she replied.

As always, she looked beautiful when angry and he had to shove his hands in his pockets as he fought the urge to pull her against him and kiss away her scowl. Instead, he nodded.

'Good luck with getting the charity off the ground,' she added.

'Thanks. Would you like me to let you know when it's up and running? I think it would be good to do a follow-up article about it in the *Gazette*.'

'I think it's a great idea to do an article,' Adeline said, her tone still frosty, 'but I won't be taking on the position of editor after all. The shire has advertised the job and the volunteers will manage until a suitable replacement for Mike can be found.'

'Why? You're perfect for the role.'

She let out an amused puff of air. 'Kinda hard to be the editor of a small-town paper if you live thousands of kilometres away from said town.'

It took Holden a moment to understand what she was saying, then his chest tightened. 'You're leaving?'

'I'm heading back to Walsh first thing tomorrow morning.'

'You're no longer going to be a nu— I mean sister?'

She shook her head.

'This isn't because of what happened between us, is it?'

Adeline scoffed. 'What do you think, Holden? Sisters don't have sex. It's against their vows.'

'Yeah ... but it's not like it was your first time. You said yourself you'd slept with people before me, and that was okay because you hadn't taken your vows yet. I thought the church was supposed to be all about forgiveness.'

He didn't know why he was trying to convince her—it would be much easier for him if she was far away, living in another state. His heart might actually have a chance to recover if he wasn't constantly exposed to the woman who'd ruined it.

'You really don't get it, do you?' she said, throwing her hands up in the air. 'I *have* been forgiven, by Mother Catherine and by God, and even by myself, but what we did made me realise this is not the right path for me. I can't commit myself to the Lord in the way sisters are supposed to do. Not when I'm in love with someone else!'

Her words were worse than a physical punch to his gut. She still loved him. Even after long days apart to reassess—even after the despicable way he'd treated her—her feelings towards him hadn't wavered.

Life was so bloody unfair.

Holden wanted to tell her that he was sorry and that he was wrong and that the fact *she* wanted to be with *him* made him the luckiest man alive. If not for the sight of Ford sitting in his wheel-chair only a few metres away, he would have done so.

'I'm sorry, Adeline,' he said, his voice choked as he fought back tears. 'You're a wonderful person. Any man would be lucky to have you.'

She rolled her beautiful eyes. 'Oh my God, you're not giving me the old it's-not-you–it's-me line?'

'What if it's true?' he whispered.

Adeline shook her head. 'I'm not having this conversation with you. Goodbye, Holden.' And then, before he could say another word, she turned and hurried over to the waiting nuns. Michelle wrapped an arm around Adeline and glared back at Holden as they ushered her away.

It pained him to watch her go—to break her heart—but he knew she'd get over him. She'd find someone far better, someone who actually deserved her, and eventually she'd forget he even existed.

His hands clenched at his side, he marched over to Ford, desperate to take his sadness and frustration out on someone. 'Did you know Adeline was leaving?'

'Yes.'

'Why didn't you tell me?'

Ford shrugged. 'Didn't think you'd care.'

'I don't,' he lied, 'but—'

'But what?' Ford asked, cocking his head to one side, daring him to confess all.

'Nothing.' Holden scowled and stormed off to start taking down the barriers and shade tents. Hopefully the physical exertion would help burn off some of the tension. While it was probably a good thing that Adeline was leaving Smallton—he'd be able to walk down the main street and keep helping at the soup kitchen without fear of running into her—the knowledge that he'd likely never see her again was unlike any pain he'd ever felt before.

And that was saying something.

Chapter Forty-three

After what felt like a never-ending drive across the country, Adeline arrived back in Walsh with a sore throat and red eyes from crying most of the way. It was bad enough leaving Holden behind knowing that he didn't give two hoots about her, but saying goodbye to everyone—Ford, the boys, the sisters, Bella and the puppies—had pushed her over the edge. She hadn't known it was possible for one person to have that many tears inside them.

After a brief chat—or rather inquisition—with her parents, she'd sent an email to Meg Cooper-Jones and Tabitha McWilliams, asking if they could all meet at the tearooms at a time convenient to them. As Tab had a young baby and Meg was due to give birth any day, Adeline hadn't expected a speedy reply, yet following a shower she'd checked her email, hoping for an update from Michelle, to find one.

Dear Adeline

Tab and I will be at the tearooms tomorrow and can meet you at eleven o'clock before the lunch rush if that works for you.
Let me know,
Meg.

She'd replied immediately saying that worked perfectly, then fallen into her childhood bed and tried to get some much-needed sleep.

In the morning, when she checked herself in the mirror and discovered that she still looked like a wreck, she contemplated rescheduling her visit. Then she reminded herself that appearances weren't important but what she had to say about her grandmother and Eliza was, and she couldn't move on with the rest of her life without getting it off her chest. After a quick shower, she dressed, put on just enough make-up so she didn't look like a ghost, and climbed into her car for the short drive to nearby Rose Hill.

For as long as Adeline could remember, this 'town' had been no more than a place you drove through to get to somewhere else. All but abandoned in the late 1970s when goods and services became more easily accessible in the bigger town of Walsh, it had become a ghost town with only one resident. That is until Meg had moved in a couple of years ago taking the population to two, not counting dogs and chickens. Since then, she and Tabitha had opened a café and gallery that had quickly become a popular spot for tourists and residents in the neighbouring towns as well. The café boasted delicious home-cooked pies and cakes, and the gallery showcased artists from around the region, but Adeline suspected it was Tab's famous homemade ice cream that drew the masses from far and wide.

She parked her car across the road and tried to ignore the nerves dancing in her stomach as she headed towards the tea-rooms. It truly was a pretty picture—the old building had been lovingly brought to life again with new awnings, a fresh coat of paint and welcoming flower-filled window boxes out the front. As she neared the open front door, tantalisingly sweet scents of baking greeted her, and she took a quick breath before stepping inside.

Although she'd arrived prior to the 'lunch rush', many of the tables were already occupied with folks enjoying coffee and cake or tea and scones, but as usual the one in the far corner sat empty, a little sign atop it that read: *Reserved for Eliza*. She stared at the vacant corner and swore she could almost see the outline of someone shimmering there. Shivering, she shook herself, then wound her way through the tables towards the counter where chestnut-haired Meg was taking a payment from a customer.

As she waited for Meg to finish, she glanced into the adjacent gallery and immediately regretted it, because the paintings on the wall made her think of Holden's body art. If he put pen to paper instead of ink to skin, his work could sit perfectly alongside the other local art.

She'd hoped that coming home would begin to ease her pain because there wouldn't be reminders of Holden, but she'd only been back twenty-four hours and already, thousands of miles from Smallton, almost everything she saw led her mind back to the time they'd spent together. It began yesterday afternoon when she'd walked into her old bedroom and seen the typewriter Gran had given her sitting on her desk, which had immediately made her think of the drawing Holden had done on her arm.

Long after the ink had faded, she could still recall the feel of his pen on her skin, and she would never forget the magic that happened between them next. Last night, after falling into bed and failing to fall asleep, she'd turned on her TV and what had been playing on Channel Seven but *Lady and the Tramp*? She'd meant to switch to Netflix but accidentally hit the wrong button and changed the channel instead. The evening movie on Channel Nine was *101 Dalmatians*.

What were the chances? She'd almost fallen off the bed. Why did life have to be so cruel? The longing for Bella had unravelled her once again. She desperately wanted to know how the puppies were doing but didn't even trust herself to message Ford.

'Hi Adeline. Sorry to keep you waiting.'

She started at the sound of Meg's voice and turned her attention on the other woman, trying not to stare at her enormous stomach. 'It's fine. Thanks for seeing me,' she replied. 'Should you still be working in your condition?'

Meg chuckled and placed a hand on her bump. 'You sound like Lawson. Don't worry. Today's my last shift. Tab and I have hired a manager for the next six months.'

'That's great. This place seems to be going from strength to strength. I'm really pleased for you both.'

'Thank you.' Meg half-smiled as she looked at Adeline with what could only be described as wariness. 'I must say you surprised us with your email. We hadn't heard you were coming home.'

'I didn't tell anyone.' If she had, the news would have been common knowledge before she'd left the outskirts of Smallton. Adeline's chest squeezed as she thought about that faraway place and all she'd left behind. Pushing that thought aside, she peered through the open hatch into the kitchen behind them. 'Is Tabitha here?'

'She's just upstairs changing Daphne, but she'll be down in a moment. Can I get you a drink or something to eat?'

Adeline eyed the glass cabinet of cakes and the wide selection of ice cream beside it but didn't think she'd be able to eat a thing until she'd said what she'd come to say. 'Just a cup of tea, please.'

Meg called through the order to a young girl out the back— Adeline was surprised she didn't recognise her considering she'd only been gone a few months. 'Do you want to sit? Tab should be down any second.'

'That would be great,' she said, and followed Meg over to a table that had just been vacated by the window.

Seconds later, another waitress—Becki, a teenage girl Adeline used to babysit when she was a toddler—swept over, cleared the table of the used plates and wiped it clean. Meg thanked her then looked back to Adeline. Moments of awkward silence followed and then they both spoke at once.

'Do you know what you're having?'

'So, what happened to joining a convent?'

They laughed, slightly easing the awkwardness.

'I'm having a boy,' Meg said. 'We're calling him Alby. His name was supposed to be a secret, but we told Ned and he was so excited, he let it slip.'

'How is Ned?' Adeline asked. He'd always been such a cute kid.

'Adorable as ever. He's just started learning to play the piano accordion with Ferg. Anyway, I want to hear about the convent. You're the first person I've ever known to join one. I didn't know you were so religious.'

Adeline shrugged. 'My faith is strong.' Despite everything that had happened, she didn't blame God. 'Although I can understand why you might not have known that.'

Before she could begin her apology, Meg said, 'So, why are you back? Wasn't it what you expected?'

'The convent exceeded my expectations. The sisters were wonderful, and I learned so much about myself, but in the end, I realised it's not where I'm meant to be.'

'I see,' Meg said. 'That's here then?'

'I don't think so,' Adeline replied. 'I'm only home to sort out a few things while I look for a job in the city. One of those things is saying sorry to you.'

'What?' Meg's mouth dropped open, then she asked, 'What for?'

Adeline inhaled. 'For how I treated you when you arrived. I've got no excuse except that I was jealous that Lawson liked you because I'd had a crush on him forever. But that isn't really an excuse. And I truly am sorry.'

She wasn't going to ask for forgiveness—not wanting to put Meg in such a position—and she never imagined they'd be friends, but she wanted her to know she'd seen the error of her ways.

'Thank you,' Meg said. 'I appreciate that. And to be honest, I understand you liked Lawson—who wouldn't?—and you were looking out for him. You weren't wrong that I had something to hide, and I'd have had to tell him eventually. You just sped things up a little.'

Meg was being very magnanimous. She might have had to tell Lawson about her past, but she'd been under no obligation to tell anyone else. She'd done her time. As if Meg could read Adeline's mind, she added, 'And we both know everything comes out eventually in a small town.'

'Isn't that the truth,' Adeline said; she'd bet by now someone in here who'd seen her had text messaged someone else, who'd called someone else, who'd told someone else when they bumped into them in the supermarket, and half the town would now not only know of her return, but also that she'd been seen having what looked to be a serious conversation with Meg Cooper-Jones.

'Tea for one,' said Becki, delivering a dainty China cup and a teapot dressed in a cute, crocheted cosy that looked like a koala—one of Meg's creations no doubt.

Adeline smiled, the koala reminding her of Michelle and her substitutes for swearwords. It was the first time she'd thought of something to do with Smallton without feeling desolate. Maybe there was hope for her after all. 'Thanks, Becki.'

'No worries,' grinned the teenager. 'And a decaf cappuccino for you, Meg, and water for Tab.' She put both on the table and then, hugging the tray to her chest, walked away.

Adeline had barely lifted the pot to pour some tea into her cup when Tabitha joined them, a dark-haired, full-faced baby resting in the crook of her arm. It was the cutest little thing Adeline had ever seen. 'Oh, my goodness, congratulations,' she gasped. 'Daphne is adorable. You and Fergus must be so happy.'

'We are.' Tab lowered herself onto a chair. She held Daphne safe with her little arm, while lifting her shirt and positioning the baby at her breast. Once the baby was suckling, she picked up the glass of water and took a large sip.

It always amazed Adeline what Tab could do, despite her disability. If she were honest, any nastiness she'd shown towards her when they were growing up was because she was jealous of how capable, talented and self-assured Tab always was. And when she'd lost her arm, little had changed in that department.

Putting the glass back on the table, Tab looked to Meg and then back to Adeline with a guarded expression. 'What's this visit about? What's going on?'

'Um …' Meg looked unsure whether she should say something or wait for Adeline.

Adeline cleared her throat. 'I've just apologised to Meg for the way I treated her, and I want you to know, I'm sorry for always being a bitch to you as well.'

Tab blinked. 'You're sorry?' she said eventually.

'Yes. For all the bitchy comments and mean things I said to you while we were growing up.'

'And since,' added Tab.

Adeline nodded. 'For always. I was jealous of you growing up; you had a loving family, lots of friends, whereas I've always struggled to be close to anyone. I was your typical bully; trying to hide my lack of confidence and self-worth behind bravado. And I'm also sorry about Ryder. I think you guessed I went out of my way to convince him to come play at the Walsh Show because I knew it would make you uncomfortable.'

'Heard that didn't work out so well for you either,' Tab said sharply, confirming Adeline's suspicions that everyone knew what had happened between her and the country music singer.

She blushed. 'No, not exactly.'

'It's not just me you were a bitch to,' Tab added. She seemed more wary, less likely to forgive than Meg, and Adeline didn't blame her—they'd known each other longer, which meant she had more grudges to hold.

'I know,' she agreed. 'And I'll be working through a list, but I'm starting with you two and ... Eliza.'

'Eliza?' Meg and Tab said in unison, their gazes drifting towards the corner table.

'Yes, because I'm almost certain my grandmother killed her,' Adeline confessed in a low voice.

If the other women had looked shocked by her apologies, now you could knock them off their seats with a feather. Silence rang between them all a few long moments, then both spoke at once.

'What makes you think that?' Tab said.

'You *knew* that?' Meg asked.

Now the other two weren't the only ones stunned. '*You* knew?' Adeline replied.

'I think we need cake to get us through this.' Tab shoved her hand in the air and then called to the counter. 'Becki, can you bring us a massive slice of red velvet mud cake and three spoons, please?'

'I know you suspected Eliza was murdered,' Adeline said to Meg as Tab switched Daphne to her other breast, 'but are you saying you guessed it was my grandmother?'

Meg nodded. 'I don't have any actual evidence, but one night while I was researching about Eliza, I had a dream, or rather a vision. You came to visit me, and we had a fight, which ended in you throwing me down the stairs. When I woke up and realised I was dreaming, it suddenly clicked that it wasn't you and me I was seeing, but Eliza and your grandmother. Then—' she shrugged as if she knew how crazy what she was saying sounded, '—I asked Eliza myself. The hall light flickered on and off in reply. And I knew I was right. She killed her so she could have Henry, didn't she?'

Adeline nodded.

'Did Penelope tell you that before she died?' asked Tab.

Adeline shook her head. 'You know she was as good as mute her last few years. After she died, I was reading her journals and found what is essentially a confession.'

The other women exchanged a look, their eyes widening.

'You're right,' Adeline continued, 'Gran was furious when Granddad broke off their engagement for Eliza, so she fixed things so that they couldn't be together.'

Thunk.

They all jumped as the *Reserved for Eliza* sign fell right off the table. Despite the open front entrance, there was no wind outside and no fan or anything inside to have caused it.

Adeline stood, crossed over to Eliza's table, picked the sign off the floor and put it back in its position.

'I'm so sorry,' she whispered. It felt silly talking to someone she couldn't see but she *could* feel her presence, and even dead, the woman deserved acknowledgement of what had happened to her. 'I'm sorry my grandmother robbed you not only of life but of love, and I want you to know I'm going to make sure the truth is told.'

In reply, the lights above flickered briefly.

Adeline looked back to Meg and Tabitha. 'Did you see that, too?'

They both nodded, and this time Tabitha actually smiled at Adeline, then gestured to her to join them again. 'Come have some cake?'

'Thank you.' Adeline sat back down at the table and let out a long deep breath.

'What did you mean you're going to make sure Eliza's truth is told?' asked Tab, picking up a spoon and digging it into the cake. Daphne had finished feeding and was now sitting up in the crook of Tab's little arm, sucking happily on a dummy.

'I'm going to write an expose for the *Whisperer* putting forward all the evidence I found in Gran's journals showing what really happened. If it's alright with you, Meg, I'd love to look at what you found that made you believe Eliza was pushed and also interview you about exactly what led you to believe the murderer was Penelope Walsh.'

Meg's eyes widened. 'I'm happy to help you, but what's your family going to think if you do that?'

'I don't care,' she replied. 'It needs to be done. Eliza and *her* family never got justice. Penelope can't be convicted by a court, but I owe it to her victim to make sure the truth is out there.'

'You've really had a transformation, haven't you?' Tab said, digging her spoon once again into the cake. If Adeline wanted some, she'd better hurry, but as good as it looked, food was the last thing on her mind right now, and Tab probably needed it more than she did. Breastfeeding looked like hungry work.

She smiled, then asked, 'Would you like me to hold Daphne while you eat?' Hopefully, Tab wouldn't be offended by the offer, but a few crumbs had just landed on the baby's head, and Adeline had heard new mothers rarely got the chance to eat in peace.

'Sure, that'd be great, thanks,' Tab said as she put down the spoon to safely hand Daphne over.

Adeline felt a pang in her heart as her arms closed around the little bundle. She was squishy and warm and smelled that divine fresh baby smell. As she stared down into Daphne's big, brown eyes—her lashes thicker and longer than you'd think a baby would have—she imagined what Holden and her child would look like. It hurt that she'd probably never get to experience what it was like to hold a baby of her own.

Perhaps she shouldn't have taken the morning-after pill.

'Are you okay?' Meg asked, just as a tear plopped down onto Daphne's nose.

Adeline hadn't even realised she'd been crying. 'Oh my God, sorry.' She wiped away the tear with her thumb and then swiped at her own eyes.

'It's fine,' Tab said, offering her the serviette that had come with the cake. 'I was a bawling mess most of the first few weeks of Daph's life; I'm sure she swallowed more tears than milk. It's you we're worried about.'

Those kind words and Meg's nod of agreement only made Adeline sob harder. 'I'll be fine. I'm just … I'm just a little emotional at the moment.'

'Has this got something to do with you leaving the convent?' Meg asked.

She nodded. 'I really miss the sisters.'

'Then why'd you leave?' This from Tab.

Adeline swallowed. 'I fell in love,' she said.

'With another nun?' asked Meg, leaning forward in interest.

'No.' Adeline let out a puff of amusement. 'With a guy I helped organise a fundraiser with.'

'So that's why you left?' Meg mused, and Adeline nodded.

'Not a happy ending, I'm guessing?' Tab asked, her expression kind.

'No.'

'I'm sorry,' they said in unison.

Then Meg added, 'You know, you don't have to talk about it if you don't want to, but both Tab and I have experienced our share of heartbreak, so if you ever do need a shoulder to cry on, we're here.'

'With cake,' added Tab, gesturing to the plate, which now only held a few brownish-red crumbs.

Adeline smiled. 'Thank you. That means a lot.'

But she didn't see how rehashing it all would help and didn't dare hope she'd ever be as lucky as these two, who had found their Prince Charmings and were currently living happily ever afters. This time she meant it when she resolved to be done with men. Once she found a job, moved to Perth and settled into a new place, she'd get another dog. Although this time, after seeing Bella's bitza puppies, she decided that rather than buying a pure-bred, she'd go to the RSPCA and adopt a dog that needed her as much as she needed it.

Chapter Forty-four

After a long day sawing timber for the first tiny house, Holden showered, ready to head into town with Ford and the boys to help at the soup kitchen. Now that Rocky had found his feet at school, he'd asked if he could help too, which meant no one needed to stay home with him. Holden was looking forward to a busy evening. Ever since Adeline left town, he'd been doing everything he could to keep his mind and body occupied.

He'd taken on every shift he could at the tattoo parlour and when he wasn't there, he'd work from dawn till dusk on the tiny house, sanding down window frames, measuring and sawing wood. The boys were helping in the afternoons; they'd already put down the subfloor and tomorrow they were going to start on the framing. He wished he could send update photos to Adeline, but she deserved a clean break, so instead he sent them to Bronte.

Her replies were encouraging but sporadic. She was crazy busy as only a few days after the funeral, Tricia had announced she needed a break and had climbed in the caravan she and Bill had been doing up for years and set off on a solo adventure around Australia, leaving poor Bronte to make sure the business didn't go to the dogs. She sounded exhausted whenever they spoke, so Holden hadn't burdened her with his Adeline issues as he might have done if she were still here.

Maybe it was also because he was scared that she'd react like Ford, who still seemed to be pissed at him.

He sighed and pulled on clean jeans and a shirt, then went out to meet the others who were already waiting for him in the van.

'You're not bringing that puppy,' he said to Rocky, who was hiding one of Bella's babies under his shirt.

The boy groaned and then jogged back to the house to deposit his stowaway with its mother. Holden didn't blame Rocky wanting to bring one. They were adorable and starting to become more independent and cheekier. Hopefully the little terrors wouldn't have caused too much destruction by the time they got back later tonight.

Sam entertained them on the short drive into town with stories of a snake causing a stir in his maths class today. 'You should have seen how fast Miss Lewis jumped up onto her desk.'

'I hope you didn't catch the snake and release it into the classroom,' Holden said.

Sam gave him a sheepish look and Holden shook his head. Sam had only just finished paying him off after the pizza episode, but he supposed pizza and silly pranks were better than the things he'd gotten up to when he'd first arrived.

When Ford parked the van at the edge of the car park, Holden and the boys unloaded the food they'd brought while he organised himself into his wheelchair. As they approached the shipping container, Holden saw Sister Rita and Michelle from the convent already inside. Part of him wanted to ask if they'd heard from Adeline, but their wary looks told him such interest wouldn't be well received.

Was it a crime to hope she was doing okay?

If only they knew how much he was hurting as well, maybe they'd cut him a bit of slack.

'Toovs, you help serve tonight,' he said. 'I'm gunna do the rounds out here.'

'Serious?' Toovs asked. He'd been wanting to get inside the container since his first night helping out at the soup kitchen, but Holden wasn't sure if he was ready for it. Some of the clients could get a little aggro if they didn't feel they were getting served quick enough.

He nodded. 'Don't make me regret this.'

Toovs jogged towards the van and Holden watched as he received an apron from Takishah and slipped it joyfully over his head.

It was a cool night, but the weather was calm so there were plenty of people here for a feed and a yarn. Holden kept busy picking up rubbish, clearing away used paper plates and making small talk. Nearing the end of the evening, his ears pricked up when behind him he heard Dangerous Denise ask, 'Where's the pretty blonde one tonight?'

Sister Rita had passed him only seconds before with a big container of muffins, which meant Denise had to be talking about Adeline. He stilled as he listened for a reply.

'Unfortunately, she's gone home, Denise.'

'What? Back to WA? For good?'

He guessed Rita nodded, because Denise added grouchily, 'Well, that's a pity. I liked her. She had spark.'

Spark. That was an understatement

Keep talking, he willed them. Ask more questions, Denise.

He wanted to know if the nuns had heard from her, if she'd got home safely, and what she planned to do next. He wanted to know if she was okay. Maybe if he knew she'd managed to move on, he'd somehow be able to do so.

But Denise ended the conversation with, 'Give her my love if you hear from her, and I'll have another one of those muffins, thank you. Can't have me wasting away.'

Rita chuckled—Denise was in no such danger—and then wandered on with the container. Holden fought the urge to go after her and ask all the questions that were still unanswered. Instead, he continued cleaning, making sure there wasn't even one tiny piece of litter left on the ground when they all packed up and went home. Once there, the boys traipsed off to bed, Ford decided to watch TV to wind down and Holden went to check on Bella and the puppies.

'Hey girl, these kids behaving?'

Bella made a noise that sounded like a sigh as the one with the black heart, whom they'd named Love, climbed onto her head and started nibbling at her ear. The others were either suckling or asleep.

Holden chuckled and reached down to scoop the little guy up. 'Let me take him off your hands for a while,' he told Bella, and then headed into the kitchen, puppy squirming in his arms. He closed the door and put Love down, letting him run around and explore while he poured himself a measure of whiskey from his secret bottle—which would need replacing soon if he kept up his new nightly tipple—and took it to the table to go through that day's mail. Most bills were online these days, but they still got some by snail mail.

He groaned and had another sip, already mentally juggling his budget.

But hang on … One envelope didn't have the see-through window at the front that bills did, but there was a logo of one of the organisations he'd applied for a grant from.

What was another knockback when he was already down? He ripped open the envelope and unfolded the letter.

'Holy fuck,' he shrieked, clapping a hand over his mouth. Love looked up from where he'd been nosing at something in the corner. 'It's a yes!' he shrieked.

★ ★ ★

By the time Ford wheeled himself in from the living room and asked, 'What's going on?' Holden had read it through three times just to be sure he wasn't misunderstanding.

He grinned, then flashed the grant acceptance letter in his brother's face. 'We got one. We got a grant! Twenty-thousand dollars towards the materials for more tiny houses.'

'Well done, bro, that's awesome,' Ford said, offering him perhaps the first genuine smile since he'd yelled at him about sleeping with Adeline.

Adeline. Holden's heart squeezed at the thought of her, the joy he'd felt a moment ago fading.

'What's wrong?' Ford asked as Love darted in and out from under the wheelchair. All the puppies loved it for some reason. 'Is there a catch or something? You look like you just heard someone died.'

Holden sank into a chair and shoved a hand through his knotty hair. 'I want to tell Adeline.'

Ford raised an eyebrow. 'You really think that's a good idea?'

'She deserves to know. This wouldn't have happened without her,' he said, gesturing to the letter in front of him, all the while knowing he was just clutching at an excuse—any excuse—to reach out to her.

'Yes, but you really hurt her, Holden. Maybe it's best just to—'

'Do you think I wanted to hurt her?' he yelled. 'Hell, Ford, she's not the only one hurting. I'm breaking inside! I never thought love could hurt this bad.'

'Keep your voice down, or you'll bring the boys in here,' Ford said warningly, leaning down and scooping up Love by his feet. 'Hang on. What the *hell* are you talking about? Did you just say you *love* her?'

Shit. He hadn't meant to let that slip but now that he had, he couldn't bring himself to deny how he felt about her even one more second.

'Yes,' he confessed on a whisper. 'I love her. There's no other explanation for the fact that I can't get her out of my head. I think about her non-stop. I miss her smile. I miss her laugh. I miss talking to her. I miss her stupid non-swear words. And every time I think about living the rest of my life without touching her again, a piece of me dies. But it's more than just that. I want to sleep all night long beside her; I want her to be the last person I see when I go to bed and the first person when I wake up every morning. She's totally fucking ruined me.'

Ford shook his head—he looked utterly perplexed by what Holden was saying. 'If you love her, then why on earth did you tell her you didn't? Why did you send her away?'

'Because I don't deserve her!' He reached for his glass and downed almost all its contents in one gulp.

'Are you crazy? Of course you deserve her. You deserve *love* more than anyone I know.'

'How can you say that after what I did to you? I ruined your life and if *you* can't have love, then why the hell should I get it?'

Ford's eyes narrowed and Holden saw his knuckles whiten as he gripped his wheelchair handles. 'Are you fucking kidding me?'

'I …' Holden didn't know how to react to this outburst.

Ford rarely swore, rarely raised his voice, rarely even got angry, but there was fire in his eyes right now. Love scrambled off his lap onto the floor.

'Who said I can't have love?' he demanded. 'I might not have found my Mr or Miss Right yet, but I haven't given up. I know they're out there and when I find them, I sure as hell won't be as stupid as you. So don't put this on me! I asked you to come live with me because I missed you and I wanted a relationship with my big brother again, but I don't want to spend my life feeling like some kind of burden around your neck, feeling pitied and—'

'That's not what I—'

'Shut the fuck up and hear me out. I've made the most of my life. I may not have the use of my legs but I'm fucking alive. I got in that car willingly, so it's as much my fault as it is yours. I forgave you for this—' he gestured to his legs, '—years ago. I know it only happened because you were rescuing me and for that I'll *always* be grateful. Can you imagine what would have happened to me—to my mental health—if you hadn't come for me that day? It's time for you to forgive yourself. If you truly love Adeline—and suddenly your grumpy-arse attitude over the last couple of weeks makes so much sense, so I guess you do—then don't use me as an excuse to push her away. Don't be a coward. Get on a plane and go tell that amazing woman how you feel about her. Go on, bro, give love a chance.'

'But what about the boys?' Holden said, everything his brother had just said spinning in his head. 'They're supposed to be my focus.'

'The boys and I will be waiting here for you when you get back with Adeline. We're all pretty fond of her as well, you know.'

'What if she doesn't want to come back here?'

Ford shrugged. 'You won't know if you don't ask her.'

'What are you two arguing about?' said a sleepy Rocky, rubbing his eyes as he appeared in the doorway. Love darted over to him, and he picked him up, cradling him to his chest like a teddy bear.

Toovs and Sam were right behind him, anxious expressions on their faces. Until now, any disagreements Ford and Holden had were always minor and they were always careful not to air their grievances when the boys might hear. These kids had experienced enough conflict in their lives.

'Sorry,' Holden said, swallowing. 'It's nothing you need to—'

'We were arguing,' Ford interrupted, 'about whether Holden should ring Adeline up and tell her about the successful twenty-thousand dollar grant she helped us get, or whether he should fly over there and tell her the good news in person.'

'And?' the boys asked in unison.

'And …' Holden pushed to his feet, adrenaline pulsing through his veins. Thanks to Ford, he'd seen the light. 'I'm off to book a flight.'

Chapter Forty-five

'Sorry I'm late,' Sally said as she rushed into A Country Kitchen, Walsh's much-loved café on the main street, and joined Adeline at a table by the window. 'I was on the phone to my lawyer.'

Adeline stood to kiss her ex-sister-in-law on the cheek. 'All good. I've already ordered our usual. Was it a good call?'

'The best.' Sally grinned as they sat down. 'Our settlement is finally done. I no longer have any financial or property ties to your brother.'

'Oh my goodness, congratulations,' Adeline said.

'I feel lighter already. Is it too early to go to the pub to celebrate?'

Adeline made a show of glancing at her watch. 'Hmm … let's see. 10 am. I don't think the pub's open yet.'

'Bummer. Guess I'll just have to make do with coffee and carrot cake.'

Right on cue, Raelene, owner of the café, arrived with exactly that, times two.

'Thanks,' they both said, and Raelene winked before heading back to the counter.

Adeline lifted her mug and held it up in a toast. 'Congratulations again.'

'Why, thank you.' Sally beamed as they clinked mugs. 'At least my sham of a marriage wasn't a total waste of ten years. I mean I got Levi and Tate out of it, and I got you. To friendship.'

'To friendship,' Adeline echoed.

As they got stuck into their cake, which everyone unanimously agreed was the best carrot cake in the southern hemisphere, Sally said, 'How are you anyway?'

There was no need to say what she was referring to. Adeline had spilled her sorry story about falling in love with Holden Campbell to Sally over wine and cheese the night after she came home.

'I'm doing okay,' she lied. 'I miss the sisters.' At least Josey and Michelle were keeping up the posts on NunTok. They were doing an amazing job and watching them was providing her only real joy. 'But I'm trying to focus on other things. I've applied for two jobs this morning and my exposé about Penelope and Eliza is coming along well.'

'You're a very brave lady. Jane is going to skin you alive when that's printed.'

Sally was right. Dad might forgive her—even though Penelope was his mum, he didn't care about much besides the farm—but her mother would be furious about the shame it would bring on the revered Walsh name. Adeline shrugged. 'Won't be the first time she's been disappointed in me. But it's time the truth came out.'

'Are you going to give her a heads-up?'

'I don't know.' She sighed. 'Anyway, now that you're officially free of my brother, what are your plans? Do you think you'll start dating again?'

'Are you kidding?' Sally looked horrified. 'One, the pool of men around these parts is ridiculously small. Two, I'm done with the whole lot of them. No offense, but your brother scarred me for life.'

'No offense taken, and I'm with you. Men are way more trouble than they're worth.'

'Amen to that.' Sally forked off another piece of carrot cake. 'The small blokes in my life keep me busy enough, anyway. So, tell me about these jobs?'

She told Sally about the two entry-level journalism positions she'd applied for—one at *Perth Now* and one at *Business News*. Neither of them had long-term appeal, but journalism jobs were few and far between these days, so she just needed to get her foot in the door.

'If nothing comes of them, I'll look for something in a shop or bar and write freelances articles on the side while I wait for something better. I don't want to give up on the dream, but I need an income so I can move to Perth and—'

Sally halted Adeline's words with a hand on her arm. 'Don't look now,' she said, leaning in close, 'but there's a spunk of a man at ten o'clock.'

Adeline rolled her eyes—hadn't they just agreed that all men were wankers?—but curiosity got the better of her.

'I said, *don't* look,' Sally laughed. 'Now he's caught us staring.'

But Adeline barely registered her ex-sister-in-law's reprimand. 'Jack?' she breathed.

'You *know* him?'

She shook her head. Her eyes had to be deceiving her.

While this man resembled Holden, he was clean-shaven, and his dark hair was cropped short. If anything, he looked more like Ford. Her gaze dropped to his arms, which were bare until the sleeves of a black t-shirt, and her heart literally stopped beating as she took in the tattoo of Guru on one arm and the lizard on the other.

Despite this, it was only when he said, 'Maria', and took a step towards her table that she really believed he wasn't a mirage.

'What are you doing here?' she breathed, slowly rising from her chair.

In reply, he held up a piece of paper and grinned. 'We got the grant.'

She couldn't believe what she was hearing. 'You came all this way to tell me we got a *grant*?'

'Well, that's part of it,' he replied.

She meant to ask about the rest, but instead she reached up to his face and touched his cheek, partly to check that he wasn't a figment of her imagination. 'What did you do to your beard?'

'I knew how much you hated it, so I got rid of it.'

He got rid of it because of me. Hope danced in Adeline's heart. Was she asleep and dreaming?

'I didn't hate it,' she admitted, although he might be even more good-looking without it. 'No more than I hated your tattoos.'

'I see.' He half-laughed. 'Well, I'm glad to hear you're not as averse to them as you made out, because I got another one.'

Gasps went up around the café as Holden grabbed at the back of his shirt and ripped it right up and over his head. Adeline swore she heard the click of a phone camera and one of the Stitch'n'Bitch members, Mrs Howard, murmuring about no one having any decency anymore, but all she could focus on was the tattoo of a very sexy nun and the word *Adeline* scrawled beneath it.

'Oh my God!' She felt his skin shiver beneath her touch as she brushed her fingers over her name. 'Is that real?'

He nodded. 'As real as the blood that courses through my veins. As real as my feelings—as real as my love—for you.'

She squeaked, yanking her fingers from his chest as if they'd been burnt. 'Did you just say you loved me?'

He chuckled, his eyes sparkling with warmth and amusement. 'Not loved, *love*, and whatever the future tense of it is as well. Why else do you think I'd get your name tattooed across my heart and come all this way?'

'I ... I ... I don't understand.' Perhaps she should pinch herself because surely this wasn't real.

'Do you think we could take this outside a moment?' he asked, gently taking hold of her hand.

Adeline nodded. His grip *felt* real, but if it wasn't, she didn't want to wake up.

When they were on the verandah, all eyes inside peering out the window to see whatever this good-looking, bare-chested giant wanted with her, Holden said, 'I lied when I told you what happened between us was just sex. It was a cruel thing to say, and I'll forever be sorry for hurting you like that, but I didn't know how else to push you away. The truth is; it meant every-thing to me.'

'But if you liked me, *why* did you want to push me away?'

'I don't just like you, Maria. I told you, I fucking *love* you. I love everything about you. I think I loved you from the moment you came looking for Bella all those months ago, but those feel-ings have got bigger and bigger every day, every hour I spent in your presence. And they haven't stopped since you've been gone. But I ... I didn't think I was worthy of your love.'

'What?! I—' She shook her head and then it clicked. 'This is because of Ford. Because of the accident?'

He nodded. 'Yeah. I thought because I'd ruined his life, I didn't deserve happiness or love.'

'So what's changed?'

'To be honest ... nothing, but Ford had a few choice words to say to me when he realised what was going on and the truth is, whether I deserve you or not, I *want* you. I want you so bad. And

I hope your name etched permanently above my heart proves that to you.'

Her eyes went back to the sexy nun on his sculpted pecs and she couldn't help smiling. 'What if I told you I've changed my mind? Realised I don't love you.' She shouldn't make this too easy for him after all the torture he'd put her through. 'What if I told you that coming home has made me realise you were right—it was just good sex, nothing more, nothing less.'

'Then I'd call bullshit and my heart would be broken, but it would still belong to you.' He paused and pointed to her name. 'And this would forever be a reminder of what an idiot I am for letting the best thing that ever happened to me walk out of my life.'

Then she was crying again, but this time they were happy tears. 'Do you really mean that?'

'I really do,' he said, cupping her face in his big hands and staring into her eyes. It was impossible to deny his love because what she saw there matched what she saw in the mirror whenever she thought of him. 'Which is why I'm hoping you'll agree to come back to Smallton and move in with me. Well, me and the boys, and Ford and the dogs; unfortunately we're a package deal.'

'Luckily, I've always loved a bargain.'

He grinned. 'Good, because there's something else I'd like to throw into the contract.'

'Oh? That sounds very official.'

'It is,' he said, dropping onto one knee. 'Adeline Walsh, will you marry me?'

Holy koala.

She gasped as his hand went to his pocket—'I don't have a ring; didn't have time to organise one. Besides, I thought it would mean more if we chose it together'—and pulled out a pen. 'But if you say yes, I'll draw a temporary one on.'

Aware of the eyes of half of Walsh staring at them over the tops of their coffees and carrot cake, Adeline laughed. 'Are you crazy? We've never even been on a date.'

'I'm hoping to fix that tonight, because you deserve all the romance in the world, but no number of dates is going to change how I feel about you. I love you, Maria.'

Oh Lord, her heart felt as if it might burst.

'I love you too, Jack,' she said, pulling him up so she could kiss him as cheers erupted from inside.

'Is that a yes?' he whispered, his lips still only millimetres from hers.

'It's a *hell* yes,' she replied pulling back and thrusting out her hand so he could draw on the ring. Marrying someone she'd only known a few months wasn't the craziest thing she'd ever done, but she already knew it would be the best.

'Thank fuck. Sorry, thank *koala*,' he said and began to draw.

As she watched him work, she asked, 'How did you know to find me here? At the café?'

'I didn't. It was just luck.' The black pen tickled her skin, reminding her of that wonderful night in the shed. 'I came in here hoping someone might tell me where you lived, and there you were.'

'Yes. And here you are,' she sniffed, still bamboozled, amused when he didn't stop at a simple band but added a diamond as well. 'It's almost as if God brought you here.'

'Excuse me?' Sally cleared her throat and Adeline turned to see her ex-sister-in-law standing right behind her, sunglasses lowered as she peered over the top of them like a disapproving old lady. 'Are you going to introduce us?'

Adeline beamed and wrapped her arm around Holden's waist, drawing him to her side. 'Sally, this is Holden Campbell. My *fiancé.*' No word had ever sounded sweeter. She thrust out her ring finger to show her.'

'I—'

When Sally couldn't seem to find the words, Adeline continued, 'And Holden, this is Sally Walsh, my best friend and sister-in-law.'

'Pleased to meet you,' he said, offering her his hand.

'Actually, it's *ex*-sister-in-law and I'm Sally Keyes now, remember?' she said as they shook. 'And what happened to our pact to swear off men?'

'Whoops.' Adeline shrugged and couldn't stop smiling. 'Isn't it a woman's prerogative to change her mind?'

Sally pretended to scoff, but then she drew Adeline—and Holden by default—into a hug. 'Congratulations, sis. And you too, Holden. That was a pretty impressive arrival, and the tattoo tells me you're serious about my bestie, which you'd better be, because if you break her heart again, I swear I will hunt you down and kill you.'

'I promise that's not going to happen,' he replied. 'But do you mind if I whisk her away now? It's time I showed her some romance.'

Sally raised an eyebrow. 'Romance? Is that code for make-up sex?'

He chuckled. 'Oh, I promise you there'll be that and more involved.'

Sally sighed and shooed them away with her hands. 'Go on, then. Have fun, kids. And Adeline, you better tell me all about it later, so I can live vicariously through you.'

'Deal.' Adeline hugged her then they went back inside to grab her bag, before she and Holden left, walking hand-in-hand. She never wanted to let go. 'What now?'

'Now,' he said, 'we start the rest of our lives.'

She laughed. 'That sounds good, but I was meaning *right* now. Do you want to come back to the farm? Meet my parents. Chat about the logistics for my—'

He yanked her to him again and pressed his mouth against hers. 'That all sounds very sensible,' he said, barely lifting his lips, 'but I meant it when I said I planned to romance you. I hope you don't have anything on tonight or tomorrow because I've booked us somewhere to stay.'

'Oh? Where?'

'It's a surprise.'

Adeline bit down on another smile—she didn't think she'd stopped smiling since he'd shown her his tattoo. No one had ever *romanced* her before. The few times she'd gone away with a boy-friend, she'd been the one to organise it. 'Can I go home quickly and pack a bag?'

He nodded. 'I'll follow you. Do you think we could take your car on our trip, and I leave the motorbike there?' He gestured to a big shiny bike parked on the other side of the car park.

'You rode all the way here?'

Holden chuckled. 'No, that would've taken too long and once I'd realised what a dick I was, I couldn't get here fast enough. I flew, then rented the bike in Perth.'

'And you're still not going to let me ride it with you?'

'No,' he said seriously. 'I'm not quite ready for that yet, but maybe one day.'

She squeezed his hand. 'We can take my Prado.'

They reluctantly parted for the ten minutes it took to drive from town to the farm and then she took his hand and kissed him once more before leading him inside to meet her parents. As it was the middle of the day, they were both at home.

'Mum? Dad!' she called as she pushed open the front door.

Her mother's voice drifted back. 'We're in the kitchen. What's going on? I thought you were out today with Sally.'

'Change of plans. I've brought a visitor. Someone special I want you to meet. Tada!' she said as they emerged into the kitchen to find her parents sitting at the table, remnants of morning smoko on the table. Dad was reading the paper and Mum had been doing a crossword puzzle, which she abandoned as she laid eyes on Holden. 'I'd like you to meet my fiancé, Holden Campbell.'

'Pleased to meet you Mr and Mrs Walsh,' Holden said.

Jane stood and dusted her hands on her trousers as if she'd been peeling vegetables rather than doing a crossword, but she didn't offer Holden her hand as would have been polite. 'Why didn't you tell me you were bringing someone round? The house is a pigsty.'

'I didn't know I was going to be,' Adeline said. Besides, their house was never a pigsty. Her mum had cleaners that came twice a week. 'And did you hear what I just said?'

Dad looked over the top of his paper, barely lowering it. 'Fiancé? What happened to becoming a nun?'

Had he even noticed she'd been home for weeks?

Adeline rolled her eyes at Holden as if to say, 'See what I have to deal with?' and then laughed. Nothing could burst her bubble today. 'I told you that's not happening anymore, and here's the reason why.'

Her mum looked Holden up and down and frowned, her eyes focusing on his tattoos. Imagine if she'd seen him before he'd shaved his beard and got a haircut. 'You're marrying this man?'

'Yep.' Adeline grinned. 'As soon as koala-ing possible.'

Her parents exchanged a look that suggested she'd gone mad, and she heard Holden smother a laugh.

'Well, are you going to offer your future son-in-law a drink while I go pack a bag?' she demanded.

'You're leaving *now*?' asked her mother.

'I'm taking Adeline for a night away to Margaret River,' Holden explained. 'After that we'll make plans for the future.'

Adeline gave him a nod of approval. 'Margaret River? Nice.'

Mum sighed. 'Well, I suppose congratulations are in order.' She finally offered Holden her hand and then nudged her husband to abandon the paper and do the same. No matter what she really thought of Holden—or at least his appearance—the etiquette she'd learned at her posh private girls' school had kicked in.

'Thanks, Mum.'

'Yes, thank you very much Mrs Walsh. I know I'm the luckiest man alive now that Adeline has agreed to be my wife.'

Jane made a weird noise and then clapped her hands. 'Right, let's get you a cup of tea and you can tell us all about yourself, because Adeline certainly hasn't.'

Adeline kissed him on the cheek then slipped off to pack that bag as quick as humanly possible. Too long in her mother's company and Holden might change his mind.

Six and a half minutes later—which had to be some kind of record—she returned to the kitchen with her overnight bag on her shoulder. 'I'm ready. Let's go.'

Right now, she didn't want to share him with anyone, least of all her parents.

Holden thanked Jane for the tea and promised next time he'd stay long enough to drink all of it, and then they headed outside to the Prado with Jane calling out things they needed to get onto ASAP for the wedding.

'Sounds like you won her over,' Adeline said, laughing as they both climbed into her four-wheel drive.

He grinned and snapped his seatbelt into place. 'I'm very charming when I want to be. Besides, they're not as bad as you made out. When I apologised for not asking their permission for your hand in marriage, your mother swooned, and your father actually put down his newspaper and asked me about my line of work.'

Adeline snorted. 'Give them time. Thankfully, we'll be living across the other side of the country, so we'll probably never see them.'

'Unless they take up my offer to visit whenever they want for as long as they want,' he said, his tone teasing.

'Thank God they're dairy farmers and have taken a grand total of two holidays in their lives.'

The hour and a half it took to drive to Margaret River through luscious eucalypt forests and cute country towns went both quickly and torturously slow. They had so much to talk about—so much to catch up on—but with Holden's hand on her knee the whole time, Adeline found it hard to think about much besides getting him naked again.

She hoped he didn't have too many other plans for their date.

'Turn off here and our accommodation should be three hundred metres on your left,' he directed.

A minute later Adeline gasped as they turned down a gravel drive following a sign that read 'Glamp the Night Away', the photo of a beautiful domed tent beneath it.

'Oh my goodness? Dome glamping? I've wanted to do this ever since I saw it on *Farmer Wants a Wife*!'

Holden squeezed her knee. 'Well, I like camping, but I know you're a five-star resort kinda gal. Hopefully this is the best of both worlds.'

'It most definitely is,' Adeline said as they emerged into a clearing which held their accommodation. 'It looks like something from another planet.'

'Wait till you see inside. That's if it lives up to the online photos.'

They parked and then found the key box. Holden punched in the code the owners had given him and led her inside.

'Wow,' she said, turning slowly around, admiring the king-sized canopy bed and the Scandinavian-look décor with soft throw rugs and gorgeous cushions. The exquisite forest view out the front took her breath away. If this was camping, she never wanted to stay in another five-star hotel in her life. 'I don't think any photo could have done this justice. Can we live here forever?'

He laughed and closed the distance between them, taking her hands and pulling her to him. As his delicious heat seeped into her, the smell of him drove her wild and all thoughts, except the bed and making love in it, evaporated.

They could be in a run-down shack in a post-apocalyptic world and she wouldn't care as long as she was with him.

Hours later, after devouring a romantic picnic dinner that had been delivered to the deck while they'd been getting busy inside, they soaked in the outdoor bath under the stars, with only the occasional hoot from an owl to remind them that they weren't the only creatures in the world.

'How bad does it hurt getting a tattoo?' Adeline asked, tracing her fingers over the new semi-sacrilegious image on Holden's chest.

He frowned. 'Why? You thinking of getting one?'

She nodded. 'Yep. My mother will have a heart attack—she thinks they're the work of the devil—but I want to get a real version of the typewriter you drew on my arm, and I can't let you be the only one with someone's name scrawled across your chest. I'm going to get a lumberjack with your name beneath it, right here.'

She pointed to her naked right breast as Holden's eyes widened.

'Lumberjack?'

'Yeah, because the first time I saw you, that's what you reminded me of. A very *sexy* lumberjack.'

She saw the moment realisation dawned in his gorgeous eyes. 'That's why you call me Jack?'

'Yep.'

He threw back his head and laughed, making water splash over the sides of the bath. '"Maria and Jack". Has quite a nice ring to it, don't you think?'

'I do,' Adeline replied, and then she snuggled against him.

It was the first night of the rest of their lives and she couldn't wait for what was to come.

Epilogue

'Happy birthday to you, happy birthday to you, happy birthday dear Rocky, happy birthday to you,' Adeline sang along with her closest friends, family, and Rocky's friends too. Some of the dogs even barked, as if not wanting to be left out.

It was a Saturday night, two weeks before Christmas, and they'd all gathered in the front garden to celebrate not only Rocky's birthday but also his recent graduation from school and his early offer into veterinary science at the University of Melbourne.

Behind them was the house where Adeline now lived with Holden and—at present—two brothers who'd come to stay with them after their parents had died in a horrific car accident. These kids, seven and thirteen respectively, were messed up in different ways, but with the help of two rescue pups, they were slowly learning that she and Holden wanted them to be part of their family. The shed and the training yards where Holden worked with the boys and the dogs were off to one side, and on the other was a row of tiny houses, each accommodating an ex-foster kid.

This was *her* home. These were her people. And she loved them all.

Holden cupped his hands on either side of his mouth and shouted, 'Three cheers for the man of the moment!'

The guests—of which there were many—echoed back, 'Hip hip hooray, hip hip hooray, hip hip hooray!'

Rocky leaned forward and with one big puff blew out the eighteen candles on the caramel mud cake Ford had made to celebrate his special day. He ruffled Bella's head—she was never far from his side—and then beamed at the crowd. 'Thanks everyone.'

'Speech!' cried Mitch. He was standing to the side with a cute, button-nosed, blonde-haired cherub of a toddler on his hip. She was the spitting image of his long-time girlfriend, Tarryn, who looked elf-sized standing next to him.

Rocky ran his hand through his scruffy red hair. 'I don't know where to start.'

But then his gaze zeroed in on Adeline and Holden at the front of the crowd and she felt a lump form in her throat.

'Actually, yes, I do.'

Rocky might not be her flesh and blood, but all the boys that she and Holden fostered were her children and she couldn't have been prouder if she'd pushed him out herself.

Holden squeezed her hand and pulled her closer into his side. Even after four years, her nerve-endings still tingled every time he touched her.

'Apologies everyone for the mushy stuff you're about to hear. I'll try to keep it short.'

'Yeah, right,' shouted Toovs from the middle of the crowd. He now lived in Queensland, working on a cattle station and loving it, but he'd made the trek back for tonight and was staying in Smallton with Sam, who'd just finished his apprenticeship with a cabinet maker and had recently moved out of his tiny house and into a small unit in town. While working on the first house with Holden, Sam had discovered not only a passion but also a talent for building, which had kickstarted his career and channelled all his energy into something positive.

Of the boys who Adeline had met when she'd first arrived in Smallton, Luka was the only one not with them tonight, but it was a long way to come from London, and this close to Christmas he couldn't get time off from his role as the lead in a West End pantomime.

'I don't know where I'd be today if Holden and Ford and then Adeline hadn't taken me and loved me even when I didn't make it easy for anyone to do so,' Rocky began, 'but I'm pretty sure I wouldn't have finished school. And I'm certain I wouldn't feel part of a family like I do now. These three not only loved me unconditionally, even sacrificing their own needs for mine, but they encouraged me to work hard, taught me life lessons and so much more.'

He went on to share some of his favourite memories from the past few years and by the time he'd finished, Adeline was crying, and she wasn't the only one.

She looked over to where her mum was sitting on a milkcrate next to Sally and Ford, bouncing their three-year-old daughter Chloe on her knee. Ford sat in his wheelchair with Sally in his lap and both women were dabbing tissues to their eyes.

Yep, life was full of surprises.

This wasn't Jane's first trip to Smallton—ever since Adeline's article about the murder of Eliza had appeared in the *Whisperer*, things had improved dramatically between them. Adeline had expected her mother's anger, but got the opposite instead. Jane had been horrified to learn of her mother-in-law's actions, but had admitted that she'd never really liked Penelope. She'd always felt there was something off about her. She'd put it down to Penelope not thinking Jane was good enough for her darling son, but now she felt justified in her dislike. Adeline had been even more shocked when her mother admitted that she'd always felt jealous of the close relationship she'd had with her grandmother, and apologised for letting her own issues come between them.

Adeline's drastic life changes had inspired her mum to make some of her own. Jane had left the farm and her husband, bought a vintage caravan, flashed it up and now travelled around the country, taking photos of rural Australia that were so good she sold them online. Adeline wouldn't say she and her mother were exactly close, but they understood each other a lot better than they had before and had deeper, more meaningful conversations on the regular.

And as for Sally? Well, she'd met Ford at Holden and Adeline's wedding and after a mere ten minutes of conversation had declared to Adeline that her man ban was lifted. Later they'd found out that at the very same time, Ford had been telling Holden that he'd finally met his person. A courtship via text and many FaceTime chats had begun and within six months, Sally and the boys had moved to Smallton and into a house in town with Ford.

Adeline adored having her best friend, nephews and now niece close by.

'I need another drink after that,' announced Bronte, when Rocky finally finished singing the praises of what seemed like each and every person in attendance. 'Don't think I've cried as much since I watched *Dumbo* as a kid.'

Holden chuckled. 'You must be getting soft in your old age. I'll get you another beer.' He nodded to Adeline's wine glass. 'Want a top-up?'

'Does a bear shit in the woods?' she said, using one of his favourite phrases.

He took her glass and went over to the drinks table.

'Is Jack managing to hold the fort on his own?' Adeline asked Bronte.

In a bizarre turn of events, Bronte had met her own 'Jack' in Middle of Nowhere, but his name really was Jack. They'd been an item almost as long as Sally and Ford, but the only problem with owning a small business far from civilisation was that they rarely got to escape together. Bronte's mum Tricia gave them a reprieve for a few weeks a year, but she was currently on a cruise in the Bahamas. Lucky woman!

Bronte bit her lip and Adeline could tell she was trying to tame her grin. 'Yeah, course he is. He's awesome. But damn, I miss him. I never thought I'd like someone enough that I wouldn't get sick of having them around, but I feel like I left my right arm behind.'

'I'm happy for you,' Adeline said.

Holden returned with the drinks, and she left him and Bronte for a rare one-on-one catch up. She heard Bronte asking about Home Sweet Tiny Homes as she went across to talk to Sister Michelle, Sister Lola and Sister Rita.

She knew he'd be modest in his reply, but the truth was their charity kept going from strength to strength and had become a full-time job. While Adeline still ran the *Smallton Gazette*— and loved every minute of it—Holden only did tattoos if his old boss needed a holiday. The tiny houses on their property were only five of many that had been built in the region over the last few years, and she couldn't be prouder of what they'd achieved together. Of course, the generous donation that Sister Josey had left them in her will had helped a lot, and the tractor pull had become an annual event, drawing a bigger and bigger crowd each year.

'Congratulations,' she said to Michelle. 'I see you just hit one hundred thousand followers. That's koala-ing amazing.'

Michelle made a face. 'Still nowhere near as many as Kim Kardashian.'

'Does the Pope follow Kimmy?' asked Rita, poking Michelle in the side.

'What?' exclaimed Adeline. 'The Pope's on TikTok?'

The sisters nodded, then Lola leaned in and whispered, 'But between you and me, we're pretty sure he doesn't choreograph his own dances.'

Adeline laughed. 'I love you guys. Thanks so much for coming, and thanks for everything you've done for all of us over the years.'

She felt herself getting teary again and wondered why she was so damn emotional; maybe it was that time of the month.

Holy koala.

It wasn't that time of the month; it was two weeks *past* that time of the month! And she'd never been late in her life. A shiver went through her body at the realisation of what this may mean, and she immediately put down her wine glass.

She and Holden hadn't been trying for a baby, but they hadn't *not* been trying either. Although he used to think he didn't want kids, he'd changed his mind when Chloe was born, telling her he wanted a miniature Maria, just like Ford had a miniature Sally.

It was one of the many cheesy but adorable things he told her on a daily basis.

'Are you okay?' asked Michelle, frowning. 'You look like you just remembered you forgot to send the paper to print.'

'I'm fine. Yes. Good. I'm good. I've just got to ... I need to speak to Holden.'

He was gathering up paper plates that were scattered around the garden, trying to stop the dogs from eating them, when she found him. 'Where's Bronte?' she asked.

'Jack called. She asked if she could use our bedroom to talk to him.' Holden made a face. 'I'm trying not to think about what she might be doing in there.'

Adeline stared at him, that stupid emotion getting the better of her again. He might not have had the best example of a father, but she'd already seen him in action with their foster kids and knew that if there was a little life growing inside her right now, they were going to have the best dad on the planet.

'Oh Maria.' He dropped the plates to the ground and took her into his arms. 'What's the matter? Why the tears? Is it 'cos of Rocky? We'll visit him heaps in Melbourne and I'm sure he'll come back for holidays.'

She sniffed and shook her head. 'Nothing's the matter. Jack, I think I'm pregnant!'

'What? You serious?'

When Adeline nodded, Holden's whole face lit up as he swung her into the air, then carefully placed on the ground. 'And here I was thinking I couldn't get any happier!'

The tenderness in his eyes took her breath away. 'Me too,' she said. 'Me too.'

Author Note

I've lost count of the number of times I've watched *The Sound of Music*. As a kid I used to watch it over and over again, singing along at the top of my lungs, wishing I was one of the Von Trapp children. At seven I even auditioned for the part of Gretel in a theatre production—sadly I didn't get it. At nineteen I travelled Europe on my own and visited all *The Sound of Music* sites (from the movie) in Salzburg. I didn't realise until I was halfway through writing *Talk to the Heart* that it is perhaps my Aussie rural version of *The Sound of Music*. Adeline is, of course, Maria; Holden, the Captain; the boys and dogs, the Von Trapp kids; Ford, Uncle Max, and Bronte, the Baroness. And instead of singing nuns, we have TikTokking ones. I hope you enjoyed the story, whether you're a fan of *The Sound of Music* or not.

Author Note

Acknowledgements

I would like to take this opportunity to thank the below people for helping me write and publish another book:

To Sue Brockhoff, my wonderful publisher, and Helen Breitwieser, my fabulous agent—thanks to both of you for not telling me I was absolutely bonkers when I said I wanted to write a romance novel about a nun! Your faith in me is always so encouraging.

To the rest of the team at HQ—especially Annabel Blay, Jo Munroe, Sarana Behan, Karen-Marie Griffiths and all the state sales managers for your hard work in the editing and marketing of this book.

To my brilliant editor, Lachlan Jobbins—you have such a wonderful skill to uplift me and make me feel confident about my stories and writing, while also encouraging me with your wisdom and insight to improve them. Forever grateful. And a massive thank you to Kate James and her eagle-eye proofreading skills.

To the authors who support me on a daily basis—especially to Rebecca Heath for reading everything I write before anyone else, Anthea Hodgson, Fiona Palmer and Tess Woods for listening to me whine on a daily basis and being great brainstormers, and to

Writers Camp (Emily Madden, Amanda Knight, Lisa Ireland and Rebecca Heath) for so many laughs and cries over the years and for always having my back. I've got yours too. And to all the other wonderful writer friends of which there are too many to name—I LOVE our author community!

To Jem Gowen, who generously provided lyrics from her own writing for Ryder O'Connell's songs—thank you for being better at writing songs than I am.

To all my readers—without you I wouldn't be able to write for a living and for that I'm super appreciative. Thanks for buying, borrowing, reading, loving and spreading the words to all your friends about my stories. Massive thanks to Brooke Testa and the Rachael Johns' Online Book Club as well.

To my family—to Mum, Craig, and the boys! I'm not sure there's any different way to say what's already been said in all the books before this one, but I love you all and thank you for all you do both practically and emotionally to support my author life.

Other books by

RACHAEL JOHNS

 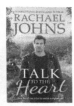

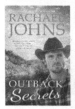 

  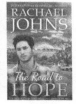

rachaeljohns.com

talk about it

Let's talk about books.

Join the conversation:

f   @harlequinaustralia

♪   @hqanz

○   @harlequinaus

harpercollins.com.au/hq

If you love reading and want to know about our
authors and titles, then let's talk about it.